For early access, extra content, and updates, follow me at:

Website: http://www.thefalsehero.com/

Patreon: https://www.patreon.com/MichaelPlymel

Facebook: https://www.facebook.com/michael.plymel.79

Discord: https://discord.gg/Wc2cYpPMt3

Reddit: https://www.reddit.com/r/TheFalseHero/

Chapter 1

The crack of thunder tore through the clear, blue sky.

Huh? Thomas thought. *Was it supposed to storm today? There's not a cloud anywhere to be seen.*

No wait, when did I start looking up at the sky?

A familiar face blocked his vision. His bodyguard. The man's mouth was moving, but he couldn't hear the sounds coming from it.

Although Thomas could read lips, he was unable to focus enough to do so.

I'm tired. So tired.

It looked as if night had begun to fall, but the truth was far more sinister. The curtains had been forcibly drawn closed on his life.

"Wake up, sleepyhead," a feminine voice called out.

"M-my schedule..." Thomas just kept lying on his puffy, white cloud.

"Hm? What about it?"

"I can't catch up no matter what I do, so just let me sleep already..."

"Oh? Well have I got a surprise for you!"

"Huh? A day off!? You should have said so from the beginning!" Thomas popped up, sanity finally returning to him.

He looked around, only for his sanity to be replaced with confusion. The way his mouth slowly opened and closed as he tried to make sense of his situation was a sight to behold.

After Thomas took a good look at the white clouds that supported his rear, his eyes fell on the set of golden gates that stood behind the mysterious woman sitting in an ornate chair before him. Even if something like this were to suddenly fall into his lap, a lifetime of movies had already prepared him for what it meant.

"Am I ... dead?" Thomas asked.

"You certainly are!" The Goddess' words were a bit too lively.

"Then that means, you're God? Or, you're Goddess...?" Thomas' face suddenly became thoughtful. "Huh, why doesn't the word 'Goddess' sound right when not paired with the word 'the'? You are God. You are Goddess. Nope, something definitely doesn't sound right..."

"Are you done?" the Goddess asked, waiting for his mind to return.

"Ah, sorry. I tend to get lost in thought sometimes."

"I am aware. I've been watching you for a long time, Thomas George Hamilton."

"That's kinda ... well, expected, I guess." He shook his head. "So does this mean I'm going to be judged for my sins?"

"Eh, I'm not really into that kind of thing. I usually just let the automated system punish the ones that need it. Besides, I'm not even your Goddess. At least, I wasn't before today."

"Huh? Sorry, but you kind of lost me..."

"Well, don't worry about it too much. The cranky old man who oversees your world has his way of doing things, while I have mine. Due to an agreement, he gave me your soul upon your death. So, here you are."

As expected of a human who'd suddenly been thrust into the machinations of the gods, Thomas showed a confused expression to the Goddess. It made her want to smile, but she held it back. It wouldn't do to appear conceited, considering the task she was about to ask him to undertake.

"So, um, why exactly did you want my soul?" he asked nervously.

"Thomas George Hamilton, Master of Economics degree and minoring in business administration. With your intelligence and dedication, you could have had a lucrative career at the corporation of your choice. Yet you stepped off the path you carved for yourself in order to become a politician. Why?"

"Why? There's no deep reason. It's just that after everything I learned at my university, I didn't like the direction of my country. I thought that maybe I could use what I knew to help steer it back on course. Guess I failed, huh?"

"Yes, you failed. Sometimes, no matter how much you desire something, it can slip from your grasp. But just because you died doesn't mean all your hard work must be wasted."

"What exactly are you saying? That I'll be able to go back?"

"No. Your time on Earth is over, at least in your current incarnation. Were you to return, it would be in the form of a newborn with no memories of your former life. However, there is another path available to you."

After hearing that he would have to start life over from the beginning, Thomas visibly deflated. After all the effort he put in to learn the economic and business theories that he thought to use in service of his country, the idea of it all going down the drain weighed heavily upon his mind.

But when he heard that there was another option, his eyes hardened, as if already prepared to grasp it, despite not even having heard the details.

"This other path, what is it?"

"I told you that I'm not your Goddess. The fact is that I oversee an entirely different world than your own. This other world is in desperate need of someone with your knowledge, someone who can prevent the collapse of their civilizations."

"Wait, collapse? How can I hope to stop something that sounds so terrible?"

"As for whether you can or can't stop it..." The Goddess' words cause Thomas to lean forward in anticipation. "...I have no idea!"

He faceplanted into the puffy cloud like a balloon that had suddenly deflated. When his head came back up, it lacked the reverence it held when he first awoke.

"You're a god, right? Can't you see the future?"

"Even we have our limits. When a chess player calculates his moves, he does so with assumptions on the path his opponent will take, knowing the limitations of their options. For us, it's no different. We see many things, but until they come to pass, we cannot be certain.

"However, in the world I oversee, nearly every path leads to the same dreary future. In it, there is famine, wars, and devastation. Left as it is, the chance that the upcoming collapse will be thwarted is miniscule, at best."

"That sounds terrible. But what am I supposed to do to stop it? I don't know anything about this world."

A smile bloomed on the Goddess' face. "It just so happens that nearly an entire family of worthless royals is about to meet their untimely demise."

"Uh, okay..."

"It also just so happens that a fresh corpse is the perfect place to cram in a wandering soul~"

"Wait, are you saying..."

"Ah, finally beginning to understand, are you? Thomas, have you ever wanted to be a king?"

His eyes opened so wide that they appeared as saucers, and his brown irises as cups filled with tea.

"I can't be a king...! They rule over subjects like a dictator! That's the worst kind of governmental system, one my ancestors fought and died to eradicate!"

"Oh, c'mon. It's not so bad. What's a few genocides between friends?"

"Are you serious!?"

"No."

"...What?"

"You asked if I were serious, and I answered."

"Y-yeah, but..." Thomas shook his head. "Forget it. I feel like I won't win no matter what I say, so let's just move on. We have an old saying on Earth: Power corrupts, and absolute power corrupts absolutely. There's a reason why my country had checks and balances put in place to prevent the concentration of power. You never know how someone will react when given free rein to do as they wish."

The Goddess nodded. "It's true that obtaining such power can lead to tyranny. But in most cases, the tyrant was always so, they just hid it beneath a veil until they were able to reveal their true selves. That saying of yours refers more so to the long-term detrimental effects of giving too much power to positions, groups, or institutions. Over time, the corrupt will flock to them and bring disaster to the people."

"Like monarchies."

"Precisely like monarchies. But although the position may draw in the worst of men, it doesn't mean it will draw out the worst of a man. You've already proven it so, have you not?"

Thomas considered the Goddess' words in silence. As a politician on Earth, he was in a unique position to abuse his power for personal gain, yet he stuck to his morals, truly wishing to use his authority to better the lives of those he represented.

Although he didn't gain the power of a king, even a sliver of that tempting fruit is enough for most men to cast off their masks, at least privately. But no matter how many bribes he was offered, he never succumbed.

"I'm not special or anything," Thomas said. "Lots of people would have done the same if they were given the chance."

"Maybe. But I'm not talking to lots of people. I'm talking to you, the one who did stand by his morals, despite the riches they offered you. And it's because you refused to sell your soul to them that I've come to you seeking aid. Earth would have been a better place had you survived. Alas, that was not to be. However, there is another world that desperately needs your help. I'll ask again, Thomas: Will you become a king?"

"I..." The resolution returned to his eyes. "If you really think I can put my knowledge to use to help the people of your world, then I'll do it. I don't want all the hard work I put in to go to waste."

"Excellent! I knew I could count on you!" The Goddess mentally wiped the anxious sweat from her forehead. "Then, whose body should I put you in~"

"Didn't you say you were going to put me in the king's body?"

"No way. That man's nearly 40 years old. You'll need all the time and energy you can get if you want to change the course of this world. One of his sons would be a much better choice!"

"So ... I'm going to be a prince?"

"Yes, but not for long. It's a monarchy, after all! Since you'll be the only one who survives, they'll have no choice but to crown you. The question is, which of the three princes would be best..."

Thomas watched as a small pool of water appeared between him and the Goddess. It shone with a faint, silvery light, resembling dew rising into the morning sky.

Within the pool, colors began to swirl. They converged into shapes, eventually taking the form of a person lying in bed, his face strained and pale. The only striking thing about him was a massive scar that ran along one side of his face. It was a brutal injury and one that had defined him ever since he received it.

"The crown prince," the Goddess said. "Twenty-one years old, thick bodied, and feared for his hot temper."

"I'm going into his body...?" Thomas obviously had his reservations.

"As the oldest, he was groomed to rule. The nobles and subjects would be more likely to obey, making your transition far easier. But his temper is famous throughout the kingdom, and you simply wouldn't be able to emulate it, which may draw suspicion due to the sudden change in attitude."

"Yeah, I'd rather not be in the body of someone like that…"

"In that case…"

The colors swirled again. When they settled down, a noticeably more youthful face appeared within the pool, but he looked just as sickly as the first.

"The youngest prince, 15 years old. He's much calmer than the first, but there's one problem…"

"W-what? Don't tell me he's secretly some kind of hardcore criminal or something, using his calm demeanor to trick people into thinking he's a nice kid."

"Wow. You've really gone off the deep end already, haven't you?"

"Well, everything's been so crazy until now that I can't help but think you're going to say something extreme again."

"You're certainly right about one thing: There is something extreme about this young prince. More precisely, he's an extreme idiot."

"Eh?"

"Dumb as a rock. Not running on all cylinders. The elevator doesn't go to the top floor. You know, that sort of thing."

"That's…" Thomas felt a bit of sympathy for the poor prince. "What's my other choice…?"

As expected, he didn't really want to be put into the body of a royal dud. So, the Goddess gave him what he wanted, a view of the final prince.

"The middle child, 17 years old," the Goddess said. "Among the citizens, he's known for his charming smile and silver tongue. Quite the looker, too. He can make nearly any lady swoon just by turning their way, an advantage he's no stranger to utilizing."

"Y-yeah, even with his sickly face, I can see that. Doesn't that mean he's the perfect choice?"

"Hahaha…"

"H-hey, why are you suddenly giving me a stiff laugh!?"

"No reason~" The Goddess simply smiled back at Thomas. "I do agree he's the best choice among the three, so why don't we go with this one."

"Okay, but I'm still a little uneasy from that laugh…"

"Don't sweat it! Just act as you normally would, and I'm sure it'll all work out. Probably."

The pool vanished, leaving nothing but a fluffy cloud in its place. With the water gone, the Goddess stood from her ornate chair and walked over to Thomas, stepping over where the pool used to be.

The middle-aged Thomas scrambled to his feet, not wanting to rudely remain seated before a literal god. A nervous bead of sweat would have slid down his face, if his body had physical form. Even without it, the Goddess could clearly see the anxiety in him.

"This task will not be an easy one," she said. "There will be many hardships, and success is far from guaranteed."

"I've already decided, so there's no going back now. But I do have one question. What's going to happen to my family on Earth?"

"As stated, it's difficult to see through the fog of time, even for me." A small smile appeared on her lips. "But most of their paths lead to a bright future. I'm certain they'll be just fine."

"I see. Thank you." Thomas relaxed. "Then I'm ready."

She raised her hand, placing her fingers against Thomas' forehead. "I can't provide much assistance, but there will be a time when we speak again. Until then, good luck in your endeavors."

A gentle force caused Thomas to tip backwards. He instinctively tried to step back to prevent himself from falling over, but his astral body refused to obey his wishes. All he could do was give himself over to the force that pulled at him, dragging him to the new world.

As the heavenly scene began to fade, the voice of the Goddess resounded one last time in his mind.

"Ah, I forgot to mention. The royal family was struck with a disease. Not by chance but by a calculated hand. In other words, they were assassinated~"

"Hey! Tell me that from the beginning!"

With that final exchange, Thomas' consciousness faded.

"Hmm," the Goddess mused. "Should I have explained the world's magic system to him? Eh, I'm sure he'll figure it out~"

"Are you a Goddess?" a youthful, male voice asked. "Or a devil?"

"Oh, my. What a ridiculous question. There's no way a devil would be able to emulate my beauty and charm, right?"

The Goddess turned toward the golden gates, which had been opened from the other side. In the doorway stood a young male, eyeing her with an exasperated face.

"You just sent that guy down there completely unprepared," the young man said. "Do you really think he can survive, given everything that's stacked against him?"

"You mean the treacherous assassins who will no doubt seek his life, the dire state of the kingdom he's destined to rule, or ... are you talking about that false god who's behind the troubles the world faces?"

"False god? You mean the God's Acolyte."

"That's the same thing, right?" The Goddess smirked.

"I'm just using the correct terminology for his classification. Stop being weird." He sighed.

"It's too soon to become an old man. You've only been immortal for what ... two months?"

"Two years!"

"Oh, yeah. Two months, two years, it's all the same, right? I mean, when you count your age in millennia like me, such a small amount of time is a rounding error." The Goddess nodded at her own words. "But if you want an answer to your question, you have only to look upon your own mortal life before ascending to immortality. Weren't you in a similarly dire situation?"

"That's ... true. But my circumstances were more a result of miscalculations mixed with necessity. You're throwing him to the sharks on purpose."

"Then..." The Goddess sat at a desk and pulled out a blank journal. "...I hope you'll watch closely and realize why I chose this path for him."

An inked quill appeared in her hand and began to slide across a blank page.

The story of Thomas George Hamilton had begun.

Chapter 2

Thomas' eyes slowly crept open, revealing a dimly lit, yet marvelously decorated room, appearing a dark and deep blue-gold in the scarce light.

Rather than wallpaper, the designs covering the walls were physically crafted and secured to the wood through some means Thomas was unable to discern. The décor's theme seemed to revolve around nature, with the walls being covered by vigorous growths of trees and other ornaments that brought to mind a cultured garden, kept by a careful hand.

Within the room proper, small tables dotted the corners, their sole purpose to carry vases, in which bloomed a colorful array of flowers. Even by the bedside, the fingers of a plant stretched, the roses having already gifted the covers with many of their fallen petals.

Finally, Thomas' eyes fell upon the sole figure sitting in a chair nearby. The aged woman sat beside a table filled with cloths set alongside a bowl of water. After shifting his body to look at her, the cloth upon him slid from his forehead, falling to the sheets.

The soft noise alerted the woman, who looked up at its source. Her eyes spoke volumes about the unexpected sight they took in, so much so that she sat frozen for several long seconds.

"P-prince Lucian!" She stood up with a vigor one wouldn't expect from a woman her age. "By the Goddess' blessing, you're awake!"

You probably have no idea both how right and wrong you are.

He was blessed by the Goddess, as she said. But it wasn't Lucian who was granted a second life.

"Were you watching over me the entire time?" he asked. "Thank you. It's because of your care that I was able to overcome my sickness."

"N-no, I didn't do anything of note..."

Lucian wasn't sure how he was supposed to act, nor did he know who this woman even was. So, he decided that softening her up with a compliment would be the best way to lead into the round of questioning he intended to pursue.

"My apologies, but my memory is a bit fuzzy. Can you give me the details of how I came to be bedridden?"

"As you wish, Prince Lucian. It was nearly a week ago when your father first felt the effects of the sickness. Only a day later, you and your two brothers also fell victim. The doctors had never seen the like and were unable to heal the disease. Since then, we've only been able to pray for your recovery."

"How are my father and brothers?"

"I'm sorry to say, but ... they've already passed..."

"I see."

A strange feeling passed through Lucian. He knew nothing of his family in this world except for what the Goddess explained, most of which was far more negative than positive. Yet he still felt a tinge of loss.

Perhaps it was his new body or perhaps it was simply due to losing two families in such a short period of time, the first being his loving wife and children upon his death on Earth and the second being the one he would never know here.

"My prince, may I have your leave to inform the doctors of your miraculous recovery?"

"Ah, yes. Please let them know. However, I'm still not feeling well enough to eat, so please don't bring any food."

"That's worrisome, Prince. But I shall inform them. Ah, of course I'll let the princess know of your awakening, as well."

Eh? Princess?

"Thanks..." He was barely able to keep the surprise from his voice.

The caretaker left, leaving Prince Lucian alone in his room. Nearly as soon as the door closed, his stomach let out a dissatisfied groan, as if protesting the request to forgo a meal.

Settle down, stomach. I'm not going to give you something prepared by a hand that could be looking to poison me again.

The Goddess had told him that the disease was spread to the royal family by an assassin. Whoever tried to get rid of him would no doubt be displeased to learn that he had survived. In his weakened state, now would be the perfect time to give him another dose and claim that his recovery was only temporary.

He had to gain back the energy of a healthy, young man. He felt fine, except for a weakness that he thought to be from hunger, but recovering too quickly would be suspicious. Eating is a crucial step toward that recovery, but he'd rather wait until news of his survival began to spread to make it more difficult for an assassin to easily finish the job.

A bit of noise could be heard outside his room, but it didn't seem like anything that required him to act, so he ignored it. But soon after, someone knocked on his door.

"Who is it?" Lucian asked.

"It's Mia, Esteemed Brother."

Mia? Lucian thought. *She called me brother, so I can assume she's the princess the servant mentioned, but...*

...Why esteemed?

As expected of a human from Earth, Lucian couldn't wrap his mind around the strange formalities of a new planet so easily. Or rather, it actually had nothing to do with formalities and everything to do with the former prince whose body he now inhabited.

"Come in, Mia."

The princess would never go to her brother's room of her own will. At least, that would normally be the case. But things like the impending death of your entire family tend to make people do crazy things.

"Esteemed Brother." The young girl stopped by his bedside. "How are you feeling?"

"Not good," Lucian lied. "But I think the worst is over."

The two siblings just stared wordlessly at each other as both of them waited for the other to continue.

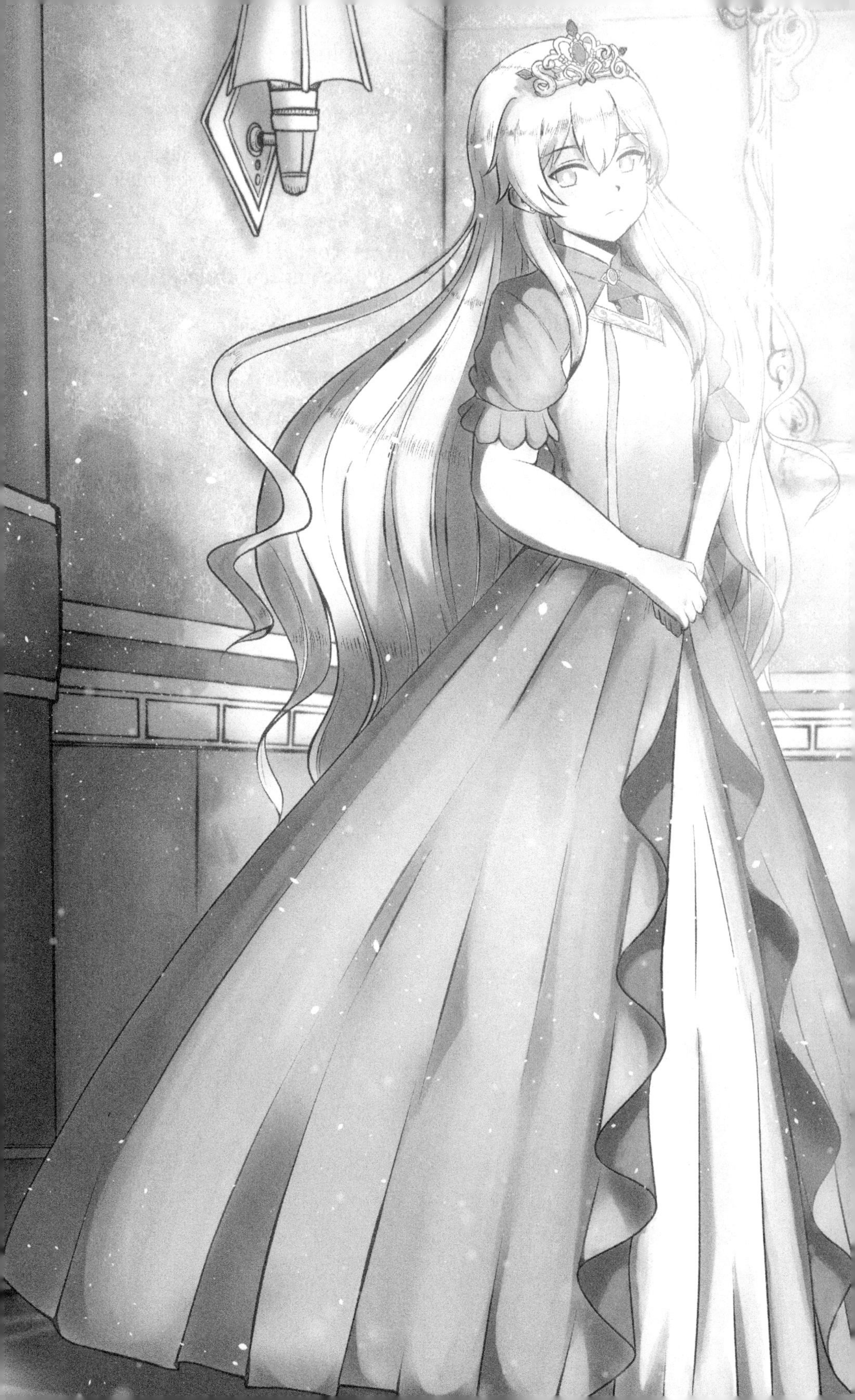

Prince Lucian's mistake was thinking that Princess Mia came to him out of a heartfelt desire to see the brother who'd miraculously survived the deadly disease. He had a lot to learn, mostly about his past self. Only there would he find the answer as to why his own sister feared him.

Mia unconsciously toyed with the skirt of her royal gown, the blue ruffles crumpling beneath her grip. This was the last place she wanted to be, yet her feet had taken her here despite her desire.

I felt ... nothing, Mia thought, looking down at her sickly brother. *Not an ounce of sadness for Lucian as he lay dying in bed.*

But without him...

Fear.

The Almekian Kingdom could only be ruled by a male heir. As the only remaining royal, Princess Mia would only become a pawn in a game of thrones, with each contestant seeking to elevate themselves to kingship through her.

Such a fate would only invite misery to the eleven-year-old Mia. She understood that well, yet she can't help but wonder if that outcome would be preferable to the one that played out in reality.

Father, why did you have to pass?

Why? Why did it have to be Lucian who survived?

Although she cared little for her two eldest brothers, Prince Lucian was the only one between them who made her feel true terror.

Though her eldest brother was scary and dominating, at least it was easy to understand what brought him to anger. The same could not be said of her middle brother, Lucian. Even as sick as he was now, she had to take care, as if the floor of his room were littered in broken glass.

As the newly reincarnated prince took in the sight of his little sister covered in a light blue gown, he was at a complete loss as to what to say. Though he had a daughter near her age on Earth, the likes and dislikes of the people in this world were a mystery for him, as were their customs and traditions.

In her posture, he saw fear. Unfortunately for him, he misinterpreted it, thinking her scared of losing her family to the deadly disease. For these reasons, the two siblings only stared at each other, neither sure how to continue the conversation.

Soon, the atmosphere grew too awkward for Lucian to bear, and he forced a simple sentence from his mouth.

"I hope you've been well, Mia. I know this must have been difficult for you."

"Yes, Esteemed Brother. I feared for the future of our family, were the disease to take you, as well."

"I thought so. But don't worry, I'm not going anywhere anytime soon. Eventually, everything will go back to how it was."

Mia flinched at the words meant to comfort her. "That would be ... most fortunate."

Again, the conversation died. But Lucian didn't intend to let the awkward atmosphere return. Instead, he hit upon a subject that he thought would both help comfort her and solve his most immediate problem.

"Hey Mia, I told the maid that I wasn't feeling well enough to eat, but I changed my mind. Do you think you could bring me some food? Anything is fine."

"You wish for me to cook you a feast?" Mia didn't quite know what to make of his demand.

"You don't have to cook it, and I definitely don't want a feast. But if you can just bring me something simple to eat, I'd be really grateful. Ah, but you have to pick it out yourself, okay? Not the cooks or maids. Just you."

"I ... understand." Mia nearly frowned at the thought of having to return to this room. "If that's what you wish, then I'll gladly comply."

"Great. Thanks, Mia. And I'm happy to see that you were left untouched by the disease."

Or rather, Lucian thought, *I'm happy that whoever assassinated the royals decided not to include you in their plans.*

With an elegant bow, Mia excused herself from the room to go prepare the food Lucian asked for.

Alone once again, the newly reincarnated prince couldn't help but think upon the most pressing subject once again. The assassination.

Surely Mia couldn't have been involved. If my own sister had tried to kill me, then things might be even worse than I imagined.

No, I can't let myself suspect her. We're the only two left in our family. We have to help each other, or else we may be brought down by whoever it was that planned my death.

Prince Lucian had no clue on where to even begin regarding the assassination of the royal family, but he drew the line at his own sister. Were he to suspect even her, he was sure that the paranoia would only cloud his mind.

Now, what in the world do I say when people start expecting me to know this world and the people in it?

A lot of problems had suddenly fallen into the former politician's lap, making him wonder if his vibrant blonde hair would soon begin turning grey from worry.

Chapter 3

Prince Lucian opened his eyes and looked around the royal room. For a moment, he lay there confused, wondering where it was that he had awoken.

He may have been a capable man, but upon waking from his first night in his new world, even his mind had trouble recalling the events that transpired the day before.

That's right, he thought. *I died.*

Throwing off the covers, Lucian stood from the soft bed. It was his first real act since coming to this world, as he was bedridden for the entirety of his opening act in his new, princely body. It was a self-imposed restriction, but one of necessity to ensure no questions would be raised about his miraculous recovery.

But such a restriction could not go on for long. There were simply too many tasks awaiting his attention. Not to mention his penchant of working himself nearly to death when he found something worthy of his time.

Though he would certainly complain about the mountain of work to anyone who would listen, even if he was the one who picked up the tasks of his own free will.

So this is my new body.

Standing in front of a tall mirror, Lucian looked at the features of the unfamiliar young man that stared back at him.

He was tall, with long, blonde hair that went well past his shoulders. Of particular note was his face. The Goddess said the prince could make a lady swoon with just a look, and now he finally understood why.

If I had this body on Earth, couldn't I be a model or movie star?

He turned from the mirror and ran his hand through his long hair, imagining the life he could have had with his new body on Earth.

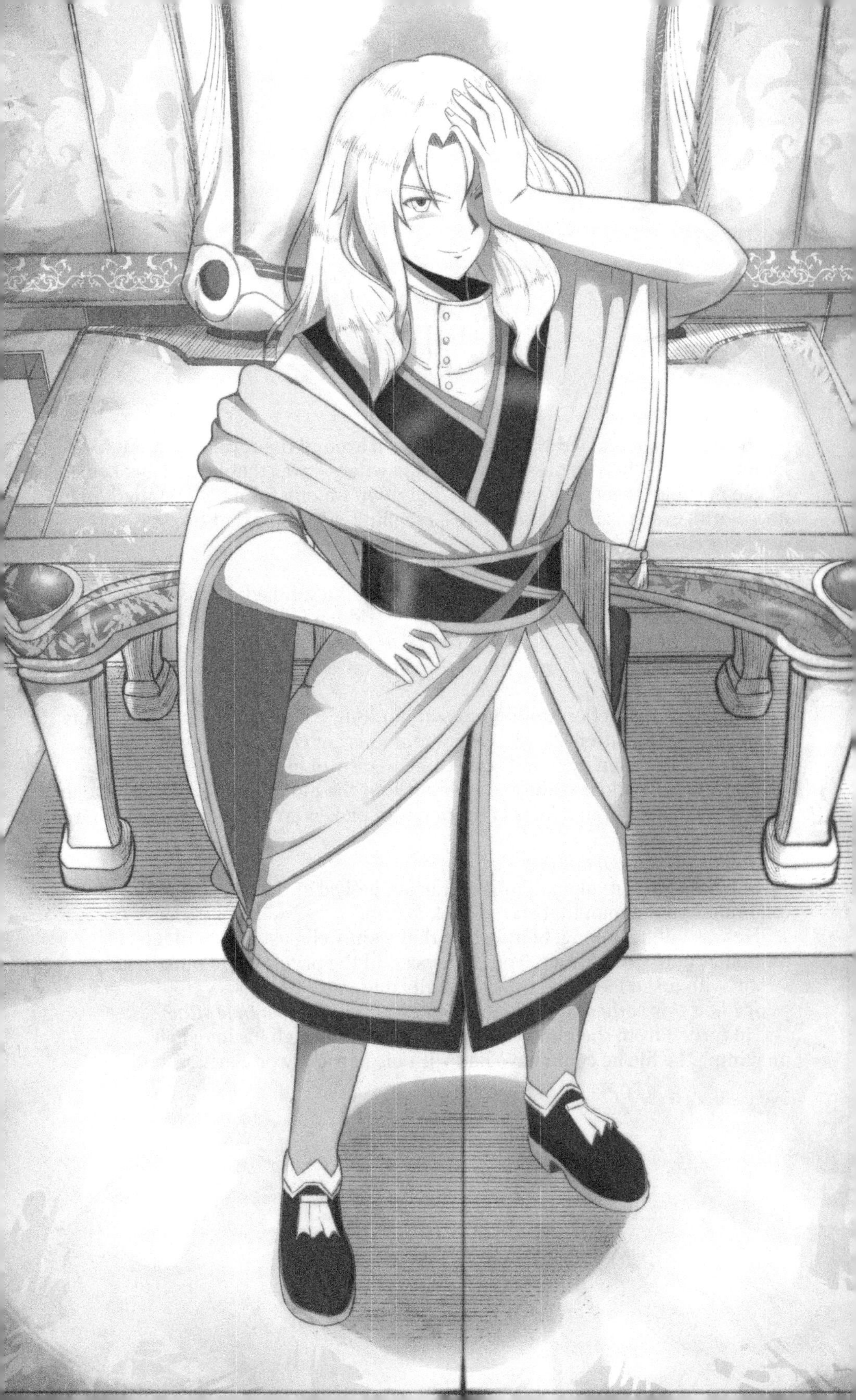

Shaking his head at the ridiculous thoughts, Lucian walked to a nearby closet and began to rummage around. He had no idea what passed for fashion in his new world, but it seemed someone had sorted his outfits so that each one was a matching set.

Thanks to that, he was able to pick one out without worrying how he might look.

Feeling like the room was getting too stuffy, he moved to the only door. He'd seen it opened several times yesterday, but the only sight visible to him on the other side was a decorative stone hallway.

If he wanted to make any kind of impact, he needed to step out into that hall and begin learning about his new world.

Many believe the first step to be the most difficult, but after taking it, the momentum would make the following ones far easier. As a man of action, Lucian didn't hesitate to follow through once he decided on a path. Turning the door's knob, that difficult first step quickly became nothing more than a memory as the decorative hallway filled his vision.

"Prince Lucian." A guard stationed outside his room saluted him. "Do you require a servant?"

"Good work keeping watch, men." He looked them both in the eyes as he spoke. "Rather than a servant, could you call for Princess Mia?"

"Right away, Your Highness."

The soldier strode down the hall, disappearing behind a corner. Lucian took note of the direction of his sister's room, though he wished he could accompany the guard to know its precise location.

But he was a royal now, and he had to act like one. Delegating tasks to subordinates was an important method to establish hierarchy. He already had such experience as a politician on Earth, so he only had to fall into those habits to ensure he'd be seen as the one in charge.

In truth, Lucian desperately wanted to be the one to complete the task. He had always found it difficult to order others around, but he couldn't deny the efficiency provided by leaving the lesser jobs to those who could complete them.

His sister had indeed brought him food the day before, as he requested. It was a simple meal, but that's precisely what he asked for. Since it filled his empty stomach, he had no complaints to offer.

As the only one he felt he could truly trust, he wanted Mia by his side during his first outing into the castle.

"Esteemed Brother." Mia gave Lucian a bow. "You called for me?"

"Hey, Mia. I hope I didn't disturb you."

"Of course not."

"Good because I was hoping you'd walk with me this morning."

"...If you wish."

Hearing her reluctant reply, Lucian couldn't help but feel as if he had in fact bothered her with this request. He felt a tinge of guilt, but he pushed it down, knowing that her support would be crucial to orienting himself in this new world.

Although Lucian knew nothing of the castle's layout, he began walking in the direction of Mia's room. His sister fell in line, though she stayed a step behind him, as if she felt she didn't belong by his side.

"Actually Mia, I have a confession to make. I told the healer last night, but … you see, I have amnesia."

"Amnesia? You don't remember anything?"

"No, except for a few details. But it seems my memory returns once I'm reminded, like a candle suddenly illuminating a darkened room."

"…"

"Because of my condition," Lucian continued after a brief silence, "I need someone to show me around and remind me of important details. Starting with the location of your room."

The siblings turned a corner, the same one the guard took when he left to fetch Mia. Lucian stopped and looked back at his sister, who seemed to have a complicated expression on her face.

The look vanished in a blink, making Lucian wonder if he had imagined it.

Claiming to have amnesia was the only way Lucian could imagine avoiding suspicion from not knowing the people and places that he supposedly lived near his whole life. But it wasn't an excuse he could use for long.

The people would expect a capable ruler to lead them, especially after the death of nearly the entire royal family. Fortunately, the soon-to-be-king had more than enough practice in memorizing large swaths of information, thanks to his years of dedicated study on Earth.

Mia took the lead, so Lucian followed. Now that he simply had to trace her steps, it gave him the freedom to examine a passing object that had caught his attention.

A small, decorative piece of metal protruded from the castle wall, looking similar to a candleholder. Yet no wax or flame sat upon its outstretched arm. Rather, a ball of glass was held in its grasp, glowing with a moderate light.

These same objects lined all the castle halls that Lucian had seen, gifting the paths with their mysterious luminescence. Even his room had them, though the ones inside didn't shine since the large window provided more than enough light to see clearly.

How do they glow like that? There doesn't seem to be anything like electricity in this world. And there's no flame inside the glass sphere.

Does that mean…

"This is the door to my room," Mia stated matter-of-factly.

"Ah, thanks," he said, dropping his thoughts. "While I'd love to see the inside, we've got important matters to take care of. Can you show me around the castle?"

"Of course, if that's your wish."

As soon as Mia stepped into the lead again, someone came from the very same corner the siblings just used. The man was old, looking like a grape that had been left out to dry.

In other words, a raisin.

"Your Highness!" The raisin-faced man shouted. "Are you feeling well!?"

"Yes. Very well, in fact. No doubt thanks to your miraculous healing."

"Is that so...? To think you could overcome that deadly disease in a mere day. And what of your..." He closed his mouth as his eyes fell on Mia.

"Speak your mind, healer. Mia already knows of my condition."

"I see. Then how is your memory this morning?"

"As clouded as ever, which is why I'm having her show me around. It seems just by laying eyes on my surroundings, my memory returns."

What a fantastic liar. Truly a model politician.

"You may be feeling better," the raisin said, "but I still wish to treat you, if you'll allow my selfish request."

"I'd be grateful, healer."

At Lucian's confirmation, the raisin raised his wrinkled hands and began to speak a special chant. When he finished, Lucian felt a warmth flow through him, filling him with comfort.

What a surprise to find out that magic is real.
I wonder why the Goddess didn't tell me...

After the healing spell filled his body, Lucian thanked the raisin before sending him on his way.

One of his visitors last night was that very same raisin. When the man began to speak his odd chant, Lucian thought it a prayer of some sort. But when the raisin finished, a warm sensation filled the reincarnated prince.

Lucian panicked at first, thinking that perhaps he had been poisoned. But the warmth seemed too pleasant to cause harm, like receiving a massage on stiff, tired muscles.

I should ask Mia some questions about magic. Chances are, it's the power behind these mysterious lights, too.

But there are more important topics to discuss first.

During his time with the Goddess, there was one topic that fell to the wayside. Thinking back on it, it's strange that he wouldn't bring it up when he had the chance.

He assumed that the upcoming civilizational collapse would be no different than the one that gripped Western Europe on Earth between 500 and 800 AD. That period of unrest was caused by the felling of the dominant power at the time, Rome.

The collapse of Western Europe's greatest culture plunged the region into chaos, where scientific and cultural advancement stagnated. Even knowing just how bad those times were for the people was difficult due to the lack of reliable writing. People were far too preoccupied with survival, after all.

"Mia, let's continue our tour of the castle. I'd like to visit any areas you deem important so I can refresh my memory of them."

"...As you wish."

Lucian fell in line beside his sister, peeking at her emotionless face. "I do remember something important. Our country, the Almekian Kingdom, is in bad shape, isn't it? How exactly did we end up in such troubled times?"

A look of concern flashed across Mia's face, but she quickly hid it. "I'm not sure. As a princess, I cannot rule this kingdom, so I was never kept informed of the details. However, when it comes to trade, food production, and public safety, each of them has quickly deteriorated. Many believe it to be the result of the Esgares Empire's recent invasions of our lands, but I can't say for sure."

"The Esgares Empire is invading us? So we're at war?"

"We're always at war. The problem is that this time, we're losing."

Could that be the reason for the coming collapse? It was the Germanic people's conquering of Rome that led to it on Earth, so this lines up nicely with our own history.

There were still many unanswered questions, but Lucian intended to seek the truth during his upcoming studies. What he needed now was a place to search for the answers. A library with historical records would be a great place to start, but his sister had yet to lead him to such a room.

"This is the throne room," Mia said, stopping in front of an ornate set of double doors.

"So this is where I'll be giving out my orders after I'm crowned."

"Yes, shall we go inside?"

"No, I'm sure I'll get my fill of it soon enough. Rather than that, I'd like to know if we have a libra–"

"Your Majesty!" A voice interrupted him mid-sentence.

Turning, Lucian caught sight of a well-dressed young man, his age matching his own. Despite being in a royal castle, he called out to the future king with confidence. The smile covering his lips said a lot, even without a single spoken word.

"Rudeus..." Mia said softly.

"My liege." Rudeus gave Lucian a bow, but it appeared more playful than anything else. "When I heard you had recovered enough to walk around, I simply had to track you down. Never thought you'd be with the squirt, though."

Lucian snuck a peek at Mia's face and saw that her expression hadn't changed, as if his rude words weren't the least bit strange.

Could it be that these two don't get along? And the fact that he would openly mock my little sister right in front of me can only mean one thing...

...Rudeus doesn't expect any sort of rebuke from me.

Knowing so little about the people around him placed Lucian in a difficult spot. If he were to act out of line compared to what was expected of him, it could draw suspicion. With his excuse of amnesia, he may be able to brush it off, but he couldn't rely on that every time.

Lucian turned to his little sister still standing beside him. "Thanks for showing me around, Mia. I'll call for you again later."

She wasted no time making herself scarce, as if she were suddenly let loose from a leash that bound her.

"What's up with you?" Rudeus asked after Mia vanished. "I don't think I've ever heard you thank her like that."

"It's because of that disease. I can barely remember anything before yesterday."

"Amnesia? Is it that bad?"

"Well, every time I see or hear about things I knew about, it seems to jog my memories. I'm slowly remembering everything, but the healer said it'll take some time."

"Hahaha! No wonder! Lucian, buddy. Have you really forgotten how much you hate your little sister?"

"I..." Lucian couldn't bring himself to agree with Rudeus.

Thinking about Mia's attitude until now, he realized that not once did she seem genuinely happy that he was alive. He assumed she just didn't show her emotions well, but now he was beginning to realize that there was another reason entirely.

A memory suddenly surfaced in his mind, one that left him feeling anxious. The stiff laugh of the Goddess when she spoke of Prince Lucian.

Lucian, just what kind of person were you...?

Well, it's not uncommon for siblings to have strained relationships. Maybe it's not as bad as I'm making it out to be.

Without knowing the details between Mia and the now deceased prince, Lucian could not fathom the depths of his sister's fear.

"Your Majesty," Rudeus said. "Now that the squirt's gone, I can really help you remember who you were before the illness."

"You keep calling me 'majesty', but I'm not the king yet, you know."

"It's fine, right? Nobody else can challenge your right to the throne. At least, not without a bloody civil war. And with the war against the Esgares Empire raging, nobody would be dumb enough to do that."

"You might be right. But in public, please use 'Your Highness'. Wouldn't want anyone to think I'm conceited enough to consider myself king before I'm even crowned."

"Don't worry, I know how important your public image is to you. I'll make sure not to ruin it. I've kept your secrets all this time, haven't I? Oh, right. The amnesia."

Lucian was barely able to keep the frown from his lips. "I'd be happy if you could remind me of those secrets when we have time."

"No problem! Leave it to your best friend!" A smile crept onto his lips. "I've got the perfect place for us right now. It was always one of your favorite pastimes, so it's sure to bring back some memories."

"That so? Then I'm interested to see what you have in mind."

In truth, Lucian wanted to go to a library. He felt that gaining knowledge on his new world was a far more important task than whatever Rudeus had in store for him. But he'd have to learn about the former prince sometime, and he didn't lie when he said he was curious about what was to come.

Since it was a destination that had tangible benefits for him, Lucian decided to follow Rudeus through the castle hallways, taking note of various rooms along the way.

Before long, they stepped out onto a second-floor balcony overlooking a large courtyard. The ground below was separated into various sections, like a flower garden and a gazebo used for outdoor dining.

But by far the most dominant section was a simple ring of dirt just below the balcony. Even though there was nothing interesting about it in particular, dozens of people were gathered around it, yelling and cheering.

That's because taking place in the center of that dirt ring was...

"A duel?" Lucian looked down at the two men, each wielding a sword and shield.

"Hah. Starting to remember yet?"

"We used to come here a lot to watch the fights," Lucian surmised.

"What better way to pass the time than a little friendly bloodshed? Though it was never enough for you."

"What do you mean?"

Rudeus gave the prince a mysterious smile. "One thing at a time, my friend."

Feeling a little uncomfortable, Lucian watched the match between the two warriors. They wore protective gear, but the armor only covered the vital areas like the head and chest. The rest was simple cloth.

Of course, Lucian had seen plenty of fights in his years on Earth. But boxing and MMA matches on a television screen were a far cry from the brutal battle taking place in the arena below him.

The light-brown dirt was already covered with a crusty red, yet the two warriors seemed determined to color the rest with their own blood.

Their speed and power are on another level. Are they really human?

It was true that stepping into a new world would really mess with someone's expectations, but if Lucian wanted to stand a chance of solving the problems he'd be encountering, he needed to change his way of thinking.

With a sudden burst of speed, one of the fighters below bashed into his opponent. The aggressive assault broke the second man's guard, leaving him open for a follow up. The fighter didn't miss the opening, his sword becoming a blur to Lucian's eyes.

A grunt, a splash of red, and a thud. At the end, the man lay defeated on the newly painted dirt ground.

There's no way a man can move with such speed. Could it be the result of ... magic?

"Bravo!" Rudeus yelled from the balcony. "Nice fight!"

The soldiers turned their faces up, realizing for the first time that the audience had increased at some point during the match. When they noticed that one of the newcomers was Prince Lucian himself, they saluted their soon-to-be king.

"Well?" Rudeus urged him with his eyes.

Lucian—or rather, Thomas George Hamilton—had given many speeches in his previous life. How could he not, considering his political career? Such experience wouldn't simply vanish, even if he was in a new world.

Fear, anxiety, hesitation. None of those struck him as he looked upon the armed men whom he would soon be responsible for commanding.

"An excellent duel!" Lucian said. "Worthy of my kingdom's warriors! To the victor, I offer my praise! Your fearless assault opened a path to victory, and such bravery is always admirable on the battlefield!

"And to the loser, take this as an opportunity to learn! It is only through defeat that you can truly grow! The next time I see you step into the arena, I hope that you will impress me with your unrivaled swordsmanship!"

It seemed his words had the intended effect, as the men let out a cheer. Even the defeated fighter seemed to have had his spirits lifted, a look of conviction in his eyes.

"Still have it, I see," Rudeus said.

"Just because I don't remember doesn't mean I'll forget."

"That's just like you." Rudeus shook his head. "Oh, what's this? Don't tell me that beast intends to do battle with a real warrior."

"Hm?" Lucian matched the direction of his gaze.

In the dirt arena, two new warriors had stepped into the ring. One was a man like any other, his muscled body no doubt a fearsome sight on the battlefield. But the other...

Are those ... animal ears? And a tail...?

He barely managed to hide his surprise at the sudden appearance of a strange looking person with fox-like ears and a matching tail. Her hair and furry tail were both strikingly white, though there was an even more surprising fact about the beastfolk warrior.

They're ... a girl? And young, at that.

Seeing the slim figure of a girl that couldn't be a day older than the 17-year-old prince himself, Lucian couldn't help but feel a bit anxious as the two warriors faced off in the center of the arena.

Though he wanted to stop the match, he felt that doing so would be a huge dishonor to the courage it must have taken the young girl to step into the ring. He could only watch on in silence, his hands tightening on the balcony's railing.

"How long do you think she'll last?" Rudeus asked.

"You say that as if the battle has already been decided."

"Do you really think one of the white haired beastfolk can defeat a trained soldier in the arena?"

"We won't know until the match is concluded." Lucian wanted to convince himself more than anything else.

"Hah. Guess you've forgotten, huh?"

"Forgotten what?"

"Just watch, and it should come back to you."

After Rudeus' words, a new voice filled the air, barely audible over the rowdy soldiers eagerly awaiting the start of the match.

A chant. So he's using magic.

It wasn't the warrior in the ring using the spell. Rather, it was one of the men in the outer ring. But even Lucian could tell that the magic was directed at the man who was about to do battle.

Unlike the large man, the fox-eared beastfolk girl didn't have anyone casting magic on her. Everyone there understood why, except for the anxious prince.

After the short preparation, the battle began.

When it came to fighting, Lucian couldn't claim to have any amount of expertise. He'd never even been in a fight before, much less a battle. The same could be said of many people who grew up in the comfort of a peaceful country like the United States. The most he could claim was a bit of second-hand experience watching boxing and MMA.

But even Lucian could tell that something was odd.

Why is she so slow? No, it's not that she's slow. She's just moving normally, like a regular person. It's her opponent that's been quickened by his magic.

So, why didn't anyone cast the same spell on her?

Realization suddenly dawned on him, sparked by Rudeus' words before the battle began.

No, could it be that using magic on one of those animal-eared people is a bad idea...?

"She's better than I thought," Rudeus says. "But it's only a matter of time."

"A matter of time before what?"

"Before she runs out of stamina. There's no way she can keep this pace up for long."

"But isn't her opponent pushing himself even harder? He's moving quicker and hitting harder. If anyone were to wear out, wouldn't it be him?"

"Lucian, buddy. You really need to go to the court mage and get a reminder of just how powerful magic is."

"Are you saying that the spell he cast not only increased his physical abilities to this degree but also his endurance?"

"Wouldn't be very useful if you exhausted yourself so quickly, would it?"

Even as they spoke, Lucian never took his eyes off the battle. His grip on the railing was so tight that his knuckles were beginning to turn as white as the beastfolk girl's hair.

She's good. Better than her opponent. But...

A sword hit the dirt. The beastfolk girl that used to hold it dove to retrieve her weapon, but a kick sent her sprawling to the ground.

The victor raised his sword, preparing to deliver a powerful blow to finish the battle.

Time seemed to move at a snail's pace as Lucian waited for the sword to fall. He could tell the swords were blunted, but with the soldier's enhanced strength, he feared what kind of damage the weapon would do to a normal girl.

I can't...!

"That's enough!" Lucian's yell was so commanding, it surprised even him.

The warrior looked up at the balcony, the sword in his hand still held high. On his face was a bloodlust that could only be brought out by a fierce battle.

"Hey, Lucian!" Rudeus yelled softly. "It's bad manners to interrupt a duel!"

"I know," he replied with remarkable confidence.

The soldier finally lowered his weapon, though he didn't seem pleased with having his victory dampened by Lucian's command. But the prince already had a plan to remedy the situation he brought about.

During his time with the Goddess, Lucian learned little about the former prince whose body he now inhabited. But one thing she was very clear about was his reputation for swooning ladies.

"It'd be a shame to mar the face of such a lovely girl," Lucian said. "Especially since I wish to make her acquaintance."

At his words, a wave of understanding swept through the soldiers below. If the beastfolk girl caught the eye of the lady-killer prince, then it'd be easy to excuse the rude interruption.

"So that's it," Rudeus said. "Should have known. You just can't help yourself when you see some easy prey, can you? Even white hairs aren't off the menu."

"I'll have you know that I plan to be a gentleman."

"Hah, right. Or do you actually believe that? Your memory problem is really screwing with my expectations. But don't worry, I'll help you remember. Just leave it to your buddy Rudeus."

Please, I really don't need this to be any more complicated than it already is...

As he looked down at the gaping beastfolk girl below, Lucian couldn't help but feel like he'd gotten himself into quite a mess.

What am I going to do about this situation now?

Chapter 4

"I-it's good to meet you, Prince Lucian! I'm Emilia!"

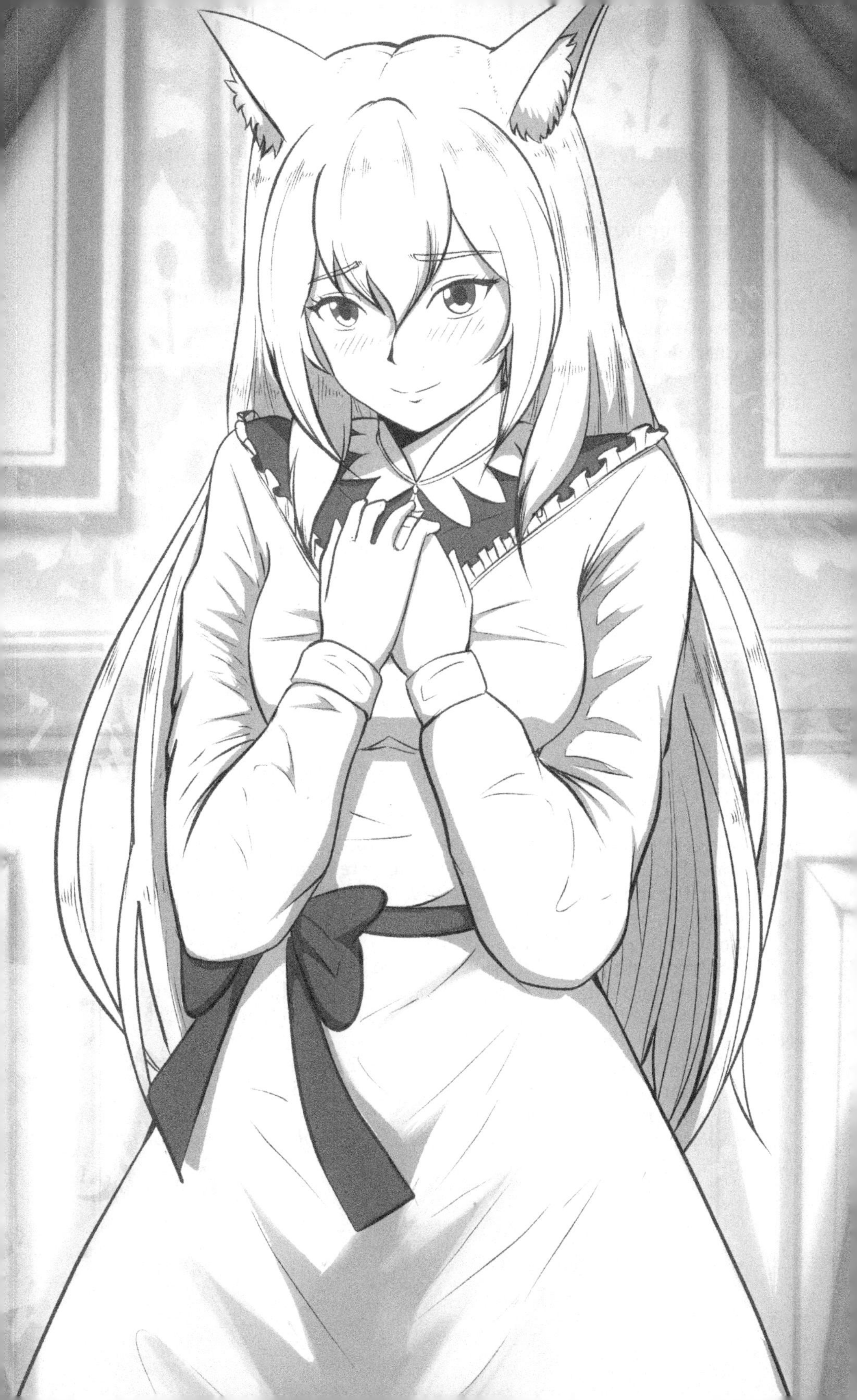

Anyone who said the foxkin beastfolk girl was nervous to meet her prince would be a contender for the title of Captain Obvious. Not only was it nearly unheard of for a commoner to be invited into the castle, but that goes doubly so for beastfolk.

Add her white hair onto the list, and it could only be considered a once-in-a-lifetime event.

Emilia made many sacrifices to obtain her skill with the sword and join the military, so this outcome could be considered a dream come true. But it wasn't one she ever imagined would happen.

After her defeat in the practice grounds, Emilia was guided into the castle proper, where she was given instructions on how to act and present herself in front of the soon-to-be king.

Though nervous, a soldier was conditioned to follow orders. Perhaps that was why she managed to not make a fool of herself, despite having no formal etiquette training.

I really messed up, Lucian thought. *Couldn't I have found another excuse as to why I stopped the fight...?*

The silly little prince ended up plopping yet another burden onto his plate. It was his own fault though, so he only had himself to blame.

Of course, that wouldn't stop him from complaining about it to anyone who would listen. The problem was, he had no such confidant in his new world. Unless he could find someone he could truly trust, he'd have to carry all his burdens alone.

"Welcome, Emilia." Lucian motioned to a nearby seat. "Please, make yourself comfortable."

"Yes, Your Highness!"

Emilia obeyed, but contrary to the fluid and precise movements she displayed in the arena, she walked to the seat with stiff steps.

She's really out of her element. No surprise, I guess. Not everyone can handle a sudden invitation to meet with royalty.

He waited patiently for her to relax a bit before continuing. "I was impressed with your battle today, Emilia. It takes courage to face a soldier enhanced with magic when you have none."

"Thanks. Though I still lost..."

"That's true, but there's still pride to be had in defeat. I'd much prefer to see your face filled with determination and focus, as it was during the match."

"I-is that so?" A bit of confidence returned to her. "In that case, I'll gladly accept your praise, Your Highness."

"That's more like it," Rudeus said. "I'm sure the prince would be happy if you carried such an expression during the dinner party tonight."

"Eh!? I'm going to a dinner party!?"

Hey, why are you even here? I don't need you to play wingman for me right now!

The unfortunate prince just had his plan foiled by his wannabe wingman. In truth, Lucian had intended to only offer Emilia praise and a bit of conversation before sending her on her way.

But now that Rudeus had offered an invitation to dinner, he couldn't very well rescind it. Stuck with yet another task to juggle, Lucian could only mentally shake his head in response. He might want to get used to that.

"Of course you're invited," Lucian said. "Consider it a reward for impressing me today."

"Thank you very much, Your Highness! Ah, b-but I don't have an outfit worthy of such a party..."

"Don't worry, we'll provide everything you need."

"Should I tell the maids to prepare a gown?" Rudeus asked.

"No, she's my guest, so I'll take responsibility for her. However, I would like you to ensure that the meals served are to my liking. You know what I like to eat, right?"

"Hah. Of course." Rudeus nodded, having picked up on Lucian's intent. "Then allow me to take care of it straight away."

He stood from his chair, gave the prince a wink, then left through the room's only exit.

In Rudeus' mind, the prince gave him two tasks. The first was obviously to make sure the food served was his favorite, so Lucian could remember what he liked to eat. But the prince really couldn't care less about the tastes of his body's former inhabitant.

Rudeus believed the real reason for the mission was to give Lucian some alone time with Emilia. The deceased prince had been quite a ladies' man before his untimely demise, so situations like this hadn't exactly been rare.

He thought to give the prince a helping hand while his memory was still foggy, but it seemed that was an unnecessary task. With a smirk, Rudeus walked off toward the kitchen.

After watching his companion leave, Lucian breathed a mental sigh of relief. Having that man's expectations hounding him was quite tiresome. Now that he was alone with someone who had no knowledge of the former prince, he felt he could truly relax.

Emilia, on the other hand, only grew more nervous. It was strange enough to be invited into such a private chamber by the crown prince, but now the two of them were completely alone.

An awkward silence began to settle, but it wasn't one Lucian picked up on. He was still enjoying the sudden relaxed atmosphere brought upon by Rudeus' departure. So, it wasn't the least bit surprising that when he finally spoke up, there wasn't a hint of unease in his voice.

"Say, Emilia. Care to join me for a while?"

"A-ah. I'd love to, Prince Lucian ... but what exactly do you have in mind...?"

"I know this may sound really boring, but I wanted to do some reading. It'd be great to have someone accompany me to answer some of my questions."

"Eh...? Reading?"

"Sorry, do you not want to?"

"N-no, that's not what I meant! Of course I'd love to go!"

"Y-you would?" Lucian was caught a bit off guard by Emilia's sudden enthusiasm. "Then, if you please."

He stood, then held out his hand. The foxkin beastfolk girl stared at it for a long second, as if unsure what the gesture meant. Though in truth, she was simply surprised that a prince would offer it to help her stand.

She really gets embarrassed easily, Lucian thought as Emilia took his hand. *It's kinda cute when her face gets flushed red. It really contrasts her white hair.*

I wonder if there are other kinds of beastfolk. And if white hair is common among them.

Unbeknownst to Lucian, white hair was in fact rare. Very rare. Though the reason for that wasn't one he'd be thrilled to learn.

"We'll be going to the royal study," Lucian said after they stepped into the hall.

"Is it fine for me to enter such a place?" Emilia looked more excited than nervous.

"Sure, as long as you're with me. In fact, I'd prefer for you to join me. I have a lot of questions, and you're the perfect person to answer them."

"Eh? Why me?"

"I've received a lot of tutoring, but what's taught to me by teachers doesn't always reflect what's going on in the everyday lives of the citizens. Having input from someone who's lived their whole life outside the castle is important to developing a well-rounded understanding of the world."

Emilia's mouth was slightly agape after hearing Lucian's explanation. "If you think I can be of any service, then I'll happily answer any questions!"

"Good." Lucian opened an ornate door.

He had finally broken down and asked Rudeus where he could find a library, but it turned out, there was no such place in the castle. The only room with a plethora of literature was the royal study, where the king stored his books and important documents.

That place now filled Lucian's vision, massive bookcases filled to the brim with literature of all kinds. Those bookcases didn't just line the walls. They filled the room from front to back, thousands upon thousands of books, documents, and papers of various natures.

They said there wasn't a library, but isn't this large enough to be considered one?

In truth, much of the literature there was simply useless documents of reports, records, and other administration paperwork. Many of them were so old that they were no longer valid to the current state of the Almekian Kingdom.

But that wasn't the case for everything. Within the thousands of pieces of literature, perhaps Lucian could find what he needed.

"Then." Lucian turned to Emilia. "Let the study begin."

"Well, this is inconvenient," Lucian said as he flipped through yet another useless document.

"Prince Lucian." Emilia's voice was laced with buried anger. "Whose job is it to organize the royal study?"

"Uh, I'm actually not sure about that..."

"Whoever holds the position is in desperate need of a reprimand! Don't they understand even the basics of how to sort literature!?"

"It would seem that the answer is ... no."

After entering the royal study with grand plans of quickly obtaining the information they sought, the two of them learned a valuable lesson. The previous monarch cared little for organizing their documents for ease of access.

The truth was that after the previous caretaker had passed away, nobody had been appointed to replace them. Seeing as how that was five years ago, the room could only be described as a disaster.

Sure, it was kept clean and tidy by the maids, but since they simply placed any books into the nearest empty space on the shelves, it wasn't uncommon to find a historical record placed next to an administrative ledger.

When faced with such thoughtless sorting, Lucian and Emilia could only randomly pick through the thousands of books in hopes of finding what they sought. Even though their search was barely more than trial and error, the two of them were bound to run across the information they needed eventually.

Currently, a small stack of books sat atop the study's desk. Lucian intended to go through their contents when he had time, which meant many late nights staring at parchment.

But as of yet, the information he truly sought had eluded him.

The task had become mindless enough that Lucian felt comfortable filling the air with conversation. He wanted to ask Emilia all kinds of questions, but he knew almost nothing about the girl herself.

Believing it to be rude to bombard her before at least getting to know her a little, he decided to start with a few personal questions. Besides, hearing of her life would help give Lucian a grasp of what kind of experiences a typical beastfolk had to deal with. That was important, if he wanted to rule them effectively.

"Emilia. What made you want to join the military?"

"Ah ... w-well, it's a bit embarrassing, but I once read a story called *The King's Journey*. He started as just a soldier, no different than any other. But he worked hard and did his best! Battle after battle, he risked his life to save as many others as he could!

"He was rewarded with recognition and promotions over and over! The men respected him, and his name even spread through the empire's towns and cities! But when the war was over, the empire tried to get rid of him! Ohhh! Just remembering it makes me so mad!

"But that didn't stop him! He fought against the charges of treason, and the people stood with him! With the citizens and soldiers at his back, he took the crown and made his homeland into a great empire again!"

"W-wow..."

But you do realize you're talking to a future king right now, don't you?

It was fortunate that Thomas George Hamilton was the one who heard her story, as the contents essentially romanticized rebellion.

However, hearing that she had such strong feelings toward a hero who stood up for what he believed in, going so far as to dethrone a tyrant, actually made him respect Emilia even more.

"S-sorry! I get a little worked up sometimes..."

"No, don't apologize. It's good to have passions to drive you."

"Ah, perhaps you're right. I mean! You're absolutely correct, Prince Lucian!" Emilia bowed her head slightly.

"Hey, don't just suddenly remember I'm the crown prince and get all proper. I'd like it if you treated me more casually when we're alone."

"Eh? Is that okay...?"

"Of course it is. But only when we're alone. We do have a rigid society, so appearances are important."

"I understand. I won't disappoint you!"

"I've got to be honest though," Lucian said as he moved on to another bookshelf. "I didn't expect you to be an avid reader."

"I love books. They take you to worlds that you'd otherwise never be able to visit. For someone like me, it was the only way to escape."

"Someone like you?"

"W-well, you know. The white hair..."

White hair? Rudeus did say something about her white hair.

Without knowledge of this world's history, Lucian could only surmise the meaning of white haired beastfolk from the few comments he'd heard.

Rudeus seemed surprised that Lucian would set his eyes on a white hair, while Emilia spoke about the subject with obvious reservation, as if it were something to be ashamed of.

With these clues, Lucian could piece together that it wasn't a point of pride. Rather, they appeared to see it more like a curse.

The connotation is obvious. But there's no way for me to guess the literal meaning of having white hair unless I ask directly.

Although he didn't want to dig up what was obviously a sour subject, he had to be fully informed about it. He had invited her into the castle as his personal guest, so he had to be prepared to deal with whatever problems came along with that.

"About your white hair ... could you tell me what it means?"

"What it means? It's just as everyone says, isn't it? The white-haired beastfolk nearly conquered the world, right? That's why they were exterminated..."

"Yeah, of course. But what does it mean for you, who's had to live with white hair your whole life?" Lucian readily agreed, then swiftly pretended as if his question was meant to be interpreted differently.

"Ah, you mean how has it affected me personally? Of course, I was ostracized as a child. My parents had no choice but to move out of our town and into the countryside. Even there, I could barely show my face. But at least I could find places where I could be alone. Though the books my parents sometimes brought home were by far the most helpful at keeping me sane."

"What a rough childhood. But it seems like you managed to grow into a capable young woman. I'm impressed."

"I-I'm not that special or anything. I just wanted to take control of my own life, so when I had the chance, I chose my own path."

"By joining the military? I'm surprised they even let you in, considering the stigma against white-haired beastfolk."

"Eh?" Emilia gave Lucian a questioning look.

For a while now, his strange comments had made her increasingly curious. To her, it sounded almost as if the crown prince had no knowledge of the world at all.

Seeing the books and reports stacked up on the study desk only further confounded the young girl. But despite her internal questions, there was no way a white hair with no military rank could voice them out loud.

If it's answers he's looking for, Emilia thought, *then maybe I can provide some.*

"My kind are always in high demand within the military. Our lineage may be feared, but at the same time, our strength can't be denied. It was the effectiveness of magic on us that allowed us to nearly conquer the world, so of course the kingdom would want that power for itself, right?"

"Right ... the effectiveness of magic on your kind."

Since it seemed he still didn't understand, Emilia continued. "Support magic has an extremely powerful effect on white-haired beastfolk. Even if we can't cast spells ourselves, having other mages enhance us before battle can create a formidable force that can be unleashed on the enemy."

"Ah, that's true. With such a powerful regiment in our ranks, our battle potential goes up dramatically."

"That's exactly right. Although the Council of Elders has fought to prevent us from being forcibly conscripted, many of my kind still end up in the military. Those who don't join are often excluded from society, labeled as cowards for not fighting to make up for our past failings."

"Yeah, I can understand that, even if I don't agree with it."

The prince finally realized just what kind of world Emilia had been living in her whole life—ostracized by those around her, yet expected to fight for them, regardless of the treatment she endured.

Considering everything she must have been through, Lucian thought, *it's a wonder she's as cheerful and easy-going as she is.*

Not just anyone would be able to live a life like that and still be able to smile.

Since the topic had gotten heavy, Lucian decided to let the air settle a bit while he focused on looking through the books and records filling the shelves.

As he worked, he stole glances at Emilia. The young beastfolk girl didn't show the slightest bit of agitation. In fact, she seemed quite happy, despite having done nothing but look through paperwork for the past hour.

As Lucian watched her, he noticed for the first time that Emilia wasn't just putting books back from wherever she pulled them from. Rather, she was placing them back onto the shelf in different locations.

Lucian couldn't see any reason for doing such a thing, as it only increased the amount of work. So, he decided to simply ask.

"Hey Emilia, why are you moving the books' locations around on the shelves?"

"Ah, my apologies, Prince Lucian. I simply couldn't help myself. When I saw how disorganized this study was, I just had to start fixing it…"

"You're sorting them? In that case, there's no need to apologize. It's a task in desperate need of completion, so I don't see a problem with continuing it."

"Thank you! I'd be happy to organize the entire study, if you wish for it!"

"Not a bad idea. It'll give you a reason to come back to the castle, at the very least."

Although he had initially intended on simply sending her away after a short conversation, somewhere along the line, Lucian had begun to think that it'd be great if they could meet again. Having so few people he could trust in the castle, someone from the outside was a welcome addition.

After all, there was no way Emilia had a hand in the former prince's assassination. That fact alone made her valuable as a potential confidant.

"Ah-ha!" Lucian pulled a particularly thick book from the shelf. "Found it!"

"Way to go, Prince Lucian!" For some reason, Emilia sounded really proud of him.

"With this, I can finally start fulfilling my role as the crown prince."

"I'm glad to hear, but why is a book filled with noble lineages so important?"

"Because it gives me a crystal-clear view of this kingdom's hierarchy. Which noble families control each territory, who their branch families are, their ranks, the titles and positions they hold, and more. It's absolutely essential that I know my own kingdom inside and out."

"Ah, so you want to fill in the gaps of your knowledge! I guess since you weren't the crown prince, His Majesty didn't give you tutoring on such subjects?"

Lucian had kept a secret from Emilia all this time. Or rather, he had kept the lie about his faulty memory from her. He didn't want news of his condition to spread too far outside the castle, so he had intended to let her leave never knowing the truth.

But if she were going to be returning, then he wanted her in on his lie.

"Ah, right. I haven't told you yet. Actually, the disease messed with my memory. I have a hard time recalling people's names, much less all the information here in this record. I need to remember all of it, or else I'll quickly be overwhelmed by those who seek my power."

"So that's why!" Emilia finally understood his strange questions and behavior.

"Yeah, though I'd like to keep it a secret from others. Can I trust you with it?"

Emilia stood up, straightened her back, and performed a perfect salute. "I swear that it will never leave my lips, Prince Lucian!"

"At ease, soldier," Lucian said with a teasing smile. "Looks like I'll be busy with these records tonight, but we still have some time to spare, so would you mind answering a few more questions?"

"Not at all! Ask, and I'll give the best answers I can!"

With his search complete for now, Lucian began bombarding Emilia with the many questions that had been on his mind.

As for the beastfolk girl, she continued to sort the royal study, even as she answered one question after the next.

Chapter 5

Whew. Lucian sighed mentally as he walked down the castle hallways. *Been a while since my university days. Study sessions are gonna take some getting used to again...*

Even after his college days on Earth, Lucian had never stopped learning. But there was a difference between doing a bit of research on the side while working a full-time job versus spending hours with your nose between a book's pages.

The nearly two hours he just spent going over his empire's nobility was just a taste of what was to come. Without a doubt, Lucian would be in for many long nights in the coming weeks.

At least it'll be much easier to find what I'm looking for when Emilia finishes reorganizing the royal study.

Since she loves books so much, I can even get her to help look over some of the information and make notes for me. That way, I can get the short version quickly.

I wonder if Mia would like to help, too...

Thinking of his sister brought to mind the tense relationship the two siblings seemed to have. Lucian still wasn't sure what to make of it, but fixing it was one of his priorities.

As Lucian continued his walk down the castle halls, he found himself standing in front of a particular door. For several reasons, he was hesitant to disturb the one inside. But at the same time, he couldn't let the uncertainty of their past relationship fester.

Besides, Lucian already had a few excuses lined up as to why he would suddenly show up unannounced. If he had the time and reasons, then he might as well put them both to use.

knock, knock

"Yes? Who is it?" a young voice asked.

"Lucian. May I come in?"

After a few seconds of silence, the pattering of soft steps was followed by the casual opening of the door.

"What brings you to my room, Esteemed Brother?"

"Hey, Mia. I wanted to check up on you to make sure you'll be ready for the feast."

"Yes. I've already properly groomed myself and am just awaiting the clock's signal."

"You definitely put in the extra effort, didn't you?" Lucian noted her elaborate dress and meticulously bound hair. "Though you seem to have a habit of looking presentable at all times."

"It's my duty as a princess to look the part, even if I have no real responsibilities."

"That's true. But maybe we can find something useful for you to do. It must be rather boring to not hold any sort of position, despite your title as princess." Lucian looked over Mia's shoulder and into the room behind her. "Mind if I come in so we can discuss a few things?"

The young girl stepped aside, so Lucian took the path offered him. As expected of an eleven-year-old princess' room, it was decorative and tidy. Though perhaps another way to describe it would be prim and proper.

On Earth, most girls her age would have toys and many other objects lying about. Lucian's own daughter on Earth was ten, and her room was always filled with various sources of entertainment. Seeing a room so cleanly kept was quite a shock to him.

That said, it wasn't like Mia's room was barren. A desk took up one of the walls, with books lined up between two bookends. A quill and jar of ink sat atop it as well, making Lucian curious what it was that Mia liked to write.

Does she need it for her studies? Or does she keep a diary?

Moving his eyes from the desk, they fell on a large fireplace, next to which was a clock standing taller than Lucian himself. The consistent clicking of the swinging pendulum emanated from the clock's base as it precisely kept the time of day, at least by the standards of this world.

A chest at the foot of Mia's bed, a dresser on one side of the room, a wardrobe indented into the wall, and a partition in the far corner. Such objects could be seen at a glance, each obvious in their use.

But there was one thing that stood out among the rest.

A stuffed teddy bear? I guess she does like cute things, after all.

The furry little head of the stuffed bear barely poked out from beneath Mia's bed sheets. It wasn't uncommon for girls her age to fall asleep with a toy in their embrace, but Lucian was still a bit surprised at the revelation that the ever-proper Mia was among that group.

It seemed his eyes lingered on the stuffed bear a little too long, as Mia gently pulled on the sheets, covering what little of its furry head once peeked out from beneath.

Embarrassed, huh? Lucian held back a smile. *So you're just a normal kid, after all.*

Lucian felt a little more comfortable, now that he'd gotten a glimpse of his sister's soft side. The fact that she tried to hide it after it was already revealed ended up backfiring, in his mind at least.

"I'm glad to see that you're prudent when it comes to preparing for gatherings," Lucian said. "That's one less thing for me to worry about. It also means I can get straight to the second reason I stopped by."

"What is it that you need? I'll help in any way I can."

Lucian ignored the complete lack of enthusiasm in her voice. "Actually, because of my memory problems, I can't even remember how to use magic. Considering how powerful spells are, I don't want word of this to spread. Hence why I was hoping you could give me a short lesson."

"You even forgot how to cast? I suppose I should have known that, considering everything else you can't recall." Mia made a complicated face. "If you wish to remember, then I will do my best to teach you."

"Thanks, Mia. I'll make sure to thank you with a gift, though I can't imagine what you'd like. If there's anything you want, feel free to share it with me."

"...There's no need to offer me a gift."

"You think so? I don't agree, so try not to be surprised if I get you one, okay?"

"...Understood." Mia barely maintained a neutral expression. "As for the magic lesson, it should be simple if all you need is a quick reminder."

"Yeah. At least I hope so." Lucian felt a sweat drop forming on his back.

The dead prince may have been able to cast spells, but the reincarnated politician name Thomas George Hamilton had only seen the like in movies. He didn't even play his world's video games, so his exposure to things like magic was very limited indeed.

Now, he was being expected to pick it up in a heartbeat.

"Do you remember about mana?" Mia asks. "If you close your eyes and focus, you should be able to feel it flowing through you."

"So that's what this strange feeling is..." Lucian focused on the warmth he felt inside his body. "But what can I do with it?"

"With the proper chant, the mana will move on its own and fulfill your desire." Mia's face filled with concentration. "Divine power, grant Lucian a cat's grace!"

Lucian silently stared at his sister for several seconds, his eyes slowly widening. As soon as she had completed the spell, he felt the magical energy pour into him, filling him with a strange sensation.

He moved his arms before him. It was a simple gesture, but even with that, he could feel the difference.

Why do I suddenly feel like I could win the gold medal at a gymnastics tournament on Earth?

No, the reason is obvious. Magic.

"I think I understand what kind of magic that was, but can you explain?"

"The chant allows the target to move more swiftly, while increasing their balance and precision. It's a common magic to use since it allows the target to appear more elegant and graceful."

"That so? Then did you cast it on me, hoping it would somehow jog my memory?"

"No. It's just that casting support magic on oneself is impossible."

Lucian looked surprised. "Impossible to use on yourself? Why?"

"Nobody is sure. Magical scholars can't agree on a reason, and I've never pondered it too deeply."

"Guess that's just how it is, huh? Well, either way, I might as well try it, too." Lucian closed his eyes and tossed aside his embarrassment. "D-divine power, grant Mia a cat's grace!"

And just like that...

...Nothing happened.

"Um..." Mia's tiny voice was like a dagger being jammed into his deflated pride. "That chant is the one I use. I don't know how effective it will be for you."

"Turns out, not effective at all. I felt the mana start to ... do something. But after the chant, it just went back to normal."

"How strange. Even if it's not an efficient chant, it should have at least activated the spell in some fashion."

"By effective and efficient, what do you mean exactly?"

"Everyone has their own chant, one that fits them. Magic scholars say that the better a chant fits the caster, the more effective the spell will be. Your position, personality, and desires all play a part on the strength of the spell."

"So, for example, a warrior may have a more aggressive chant than a priest, even if they're casting the same spell?"

"Correct. And neither one would be wrong. They are simply maximizing the effectiveness of the spell according to their own circumstances."

"Position, personality, and desires..."

"If you can't recall your chants, then you'll have to toy with your wording until you find ones that work best for you. Within the royal study is a book that lists a variety of spells, along with chants many use as a starting point to find their own. Or..."

"Or?"

"...Or you can ask Rudeus. I'm sure he remembers many of the chants you used to use."

"Rudeus, huh? I feel like he'd use it as an opportunity to have a good laugh at my expense, getting me to say all kinds of ridiculous chants. But I'll keep it in mind as a last resort. Anyway, is there anything else I need to know about how to cast magic?"

"No. If you practice from the book, you should have no problem casting. From there, it's simply refining the chant to fit you. But if you still find yourself unable to use magic, you may need to seek a teacher. Nobody can use magic without training first, so if your amnesia is blocking your spells, it may be necessary to start from the very beginning."

"Great. Thanks, Mia! I really owe you one."

"It's simply part of my responsibilities."

"Maybe, but I'll make sure to return the favor soon. Look forward to that gift!"

"..."

"Well," Lucian continued, "I'm going to get ready for the feast. I'll see you there soon."

"Goodbye, Esteemed Brother." Mia bowed her head slightly.

With that, Lucian left his sister's room. Although he wanted to go to the royal study and try his hand at some more magic, he had responsibilities to take care of.

Perhaps he had time to train a little longer with Mia, but one embarrassing failure was tough enough. He wanted to at least ensure his success before chanting in front of her again.

And so, with another task placed on Lucian's schedule, the recently reincarnated prince stepped into his own room to prepare himself for the party the nobles were throwing in honor of his miraculous survival.

Chapter 6

"That was quite a bore," Rudeus said. "But at least the formalities are over, and we can start enjoying this party."

"True." Lucian took a sip of wine. "It went on for a little longer than I would have liked. Though it did help me remember some important information."

After the celebratory party began, Lucian was stuck in his seat, greeting one guest after the next. Technically, they were congratulating him on surviving the disease and becoming the crown prince, but their ulterior motives were obvious to all.

Most nobles and otherwise powerful individuals in the kingdom had focused their attention on the king and the previous crown prince. Of course, their reasoning was to gain the favor of the current and future ruler to increase the power of their household.

But with their deaths, all that effort had gone to waste. The goodwill built up over the years wouldn't simply transfer to Lucian now that the kingdom was his for the taking. They'd have to start from scratch, and for most of them, the party was the first available opportunity to do so.

Considering that, it was no wonder that each guest had spent an exorbitant amount of time delivering their greeting. Unfortunately for them, it had the opposite effect on Lucian. The previous royal family may have enjoyed being praised to the heavens, but the new one just saw it as a needless formality.

Lucian had been to many similar gatherings back on Earth. As a politician, he had a responsibility to meet with those both above and below him on the ladder of power, so he'd seen it from both points of view.

Unlike most of the ones in power, Lucian had lived by the ideal America's Founding Fathers had envisioned upon the creation of the country. Politicians did not rule over the people; they served them. How could you serve the citizens if you were more concerned with currying favor of other politicians or large political donors?

To Lucian, such questions had an easy answer. You couldn't.

Now that I'm free to move around, let's make the most of this party.

These sorts of gatherings were often for discussing the affairs and policies of the kingdom, deepening the connections of those who already hold immense power. Even though the current party was a bit special, Lucian anticipated that once the welcome ended, the true motives of the guests would emerge.

Not one to sit passively by while the world revolved around him, Lucian decided to take the first step as soon as he found an opening. With Rudeus by his side, the prince walked over to a group who was having quite a conspicuous conversation in the center of the banquet hall.

It was high time he involved himself in the kingdom's affairs. He had only just recovered from the disease this morning, but he wanted to make a show of his healthy body by engaging in the liveliest discussion at the party.

Once again, he would have to draw upon his experience on Earth to carry him through. He had his fair share of tense debates, close races, and ruthless opponents. Something like a room full of power-hungry nobles would just be one street removed from the house he'd lived in for his entire political career.

During Lucian's recent study session, he had prioritized families and individuals with the closest connection to the royal family. He had to ensure that he'd have knowledge of the ones he would be most likely to meet, so it was the obvious choice.

He couldn't get all the information he needed about the kingdom's high nobility from a book of records, but meeting them in person would ensure that he would get to know them much better. However, until Lucian was comfortable in his understanding of the kingdom, he intended to put Rudeus to use, hence why he had the young noble accompanying him.

I might be relying on Rudeus for a while. I'll just have to get used to dealing with him.

The men he came to meet were speaking around a large, oval table, though the ones sitting at it were of far more importance than the table itself. Despite there being many seats, only four were in use.

The Minister of War dominated his chair, making it appear as if he would crush it under the weight of his large frame. But the wood used in its construction was surprisingly thick, which could be expected for furnishings used by this kingdom's most powerful nobles and royals.

The Minister of Production was also a large man, though for an entirely different reason. The chair was wide, but he filled nearly every inch of it with his round body.

The Minister of Finance was almost the polar opposite. Tall and lanky, the man's sunken eyes and pale complexion made Lucian wonder if he had been lacking sleep.

Lastly, the Minister of Domestic Affairs could only be described as normal when compared to the rest of them. If the man were part of a crowd, Lucian was sure his eyes would roll right over him.

So these are the four ministers in charge of this empire's most essential matters. And as king, I'll be tasked with directing them, just as they're tasked with advising me on the course the kingdom should take.

Lucian walked to the table, which grew quiet at his approach. Taking a seat, he met each of their eyes in turn, ending on the man who seemed most ready to speak. In fact, that man looked as if he were barely able to contain his tongue during Lucian's casual walk to his chair.

However, the prince tore his eyes away from the Minister of War and instead set his gaze on the Minister of Domestic Affairs.

"How have the people taken the news of my father and brothers' deaths?"

"Your Highness," he responded in a surprisingly casual tone. "Many feared the kingdom would fracture when the royal family fell ill, but they've since calmed down after learning of your survival. As of now, they're awaiting news of your official coronation to ensure that stability will be maintained."

"That's to be expected. Release an official statement saying that after one month of mourning, I will receive the crown."

"Alright. As soon as the news spreads, I'll gauge public opinion again. Though I suspect they'll be thrilled to learn you'll be king soon enough, considering your reputation among them."

"Good. I didn't expect my popularity with the people to come into play like this, but I'm grateful that I spent the effort to build it."

I don't know how I did it, though...

"Then," the prince continued. "Let's hear about the state of the war, Marcus."

"About time," the Minister of War, Marcus, said. "Nothing else matters if we don't defeat the Esgares Empire's troops!"

"It's a matter of grave importance, I'll give you that. But so is the internal stability of our kingdom. In fact, we cannot wage war if there's one brewing at home."

"Winning the war is the best way to stabilize the kingdom under your rule."

"Only if there is a kingdom left for someone to rule." Lucian shook his head. "But enough of that. What's the state of the war against the Esgares Empire as of now?"

"We're going to show those bastards why their grandfathers feared our kingdom. Their empire may be twice our size, but the quality of their troops can't compare! After the winter, our nobles will be able to conscript enough men to push back their assault, and that'll be the end of their conquering."

"That's in the future. What about today?"

Marcus frowned. "They're still camped in the Ezra province. But now that we've lost a province to their invasion, the people will be more willing to fight and retake it. If we can get the equipment and supplies we need, I know we can retake it in the spring."

So, Lucian thought. *We lost territory to their army already. If we don't stop the invasion, we'll just lose more and more land, until the entire kingdom crumbles.*

"You have a stockpile of emergency rations available for the new soldiers," the Minister of Production said. "So I hope you weren't referring to me when you insinuated the loss stemmed from a lack of supplies."

"Morale won't improve from eating bread as hard as bricks. I'm surprised you even have the gall to speak so arrogantly. How many starved this winter, thanks to your poor harvests?"

"It's not my fault that the Goddess cursed our lands during harvest season. Or are you suggesting that we should be angry at her divine will?"

"How convenient. You sure like to push the blame onto others, don't you?"

"I have no idea what you're talking about. Though in truth, if the finances were in order, we could have imported more food from the surrounding nations to make up for the poor harvests."

All faces turned toward the Minister of Finance. However, the man didn't seem the least bit interested in getting involved with the increasingly heated discussion. He merely stared at the two with his dark, sunken eyes.

"Well?" Marcus frowned again. "You got anything to say?"

"Nothing in particular."

"If you hadn't nearly bankrupted the kingdom, we could afford better gear and pay for the soldiers. Maybe then, we wouldn't have lost the recent battle!"

"That's unfortunate."

"Tch. Always with that same attitude. You'll–"

"That's enough," Lucian said.

"–get what's coming to you one day," Marcus continued, ignoring the prince. "I don't know why His Majesty kept you around, but I hope our new king has more sense!"

Lucian sighed. "We're in tough times. Left as is, it will only get worse. But I don't intend to sit idle while my kingdom crumbles, so I expect the four of you to get along and work toward rebuilding our country."

Not a single one of the ministers looked pleased at the thought of playing nice. To them, Lucian was still a kid, and not even one who was destined to hold the crown. Yet now he stood above them all. Such a rapid change in power was a tough pill to swallow, especially for those who think themselves more able.

However, unlike the masses, some of the ministers there knew that the deceased prince wasn't the gentle, caring man he pretended to be. Beneath their displeasure was a hint of fear, as if they expected the ground could fall out from beneath them at any time.

Although Lucian himself didn't pick up on their hidden fear.

Was it one of you? Lucian thought. *Did any of you have a hand in the death of nearly the entire royal family?*

Although there was no proof, Lucian believed the ones closest to the crown would be far more likely to benefit from the vacuum of power left in the wake of the king's death.

"Now," Lucian continued. "Let's discuss these matters in more detail. There are many things I wish to know."

The conversation continued for a while, which was exactly what Lucian wanted. He needed to learn about the state of his kingdom, and what better place to hear it than the mouths of those who control its most major functions?

However, this was a party to celebrate his survival, so he didn't intend to spend the entirety of it speaking of political matters. So, after obtaining a wealth of information, Lucian bid the men farewell and stood from his chair.

Things are bad, Lucian thought. *Really bad.*

The people are starving. Not just metaphorically. They're literally dying from starvation.

Can these people really enjoy such a lavish feast while the ones they're supposed to be protecting are dying from a lack of even the most basic food?

No, this isn't Earth. These people don't even have to pretend to care about the citizens. As long as there's no threat of a rebellion, they'll probably continue with this lifestyle until the very last person in this kingdom dies.

I can't rely on them to have a sudden change of heart, which means I have to be the one to act.

Before Lucian could even decide on his next conversation partner, a man approached him.

"Archduke Henrik Mathison Almekia," Rudeus reminded Lucian. "Your uncle."

"Ah, Uncle Henrik." Lucian gave him a slight nod. "It's good to see you."

"Your Highness, Prince Lucian." Henrik's formal bow made Lucian's small nod look almost rude by comparison. "It brings me great pleasure to see that at least one of the main family's heirs was able to survive the disease. I shudder to imagine what the kingdom would have to suffer through, had we lost you, as well."

"Perhaps this was simply the hand of the Goddess at work." Lucian held back a wry smile. "The Divine works in mysterious ways, after all."

"Yes, and I pray that her boons continue to fall on you in the future. We certainly need them in these uncertain times."

"Thank you, and I hope your magitech business continues to flourish. Your inventions have really been the saving grace for our kingdom this past decade."

Lucian had read a bit about Henrik's thriving magitech business during his study. The document stated that his uncle had made so much money from the creation and sale of magitech items that he had become famous even in the surrounding countries.

If it weren't for the trade and prestige brought into the kingdom through Henrik's efforts, Lucian wondered just how much worse their situation would be right now.

"Think nothing of it, Your Highness. I am merely doing my part to spread prosperity through the kingdom. Though if I could be so bold to speak freely, I do believe my magitech business is on course to become the greatest in the entire world."

"That would be an amazing feat, Henrik. If there's anything I can do to help, please don't hesitate to ask. It's a matter of national pride to have a world-class business, and it would surely help raise us from the depths we find ourselves in."

"As you wish, Your Highness."

The two gave parting gestures, then moved on, with Lucian seeking out other guests. He had already picked up on which ones held the most power, though he was still fuzzy on the finer details.

Regardless, he did his best to approach them in the appropriate order, so as not to offend the ones who expected special treatment. Even if he'd be king soon, Lucian still had to respect the hierarchy that existed in the kingdom.

Eventually, he felt he'd engaged in an adequate number of conversations, so he looked to the person that had been on his mind for quite a while.

He had dumped the young Emilia with a group of maids before the party, giving them the order to instruct her on how to present herself during the feast. In truth, Lucian wanted to join in to learn the etiquette himself. He still had little knowledge of the customs and expectations of this world's culture, so his biggest fear was making a fool of himself without even knowing it.

But since there was no way he could ask the maids to educate him, he had to do without. Besides, Emilia would be cleaned and dressed during that time, and he couldn't very well be present for that.

"Emilia's looking really pitiful, isn't she?" Lucian said, looking her direction.

Rudeus turned toward the far corner of the room. "Well, you were the one who placed her in such a sad position. Didn't I suggest having her sit next to you?"

"Yeah, you did. But I know a thing or two about power structures, and having her in such a spot would only draw their hatred toward her."

"Well, yeah. But that shouldn't matter, right?" Rudeus gave the crown prince a mysterious glance.

"Of course it matters. With her rank, it should already be impossible for her to attend such a party. I don't want to make it worse for her by suggesting that she's above the most powerful people in this kingdom."

"Man, Lucian. I just can't figure you out, buddy. Are you playing games again? If so, I'd really appreciate it if you could let me in on the joke..."

"You'll figure it out eventually, Rudeus." Lucian certainly didn't know what the young noble expected of him, which bugged him immensely. "But for now, I'm going to go keep her company. Care to join me?"

"I'd love to, since getting to know her could come in handy for later." Rudeus looked toward a certain noble. "But I should accompany my father for a while. I've got my own duties to attend to, believe it or not."

"I see. Well, give him my greetings."

"Will do, buddy. Have fun." Rudeus winked, then walked off.

Just what is that guy expecting...?

Putting Rudeus out of his mind, Lucian turned toward the white hair girl sitting alone at a distant table.

Emilia spent the entirety of the party trying to look as inconspicuous as possible. She knew exactly one person here well enough to actually engage in discussion. Unfortunately for her, that person was the prince, who could only move around greeting one noble after the next.

Sitting awkwardly in the corner of the large ballroom, Emilia simply prayed for someone to come save her. Sadly, nobody at the party wanted to get involved with a white hair soldier. Especially one brought in by Prince Lucian himself.

The only one who had spent any time with her was the representative from the Council of Elders, a group that represented the beastfolk race within the Almekian Kingdom's political structure. But that man had his own duties and couldn't accompany her for long.

So when Lucian finally arrived at her table, she latched onto the lifeline with every fiber of her being.

"Prince Lucian." Emilia bowed her head.

"Please, relax." Lucian took a seat. "How's the party been?"

"I-it's been fantastic."

"Heh. You should be more honest when it's just the two of us."

"Ah ... haha..."

"Sorry for putting you through a boring party like this. I'll make it up to you afterwards, though."

"No, it's perfectly alright! I'm honored to even be invited to such an event! B-but what exactly do you have in mind after this...?"

"I'm going back to the royal study to get some more reading done. I was going to bring you along, if you wanted to go."

"Ah, of course! I have so much more sorting to do!"

"Haha, good. I'll be counting on you to organize it so I can find what I need at a moment's notice."

"I'll do my best!"

Lucian's eyes moved toward a particular girl who'd been stealing glances their way, but as soon as their gazes met, she turned away.

His sister, Mia, had said that as a princess, she couldn't rule this kingdom and therefore was given little training or information regarding matters deemed important for kingly duties. Yet due to her close proximity to the crown, Lucian surmised that she would be of great help to him.

I just need to fix our broken relationship. I really need to get her that gift. She's been helpful already, so it's not like I'm doing it just to buy some goodwill from her.

But what would a young princess even want or need...?

I was hoping Mia would take it up on herself to keep Emilia company while I was busy, but I guess even she doesn't want to get involved with a white haired beastfolk.

I'd rather she not be so distant if Emilia's going to be coming to the castle from now on, so I should at least introduce them.

As if his thoughts summoned her attention, Mia's eyes once again turned in their direction. This time, Lucian was quick to motion her over, and the reluctant princess had no choice but to obey.

"Do you need something, Esteemed Brother?"

"Hey, Mia. I'd like you to meet Emilia. She'll be helping me out from now on, so please try to get along with her."

"Understood..." Mia turned to Emilia, but her eyes seemed even more empty than usual. "I'm Princess Mia. Pleased to make your acquaintance."

"It's an honor, Princess Mia!" Emilia showed off the bow she'd been forced to practice from meeting so many nobles and royals recently.

Lucian was hoping the two would somehow hit it off, but after the short introduction, there was nothing but silence between the two girls. Sensing the approach of an awkward atmosphere, he had no choice but to drive the conversation onward himself.

"Emilia will be helping me organize the royal study. Did you know how badly it's been neglected?"

"Yes. Since it doesn't get much use, Father refused to hire a caretaker. It's been in such a shape for a long time."

"Well not for much longer. We're going to get it in working order, right Emilia?"

"Yes, Your Highness!"

"I see." Mia was completely unenthusiastic. "I wish you luck in your endeavors."

Hmm. Could it be Mia really doesn't like white haired beastfolk? It can be hard to go against deeply ingrained beliefs, so it might take her a while to come around...

Lucian didn't want to force the issue at the moment, so he gave Mia her leave.

For her part, Emilia had picked up on the princess' reluctance, but she could only stare at her retreating back with sad eyes.

The rest of the party passed far too slowly for Lucian's liking. But eventually, the time came to call an end to the event.

Nobles filed out, many leaving empty words before exiting. Lucian took them with a smile, playing the part expected of him. In his mind, it was his duty to play by the rules that existed in this world. Or rather, to be the prince they expected him to be.

But it was yet to be seen if that kind of strategy could really lead him to the future he desired.

Chapter 7

"Fresh air," Lucian said, putting down the book he'd been reading. "I really need some fresh air."

"Um." Emilia tilted her head just a bit. "A balcony, perhaps?"

"Not good enough. I want to really clear my head, so something like a balcony just isn't good enough. I was thinking about going for a walk. Want to join me?"

"O-of course! Where are we going?"

"To town. I want to see the city with my own eyes."

"I'd be happy to accompany you, Prince Lucian."

After cleaning up the desk, the two exited the royal study. They'd need guards, as it was unheard of for the future king to simply wander the streets without protection.

Lucian often went on walks when he had difficult problems that he didn't have the answers for. And right now, there were plenty of them.

As expected, when the crown prince wanted to leave the castle, the guards gathered to escort him. But he didn't want a small army walking the streets with him, so he picked six of the nearly two dozen men to go with him.

The royal family had many carriages. Some were for long-distance trips through the kingdom, while others were for luxurious outings in the city. Of course, Lucian didn't know any of that, so when he was brought to choose a carriage, he left the choice up to Emilia.

The foxgirl was a bit flustered at having to choose from among the fancy rides available only to the royal family, but Lucian was sure she'd have a better chance at picking the right one compared to him. Plus, he figured it'd be fine even if she only picked the one she liked most.

And so, after a short trip through the inner wall, Lucian got his first glimpse of the city that surrounded the castle. He expected a dreary scene, with dirty streets and sour faces, so the vibrant atmosphere that filled the shopping district was quite a shock.

These people don't look the least bit worried about the state of the world, Lucian thought. *Don't they understand how bad things are outside the walls?*

Many of them did in fact know. However, most believed their wealth and status was a sufficient buffer between them and the catastrophic events building upon the horizon. After all, he and Emilia did travel to the wealthiest merchant district in the city. Of course a distant war and some starving peasants wouldn't affect their livelihoods.

No sense getting worked up over it. I have a guest to entertain, so it'd be rude to ruin the mood.

Though I do need to keep at least part of my mind focused on the details since half the reason to come out here was to see the state of the city and its inhabitants.

The carriage the two were riding in came to a stop. They'd reached their first destination, though Lucian didn't know where exactly that was. How could he, considering he knew virtually nothing of the city.

So rather than look foolish, he allowed Emilia to pick the first stop. When Lucian told her it could be any place she desired within this shopping district, a sparkle had entered her eyes.

"Hey," Lucian said, looking out the carriage window. "You don't intend on making bread for a living, do you?"

"No way! I'm a soldier, not a baker!"

"Then we're not going to a pastry shop so you can study the art of breadmaking?"

"Why would that be the first reason to cross your mind!? Most people come here to eat, you know!"

"Ah, guess that's true. It's still a little suspicious, though."

"Mrrr." Emilia puffed up her cheeks. "I feel bullied."

"Nonsense. It's just your imagination."

Lucian was in fact bullying her. For reasons unknown to him, he couldn't help himself. Though the truth was that he was suffering from the physiological effects of youth.

Despite having the knowledge and wisdom of a 38-year-old adult from Earth, his body was now that of a 17-year-old young man. Of course there would be some changes to his personality, thanks to the excessive amount of hormones coursing through him.

On top of that, the deceased prince whose body he now inhabited was quite the womanizer. Those kinds of habits wouldn't simply vanish into the void, even when a new soul was crammed inside.

Lucian wasn't aware, but his actions up until now had also been subject to minor alterations for the same reason. And in the future, that would only become more apparent. After all, the deceased prince wasn't the loving man he portrayed himself to be, so would it be any surprise to learn that his reincarnated self was a bit more comfortable with violence?

"We can't enjoy the bakery from in here." Lucian stood and offered his hand to Emilia. "Why don't we see what this place has to offer."

Emilia slowly raised her arm, until her fingers rested atop Lucian's. "I-I'm looking forward to it, Prince Lucian."

"Ah!" Emilia suddenly remembered something. "I don't have my cloak…"

"To hide your white hair? Don't worry about that."

"Are you sure? I don't want to cause you any more trouble…"

"It's no trouble. Sure, I've heard the rumors that have begun to spread, but that kind of thing will fade once people get used to seeing you around the castle."

Emilia had a complicated expression, but since she didn't want to ruin their time out in the city, she pushed her feelings aside.

I'll have to do my best, Emilia thought. *The heroes in my favorite stories wouldn't be afraid of their accusatory eyes, so why should I?*

After building her courage, Emilia followed Lucian out into the light of day. She rarely walked among the people of the city, preferring to stay with her comrades in her beastfolk division at the garrison.

Of course, each of them had white hair, as well. The army kept them separate from the rest of the military units, though they weren't technically restricted in any way, save for the universal laws that bound all white hairs.

The street the two stepped out on was lined with lamp posts to provide a source of light in the evening. However, there was no such thing as electricity, so they were powered in other ways.

In short, magic.

Empowered glass, Lucian thought as he looked upon the lamps. *Magically infused so when the ambient light fades, the spell within will activate.*

I wonder how such magic works. It'd be great if I could figure out how to cast spells…

Despite several attempts, Lucian had not yet managed to conjure forth a single ounce of magic. To him, it almost felt as if his spells were blocked by some unseen force.

The lamps weren't the only magically infused objects littered through the city. A rudimentary sewer system was powered by magical pumps, while many buildings were warmed with mana-infused heaters.

Though the world lacked many amenities that Lucian was accustomed to on Earth, a surprising number of them had been recreated using magical technology. It was these very devices that his uncle, Archduke Henrik, researched and constructed with his massively successful magitech business.

After taking note of some of the fantastical creations the people of this world managed to build to advance their society, Lucian slowly refocused on the reason they stopped there in the first place.

"It's nice," Lucian said as he walked inside the bakery. "A bit overly decorated for my tastes, but that will make for a memorable visit."

"Right?" Emilia looked around the interior. "This shop is famous not just for its sweets but also its atmosphere. Though to most, it's just a rumor since it's rare to actually be able to eat here."

"Yeah. Not only is it in the highest-class merchant district, but the prices are a little ridiculous."

"Um, I hope that's not a problem…"

"Of course not. I brought more than enough coin to cover something like this. But what should we buy? There are quite a few options here."

Lucian eyed an artistic display, where various paintings illustrated the shop's baked goods. Each one looked to be a carefully constructed combination of bread, jellies, fruits, creams, and other ingredients.

"Actually!" Emilia skipped up to the display. "I already know which one I want!"

Lucian followed her, his eyes falling on the one Emilia was intently staring at. "A cream-filled jelly pastry, huh? Guess they are a classic."

"I heard the way the cream gushes out with each bite and mixes with the sweet jelly just melts the inside of your mouth!"

"I think I'll get this blueberry danish. I love snacks that are made sweet from natural fruits."

"Ah, that looks tasty too."

"Then how about we share a bite with each other. That way we can both try two different pastries."

"Eh!? W-well, if you insist..."

"Then it's settled." Lucian motioned to the man behind the counter.

The shopkeeper was busy dealing with other customers since the store was quite busy. But having already seen that a VIP had entered, the man had been secretly keeping an eye on him to ensure he would be ready to meet his needs.

Although the shopkeeper didn't know who Lucian was, having someone walk in with a retinue of guards was a rare occurrence, even in a high-class shopping district like this. He knew that could only mean Lucian was a high noble, foreign dignitary, or perhaps even a member of the royal family.

But he never imagined that it was the crown prince himself. This was a world without photographs, and the second prince was never supposed to be an important man, so he wasn't paraded around in the public eye like the king had done for the first prince.

Even though the deceased second prince had carefully curated his public image, there were still many who had no idea what he truly looked like up close. Hence, it wasn't uncommon for people to assume he was merely wealthy or powerful, rather than their future ruler.

"How may I help you?" the shopkeeper asked.

"We'd like these two pastries, please." Lucian pointed toward the ones they had decided on.

"Ah, my apologies. We don't have any of the cream filled pastries at the moment. We simply can't get the specialized bread needed to make them, you see."

"That's ... unfortunate."

"I-it's fine!" Emilia said. "I'll um ... I'll take this one, then!"

"Certainly ... miss." The shopkeeper couldn't help but stare at her white hair and fluffy fox ears.

Ignoring that, Lucian and Emilia stepped back from the counter as the man relayed their order to the baker. Since it was just a couple bread-based snacks, it wasn't long before the man happily handed the two their fresh, warm pastries.

On their way out the door, Lucian overheard the man behind the counter telling another customer that their desired snack was also unavailable. It seemed quite a few were out of stock due to a lack of ingredients.

The food shortage hits everyone, Lucian thought. *If a high-end shop like this can't get their ingredients, then I can only imagine how bad it must be for others.*

Since it was such a nice day out, Lucian decided to walk the streets, rather than get back into the carriage. Of course, he also wanted to get more familiar with his new world, and this outing was the perfect opportunity.

Considering that the entire royal family was recently assassinated, it may have been risky to walk around so carefree, but Lucian wasn't about to be holed up in the castle, stricken with fear.

Besides, who would openly attack a crown prince in the middle of his own capital city?

"Delicious!" Emilia's eyes practically had stars in them as she took a bite of her strawberry shortcake.

Lucian followed suit. "Yeah, it's surprisingly good. The blueberries are especially sweet."

"Right!? It's the same for my strawberries! That shop really is the best!"

"I'd like to perform a thorough evaluation of other establishments before coming to a conclusion." Lucian turned his head ever so slightly toward Emilia. "I hope you'll join me when I come back to study them."

"Mmm!" She could only give such a response, since she had her mouth full of strawberry shortcake.

The district had quite a selection of shops, but Lucian wasn't interested in most of them. Clothes, accessories, furnishings, and other such items were quite mundane. But he did happen across a particular store that caught his eye.

A talisman shop, Lucian thought. *Now that's something worth checking out.*

Lucian stopped his steps. "Emilia, let's see what kind of talismans this place has in stock."

She looked at the shop door with a conflicted face. "Okay, Prince Lucian. I know this kind of place is important for the kingdom."

"Yeah. I'd like to see with my own eyes what the local mages are selling to the citizens. But first..." Lucian held out the remainder of his blueberry danish.

Emilia eyed it, then suddenly realized why he was offering it to her. "W- we're really trading pastries!?"

"I was serious, you know. I'm interested in how yours tastes, and I know you have to feel the same for mine."

"Yes, but..." A tinge of red crept into her face.

Despite that, she held out her strawberry shortcake, and the trade was made. She looked at the mostly eaten danish in her hand, but it didn't move any closer to her mouth. As for Lucian...

"It really is delicious. I think I liked yours more than mine." He wiped his mouth with a handkerchief.

He really ate it without hesitation, Emilia thought. *Maybe I'm the strange one here...*

Clearing her mind, Emilia stuffed the danish into her mouth. As expected, the sweet blueberries and honeyed bread were a shock to her senses, in a good way.

"Ahhh~" She let out a satisfied sound.

"I'm glad you approve. Next time, let's try something new."

"Yes, I'm looking forward to it!"

The two of them stepped into the talisman shop, followed by their retinue of guards. It was a small building, which wasn't surprising considering the merchandise was just small slips of paper hanging from the walls.

Of course, they weren't just normal strips of paper. Each of them had words painted on one side, some just a single word, others two or three. Looking around, Lucian noticed they said things like 'Strength', 'Agility', 'Grace', 'Wit', and much more.

For the ones with multiple words, it was common to see simple phrases, such as 'Great Power'. The combinations were all slightly different, as we're their effects, and a buyer could choose from among the vast selection to get the talisman that fit their needs.

Held within the talismans were spells, waiting to be released. The effect depended on the words written onto the paper, with more words leading to more powerful magic–to a degree.

The downside of talismans was that the spell effects were reduced compared to a properly trained mage casting them with their own mana. Of course, they were still useful for those who were unable or unwilling to train in the ways of magic.

But more importantly, a talisman could be used on oneself. It was the only known way for a person to cast magic on themselves. Because of that, it was common for people to carry at least a few of them at all times.

Those that could afford to do so, at least.

"Not bad," Lucian said. "Lots of talismans in here. Though I won't know their strength until I test them."

"Yeah..." Emilia looked a bit uncomfortable.

"What's wrong? I was thinking of buying you a couple, too."

"No, please don't do that! I would ... be greatly inconvenienced."

Emilia realized that she never told the amnesiac prince about another peculiar effect of magic on white haired beastfolk.

"Actually," Emilia whispered. "I forgot to mention last time, but white hairs like me tend to ... lose control when enhanced with magic. Because of that, we're forbidden to even carry talismans."

"Lose control? What do you mean, exactly?"

"I told you we gain far more strength than others when enhanced, but it comes with the cost of becoming temporarily reckless. It's a status commonly known as Berserk, and when afflicted by it, we tend to cause trouble…"

"When you say Berserk, do you mean you lose all control?"

"Not exactly. It's different for every white hair, with some retaining more sanity than others. Fortunately, I can still think somewhat clearly while Berserk. But that doesn't mean I won't act impulsively and cause problems."

"Yeah, I can see why that'd lead to trouble."

Lucian went silent, pondering on the challenges white-haired beastfolk like Emilia must endure.

It'd be tough, knowing you'll lose most of your sanity during battle, Lucian thought. *That's the last place I'd want to go berserk.*

I wonder why she would even join the army, if that's the fate that awaits her.

There's nothing Lucian could do to change the reality of this world, so he could only accept things as they were. Since he didn't want to add weight to her mind, he decided it best to hurry and buy a few talismans, then take his leave.

The shopkeeper recognized him this time, which was probably fortunate. If anyone other than the crown prince were to bring a white-haired beastfolk into a talisman shop, people might have asked questions.

With several talismans in his possession, the two of them left the shop and continued down the street. They passed by a few more stores, but once again, none of them were of any interest to Lucian.

Still, he wanted to make up for the somewhat sour mood brought on by the trip into the talisman shop, so he kept an eye out for something that would wash it away.

That's when he saw it. Or rather, it was as if his eye was drawn to it, whether he liked it or not.

A fortune teller? Lucian thought. *I wonder if the people of this world believe in that kind of thing.*

Even back on Earth, there were those who sought such mystical arts, though they had long since fallen out of the mainstream. But this was a world of magic, and its lack of scientific progress left many mysteries in the world that were unexplainable to its inhabitants.

For that reason, or perhaps another of which he was unaware, Lucian stepped toward the woman who sat in a strange, tent-like stall on the street corner. Rather than a door, the entrance was covered in beads which hung from the tent on strings.

Pushing the beady strings aside, the two entered the mystical interior of the fortune teller's stall.

"Ah, come seeking guidance, have you?" The woman asked in a melodic voice.

"Yeah. We'd both like to hear what life has in store for us."

"If it's the future you want to see, then you've come to the right place. Which among you wishes to learn of your destiny first?"

Lucian looked to Emilia. "How about it?"

"Sure! Sounds like fun!"

Fortunately, Emilia was interested in mystical arts like this, so after paying the fortune teller's fee, she happily sat down in front of the seer.

From Lucian's perspective, the fortune teller simply made a show of waving her hands over her crystal ball. But Emilia was captivated by the display, eagerly awaiting to hear of her future.

These kinds of people usually tell others what they want to hear, Lucian thought. *The Barnum effect, as it's known. Just say some general stuff that probably relates to anyone, and people will find ways to apply it to their personal lives.*

The seer had her eyes closed now, still waving her hands around the crystal ball, just a hair from touching its surface. A small hum could be heard coming from her lips, and it almost seemed as if she was speaking softly, though it was inaudible to anyone in the room.

Finally, she stopped and opened her eyes. "Young beastfolk. You will soon be met with a great challenge. One that will test both your mind and body. Should you fail the test, your life will be forfeit. However, if you overcome it, the world you've long since desired will open before you. Though the path you will walk shall be a thorny one."

What the hell!? Lucian could barely believe his ears. *What kind of fortune is that!?*

He turned to Emilia, sure she'd be disappointed to be told that she potentially had such a bleak future ahead of her. However...

"I won't fail," Emilia said. "No matter what, I won't fail!"

The seer simply smiled in response.

Emilia stood from the chair and walked back to Lucian's side. She peered up at him, and he could see expectation in her gaze. Holding back a sigh, Lucian sat down to have his fortune told, prepared for another such ridiculous telling.

"Ah." The seer made a strange noise. "We've got ourselves quite a unique specimen here. I can already feel the weight of destiny hanging over you. This will be an interesting reading, indeed."

"Thanks, I think."

"Hohoho." She let out a strange laugh as she began waving her hands over the crystal ball.

Lucian was treated to much the same scene as before, except he had a better view of it this time. In just a few seconds, her eyes snapped open and grabbed his gaze with a powerful focus.

"A great upheaval will soon begin, one that has the potential to shatter the world. At its center, you stand. Alone, you are crushed by the immensity of your foe. No one man can stand against he who holds the knowledge of the gods.

"Three guardians. No more, no less. With their strength, you may yet bring this world back from the brink. Without them, all hope is lost."

Her gaze returned to normal, and another smile formed on her face. "How about it? Did you find the answers you needed?"

"Y-yeah." Lucian couldn't help but respond in such a way.

"Good, good. Then..." She pushes a bowl toward him. "I'm accepting tips."

Hey, don't ruin the mood...

With a sigh, he put a few silvers into her bowl, then stood. Many thoughts were running through his mind, but he still had a guest to entertain, so he saved the heavy thinking for later.

"Oh, one more thing," the seer said as the two were about to leave. "As thanks for the tip, I'll tell you something good. The first man is a distraction. The real threat comes after."

"What do you mean?" Lucian asked.

"You'll find out soon enough." The smile returned, larger than ever.

With that, Lucian and Emilia exited the seer's tent and stepped back onto the street beyond.

"What a strange fortune teller," Lucian said.

"Bring it on!" Emilia was still fired up over her fortune. "I won't lose!"

Lucian didn't want to rain on her parade, so he kept his somewhat melancholy mood to himself. He was never one to put much faith in a soothsayer, but before his reincarnation, he would have said the same of Goddesses and other worlds full of people.

Could it be that magic actually lets some people see into the future? Her words really did seem...

He cut that line of thought for now. After all, he was still on his city stroll, and he wanted to end it on a high note.

But where should our final destination be? It's tough when I barely know anything about the city...

I wonder if we should stop by a clothing store so I can buy Emilia an outfit. A gift like that will probably make this outing one to remember.

Not to mention, she can get some use out of it. In fact, I can play it off like I'm getting her something nice for her to wear when she visits the castle.

It'd be weird if she got the wrong idea, so having an excuse like that would be–

"I-it's Prince Lucian!" A voice interrupted Lucian's thoughts.

"That's far enough." One of the guards blocked his path.

"A-ah, sorry! I just got a little excited at the thought of meeting him." The man looked Lucian's way with a hopeful expression.

"It's fine," Lucian said to the guard. "You can let him in."

"Thank you, Your Highness!" He stepped within the perimeter the guards maintained for the two.

They had been greeted by others, and there were even a few following from a distance, curious about the prince's destinations here in this shopping district. Of course, the fact that he had a white hair accompanying him only added to their curiosity.

But as of yet, nobody had been so bold as to try to gain access past the guards that surround the two. Seeing the man's determination, Lucian thought it a good opportunity to show that he is a man of the people, one willing to listen to others.

Of course, this was a tactic he often used back on Earth. By openly speaking to his supporters in public spaces, he was able to gain the reputation as a down-to-earth man.

"Your Highness!" The man bowed. "I'm honored that you would talk to me."

"It's only natural to speak to my citizens, isn't it? What better way to understand your desires?"

He raised his head but kept his hands close to his body. "Your reputation holds true, then. Perhaps the kingdom really is in good hands."

A strange feeling began seeping into Lucian. "I certainly hope so, since I plan to bring the kingdom back to its glory days."

"Truly!?" The man stepped closer. "I was worried about where the kingdom was heading, but it seems those fears were unfounded!"

"Yes..."

What's going on? Lucian thought. *Why is this man making me feel so anxious?*

A memory surfaced with Lucian. The very last moments of his life on Earth.

Wasn't I talking to one of my constituents just like this, just before...

"It's a miracle that you managed to survive, Your Highness." The man said with a smile. "Surely the Goddess herself was looking out for you."

"Which makes it unfortunate that..." His smile faded. "...You have to die!"

The man's hand lashed out, now holding a long dagger.

Lucian had no combat training on Earth, so his reaction was understandably slow. Luckily for him, he was already on edge. That sense of anxiety gave Lucian just enough of an advantage for him to stumble back as the dagger sought his heart.

But there was no escape. The man moved swiftly, as one often did when enhanced by magic. Lucian could only watch on as the weapon's tip closed in, seeking to put an end to his life.

Another hand entered Lucian's vision. It wrapped around the man's wrist, then yanked it off course. The dagger pierced the air next to Lucian's torso, leaving nothing more than a small gash in his coat.

Emilia followed up her grab with a kick to the man's solar plexus, causing him to double over and sending a spray of spittle flying from his mouth.

In the blink of an eye, the guards had the man pinned to the ground as Lucian still stood in place, trying to catch up. His life had nearly come to another abrupt end, and he had barely been able to react.

"Are you okay!?" Emilia patted Lucian's side, where the dagger had nearly pierced him.

"I'm fine, I think..." Lucian slid his hand beneath his shirt, checking for blood.

He released a sigh of relief when his hand came back without a drop of red. But he couldn't relax, even as he watched the assailant getting bound with rope.

W-what's this feeling...? A tingle ran down his spine, making the hair on the back of his neck stand.

The first man is a distraction. Lucian looks around the street. *The real threat...!*

Almost. Lucian almost missed it. But his hyper attentive focus was just enough to catch a glimpse of the shadowy figure whose form seemed to merge with that of the dark building acting as his backdrop.

That figure was leaping through the sky, straight toward Lucian and the unaware Emilia. In his hands wasn't just a single dagger, but two. The blades were a pitch black, like the man's outfit, so not even a single glint of light would bounce off their metallic surfaces.

There was no time to yell, no time to flee to safety. So Lucian did the only thing he could think of. He pushed off the stone road with every ounce of strength he could muster from his legs, diving right into the shocked Emilia.

The two tumbled through the air for what felt like an eternity. Adrenaline often made people perceive time more slowly, a fact Lucian was learning at this very moment. Eventually, they hit the ground. For Lucian, it was an uncontrolled roll across the stone, but for Emilia, it was a combat maneuver.

Not only did the beastfolk girl protect Lucian's head from smacking into the solid surface, but she directed his body so that he would be behind her when their momentum came to an end. Because of that, she was able to spring back to her feet and face the assassin that still sought his life.

"Stop him!" a guard yelled.

But the assassin was no mere back-alley thug. His cloak was enchanted with an anti-detection spell, making him blurry, even when looking directly at him. On top of that, he was enhanced with powerful magic that gave him an inhuman amount of speed.

The guards were no pushovers, but they were simply a few steps too far away. They wouldn't make it in time to save their prince.

I won't let you! Rather than backing away, Emilia stepped forward.

She was unarmed and facing an opponent that leaked bloodlust, with the skill to back it up. Yet there was no hesitation in her as she raised her hand to meet the dagger that was aiming for her neck.

Knowing that evading would leave Lucian exposed and that blocking was impossible, Emilia opted to catch the blade with her bare hand. The tip pierced straight through her palm and came out the back of her hand, but not a single drop of blood spilled from her throat.

Even the assassin didn't expect such a daring move. In his mind, she would either avoid the attack or attempt to knock his arm away. In either scenario, he would be able to open a path to the prince. Yet she had chosen neither.

Having no choice, the cloaked man decided to barrel through Emilia with pure force. If he stopped his steps for even a single second, the guards would swarm him. But...

"Gah...!" He let out a pained sound as Emilia deftly landed a strike.

"Don't underestimate me!" Emilia lashed out again, but the assassin wouldn't be caught off guard a second time.

Emilia's hand found only the fabric of his cloak as the assassin blurred. She was met with his counter in the form of his second obsidian dagger, and having no magic enhancing her, she could only grit and bear it as the weapon sliced into her forearm.

Without a doubt, Emilia was at a disadvantage against this powerful man. After a few more exchanges, she would be overwhelmed. Such was the fate of white hair who did battle without magical enhancements.

But victory didn't always go to the stronger warrior.

"Kuh...!" The assassin coughed, and blood spilled from his mouth.

He looked down, where the tip of a sword stuck out from his body. Immediately after, several more weapons pierced him. His two daggers fell to the stone road, and the light faded from his eyes.

"Whew..." Emilia let out a breath as she peered around for any other potential dangers.

Not seeing any signs of a third assassin, she walked to Prince Lucian, who had only just gotten back to his feet.

"You're hurt!" Lucian's wide eyes fell on her wounds.

"I'll see a healer soon. More importantly, are you injured, Prince Lucian?"

"I don't–" Just as he was about to say no, he felt a dull pain in his side.

He once again reached under his shirt. When his hand returned this time, it was stained red.

"Oh no! We need to get you to a healer right away!"

"It's not that bad, I think..."

"Maybe so, but the daggers could have been poisoned!"

Lucian wanted to protest and say that Emilia would have gotten a bigger dose of poison, but before he could respond, the guards whisked him into his carriage. They went full speed, not stopping until they made it all the way back to the castle.

Fortunately, one of the guards was trained in restoration magic, and he used it to dispel any potential poison and to help close their wounds on the way. Once back inside the castle, that raisin faced healer appeared and used a barrage of spells on the two.

Though not instantaneous, their injuries healed far quicker than they would on Earth. It was the first time Lucian experienced the power of magic so intimately, and it made him realize just how different this new world was compared to Earth.

I really need to learn how to cast magic, Lucian thought. *I guess I'll have to swallow my pride and ask Mia for help.*

Although his trip out in the city had ended in his near demise, it was still an experience that would prove useful in many ways.

And during the course of his adventures in this new world, it certainly wouldn't be his last brush with death.

Chapter 8

"You want me to go back to my barracks?" Emilia asked, obviously reluctant.
"I'm just going to rest for a while, so I thought you should do the same."
"Ah, I see. Yes, it's important to rest while recovering from an injury, even if the wound is already healed."
"Then I'll call for you again when I need you, Emilia."
"I understand, Prince Lucian. I'll be waiting."

After a somewhat awkward bow, Emilia left the treatment room where Lucian was still resting.

Lucian sat back into the soft cushion of his chair, looking up at the ceiling.
Weak. I'm too weak.
I know I won't be able to defeat an assassin like that on my own, but if I could use magic, maybe I could at least survive long enough for my guards to save me.
If Emilia wasn't with me today, I'd probably be dead right now.
Did that stupid Goddess really mess up? Or did she block my magic ability on purpose? No, what if I simply can't cast because my soul was human to begin with...?

Lucian tore his eyes away from the ceiling and stood. Without a word, he left through the room's only door. Even though he told Emilia he was going to rest, he had other plans.

He'd be fine with letting her stay and sort the royal study while he worked on other things, but rumors had already begun to swirl about her preferential treatment. If others were to find out she had unfiltered access to the documents in the study, some people may begin to raise questions.

Plus, Emilia was still technically a rank-and-file soldier. The commander in charge of her squad may not be able to punish her for her absence, but Lucian knew that revenge wasn't always so easy to stop.

I hope she's not having too hard a time because of her close relations to me.

Lucian finally stopped his steps. In front of him was a door he'd seen several times now, but he was always a bit anxious to give it a knock. Learning that the one who resided in the room disliked him made him a bit nervous.

Despite his reluctance, he had a clear goal to accomplish. So, after pushing down his feelings, he raised his hand in order to give the door a firm knock.

"Lucian!" A voice called out before he could knock on the door.

The prince turned. "Rudeus. What's wrong?"

"What's wrong? Buddy, the talk of the city is that our crown prince was nearly assassinated in the middle of the street! What happened!?"

"Oh, that. Yeah, they got pretty close."

"What do you mean 'oh, that'? Didn't you even have your sword on you? I know you wouldn't go walking around unenhanced by magic, and your sword is one of the most powerful in the kingdom. A normal assassin would stand no chance against you, especially when you've got your guards. So, why did that white hair have to rescue you like that?"

"Right. Guess I was sloppy. I'll make sure to be more prepared next time."

"You say that like you're sure there will be a next time." Rudeus shook his head. "No, wait. Could it be ... you planned all this?"

Eh? Why would I do something like that!?

"No, I didn't plan it." He kept his thoughts to himself. "I was so shocked I could barely react."

"That's not like you at all." Rudeus suddenly had an idea. "I know! Follow me, buddy. I've got just the thing you need!"

"What is it? I was going to speak with Mia for a while."

"That runt? You got something planned for her again?"

"Not really, just had a few things to discuss."

"Can it wait? I've got a couple things to do in a while, so I'd like to get this over with quickly."

Lucian gave it a bit of thought. He wanted to get Mia to teach him how to cast spells, but he had no plans to leave the castle again anytime soon. Since he was relatively safe, he could come back in a little while and start the training.

I'm a bit interested in what Rudeus has planned. If he thinks it can help me protect myself, then I should really give him a chance.

"Fine," he said. "I'll go with you."

"Awesome! C'mon, this is gonna be fun!"

Lucian fell in line beside Rudeus, letting the young noble lead him through the halls. They ended up going into a section of the castle that Lucian hadn't been in before, though he had asked about it and decided that it wasn't a place that he really belonged.

Don't tell me...

"And here we are!" Rudeus looked at Lucian with a grin.

"We're going to ... train?"

"No, not train. Duel."

"You want to fight me?"

Suddenly, Lucian felt that coming here was a poor choice. It had already been proven that his martial skills were far below the people of this world, thanks to their years of training and powerful magic. He couldn't imagine going up against them in a fight.

But even though Rudeus had done as he pleased a few times in the past, he hadn't used Lucian's memory loss to play any pranks. The young man seemed to genuinely want to help him regain his former self.

He did say an assassin would be no match for me. He probably thinks he's doing me a huge favor...

Lucian wanted to refuse and go back to Mia's room where he could hopefully learn some magic. But Rudeus was already dead set on the match, so much so that he had already picked up two wooden swords, one of which he held out to Lucian.

Ugh. What a pain...

No, wait. This could be a blessing in disguise. If I lose quickly and decisively, then it'll make sense later when people realize I'm such a weak fighter.

I can just say that the disease somehow made me forget most of my training. That'll be a convenient excuse, and Rudeus can back me up after I make him feel bad for beating me up here.

As usual, Lucian was thinking of a way to turn the bad situation to his advantage. A sly devil, he was.

"Alright, I'll do a match." Lucian grabbed the wooden hilt.

What...? He looked at the sword in his hand. *Why is it so comfortable?*

Lucian twirled the sword, then passed it from one hand to the other. His grip felt just right, and his body seemed to fall into what he could only see as a combat stance.

Could it be...!

Lucian was remembering a documentary he once saw back on Earth. It spoke of a master pianist who sustained a head injury and was in a coma for years. When that man awoke, he had complete amnesia.

His profession, his family, his name, and every other aspect of his life was wiped clean. Yet when that man was put in front of a piano, he would play masterpieces.

This body. Lucian held the sword before him. *It remembers?*

"Looks like it's coming back," Rudeus said. "You ready, then?"

"Yeah. Yeah, I think I am."

"Good, but I'll say this right now. Don't get angry at me when you're eating dirt."

"I'm prepared to lose, as long as I can get the feel for the sword in the process."

"In that case, I'll start slow." Rudeus raised his wooden sword. "Here I come!"

True to his word, Rudeus charged. The young noble wasn't just competent with the blade, he was a near prodigy. If he had more aptitude for magic, he may have even been considered for the title of Heavenly Sword, the highest rank of swordsman in the kingdom.

The now deceased Lucian wasn't a slouch, either. Though his advantage lay in the potency of his magic to make up the difference in raw potential between him and Rudeus.

When the two dueled, it was often quite a spectacle. Though the power of his magic often saw the prince to victory. But right now, Lucian didn't have that luxury.

Fast...! Lucian intercepted the first attack. *And this is him holding back!?*

Despite his complaint, Lucian knocked away a second attack, then a third. He seemed to find a flow, as if a current of water were directing his movements.

But even though his body knew what to do, his mind was still uncertain.

"Are you just going to block?" Rudeus asked, even as his sword lashed out again. "The Lucian I knew would take every opening he could find!"

He ignored the taunt, focused only on deflecting the ever-quickening strikes coming his way. He let the flow take him, direct him. It was comforting, like hearing a song for the first time in years and suddenly remembering how much you loved it.

But just as a song must come to an end, so too does a battle. And only one man can emerge the winner.

Now...!

Seeing an opening, Lucian struck out for the first time. His wooden sword closed in on Rudeus, completely bypassing his defense. Or so he imagined.

But the scene that played out in his mind didn't match reality.

"It's my win." Rudeus lowered his sword, which had been at Lucian's throat.

As for the prince's weapon, it missed its mark by a hair's breadth. Now that the moment had passed, Lucian knew he'd been played for a fool.

"You never would have fallen for such an obvious trap before you got sick, buddy. You still got your skills, so I hope the rest comes back to you soon."

"Yeah, me too." Lucian took one last look at his wooden sword before placing it back on the rack.

"Don't worry. I'll be here to train with you whenever you want! Maybe next time, we can spar with magic enhancements!"

"I'll consider it."

"You know what? I think I know what would *really* cheer you up."

"Didn't you say you had something to do?"

"It can wait, man. This is more important! Just give me ten minutes, and I'll come get you. Where you going to be?"

"Hmm. In my room getting refreshments, most likely."

"Perfect! I'll see you soon!" Rudeus took off, heading toward some unknown destination.

That guy sure is a handful...

But he showed me something good. Maybe I'm not so weak after all.

Chapter 9

After getting back to the castle, Emilia had been dismissed by Lucian to go back to her barracks. She would have rather stayed with him, but an order was an order.

As she walked down the castle halls, the footsteps of a single guard echoed behind her. She was in front of him, but she wasn't really leading the way.

In a way, the guard was escorting her. If Emilia were to try to enter any of the other rooms without Lucian by her side, she wasn't sure what kind of reaction the guard would have.

Regardless, the escort was their way of saying that her business in the castle was finished, so she should leave quickly.

It's rare for a white hair like me to even step foot inside the castle.

I hope I'm not stirring up too much trouble for Lucian because of what I am.

Emilia left through the main entrance, with her escort staying inside as the castle's massive doors closed behind her.

She was technically allowed in the courtyard, though her kind was always treated with suspicion. Or perhaps it'd be more accurate to say they feared the strength white hairs had when Berserked.

A wall surrounded the castle grounds, separating it from the city. Because of the fear people had for white hairs, their barracks and training grounds were located outside that wall.

Emilia stepped up to the southern gate. The guards there had harassed her the first few times she came through, but they had long since gotten used to her coming and going.

Though recently, they had been avoiding her. The guards stationed in and around the castle were starting to wonder how they should treat her after the crown prince took a liking to her.

Emilia imagined their hesitation would only grow once news spread of how she saved Lucian's life.

She made it to the other side of the gate without issue, continuing on to her barracks. Fortunately, it wasn't far. Even if they didn't want white hairs within their walls, they did like to keep a short leash on them.

Another wall appeared before her, though it couldn't even come close to comparing with the one surrounding the castle. It was barely twice Emilia's height, meaning she could jump it in a single leap if she were enhanced.

But it acted as an obvious sign that trespassing wouldn't be tolerated. After all, just behind the wall was the barracks and training grounds Emilia used on a daily basis.

As this was her officially assigned station, she had no trouble getting in. Her feet didn't stop, carrying her past the large dirt pit where most of her fellow trainees were doing drills.

Normally, she'd be standing alongside them. But when the crown prince called, everything else had to wait.

One of the trainees caught sight of Emilia and waved, which she returned with a stiff smile. The friendly girl started her training at the same time as Emilia, so the two became friends.

Sara is as straightforward as ever, huh?

Her friend had a tendency to do what came to mind, sometimes without thinking it through. She was happy to see Emilia had returned, no doubt wanting to hear of what she had done while she was with Lucian.

Sorry, Sara. I was told not to talk about the attack, so you're going to be disappointed.

Emilia kept walking. She wanted to join in on the training, feeling guilty that she had skipped so many training sessions to be with Lucian. That was the reason why her smile was stiff when she waved back to Sara.

Of course, Emilia made up for her lost training by staying up late to practice on her own. Even though Lucian had sent her back to rest, she had no intention of doing so. She was already falling behind.

At least, that was how Emilia felt. In truth, her skill with the sword was already beyond that of a mere trainee. She began her training years before she stepped foot into these training grounds, after all.

But before Emilia could join in on the training, she had to report to Lily.

Hm? Emilia looked around. *Where is Lily?*

And isn't there someone else missing from training?

Emilia walked up to the barracks where she and the other white hairs eat and sleep. It was a simple building, providing only what was necessary for their daily needs.

Just beyond the front door was a communal room, where the trainees could gather to talk or eat. The only other door led to a kitchen and storage area.

The trainees were expected to clean the barracks themselves, but the cooking was done by permanent staff at lunch and dinner. If they wanted breakfast, they'd have to get it themselves, and they weren't allowed to use the military's stock.

Although the trainees did earn some pay, most white hairs agreed that it was better spent elsewhere. After all, the military did feed them surprisingly well.

Even though the white hairs were feared and despised, they were also the most powerful force on the battlefield. Any nation that treated them too poorly had already been conquered by those who provided some nourishment for their weapons to grow.

But weapons they were.

Emilia continued past the empty communal room. There weren't any more doors, but there was a hallway on the other side. It was short, only a few paces long, and ended in a T-intersection.

She looked down the path on the right. Normally, she'd head that direction, since that's where the female sleeping quarters were. But her feet remained planted at the intersection.

Voices? Emilia's fox ears twitched. *Lily. And Sigurd. So that's why he was missing from the training ground.*

Emilia turned left, toward the boys' quarters. After turning a corner, she saw exactly what she expected.

Lily and Sigurd heard her footsteps echoing down the stone hall, so by the time she saw them, they'd also seen her.

"Emilia," Lily said. "Welcome back."

"Thanks, Lily. And I've got quite a report for you this time..."

Lily and Sigurd looked at each other, but Emilia was sure that neither one was expecting to learn she had saved the Crown Prince from assassination.

"Did something happen?" Lily asked.

"Yes, but it's not something I can speak about openly, so..." Emilia looked to Sigurd.

"To think you'd be learning secrets from Crown Prince Lucian himself." Sigurd shrugged. "It's a good thing you didn't listen to me when I told you not to go to the castle courtyard and challenge the soldiers."

"Haha. It really was good advice, but I'm just a little stubborn. Oh, but what about you? If you're skipping training, then does that mean you've got something to do?"

"I'm leaving in two weeks, and Lily was helping me get a few things ready."

Emilia eyed the paperwork in Lily's hands. "Ah, that's right. Your six months of training are almost over."

Trainees came and went. Each one spent six months at the barracks, but after that, they were shipped off to the front lines. Or picked up by a wealthy noble as a personal bodyguard.

To discourage individuals from hoarding the kingdom's precious supply of white hairs, they charged a massive tax for each one under a person's employ. The sum was large enough that only those with deep pockets could afford to hire them. Though there were people wealthy enough to have more than one.

Archduke Henrik, Lucian's uncle and owner of the kingdom's greatest magitech shop, was said to have three white hairs under his personal command. But the majority were with the military, as Almekia's kings desired.

Among the thirty white hairs at the barracks, Sigurd was the closest to graduation. Emilia was coming up on her fourth month, which meant she'd start seeing real combat experience in just a couple months.

"It's not going to be the same around here without you, Sigurd."

"What are you saying? I'm sure you can whip the new recruits into shape without me. Besides, I need to leave before you have a chance to even up the score."

Emilia perked up. "That's right! I'm going to win next time! I can't let you leave while you're ahead!"

Sigurd was by far the best fighter among the trainees. Until Emilia arrived.

When Sigurd first laid eyes on her, he couldn't help but shake his head at seeing such a soft looking girl joining the military. It was something he'd seen quite often in just the two months he'd been training at the time.

But when he stood against her in her very first duel as a trainee, he was quickly made aware of his mistake.

Her stance was refined, and her attacks sharp. It was obvious she had training, like he had. But he didn't recognize the style, and Emilia had dodged the question when he asked.

Although he won their first combat, many more followed, with Emilia improving at a rapid pace. Over the next three and a half months, he lost more and more often.

It was just two weeks before Sigurd was scheduled to be sent off, and Emilia only needed two wins to tie him. But since she'd been so busy accompanying Lucian, she hadn't had time to duel him.

"I'm done here anyway," Sigurd said, stepping past Emilia. "Once you finish your report, I'll be waiting in the training grounds."

"Alright! I won't lose!"

Sigurd turned the corner, his footsteps slowly fading into the distance.

Lily sighed. "Losing him is going to be rough. Not only does he help with training the new recruits, but the others look up to him."

"Yeah, he'd make a great captain for a squad. If we were allowed such positions, that is."

"The others respect you too, Emilia. After he leaves, maybe you can take over."

"Eh? There's no way. I'm not really the leader type..."

"But you're strong like Sigurd." Lily clasped her hands. "They'll listen to you, I'm sure."

"Haha. Maybe..."

Lily suddenly remembered something. "Ah, right. Your report. Let's go to my office for privacy."

Unlike the white hairs, Lily didn't stay in the barracks. She had her own home in the city, but she sometimes slept in her office instead.

As the representative for the Council of Elders, Lily was more of an administrator than part of the military. Though she did have a rank, it was a special one that put her outside the normal command structure.

After leaving the barracks, Emilia saw Sigurd already back with the other trainees. But unlike them, he was helping train others as much as he was training himself.

Emilia still had things to do, so she'd have to leave them be for a while longer.

Near one of the small walls that surrounded the barracks, another building could be seen. It grew larger in Emilia's vision as she followed Lily to its entrance.

"Um." Lily stopped just before opening the door. "It might still be a bit messy..."

"Not again, Lily..." Emilia shook her head.

"It can't be helped. I got up late, and I've been busy all day."

"That's precisely why I've been telling you to get an assistant. It's too much for one person."

"I'll be fine!" Lily opened the door. "Come in, come in."

Emilia stepped inside, as she had done many times before. It was only a single room, but as mentioned, it was cluttered.

As expected, Lily must have worked deep into the night. That's why she got up late and didn't have time to put up her bed.

When Lily slept in her office, she used a bedroll. It still lay unrolled on one side of the room, the covers tossed aside as if the occupant had thrown them off in a hurry.

Stacks of paper were piled up on her desk, work she had been trying to finish the night before. But from how it looked, Lily would be pulling another late night.

"Ah, please wait a moment!" Lily ran to her desk and grabbed an armful of books and documents. "I'll clean this up in a hurry!"

The squirrel-eared young woman began to clear off the desk with practiced movements, almost as if she'd been forced to clean up in such a fashion many times before.

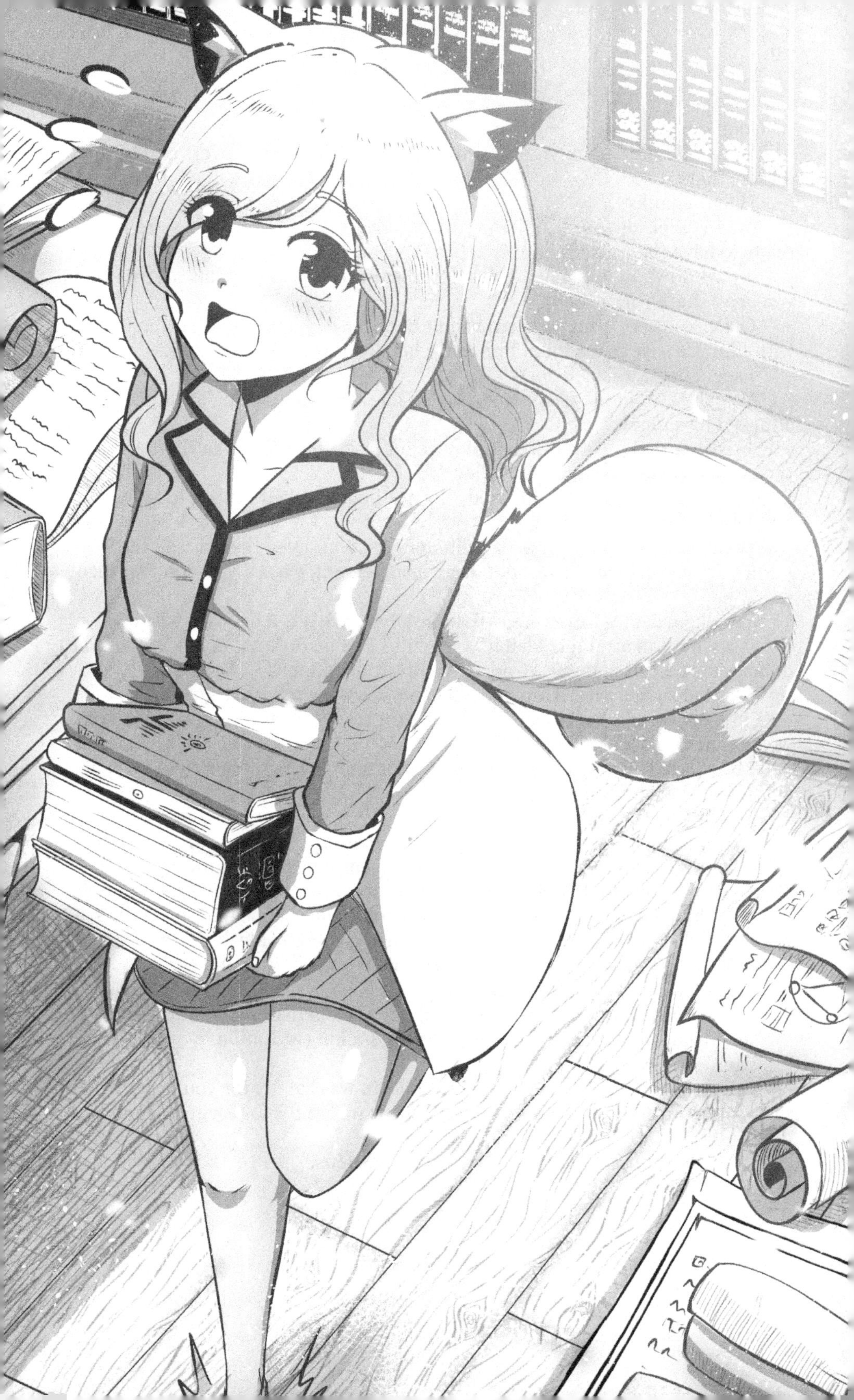

Good grief...

"Here, I'll take care of your bedroll." Emilia grabbed the covers and began folding them.

"Haha. Thanks~"

After a quick cleaning and reorganizing, the two beastfolk girls were finally ready to have their discussion.

Lily sat down in her chair. "Well, let's hear this report that has information you can't share with others."

"Okay. You see, Prince Lucian went out to the city, and he asked me to go with him. Um, we had a lot of fun, and I had a strawberry shortcake."

"I see. I bet it was delicious."

"Y-yeah." Emilia fidgeted. "Anyway! While we were walking around, we were attacked by assassins..."

She recounted the events that played out just a short while earlier. As she spoke, Lily's eyes continued to widen.

"...and before I left," Emilia said, "Prince Lucian asked me not to tell anyone the details except you."

"What a story..." Lily sat back in her chair. "You saved the prince's life, even. I don't think you'll be able to hide your involvement, even if you don't speak of it."

"Yes. Sigurd and the others will definitely figure it out once they hear about the assassination attempt. That's why Prince Lucian ordered me to tell you the details, so you can help me avoid any probing questions."

"Ah, that's true. I'll tell anyone who comes asking to buzz right off!"

Emilia covered a soft laugh. "I wonder if Prince Lucian would let me carry a weapon next time."

"I don't see why not, if he trusts you." Lily sat back up in her chair. "What about you? Do you trust him?"

"Hm? Why wouldn't I?"

"No reason. But Emilia, let me tell you something. I've been around nobles all my life. Some of them are very good at appearing gallant and virtuous. Terrifyingly good at it. But very few actually are. So, just be careful."

"Ah, I know what you mean." A certain noble's face appeared in Emilia's mind. "I'll do my best to keep Prince Lucian and myself safe."

"If it's you, I'm sure it'll turn out just fine. If you—"

A knock on the office door cut Lily off.

After receiving a nod, Emilia reached out and opened the door.

"Just who I was looking for," Sigurd said, looking at Emilia.

"Me?"

"A noble showed up and said Prince Lucian was calling for you." Sigurd motioned toward the training ground. "Guess we'll have to reschedule our duel."

"That's..." Emilia looked at the noble. "...Rudeus."

Chapter 10

I really worked up a thirst from that short battle.
Lucian walked to a marbled arm sticking out of the wall. At its tip was a blue gem, positioned just above a sink. After placing his hand on the gem, the power inside activated, releasing a stream of cold, refreshing water.

Lucian was surprised to learn just how advanced this otherwise medieval world was. The sink even drained to a complicated system, which flushed the water into an underground sewer. There were even toilets attached to that same sewer system, making life rather convenient.

After splashing water on his face and taking several, long gulps, Lucian sat down on the comfortable sofa.

Should I get changed?
Well, maybe after whatever else Rudeus has planned. Don't want to get another outfit sweaty...

As he looked at his clothes, an idea occurred to Lucian. He reached into one of his pockets and pulled out something he had recently obtained during his trip to the city.

I wonder... Lucian eyed the talisman in his hand. *If I can use the magical gems that power the devices in this world, then does that mean...*

"Strength." Lucian recited the word listed on the talisman, and immediately after, power flowed into him.

Woah! It worked!

He stood from the sofa and turned, taking in the blue thread used in the furniture's design. Kneeling, he reached beneath the heavy couch and wrapped his fingers around the thick piece of wood that made up part of its frame.

Then, he lifted it.

It's...
...Still heavy!

Setting it back down, Lucian let out the breath he was holding.

But I'm definitely stronger than I should be. Maybe if I used a better talisman, I could get even stronger!

A talisman's strength was determined by many factors, including the magical power of the craftsman and the words imbued on the paper. Lucian learned a bit about them when he was reading books on how to cast magic, but he had skimmed those parts since they weren't directly helpful to him at the time.

I gotta find more information on talismans. And I need to order some powerful ones in case I never learn how to cast spells myself.

He wanted to dash to the royal study this very moment, but...

knock, knock

"Who is it?"

"Rudeus. I'm ready to go when you are!"

"Alright. I'm coming."

Guess it'll have to wait until after this.

For the second time in under half an hour, Lucian got led around the castle by Rudeus. However, he quickly noticed something about their destination.

Are we going to the dueling grounds again? Why leave if we're just going to be heading back right after?

Rather than ask, Lucian decided to just let it play out. Rudeus was being a bit secretive, so he assumed the young noble wanted to surprise him with another tactic to jog his memory. Since the last several times Rudeus led him to unnamed destinations had proven quite useful, Lucian was hoping for another beneficial discovery.

I met Emilia because of him, and I learned that I know how to wield a sword. So I guess I'll let him have his fun.

As expected, Lucian stepped back into the dueling arena. Like before, nobody else was inside, so he was quite curious what was so different about this trip compared to the last. To Lucian's surprise, Rudeus made no indication that he intended to stop in this room. He kept walking, his eyes focused on a very particular spot.

Ah, that's right. There's a door on the other end of the dueling arena. I wonder what's inside...

He assumed it was training equipment or other such items, but Lucian was wrong. Very wrong.

"With this..." Rudeus placed his hand on the doorknob. "...You should remember everything."

The door opened, revealing a set of dimly lit stairs. Since the dueling arena was on the castle's second floor, it could just be another staircase leading down to the ground floor.

But Lucian felt that something was different about this one.

It didn't take long for them to reach the bottom, where another door waited for them. Rudeus opened it without fanfare, and the two young men stepped into a wide room that sloped downward toward the center.

At that center, the floor disappeared, replaced by a pit which Lucian couldn't see clearly from his vantage point near the entrance. But as he walked closer, he realized what that pit was—or rather, he realized what this room was used for.

A gladiator's arena? Then these seats lined up on the sloped floor are for people to watch as gladiators fight?

But why did Rudeus bring me here? Nobody else is here, so does he want to duel me in that pit?

No, that doesn't make any sense...

Just as Lucian's alarm bells started ringing that something bad awaited him, he heard the opening of a door. He turned toward the sound, his eyes growing wide when he realized who just arrived.

"M-Mia!? What are you doing here!?"

Lucian's younger sister, Princess Mia, walked toward him and Rudeus. However, her steps contained none of her usual grace. It was as if she had given up on maintaining the proper appearance of a princess which Lucian had come to expect from her.

"Mia is here," Rudeus said, "because you always loved to make her watch. Isn't that right, runt?"

"Yes..." Mia's voice lacked any energy.

Looking closely, he saw that his sister's eyes stared lifelessly into the distance, as if she didn't want to see whatever it was that was about to happen.

"Rudeus, what's going on? Why did you bring us here?"

"Still don't remember, buddy? Well, don't worry! Your pal Rudeus will help you out, no matter how long it takes."

"Remember what?"

"Your favorite hobby." Rudeus stepped toward a wall, where a lever protruded.

He pulled the rod down, and the creaking of metal could be heard coming from the pit.

With a feeling of dread now clearly hovering over him, Lucian turned to the gladiator's fighting area. There, on one side of the pit, a metal gated door swung open. A few seconds after, someone stepped out onto the dirt ground that covered the arena.

"Emilia!? What are you doing down there!?"

"P-Prince Lucian! I don't know, Rudeus told me you wanted to see me, and led me to some strange room..."

"Rudeus, what are you...!"

clank

Lucian eyed Rudeus' hand, which he had just used to pull another lever. Like the first time, the creaking of metal could be heard from within the pit.

Turning back, Lucian saw that the second metal gated door on the other side of the gladiator's arena had swung open. With a gulp, he peered into the darkness beyond, unable to turn away.

Then, footsteps. Not that of a man. No, the footsteps shook the very room in which he stood. A creature capable of sending such a powerful tremble through the stone floor would have to be gigantic.

As Lucian watched the darkness beyond the open door, an arm appeared. Even from a distance, Lucian could tell that the arm was longer than a man is tall, with bulging muscles that could crush bones. The skin was covered in fuzzy, brown fur, making it look half man, half beast.

A leg came next. It had two joints, like a goat, and it ended in a massive hoof capable of trampling a full-grown man with ease.

Finally, its head and torso emerged from the darkness. Now that Lucian got a good look at it, even someone not well versed in fantasy lore could identify the creature.

"Is that ... a minotaur!?"

"The king's pride and joy," Rudeus said without an ounce of care.

"Stop that thing! Emilia's down there!"

"Stop it?" The young noble looked truly surprised. "Why would you want to do that?"

"Because it's going to kill her!"

"Well yeah, that's kind of the point, right? You always enjoyed this moment of betrayal after getting a girl to fall for you. Don't you remember?"

"No...! I-I don't want to remember something like that!" Lucian turned to his sister. "Mia! How do we stop it!?"

The young princess' eyes were vacant. She had retreated somewhere in her mind, not wanting to witness such a cruel fate again.

"It's useless," Rudeus said. "She always gets like this when we bring her down here."

"Dammit!" He ran to the edge of the pit next, looking down at the dirt floor far below. "Emilia! Escape! Run!"

"I-I can't! The walls are too high to jump, and there's no handholds! There's no way out from the room behind me, either! Rudeus locked the door inside!"

"Rudeus, you bastard!" Lucian ran to the noble and picked him up by the collar. "Stop the minotaur!"

"I-I can't. Once it's out, it will only go back into its cage after it kills its prey."

"Then go kill it yourself! You're strong, right!?"

"Battle a minotaur alone!? Are you crazy!? Even with my full set of equipment, I wouldn't fight that thing alone!"

"Grrr!"

Lucian peered back down into the pit. The minotaur was still slowly stepping toward Emilia. The beast seemed to be enjoying its hunt, unwilling to end it too quickly. That gave Lucian a chance.

But ... what can I do!?

Looking around the room, Lucian caught sight of a possibility. On the walls were weapons of all kinds, meant to add a war-like decorative theme to the battle arena. But to Lucian, they were like a sip of water after a long trip through a desert.

Tossing Rudeus aside, Lucian ran to the nearest wall and pulled a sword free from its display. With the Strength talisman still enhancing him, it was an easy enough task.

"S-stay away!" Emilia yelled.

With her screams as fuel, Lucian ran toward the pit in the center of the arena and leaped inside, straight at the minotaur.

I'm dead, Lucian thought. *I'm actually going to die.*

The prince had grabbed the sword and leapt into the pit without a second thought. But now that the uncontrollable force of gravity was pulling him straight toward the fearsome minotaur, his actions caught up to him all at once.

There's no way I can beat this thing! What the hell was I thinking!?

Some people claimed that time slowed moments before death. Perhaps that was currently playing out for Lucian, as his fall seemed to take an eternity. During that time, his eyes flicked toward Emilia, who only just now caught sight of her prince's figure coming down from above.

In her eyes was the fear one would expect from someone facing a monstrosity intent on crushing her. But it was slowly being taken over with the horrifying realization that Lucian would soon be joining her in that fate.

As dumb as jumping in here was, Lucian thought, *I'd do it again in a second!*

He finally reached the minotaur. The creature was still unaware of his approach, its entire focus squarely on Emilia. That gave Lucian a chance to land a clean first strike, one that he had to make count.

"Raaaah!" He yelled as the tip of his sword sank into the base of the creature's neck.

The hairy, leathery flesh ripped open under the combined force of his thrust and the gravity that pulled him down. It was a strike that would undoubtedly fell any man unenhanced by magic.

But the minotaur was no man.

The beast let out a throaty howl and shook. Lucian held tight onto the hilt of his sword, which still sat embedded in the creature's neck. But the force of the monster's movements tossed his body around like he was no more than a stuffed toy.

Unbeknownst to Lucian, the fact that he became a ragdoll holding on for his life ended up saving him from the minotaur's hand, which swept just above his head in search of the one who dared to strike a blow against it.

Even though his attack was powerful, it was far from a killing blow. He thought to weather the storm until he could get his footing, but the universe didn't always follow the plans of those in dire situations.

The sword hadn't sunk as deep as he expected, and with the beast thrashing about, it came free from its flesh. In a blink, Lucian was once again in the inescapable hands of gravity as he fell from the minotaur's shoulder.

He hit the ground in a heap, tumbling over the dirt several times before coming to a stop.

Ugh. That hurt...

The fall was rough, but the adrenaline pumping through his body was enough for him to keep his senses.

He stood but came face to face with a monstrosity over twice his size and many times his weight. One look at the creature was all Lucian needed to understand what fate awaited him.

Despite that, he raised the sword. Whether by luck or his body's combat experience, he managed to keep hold of it during his tumble. It was just a normal chunk of steel with no magical enhancements. Compared to the massive minotaur, it might as well have been a butter knife.

But it was all he had.

"Prince Lucian!" Emilia yelled from the other side of the beast. "Please run! I'll distract the minotaur!"

"No! I'm not going to just leave you here! And where would I run!?"

"Mia's up there, isn't she!? Maybe she can–"

That was all Lucian was able to hear before the roar of the minotaur drowned her out. Wounding it drew its anger, and it was about to take its revenge.

His words were bold, but the truth was that Lucian would like nothing more than to throw the sword away and run as fast as he could. But the logical side of him already understood that such an action would be a futile effort.

If I'm going to die, then I'll go down swinging!

With each of the minotaur's massive steps, the ground shook with enough force to nearly break his combat stance. But his body automatically made adjustments, as if it had been through similar battles in the past.

His mind, however, couldn't keep up. With the scarce time he had before the beast reached him, he hoped he could come up with a plan. Something. Anything to increase his chance of survival.

But nothing occurred to him. He could only imagine himself getting trampled beneath the giant hooves that carried the beast closer with each step.

In the end, he could only rely on his body to make the right moves, hoping that he could pull off a miracle.

The minotaur wasn't content with just rushing him down. When it finally got close, it swung its massive arm. The hand's weight alone would be enough to knock him to the ground, but with the force of its attack added to it, the resulting injury would likely end the battle in an instant.

The prince lashed out with the sword, even as he leapt. He felt it hit flesh, but he didn't have attention to spare to check if the wound was even effective. The creature was big, but it was also quick. Even before Lucian could land and regain his stance, another hand was heading his way.

He didn't even have time to swing. Giving up on attacking, Lucian just barely managed to slip out of its range before it connected.

What the hell!? A monster this size shouldn't be so fast!

Protest as he may, he could only admit that reality didn't conform to his expectations. Forced into yet another disadvantaged encounter, Lucian could only release a futile attack, knowing that such a half-hearted strike would scarcely break the monster's thick skin.

One mistake. All it would take was one misstep and Lucian's life in his new world would come to a quick end.

His reliance on his body's battle instincts had saved him so far, but he should have known. He should have realized that when the mind and body weren't in sync, then it would only be a matter of time before the cracks would lead to disaster.

Maybe Emilia can jump out if she's standing on the minotaur's shoulder. If she can make it, then I can run into the room, and she can pull the lever to close the door.

It's a long shot, but it's the only one I can–

Something smacked into Lucian, ending his thoughts in an instant. Or rather, it was Lucian that smacked into something. The arena's wall.

He'd been so focused on the minotaur that he didn't spare any thought for his surroundings.

Crap! Can't dodge!

Lucian held the sword up, putting it between him and the oncoming hand. The metal dampened the force of the impact, but the blow still caught him square in the torso.

He tumbled, and his vision whirled. Even his thoughts became a jumbled mess, like the world that spun around him.

The dirt finally got a good grasp of him, and its friction brought him to a stop. Somehow, he had enough sense to stand, but just because you want to do something doesn't mean you will be able to.

The leg he managed to get under him crumbled under the weight of his body, and a sharp pain nearly made him cry out.

The sword he had used to block the attack lay tantalizingly close, but even if he had it in his hand, there was nothing he could do. He didn't know if his leg was broken, but it wasn't the only part of him that hurt. There was no way he could fight in his condition.

Emilia, Lucian thought. *She needs to use this chance to escape...!*

He caught sight of the fox-eared girl, and he realized suddenly that she'd been trying to get through to Mia while Lucian held off the minotaur.

His sister stood at the very edge of the pit now, staring down at him. Even from here he could see that the light had returned to her eyes. But it was too late. Lucian looked at the approaching minotaur and knew that his time was up.

Dammit. What did I even manage to accomplish in this world?

Am I just going to die a pitiful death, unable to even save the girl who put her trust in me!?

Nothing but regret filled him, but there was no longer anything he could do. The minotaur raised its hand, obviously enjoying the rush of battle. In its balled fist was Lucian's death, as assuredly as the sun setting after a long trip across the sky.

But there was someone else there who wouldn't let him go so peacefully into the night.

"Don't touch him!" Emilia appeared before him, the sword moving in a wide and powerful arc.

By some miracle, the blade managed to knock the oncoming fist aside, causing it to smash into the ground just beside Lucian's body.

"No! Run, Emilia!"

"I won't! I won't leave you here to die!"

He could only watch on as the white-haired foxgirl clashed with that powerful minotaur, just in front of his battered body.

However, even if she had the technique of a master swordsman, she wasn't enhanced by magic. After only a few, brief attacks, Emilia's body began to run red with blood.

No, it can't end like this!

Magic! Please, I'll do anything, just let me cast one spell! One single spell!

Lucian closed his eyes and reached deep, clawing at every ounce of mana he could feel flowing within him. With pure will, he sought to command the energy to move, to give life to the spell that would ensure Emilia's survival.

I feel it...! I can feel it flowing!

But the rules that bound him refused to change.

No...!

Why!? Why won't it come out!?

He had failed. Like every time before, he had failed.

He opened his eyes, all hope of a miraculous survival having faded. And yet...

If we're going to fall here, then I'd rather die fighting by her side instead of crawling on the ground!

He got his good leg beneath him. He could tell now that his other wasn't broken, but that realization didn't lessen the pain as he slowly pushed himself to his feet.

I'll sacrifice this broken body, even if it's just to put a single scratch on that minotaur!

The fear and hesitation were gone, replaced with only the desire to make use of what little he had to offer to the girl who stood before him like a human shield. However...

W-what!? What are these words!?

Something blocked his sight, nearly covering the entirety of the battle taking place right in front of him.

Congratulations! You leveled up!

Please select a skill from the list below.

[Extended Chant I] [Magic Resistance I] [Support Magic I]

As he moved his eyes around the strange box of text that seemed etched onto his very vision, more words came and went. Various descriptions of what was happening sought his attention, as did explanations of each of the skills listed on the screen.

But Lucian didn't have time to read any of it.

There...!

He focused on a single line, and a torrent of information flooded him.

This ... this is...!

While Lucian was dealing with the sudden appearance of a mysterious box of text, Emilia was still facing off against the fearsome minotaur by herself.

Is this how it's going to end? Emilia thought. *Killed by the former king's pet minotaur!?*

Emilia never had any illusions about what her fate would be, considering her position in the military. But she at least imagined that she'd be cut down in a real battle, not some arena that she stepped into due to a noble's foul tricks.

I knew Rudeus was no good. But...

She had still listened to the man, despite her instincts. The reason for that was none other than Lucian, who seemed to trust him. She figured if someone as bright as him put his faith in Rudeus, then she could too.

What she didn't know was that Lucian had also ignored his instincts. Because of their failure to listen to their guts, the two of them ended up in a hopeless battle.

Now she was badly injured, while the minotaur before her had little more than flesh wounds. It was obvious how this battle would end.

If only I were stronger...! No, if only I could cast magic!

She didn't know why the white haired beastfolk were denied the ability to cast spells. In her mind, perhaps it was punishment for their past transgressions or simply fate's way of denigrating the ones who lost their self-control when enhanced with magic.

Either way, the result was the same. She couldn't overcome the minotaur with physical strength alone, not without a mage's enhancement magic.

Emilia spared Lucian a glance and saw that the prince was too injured to fight. However...

He still won't cast magic on me. It's as I thought, then.

Emilia found it strange that Lucian hadn't used magic a single time since she'd met him. He'd even left himself vulnerable to that assassin, despite having a reputation as both a competent warrior and mage.

He can't cast magic. Is it because of his memory loss?

Enhancing a white hair was a high crime. The result would be a powerful and Berserked warrior rampaging about as they pleased.

But Lucian was the crown prince, and Emilia was certain he understood that death awaited them in the immediate future. Yet he still refused to cast magic on her.

Maybe Mia can—

That was as far as her thoughts could get before she was forced to focus on her opponent. The minotaur had been enjoying the battle, giving her injuries but not killing her outright. It wasn't as dimwitted as a common beast, which was another reason why the creature was feared by most.

The minotaur understood that its prey had been cornered, and it was in no hurry to end the fun too quickly. But its aggressive nature was constantly pushing it to attack, and it could only hold back its thirst for so long.

A second, Emilia thought. *If my life can buy Lucian even a single more second, then it won't be wasted.*

Despite knowing that death itself loomed over her, she ignored her injuries and stood firm against the fearsome creature. The sword in her hand was more ornamental than practical, but it was the only weapon she had. And she planned to stick it as far into the monster's gut as she could, hoping it would be enough to bring about a miracle.

Here it comes!

The minotaur's clawed hand fell. It no longer sought to toy with her. This time, it was coming for her life.

But fate had other plans for her today.

"Give Emilia..." Lucian's voice suddenly called out. "...Everything!"

Emilia gasped.

Her vision flared, as if she had been cast headlong into the sun itself.

Her ears rang with the deafening sound of a tornado ripping through the landscape.

Her mind exploded with sensations, drowning her with a torrent of information.

For a fraction of a second, Emilia thought she'd been hit by a fire spell. But nearly as soon as the thought passed through her mind, realization dawned on her.

She wasn't being blinded by the sun. Her vision had merely been enhanced to such a degree that it had overpowered her senses. Now that a fraction of time had passed, she could see the world as she never had before.

The vibrancy of colors, the clarity of details, the faintest of movements. It flooded her, a tsunami of visual information that she'd never experienced, even with her captain's magic enhancing her.

The same was true for her hearing and mind, both of which came to life in extraordinary ways. Such a barrage hitting her senses should have been too much for the young foxgirl, but as she was now, it felt perfect.

The minotaur's clawed hand that seemed so quick before now moved painfully slow. It was nearly upon her, but Emilia didn't feel an ounce of urgency.

With a casual movement, she placed the sword between her and the attack. When the claw finally reached her, the minotaur's massive strength and weight completely blew her body away...

...was what should have happened.

But no such scene played out. The enormous hand rested atop the sword's blade, the nails a hair's width from sinking into Emilia's face.

"You..." Emilia's voice contained a razor-sharp edge. "...Dare to challenge me!?"

The sword vanished. At least, that's what it looked like to all the others in the room. But the truth was...

"Such soft flesh." Emilia snatched one of the minotaur's dismembered fingers from the air. "And you consider yourself a hunter?"

Her strike was so quick, even the minotaur couldn't react in time. The creature recoiled its arm, the hand attached to it now missing two of its five fingers.

She tossed the chunk of flesh to the ground. "I'll show you what it means to face a real predator!"

Despite being over twice her height and many times her weight, the minotaur sensed the dangerous aura leaking from Emilia. For the first time since it emerged from its cage, it took a step back.

But power and pride often go hand-in-hand. A creature as intelligent and fearsome as a minotaur wouldn't cower just because it faced a formidable opponent. The beast let out a booming roar. Not to scare its foe but to show its will to meet Emilia's challenge head on.

"That's more like it." Emilia readied her sword. "Now give me a battle worth remembering!"

What the hell!? Lucian thought as the two warriors clashed in the center of the arena. *This is Emilia!?*

He hadn't forgotten her warning back when they visited that talisman shop. She told him that white haired beastfolk went berserk when enhanced with magic. But this was far beyond his expectations.

She's like a completely different person. Her personality, her posture, her voice ... everything.

And this strength. Isn't it too much!?

He had literally given her everything. So much so that he had fallen back to the ground, and it was all he could do to not pass out from what he would later learn was mana exhaustion.

No normal mage could bring out such power in a single cast, though Lucian was still unaware of just how different his magic was compared to the others in his new world.

Now that he had been involved in a few fights, he thought he had a fundamental grasp of what to expect. But the battle taking place in front of him went beyond what he anticipated, even from magically enhanced warriors.

Their speed is ridiculous. Even my eyes can barely keep track of what's going on. There's no way I could fight someone like that without being enhanced.

No, even if I were, I'd be no match for them...

As Lucian watched Emilia, he couldn't see any of her former technique. The skills she put on display for him ever since he first saw her fighting that nameless soldier in the sparring arena were nowhere to be seen.

Right now, Emilia was a force so powerful that even the minotaur couldn't stop her. But she wasn't fighting with her head. It was as if she were relying only on instinct to see her to victory.

That carelessness had already cost her several times, with the minotaur adding to her already serious injuries. Yet it was as if the foxgirl wasn't even slowed by her wounds. No matter how much blood dripped from her, her assault only intensified.

The sword had long since broken, yet she held onto the hilt, using what little was left of the blade to clobber the minotaur time and again.

As bad a shape Emilia was in, her opponent was worse. The monstrous creature was covered in so many wounds, its brown skin had essentially turned red from blood. Though the battle still raged, even Lucian could tell how it would end.

"Is that all!?" Emilia yelled. "I expected more from you!"

She had landed a devastating blow, and the minotaur finally collapsed.

"Groooar..." It let out a noise that sounded oddly satisfied, despite having lost.

"If that's all you have to say." Emilia raised the broken remains of the sword. "Then goodbye."

A blur, a splash of red, and the final thump of the minotaur's body going limp.

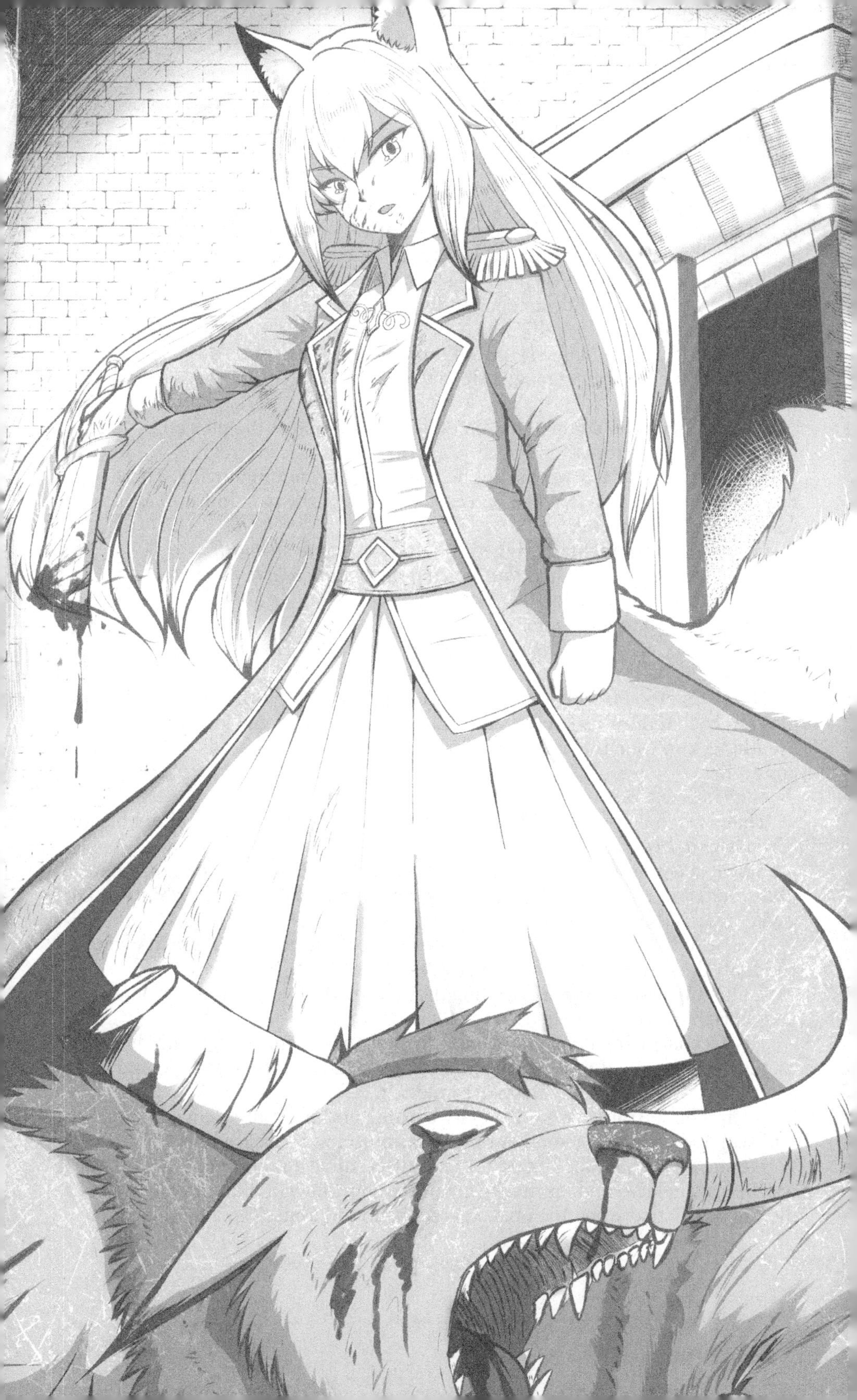

The silence was deafening. After a life and death battle that left Lucian heavily injured, it felt strange to not have a rush of noise and adrenaline. Now, he just felt drained.

With the minotaur defeated, Emilia walked over, the broken sword still held in her hand. She stopped right next to Lucian and looked down at him.

"E-Emilia?" He stared back at her blood-red eyes.

"...Enemy ... defeated." With that, she collapsed.

"S-she passed out." Lucian could only quietly voice his thoughts. "Wait, her injuries! Isn't this really bad!?"

Lucian's [Support Magic I] only allowed him to place buffs on people. It didn't let him cast healing magic. However, there was still another person here in the arena.

"Mia!" Lucian yelled up at his sister, who still stood at the pit's edge. "Cast healing magic on Emilia!"

He couldn't hear her words, but he could see her mouth moving. There was no visual confirmation that she had cast a spell, but the pain in Emilia's face seemed to ease just a bit.

Whew... Lucian mentally sighed. *What a fearsome strength.*

You even had me worried that you'd gone completely berserk, but...

He ran his hand through her messy hair.

Thank you for saving me.

"Hey, Mia!" He raised his head, looking up at her. "How do we get out of—what the...?"

His sister stood frozen, still as a statue. And she wasn't the only one. Moving his eyes back to Emilia, Lucian saw that she too was frozen. Her hair, her breathing, and even the blood that was flowing from her wounds. All of it had gone still.

What's going on!?

That's when he realized that he could see himself. He sat just behind his fox-eared friend, his face filled with confusion.

Slowly, he grew smaller. Or rather, more distant. Lucian looked up, where Mia stood. Soon, he was at eye level with her, and he saw the uncertainty in her gaze.

But he didn't stop there. He continued to float upwards, as if gravity had suddenly decided to suspend its ever-present hold over his body.

To his surprise, the arena's ceiling didn't provide even a bit of resistance. He passed right through it, like light through a clear glass.

His ascension sped up, and the sky quickly opened up above him. The huge castle where he spent most of his time in this world started to shrink, and he got a bird's eye view of the city that surrounded it.

Even then, he didn't stop. That city became nothing more than a blot on the landscape, growing ever smaller until a passing cloud obscured his vision.

He stayed in that foggy cloud for an indiscernible amount of time. Perhaps it was just a single second, or maybe an entire hour. Lucian didn't know. What he did know was that when the mist cleared, he found himself in a familiar room.

Looking around, he saw two figures. One he recognized, one he didn't.

But the fact that he was back in this room made Lucian's heart sink. He could only imagine one reason for him to be here.

"Welcome back," the Goddess said. "I didn't expect to see you again so soon."

Chapter 11

"Am I ... dead?" Lucian asked.

"Dead?" The Goddess looked amused. "No, but I would suggest for you to seek a healer soon. Your body is in terrible shape, after all."

"Y-yeah, just moving hurts." He stretched his astral body. "But I feel fine right now."

"That's to be expected when I drag you to my realm. Though you do have that excruciating amount of pain to look forward to when you return."

Lucian winced, imagining its sudden return.

"Anyway," the Goddess said. "You really put me in a bad spot, you know? I can't believe what you just did."

"Huh? What exactly did I do...?"

The Goddess put on a pout. "I went through all the trouble of adding a tutorial to the Divine System Interface to explain it to you on your first level up, yet you ignored all of it!"

Lucian thought back to all the text that kept popping up when that strange box appeared. "Well, I was kind of in a hurry at the time."

"Yare yare~" Her pout turned into a smile. "Fortunately for you, I'm a forgiving god. And so, I decided to bring you here to offer you a chance to learn of the system that will be the foundation of your power in your new world."

"So that's why you brought me here. I'll be honest, I am really curious about what that pop-up was saying."

"Pop-up? Is that really how you'd refer to a Divine System Interface?"

"Well, it just kinda popped up, so...."

"Hmm. I'll choose to ignore what you just said. I'm very forgiving."

Yeah, you said that already...

"It's fine to say it as much as I want," the Goddess said. "Since it's true."

"Please don't read my mind. It's rude."

"I refuse on the grounds that it's simply too fun to watch you squirm."

Lucian let out a sigh, suddenly remembering how mouthy this world's goddess was. "Speaking of magic, why couldn't I cast it before this so-called level up?"

"That's because I blocked your ability to use spells."

"I knew it! I knew I was handicapped from the start! Why would you do such a thing, knowing how powerful magic is in this world?"

"It's precisely because of how powerful magic is in your new world. Do you really believe you could learn it so easily? Most mages spend years, decades even, just to become competent spellcasters. Could you match them in a matter of days or weeks?"

Lucian's anger cooled. "I guess you have a point..."

"Indeed! Trust your Goddess a little, would you?" She nodded confidently. "Rather than having you use the same methods as everyone else, I devised a system of growth that will allow you to not just match, but to exceed even the most powerful people in your new world."

"This Divine System Interface, was it? And now you're going to tell me how it works?"

"I am." The Goddess waved her hand.

The same pop-up appeared in Lucian's vision, appearing exactly as it had the moment it showed up during the fight against the minotaur.

"Level up." Lucian looked at the strange words. "I feel like I've seen that phrase somewhere on Earth."

"It's just a term some people like to use when a person's power rises." The Goddess looked toward the other mysterious figure in the room. "Anyway, let's go through the tutorial you skipped when you leveled up so you can get an idea of how the system works."

The Goddess scanned the same text box. "Oh, my. There were some really unlucky skills here, but you were fortunate enough to get one that became the key to solving the small problem of your impending death at the time."

Lucian read out the choices. "[Extended Chant I], [Magic Resistance I], and [Support Magic I]. At the time, I barely even knew what I was looking at, but when I saw [Support Magic I], something clicked in my mind, and I knew it was the right choice."

"There had been much talk of support magic recently, so perhaps that was the reason."

As he looked at the skills, more text began to pop up. "Let's see. [Extended Chant I] increases the number of spoken words available for magic to reach its maximum efficiency. Um, what?"

The Goddess began twirling her hair. "You know how people chant their spells? Well, if your chant is too long, the magic will become weaker. But with that skill, you can string more words together, meaning you can give your spells more effects without a loss in power."

Lucian remembered reading something like that when he was studying how to cast magic. A simple chant like 'Give me strength' would simply increase the user's physical power. Whereas a chant like 'Grant me the strength and speed of a warlion' would enhance both power and agility to an even greater degree.

The more words you used in the chant, the more varied the spell will be, but at a certain point, it began losing its power, becoming less effective. That's why most chants were between three and ten words. Enough to clearly state the magic's goal but not so much as to lose its effectiveness.

"So this will let me increase the length of my chants and add more effects to my magic? That's great, but does something like that really matter?"

"Who knows. Maybe one day, you'll find out."

Lucian continued to the next skill. "[Magic Resistance I] says it makes me resistant to offensive magic. That sounds good, actually. Anything that can help me survive is a welcome addition, but I mean ... nobody's used offensive magic on me since my reincarnation, so..."

"The day will come when you feel the force of magic with your own body, so look forward to it."

"I don't see how that's something to look forward to..." He eyed the last skill on the list. "[Support Magic I]. Enhances allies with magic, empowering their physical or mental abilities. This is the one I chose, obviously."

"A wise choice. Without it, you would certainly have perished."

"Yeah. But I was surprised about what showed up next."

"Ah, you mean how after picking the skill, another one appeared in its place?"

"Yeah. What was it, again? [Command Magic I]?"

The Goddess nodded. "Yes, a very unique school of magic. The chance of it appearing is rather low, so even I was surprised to see it on your first level up."

"So does that mean it's strong?"

"I hope you'll play with it and unlock its true potential."

"Right. I guess I'll make time to practice it, then. But does this mean I'll get to choose two skills with each level up?"

"Indeed. But the choices are random, so don't expect to always get what you want."

The Divine System Interface had changed, showing him the [Command Magic I] skill that he picked as his second skill.

"Let's see. Says here [Command Magic I] infuses inanimate objects with power, allowing the caster to command them. Kind of vague, but it's magic, so I have high hopes for it. Though I only picked it to get the pop-up—I mean the Divine System Interface to go away."

"You did that on purpose." The Goddess pouted again. "But I'll let it slide. After all—"

"You're a forgiving Goddess," Lucian finished for her.

"It's good that you understand so quickly." She nodded. "From now on, you can call upon the interface when you please. I even added some useful information to it, like a title to show your progress!"

"A title?" Lucian looked around the screen. "Pauper Prince? What kind of title is that!?"

"It's true, isn't it? In more ways than one. Your kingdom is nearly bankrupt, and you have a pitiful selection of skills at your level. I'd say it's accurate~"

Even if he wanted to argue, Lucian couldn't say anything against her logic. "It wouldn't have been so difficult for me if you just gave me some skills in the first place..."

"Eh?" The Goddess' lips curled. "But watching you struggle is always so fun!"

"I knew it was something like that!" Lucian recalled her strange behavior from his first visit here.

"Teehee~"

Two sighs filled the air at the exact same time, which only caused the Goddess' smile to widen further.

Lucian looked to where the second sigh came from and saw the other mysterious figure looking as disappointed as he himself felt.

Who is he? He's a couple years younger than me, even. Is he some kind of apprentice?

"You could call him my apprentice," the Goddess said. "Though his training is both a reward and a punishment."

"I'm starting to wonder if agreeing was a mistake," the young man said with a tone as if he'd given up on something.

"Oh, my. You keep saying that, but you always come crawling back, don't you?"

"Who's crawling? Maybe you're finally starting to go senile? If that's the case, I don't mind helping you fix the mess your world is in, since you're obviously not up to the task."

"And whose fault is it that my world was invaded by the God's Acolyte, hmm?"

"Tch. I make one little mistake, and you just won't let it go. How petty."

"Trying to take the high ground? That might have saved Owi-Ban Shinobi, but it won't help you against me~"

"Stop using that reference. It's old, just like you."

"Hohoho. As expected of a young one. You simply don't understand that the divine age like fine wine."

"Whatever. Don't you have something left to do, or have you forgotten already?"

"As if someone as beautiful as me would forget." She turned back to Lucian. "Anyway, if you wish to continue advancing in power, you will have to become a true king."

"What's that mean?" Lucian asked.

"It means many things. Solve the food shortage, balance the budget, secure the borders, obtain the people's faith, and more. With each step you take toward rebuilding your kingdom, you will gain another level. If you want to look at your quests, simply check your Divine System Interface later."

"So, just make the world a better place, huh? That's simple enough, I guess."

"You've got the right idea, though you may want to keep your mind open, as some of your level up conditions may contradict each other. For example, re-establishing a friendly relationship with the Dark Elves will grant you a level, but it will assuredly be unpopular with the humans, lowering their faith in you."

"I see. I'll keep that in mind." A question occurred to Lucian. "By the way, if I have to accomplish something of that magnitude to level up, then how did I reach level 2 during the fight?"

"Ah, one of your level up conditions was to step forward in the face of your immediate demise. Even I wasn't expecting you to achieve it as your first level up, though that also means you can't rely on it the next time you're about to get smushed by a powerful opponent."

"I really hope that doesn't become a theme..."

"Who knows~" The Goddess gave him a mysterious smile. "But with that out of the way, it's time for you to return. Are you ready?"

"Yes. I finally have some strength and a path to grow even stronger."

"Then." The Goddess gave his head a gentle tap. "Until we meet again."

Lucian's astral body fell backwards, and his form began sinking beneath the clouds. Soon, he was gone, on his way back to his physical body below.

"Forced tutorial levels are really annoying, you know." The young immortal frowned at the Goddess. "You should have just given him the strength he needs from the beginning. Why force him to level up at all?"

"You still don't get it, huh? Well, you wouldn't be training under me if you understood how to properly rule over a world, so I suppose I'll enlighten you. I hope you're grateful!"

"The only thing I'm going to grate is your smug face."

"You see," the Goddess said, ignoring his retort, "We Gods have our own restrictions. Or rather, we have rules of our own creation that we must follow. For example, when you accidentally sent the God's Acolyte to my world, the God he follows used it as justification to challenge me for the right to rule this world.

"Once a challenge has been declared, I'm not able to intervene on my own. Hence, why I had to choose a hero to fight on my behalf. And that hero must obtain the strength to defeat the God's Acolyte on his own, under the rules of the system that I create. In other words, Lucian must gain the power he needs with his own two hands, using the Divine System Interface."

The young immortal rubs his bare chin. "But how is that fair? The God's Acolyte is so much stronger than Lucian, and he's had months to expand his influence before Lucian even arrived on this world."

"The challenger often has such advantages, but they also have their own disadvantages to match. It's true that I was rather late choosing my hero, but it's fine. I have faith that Lucian can close the gap and become a force powerful enough to battle against the God's Acolyte. After all, he's—no, I'm sure you'll figure it out on your own."

"Don't just say mysterious stuff like that. I swear, you're just like her." The young man sighed again. " Though I guess Lucian's story is getting pretty interesting."

Chapter 12

"We made it," Lucian said as a door closed behind him. "Didn't think sneaking around my own castle would be so stressful."

"Better than explaining that." Mia looked at the still unconscious Emilia, carried in Lucian's arms like a princess.

The prince set her down on Mia's bed. "True, and sorry if we bloody up your sheets."

"It's fine..."

Lucian could still detect some hesitation in Mia. After the battle with the minotaur, she had helped heal Emilia's wounds with her healing magic and unlocked the door so he could escape the arena. She had even fetched him and Emilia cloaks so they could hide their injuries and was their lookout on the way back to Mia's room to ensure they didn't run into anyone on the way there.

But she couldn't shake the feeling that her brother was playing another one of his terrible games.

Why did he jump into the pit? Mia watched on as her brother got the white hair comfortable on her bed.

If it was part of some horrible scheme, then it was an extremely risky one. He normally doesn't take such gambles, preferring to set up the field to ensure his victory.

So why would he suddenly partake in such a perilous plan?

"That should do it," Lucian said after getting Emilia's pillows just right. "How long do you think it will take for your magic to heal her?"

"Her injuries were far worse than yours, but she'll be better soon."

"I'm glad to hear that." Lucian turned to Mia. "By the way, thanks for all your help."

"It was nothing..."

"That's not true. If you weren't there, I don't know if Emilia would have survived since we had no way out of that pit. I'd say that's something, at least."

"I ... see."

Lucian had found himself in an awkward silence with Mia several times now. The little princess was prone to answering with the bare minimum responses and then just leaving the silence to fill the room.

But he didn't want it to come to that this time.

"Mia. I'm sorry for everything that you went through."

"What ... do you mean?"

"I heard from Rudeus that you were brought to that arena and forced to watch as ... well, as that minotaur was let loose on an unsuspecting girl who'd been tricked..."

"..." Mia turned away, but not before Lucian caught a glimpse of fury in her eyes.

"I ... want to make it right..."

"Make it right?" Mia asked softly. "Do you intend to turn back time?"

"I wish I could. Nobody deserves a fate like that..."

"Says the one who put them through it!" Mia suddenly began yelling. "Do you know how much they suffered!? How much I suffered!? And you think you can just make it right!?"

Even though Thomas George Hamilton had nothing to do with the events that happened before he took over Lucian's body, he still wanted to make amends for the things the prince did while he was alive.

Of course, such feelings toward his now biological sister should be obvious, but it didn't end there. The prince had clearly been a disturbed man, and Lucian wanted to counteract his evil actions with ones that would leave a positive mark on everyone's lives.

"You're right," Lucian admitted. "There's no way to undo the things he did. But ... as long as I'm still alive, I'm going to work toward improving the lives of the people who've suffered because of his terrible actions."

"He!? Why are you speaking as if you weren't the one who—"

"Ugh..." A strained voice silenced the furious Mia.

The two royal siblings looked to the source and saw Emilia's eyes slowly open. She looked around Mia's well-kept room, the confusion made obvious by the blank expression on her face.

Eventually, the fox-eared soldier's gaze fell on the two siblings, and her blank stare slowly began to fill with understanding.

"A-ah! Pardon me!" Emilia immediately scrambled to stand.

"Hey, take it easy." Lucian put his hand on her shoulders before she could hop out of bed. "Your injuries may be getting better, but you shouldn't overexert yourself."

"Sorry." She remained seated on the edge of the bed.

"Don't worry about it. We're safely back in Mia's room, so just relax for a bit."

"Thank you." Her face suddenly began turning a deep shade of red. "Ah! W-what was I thinking!? I'm so sorry!"

"Huh? What's wrong?"

"You saw it, didn't you? How I get when I'm enhanced with magic..."

"Ah, right. I was surprised by how aggressive you got. You said some weird things, too."

"Awawawa." Emilia made a strangely cute noise.

"Is it that embarrassing?" Lucian looked to Mia.

"There's a lot of stigma attached to their Berserk state," his sister answered, the fury now buried. "Everyone is taught to hate and fear it from a young age, especially the white hairs themselves. Because of that, some of them have ... strange reactions after using it."

"That so? Well, I thought it was amazing, like a scene from an action movie."

"A what?"

"Ah, nothing." He turned back to Emilia. "I don't think there's anything to be embarrassed about. In fact, you should be proud. I doubt many people could beat that fearsome minotaur in single combat like that."

"Y-yeah." Emilia regained a bit of her composure. "That reminds me! Prince Lucian, your magic is really powerful!"

"Is it? I don't really have much to compare it to, so I guess I'll take your word for it."

"We sometimes get magically enhanced during our training, but I never felt anything like I did when I fought the minotaur. It was a little overwhelming, even."

Could this be because of the Goddess? Lucian thought. *She really made things difficult until now, but it'd make sense for her to give me some perks if she wants me to save the world.*

And she did say that I should be able to exceed other mages. Does that mean I'm already more powerful than them?

A brief silence filled the room. The three of them had just shared a dreadful encounter, but they weren't the only ones there. One other person had been in that room, though he was nowhere to be seen after the battle ended.

"Mia," Lucian said. "What happened to Rudeus?"

"I ... think he ran after you jumped in." Mia looked thoughtful. "Yes. I believe he yelled something about it not being his fault, then he fled."

"That rat. Next time I see him...!"

Wait. What would I do next time I see him?

Thomas George Hamilton had been a nonviolent man. The rage that now burned inside him was a feeling he had never truly experienced before.

He may be the crown prince now, but his rule was far from absolute. There were already powerful factions seeking his life, as proven by the disease and recent assassination attempt. If he were to play his hands carelessly, then it would only empower his enemies.

If I turn on the one who was supposed to be my best friend, what would the undecided factions think?

Would they see me as too dangerous and try to get rid of me, too? Just like they did on Earth...

He had been through this before. A powerful man, surrounded by enemies. Back then, he assumed the civil nature of his country would protect him, but he was wrong. When those in power feel threatened, they will lash out, whether it's a monarchy or republic. No matter the form of government, it's ruled by people, and people don't like to have their power challenged.

This world is orders of magnitude more dangerous than America. I can't be lax here, like I was back on Earth.

No, I need to play it smart this time.

Plus, I'm already going to be making some unpopular decisions soon...

"Um..." Emilia broke the silence. "About Rudeus. What was he actually trying to do...?"

Lucian and Mia looked at each other. Emilia didn't know the truth behind Lucian's true personality, so she didn't understand why Rudeus would come up with such a convoluted setup like tricking her into facing the minotaur.

"Rudeus," Lucian said, "was doing what he thought I wanted."

"What do you mean?"

"The truth is ... even now, I have no memory of anything before the disease."

""Huh?"" Two girls said at the same time.

"I'm not regaining my memory like I claimed. I'm learning everything for the first time. Which means, I have no idea what I was like before waking up a couple days ago."

"You ... don't remember any of it?" Mia asked. "All those times you forced me to watch as an innocent girl was slaughtered by that minotaur?"

"No..."

"You don't remember giving me a kitten when I was five years old, then feeding it to that beast right in front of my face a few months later?"

"I'm sorry..."

"You ... you can't forget! Why do you get to forget it and not me!?"

"I know it's painful, but there's one thing that may bring you some peace. Mia, the Lucian you knew died that day. I'm ... not your brother."

"W-what...?"

"I died. Or rather, I was assassinated. When I came to, I was sitting in front of this world's Goddess. She gave me a second chance at life, but I had to take the body of one of your dying brothers." Lucian motioned to himself. "And this is the one I chose."

"No ... that can't be...! You're lying, like you always do!"

"I know it's hard to believe, but it's the truth. All I ask is that you keep watching me and decide for yourself. Because the Goddess didn't give me a second life for free. She gave me a mission. Mia, Emilia, I'm supposed to save this world from disaster."

The two girls looked at each other, completely taken by surprise at all the revelations Lucian dropped on them.

Emilia in particular was shocked to hear of all the terrible things Lucian supposedly did to other girls and even his own sister. She didn't want to believe any of it, considering what she'd seen of him since meeting him a few days ago.

But it was the princess who made those bold claims, and if they were true, then Rudeus' actions would make sense.

He jumped in to save me, Emilia thought. *We almost died. Both of us. There's no way that was all an act.*

I–

"I believe you," Emilia said.

"What!?" Mia yelled out. "How can you believe such an incredulous story!?"

"Because Lucian hasn't done anything bad since I met him. He welcomed me into the castle, lets me organize the royal study, took me out to the city, and even saved me from the minotaur. If he's telling me that the Goddess sent him to save the world, then I want to believe him."

"You ... don't know Lucian. He's conniving, wicked...!"

"Then until I see that side of him for myself, I will continue to believe."

"Emilia..." Lucian said softly.

"I..." Mia started. "...I will refrain from judgment for now. But know that I won't be deceived again."

"Thanks, Mia. I'll definitely live up to my words here today."

"How? If you truly plan to save this world, then you have to start with the kingdom, correct?"

"Yeah. I've been doing my best to learn everything I need to know. But I simply don't have time to put it off anymore." Lucian looked between the girls. "It's time to make my move, and I would like you two to help."

"You claim to want us to help you," Mia said. "But what can we do? A useless princess and a white hair soldier won't be able to do much against the powerful nobles within our kingdom, much less against other countries."

"First off, you're not useless. You proved that today, didn't you? The simple fact that I can trust you is enough for now, but I have a plan that requires your help. Though whether or not you'll like it is another story. But we'll get to that later."

Lucian turned to Emilia. "As for you, having a soldier by my side to keep me safe is just common sense. And the fact that you get so powerful when enhanced with magic makes you invaluable. Which is why I intend to make you the captain of my personal guard."

"Eh!? Me, a captain for the crown prince!?"

"That's right. Nobody will be able to complain about you coming and going as you please if you hold such a position."

"But my people are forbidden from holding such ranks. We aren't even allowed to lead a squad, much less become a captain..."

"I don't care. I'm going to be the king, so if it's a law that forbids it..." Lucian thought back to the words of the Goddess, who clearly wanted him to rise to his rightful throne. "...Then I'll simply erase that law."

"Erase it..."

"That's what it means to be the king. I have the power to shape the kingdom in whichever way most benefits me. If there are those who don't like it, then they can come take the throne by force."

Emilia and Mia both showed a hint of unease. Such bold actions were sure to ruffle some feathers, but the two also understood that their position in the world wouldn't allow them to just sit idle and expect everything to simply go as they wish.

It was those with the will to take decisive action who became the great figures written about in history books. Even though the two of them didn't understand the depth of the world's dire circumstances, they could feel the beginnings of something stirring.

As for Lucian...

Who was that God's Acolyte those two divine beings were talking about? They said I would have to face him, but do I have the power to fight something like that?

Lucian was anxious. He had only just learned to wield both the sword and magic, yet the threat of a foe with potentially divine power loomed somewhere in the world.

"I'll..." Emilia began. "...I'll definitely protect you, Prince Lucian!"

"Emilia." Thank you. "There's no telling when we'll be attacked by another assassin, so I'm counting on your battle instincts."

"I won't fail!"

"Oh, that reminds me." Lucian turned to Mia. "I heard from the Goddess that your family didn't fall ill. They were assassinated with a deadly disease."

"Assassinated..." Mia had a conflicted look. "So there's someone out there who's seeking the throne."

"Does that mean when we were attacked while out in the city..." Emilia trailed off.

"Yeah," Lucian said. "Someone was trying to finish the job. Chances are, it was the same culprit who spread the disease through the royal family. I plan to do some digging on the matter, but I have other objectives to accomplish first."

"What are these other objectives?" Mia asked.

"First, I need to solve our food crisis. I don't think we can survive another year of bad harvests, not with the kingdom's poor finances."

"That won't be a simple task. There are many factors that determine how much food is produced each year, some of which can't be controlled. Do you intend to ask the Goddess to give us favorable weather?"

"No, she definitely wouldn't agree to interfere to such a degree. But there's something bugging me about our crop production. I found a book in the royal study that said farms are owned by private farmers who get to decide what to plant in their fields. But even poor regions that are most affected by the famine swapped production to textiles and spices.

"Those farmers should have known that they'd be going hungry if they did that, but they swapped anyway. And that also makes me wonder where the poor farmers got the expensive seeds and extra equipment needed to plant and harvest their luxury crops. No matter how I think about it, it doesn't make sense."

"Ah, that." Mia nodded in understanding. "Farmers did indeed have control over their fields. Until Father changed the law, that is."

"What? When did that happen?"

"Five years ago, I believe. The book you read must have been written before the law changed."

"I didn't think of that. Guess that's one downfall of getting all my information from dusty books." Lucian shook his head. "But what does the law state now?"

"Father set up an administrative body to oversee each province, with men being sent to the lords in order to work with them to enhance our productive output. At least, that was the idea."

"Ugh. Centralized control over the farming industry. Of course they would run it into the ground."

"Um." Emilia raised her hand. "Is it bad for the crown to get involved?"

"Yeah. Some busybody administrative officials telling experienced farmers how to do their job can only lead to disaster. But at least this answers my question, and I even know what I need to do next. Thanks for the information, Mia."

"I-it wasn't anything special..." Mia turned away.

"Oh, and about your new position as Prime Minister. You'll have control over the day-to-day operations here at the castle when I'm gone, so I doubt you'll have time to be bored like before."

"Prime Minister...? W-wait, when did I gain such a position!?"

"Oh, right. I guess I forgot to mention it. I'm making you Prime Minister, since I need someone I can trust to watch things while I'm gone."

"But why me!? I'm just an 11-year-old princess! Nobody will listen to me!"

"They better, or they'll have to answer to me when I get back."

"That doesn't make my job sound any easier!"

"Haha." Lucian ruffled his little sister's hair, causing her frown to deepen. "Don't worry. I really just need someone that the other ministers are obligated to talk to before making any policy decisions. I don't expect you to actually run the kingdom."

"So I'm a blockade to prevent them from ruining your plans while you're out of the castle?"

"Exactly. I have a feeling they're going to try and push their garbage ideas through while I'm not here to stop them. Hence your new position."

Mia showed obvious reluctance. Her whole life, she assumed she'd simply remain an ornament. In the Almekian Kingdom, girls weren't allowed to take the crown. At best, if there was no male heir, they could marry the next king to legitimize his rise to the throne.

But now she was being given the chance to break out of that mold and take some agency for the first time in her life. Such a drastic change would be scary, and Mia was feeling the weight of that fear this very moment.

Who are you? Mia thought. *Are you really someone chosen by the Goddess...?*

Or is this just another one of your vile schemes?

She still wasn't sure what to believe. When she thought about all the things her brother had put her through, she couldn't imagine ever trusting anyone who wore his face. Yet she had seen many things today that called everything she knew into question.

I ... have to know. I absolutely need to know the truth.

"I'll accept the position of Prime Minister," Mia said. "But don't expect me to just be a blockade without any agency. If I feel the need to act while you're not here, I will do so."

"Awesome! I'm so glad to hear you say that! Thanks, Mia!"

"I-it's nothing..." She became unexpectedly embarrassed.

"Things are going to be changing around here. I'm through playing games with the people who are trying to assassinate me and murder the people closest to me."

"What do you intend to do?"

"Simple." Lucian looked at the two girls in turn. "I'm going to become a king."

Chapter 13

"Enter," Lucian said at the sound of a knock.

The door to his office opened, revealing the guest he summoned to the castle.

"Please, make yourself comfortable." Lucian motioned to the luxurious sofa placed just in front of his desk.

"Thank you for the hospitality, Your Highness."

The man removed his hat and placed it over his heart before giving Lucian a cordial bow. With his head on full display, his grey hair was laid bare for all to see. His matching goatee was meticulously trimmed, which went well with his refined and practiced movements.

He was very proud of the fine vest that covered his torso, along with the matching shirt and pants that went along with it. By all accounts, the man presented himself well. So well that it was obvious his appearance was an important part of his self-worth.

That man, Sampson, walked without a hint of fear or awe, despite being in the presence of the kingdom's future ruler. Rather, he acted as if being summoned to the king's private office was a normal occurrence, taking a seat on the comfortable sofa without care.

"Good morning, Sampson. I hope the days have been treating you well."

"Very well, thank you. I may not have a noble title or land to govern, but I find myself making ends meet one way or another."

"Yes, I've heard your business has done quite well for itself. I'm glad to see that some people have managed to prosper, even during these tough times."

"Coming from the crown prince, that's the highest praise I could ever receive. Though it's unfortunate that not everyone can say the same about their finances. Quite unfortunate, indeed."

"I agree." Lucian nodded at Sampson's words. "Those with the least are always affected the most during the hard times. It's quite a sad sight to see them suffering, wouldn't you say?"

"Oh, absolutely. I've always been a man of the people, you see. It breaks my heart to hear of their hardships during this long, cold winter."

"I knew you'd understand, Sampson. I believe that together, we can ease their suffering. You know how, don't you?"

"Of course. The crown always calls me for the same purpose, Your Highness. You seek a loan, correct?"

"I do. As I'm sure you've heard, the fields produced an abnormally low amount of crops this year. It's put a strain on our food supply to such an extent that many workers simply cannot afford to eat. However, most of the surrounding kingdoms were largely unaffected, so I intend to purchase their excess food to ease the shortage."

"And for this, you require gold. Lots of gold. Without a doubt, those countries know precisely how desperate we are for supplies, and they won't let go of them without proper payment."

Lucian opened the ledger sitting on the desk in front of him. In it was financial information of all kinds, relating to the monetary state of the kingdom. If they used the same color-coded system of modern-day Earth, then the pages would be filled with red ink indicating the tremendous losses they had sustained in the last few years.

Running a vast kingdom required an enormous sum of money. On the other hand, the land under its control would bring in an even more mountainous pile of coins. At least, that would normally be the case.

But when economic hardships hit, profits dwindle, while the costs only continue to rise. The golden eggs that once filled the Almekian Kingdom's coffers have become an endless drain that threatened to bankrupt the entire country.

Though a large part of that problem lay with the ones in charge.

"We're in need of a loan of this size." Lucian slid a piece of parchment toward Sampson.

"That's quite a hefty amount." Sampson made a showing of getting lost in thought. "We've scarcely given loans of that size before, and never during such troubling times."

"The kingdom guarantees all loans. We've never failed to pay one back."

"That's true, but have we ever faced hardships such as this? Correct me if I'm wrong, but didn't we recently lose a decisive battle against the Esgares Empire? Our people are starving, and civil unrest is rising. Under these circumstances, a loan of this magnitude is quite risky, even if the borrower is the Almekian Kingdom itself."

"Our treasury contains enough gold to cover the loan at this very moment."

"And what of the other outstanding loans? Does the treasury have enough to cover them all?"

"I'm afraid that's not something I can discuss."

Sampson pulled a small book from his vest pocket. "Well, according to my notes, the total loans we've offered you already exceed the treasury nearly 2-to-1. Since this information was proffered only two months ago, I'll assume it hasn't changed much. Though no doubt the treasury has done nothing but continue its downward trajectory since then."

Lucian was caught off-guard that this banker was so close in his estimate of the kingdom's funds. He was also right when he said that the number had decreased since then.

What Lucian didn't know was that part of the recent agreements with the bank was to share the royal family's financial situation with them so they could calculate the risk involved with the loan.

And Lucian would soon find himself forced to do the same.

"Even if the kingdom is low on funds, we will still meet our debt obligations. If we don't, trust in us will crumble."

"And how do you intend to gather the funds to pay, if things continue to deteriorate? Will you pillage it from the very people you're supposedly trying to save with this loan? Running a nation requires sacrifice. Rulers sacrifice their morals, and peasants sacrifice their lives. Sometimes, it's the only way to keep the machine running."

"There's no way I'll allow something like that. I may be young and lack the formal training my brother received, but I'm no fool. I will dig this kingdom out of the hole it's in."

"Quite confident, aren't you? But words and actions are entirely different beasts. I'm afraid that a loan of this size simply isn't worth the risk ... at least, not at the usual interest rate."

Lucian frowned. "And what rate did you have in mind?"

"I believe 20% is more reasonable."

"What!? The previous loans were at a rate of 10%! You want to double it!?"

"Oh, I don't want to. But as the owner of this kingdom's largest bank, I'm simply doing what I must. Wouldn't want my other clients to lose their shirts because I walked into a bad deal, you see."

"Tch." Lucian couldn't help but let out an annoyed sound.

The truth was, Lucian understood the man's position. In fact, he agreed with it. The kingdom truly was in a terrible spot. Any loans made to it had a real chance of going under. After all, the entire royal family had nearly been wiped out recently, and there was no telling if Lucian's reign would last.

In the worst-case scenario, a new monarch could take power, and there was a chance he wouldn't honor the loans of the previous ruler if it meant bankrupting the treasury. Knowing this, Lucian couldn't blame the man for gouging the loan's rate.

But that didn't mean he was happy about it. Nobody liked being on the wrong side of a bad deal.

"Fine," Lucian said. "I'll pay your 20%."

"Oh-ho. I knew you'd see the wisdom in my words, Your Highness. You will certainly make a fine king in a month's time."

"Thank you for the kind words, Sampson. I'll make sure you won't regret your decision here today."

Although Lucian's mood had been dampened by the raw deal and terrible state of the kingdom, he hadn't forgotten the necessity of playing the political game. It was important to appear cordial, even if that was the last thing on his mind.

The rest of the meeting was a boring slog of financial speech. Though for someone with a Master of Economics degree like Lucian, it was like coming home to a warm fireplace. Eventually, the deal had been struck, and the gold would soon be delivered. The starving masses would get their food, at great cost to the kingdom.

As for Lucian, he wished to cleanse his palette with something more pleasant. So, he sent a maid to fetch Emilia, who was lounging in a nearby room.

He considered having her sit in on this meeting, but in the end, he decided against it. He hadn't yet announced her promotion, and he was starting the negotiation from a disadvantaged position. Having a white hair lording over the banker could be interpreted as a threat, which would only hurt his chance of striking a favorable deal.

But now that the meeting had ended, he wanted Emilia by his side so the people in the castle would get used to having her around. That'd make the upcoming declaration of her promotion a little easier.

"How did it go, Prince Lucian?" Emilia asked.

"Not as good as I hoped. He really gouged me on the interest rate. It's going to hurt when the first payment comes due next year. But at the very least, I managed to secure the gold I need to buy some food for the people, so it was worth it in the end."

"Then you should consider it a victory."

"True, maybe I should. But I still want to wash the bad taste out of my mouth, so I was going to do some studying for a bit. I thought you might want to work on sorting the books at the same time."

"Yes! I made a lot of progress yesterday, but there's still so much more to do!"

"Good, that enthusiasm of yours is always a welcome sight."

The two were already walking the castle halls during their conversation, so they made it to the royal study in short order. As usual, the place was a disaster, but that's precisely why Emilia was there. With her dedication, Lucian was sure that she'd have the entire place sorted in a day if he let her stay here all night alone.

"Oh, by the way," Lucian said. "If you happen to run across a report of the kingdom's recent crop production, please let me know."

"Ah, I found it."

"Yeah, it definitely won't be easy to find among these thousands of—wait, what did you say?"

"I said I found it." Emilia stepped up to a bookcase and pulled out a thin book.

"No way. You've only sorted a fraction of the royal study, yet you happened to find the one report I'm looking for? Talk about lucky!"

"About that..." Emilia handed Lucian the report. "The study is very disorganized, but after careful inspection, I noticed that certain shelves contain more recent and important books than others. So, I focused on sorting them first, in case you asked for something like this."

"Wow, great job, Emilia. I'm impressed."

"Thanks!" A smile blossomed on her lips. "I'll keep doing my best, Prince Lucian!"

After opening the record, Lucian quickly flipped through it until he found the relevant pages. With his experience in business management, it was a simple matter to decipher the information and numbers laid bare before him.

What's going on? Lucian thought. *There's no way this report can be accurate. If it is, then that means...*

"Eh?" Emilia peered at Lucian's troubled face. "Is something the matter, Prince Lucian?"

"Emilia. Have there been any droughts or other disasters that caused the crops to fail?"

"No. I heard that we must have displeased the Goddess since most of the other countries didn't have nearly as bad of a harvest as we did."

"I somehow doubt the Goddess was to blame." Lucian flipped back a couple pages. "You said you lived in a rural area, right?"

"Yes, in a countryside between two towns."

"What kind of crops did the farmers around you grow?"

"Ah, when I left, most of the fields were growing tea, though some had spices."

"Tea and spices? Was that always the case, even when you were young?"

"Um ... no. When I was little, I remember the other kids used to always play in the corn fields. The adults would yell at them, but it never did any good."

"I see."

"D-did that answer suffice?"

"Ah, sorry. I sometimes get lost in thought. Yeah, that was really helpful. "

"Okay!" Emilia goes back to her sorting, a small hum now emanating from her.

Looks like I need to have a long discussion with the Minister of Production.

After a bit of time studying the kingdom's crop records, and a copious amount of time watching Emilia sort books, Lucian departed from the royal study. He had learned what he needed and intended to go straight to the source of the problem—Walther, the Minister of Production.

I'd like to think the ministers sincerely believe they're doing what's best for the kingdom, but that's a difficult stance to take considering how badly each of them seemed to have messed up.

We're losing a war, our treasury is nearly bankrupt, the people are starving, and public trust in our ability to rule is collapsing.

No matter how I think about it, isn't the situation already too bad to turn around!?

He suddenly began to wish that the Goddess would have reincarnated him sooner. Preferably before the kingdom began to spiral into total collapse.

Unfortunately, this was his reality now. He'd have to find a way out of this disastrous situation before the pillars that supported the nation crumbled.

Needless to say, Lucian quickly put such thoughts out of his mind. He had a mission, and distractions would only increase his problems.

He finally reached his destination, a door on the eastern wing of the castle. It looked like many others he passed by, but he anticipated that he'd be seeing the face of the one who resided behind this particular door far more often than he'd like.

As the crown prince, Lucian practically owned the castle. And since the room beyond the door was an administrative office, there wasn't any expectation of privacy for anyone within.

So, Lucian had no qualms grabbing the handle and giving it a push.

"Who—P-Prince Lucian...!" Walther, the Minister of Production, sat up straight in his chair. "If I had known you wished to see me, I would have come to you."

"I didn't want to wait. There's an important matter I want to discuss, after all."

Normally, a king would call his subjects to him. However, breaking tradition could have its benefits. It was one thing to have your boss call you into his office, but it was another thing entirely to have him barge into yours unannounced.

The sudden intrusion would leave most people on edge, wondering what it was that had their boss in a bad mood. It was precisely that unpredictability that Lucian sought to foster. Having Walther on edge would go a long way to keeping him in check.

With Emilia behind him, the sudden appearance of his ruler alongside a white hair had clearly taken its toll on Walther's mental state. The man had a tendency to fidget his fingers when he was nervous, and that bad habit was currently on display.

As the Minister of Production, he was responsible for overseeing a variety of markets in the empire, including the crafting of equipment and the routes they used to conduct trade.

However, Lucian came here to discuss a very specific topic.

"Walther," Lucian said. "I have a few questions, and I'd like some answers."

"A-ah, yes." Walther adjusted himself in the chair. "I'll do my best to provide them, Your Highness."

The chair protested as he repositioned, having difficulty handling the Minister of Production's excessive weight.

"I'm glad to hear that," Lucian said. "Because I came here to talk about a most important subject."

"And what might that be?"

"The famine."

"Ah, an unfortunate situation. The Goddess' wrath is not to be taken lightly."

"The Goddess? I don't think she had much of a hand in this particular famine. In fact, I'm quite confident in it."

"There was no drought or flood, so what else could cause such a sudden and massive decline in food production?"

"That's precisely what bothered me." Lucian pulled a book from his coat. "Which is why I began to do a little research. Turns out, the answer is quite obvious. Let me ask you, Walther. Why did you lower the number of farms producing food and swap them for luxury goods, like spices?"

"Swap farms for spices? I'm rather lost on what you mean, Your Highness."

"Walther." Lucian pushed the book toward the minister. "Can you read these numbers out for me?"

"These are..." Walther eyed the book now lying just in front of him.

"These are the records of the productivity for all the farmland in the kingdom, going back over two decades. Interesting, isn't it?"

"Where did you get this? Only a few copies exist, and I'm sure nobody has come asking for them recently."

"Where it came from isn't important. What is important are the figures you see here." Lucian pointed to a row containing a particular set of numbers.

"The total productive output, categorized by type. I've already poured over these exact figures many times, so I don't quite see what you're getting at."

"Then let me enlighten you, Minister of Production. Follow along and let me know if I make any mistakes, will you? I'll be recalling them from memory, after all."

Walther hid the frown on his face by hovering it over the book. The previous king seemed to care little for the kingdom's details. The man was too absorbed with his own ego and personal desires.

Most thought Lucian would follow in his father's footsteps, but the young prince had already surprised Walther with his unpredictable actions. The minister had presumed that Lucian was simply doing as he pleased, drunk on his new power and unsure how to use it.

But those thoughts were beginning to fade.

Just what happened to the prince? Walther thought. *Did the disease change him this drastically, or was his old persona merely a ruse to begin with?*

There's no way he could fool us all so completely for the entirety of his seventeen years of life. But then, why does he seem like an entirely different person now?

Lucian didn't miss the hesitation in Walther. As a former politician on Earth, reading people's moods and thoughts was essential to his success. So much so that he became frighteningly adept at understanding a room's atmosphere at a glance, enabling him to quickly adapt to nearly any circumstance.

The nobles in his new world may be great with their games and schemes, but compared to the skills needed to fool an entire population of democratic voters, they could still be considered lacking.

Could someone so adept at trickery really be considered a good guy? Thomas George Hamilton asked the man in the mirror that very question many times through his years. And yet, no matter how many times he fretted over it, he could never come to a satisfactory answer.

"First," Lucian said. "This year's grain harvest was 27% lower than average. Last year, it was 16% lower than average, and the year before that, it was 13%. Are those numbers correct?"

"...Yes, Your Highness."

"In other words, not only has this year's harvest been exceptionally poor, but it's been on a steady decline going back half a decade. Do you agree?"

"I do."

"Now, take a look at the non-food crops, listed here." Lucian pointed his finger at a column of numbers. "Tell me what you see."

"The yearly harvest has also been on a decline."

"Wrong."

"What do you mean I'm wrong?" Walther tapped his finger on that same column. "It says right here that we've harvested less and less the past few years."

"Yes, but only 2 or 3 percent below average. That's within the statistical margin of error and is likely caused by other factors. Which brings me to my point. The kingdom is in steady decline. Finances, standard of living, morale, and more are all collapsing. At the same time, crime is getting out of control. By all measures, the non-food crops should have taken a much larger hit to their productivity. And yet, they've barely fallen.

"So," Lucian continued. "I'll ask you again, Walther. Why did you order the farms producing food to swap production to non-food crops during a time of increasing famine?"

For the first time since the meeting began, a bead of sweat rolled down the Minister of Production's face. It even made it past both of his chins, nearly falling onto the book still lying in front of him.

"Y-Your Highness, I know it looks bad, but I swear, there's a reason why we had to keep up production of our spices."

"Then let's hear it. What was so important that you were willing to throw away the lives of an untold number of citizens through starvation?"

"To pay for the kingdom. A field producing grain may feed a village, but that same field can make us several times that in gold if it's producing a spice or textile. With how heavily in debt we've become, we couldn't afford the loss to our income. We're running a massive trade deficit, as it is! We'd be financially ruined if we didn't take drastic measures!

"Then there's the war," Walther continued. "Do you know how costly it is to battle another major power like the Esgares Empire? We're on a knife's edge as we are. If we couldn't afford to pay and feed the troops, we'd be forced to surrender to their assault."

Lucian stood up straight, digesting the Minister of Production's words.

He's not exactly wrong, Lucian thought. *They've probably been keeping the empire afloat with countless sacrifices just like this.*

But I can figure out a solution to those problems later. The people come first.

"Starting next season," Lucian said, "farm production will prioritize food over spices and textile. I want every citizen to at least have enough to eat."

"Your Highness! Are you really so worried about your reputation among the people that you'd risk destroying the kingdom!?"

"I have no intention of destroying it. In fact, I plan to rebuild it from the terrible state it's in, whether you like it or not."

"And how do you propose to pay for it? Will you debase the currency like your father did?"

Lucian pulled a gold coin from his pocket. As someone who earned a master's degree in economics, he already understood exactly what Walther was referring to.

Although the gold coin weighed 1oz, only 80% of that weight was actual gold. The rest was copper, making the entire coin into an alloy with barely three-quarters of it being a metal of actual value.

By lowering the amount of gold within the coins, the kingdom could issue more of them. This gave the monarchy more money to spend, as merchants were forced to accept them at face value, despite having less gold within them.

However, such practice could only bring a temporary reprieve to the kingdom's financial situation. Eventually, the markets would adjust, and the coin would lose value, forcing the monarch to continually reduce the amount of gold in the coins over time and eventually leading to a collapse in the currency.

On Earth, the Roman Empire had spiraled down a cycle of monetary debasement similar to the one the Almekian Empire was currently facing. At its peak, the Roman denarius was nearly pure silver. But after centuries of war, greed, and corruption, the Romans could no longer afford to pay for their spending.

The first such debasement occurred around 55 AD, during the reign of the famous, mad emperor, Nero. He cut the silver content of the denarius to 90%, essentially reducing its value by a tenth. This allowed him to mint more coinage, but it began the inevitable collapse of their currency as the people began to lose faith in it.

Over the coming centuries, more emperors would be forced to debase the denarius, continually lowering its silver content until the reign of Gallienus, where the once pure silver coin now contained only 5% silver content.

By the time the currency had reached such a low point, even the Roman Empire themselves no longer trusted their own coinage. They forced tax payments to be made with pure gold or silver, rather than their own issued currency. Once a nation reached that state of monetary debasement, there was simply no hope of regaining confidence.

"I will absolutely not lower the gold content in our coins," Lucian said. "I'll perish before I reduce it by a single gram further."

"Then how?" Walther asked. "Debt? Will you seek more loans from the banks who've already got a leash around the kingdom?"

"I've already taken another loan. A rather sizable one, at 20% interest."

"Are you mad!? How will we pay for it!? We can barely afford the interest payments already!"

"I'll think of a way."

"Your Highness, you're young and have great aspirations. I understand that, but try to think this through logically! If our vaults run dry, we're finished, all of us!"

"I said I'll take care of it, so drop it."

Walther was forced to bite his tongue, despite having far more to say on the subject.

"The important thing right now," Lucian said, "is feeding the people. I'll be using the money from the loan to make a trade deal with an allied nation to procure food. But negotiating, purchasing, and transporting it will require time. Time the people can't afford.

"That's why I'm allowing the release of three-quarters of our emergency food reserves. They are to be transported to the towns and villages in desperate need of restocking. Hopefully, this will be enough to stave off the starvation until the new shipments arrive."

"Preposterous." Walther shook his head. "Those reserves were supposed to be for the troops we intend to raise in the spring. Do you expect soldiers to fight on an empty stomach?"

"I will replenish them with the food arriving in the shipment. The fighting has stopped for the winter, so there's little risk of needing them before then."

"...As you wish, Your Highness."

"Excellent. Then I expect to hear good news the next time we discuss this matter."

Without another word, Lucian turned and left the Minister of Production's office, leaving Walther to wallow in the aura of displeasure that was seeping from him during the meeting.

But there were far more important matters tugging at his mind than an angry minister. Lucian looked at the gold coin still resting in his hand.

How the hell am I going to fix this mess?

Chapter 14

"Inflation?" Emilia asked, sitting across from Lucian's desk in the Royal Study. "You mean when prices go up?"

Lucian nodded at her question. "Yes, but price increases are more of a result of inflation, not the cause."

"So something else causes the prices to rise?"

"Yeah, an increase in the money supply. In our case, it's the extra coins minted when the kingdom lowered the amount of gold in them."

"More coins means things cost more. I guess that makes sense, but I still don't quite get how it works."

Emilia was surprisingly learned, considering her humble upbringing in the rural countryside. Because of her heritage as a white-haired beastfolk, she could never truly integrate into society. So to compensate, her parents brought her books, which she voraciously consumed.

She didn't just read fantastical stories of fictional characters but also records from historians, theories from scholars, and any other literature she could get her hands on.

In a world without a printing press, books were a rare luxury. Although Emilia's parents were fairly well-off, they couldn't afford to purchase one book after another.

So to give their daughter reading material, they had to trade in the previous book to afford the next one, kind of like checking out books in a library. They'd only let you take another book after bringing the previous one back.

Knowing she only had one chance to enjoy the story contained within each set of covers that came into her possession, Emilia completely immersed herself in those worlds. Compared to the average citizen, she could only be described as educated.

However, she had little control over which subjects she could devour. It was up to fate to determine which books were available in the nearby city at the time. And since Emilia herself couldn't go with her father on his trips there, she could only provide a general idea on her interests and hope for a good result.

Because of that, Emilia obtained much knowledge but also little depth. Most others would scarcely know what the word inflation even means in financial terms, but even though she was exposed to it, she never learned the details to an extent that would allow her to see just how much monetary inflation affected a nation like the Almekian Kingdom.

But being someone who willingly consumed complex information with a smile, Emilia would be a great student to someone with the knowledge to fill in her gaps.

Much like Emilia, Lucian had been a studious person in his youth. How could he not, given he spent so many years in a high-class college, studying one of the most difficult subjects. Obtaining a Master of Economics degree was no easy feat, especially considering his stellar grades that put him at the top of his class.

Seeing Emilia's potential as a student, Lucian couldn't help but want to explain the concept of inflation in a way she could understand. It was an important subject for anyone who intended to rule over a nation, and Lucian would certainly benefit from those around him realizing just how dire the kingdom's situation was.

Lucian pulled out two silver coins. "If you want to understand why price increases are simply a result of inflation, and not inflation itself, then a quick demonstration would clear it up."

"Okay!"

"Pretend you're a baker, and this is your stock of bread." Lucian pushed a stack of books toward Emilia.

"Five books—I mean five loaves of bread, right?"

"Yeah, while I have two silver coins. Let's say each loaf sells for one silver. How much money would you have if you sold all your bread?"

"Five silver."

"Correct." Lucian placed one silver coin in front of Emilia. "I'd like to buy one loaf, please."

"Certainly!" Emilia handed Lucian one of the imaginary loaves of bread in the form of a book.

"In a normal market, that's how the transaction would go each time. But..." Lucian held up his second silver coin. "Let's say this coin only has 50% silver content. Would you sell a loaf of bread to me for it?"

"Eh? No way. It's worth one coin of pure silver, right? Why would I sell it for half that?"

Lucian pulled out another coin. "What if I had two coins that each contained 50% silver? Would you accept that?"

"I guess so. Together they make a full coin, so the math works out."

"You're right. But now you've raised the price of your bread, haven't you?"

"Did I?" Emilia gave it a bit of thought. "I don't think so. I'm still getting the same amount of silver. It's just the coins are worth less."

"And that is the essence of inflation. A rise in prices does not mean that the things you're buying are more expensive. It simply means that the money you're using to pay for it has become less valuable, meaning it takes more of them to obtain the things you want."

"Ah! I get it now! So when the previous king reduced the silver content in the coins, he was able to mint more! But since the coins had less silver, the price of everything went up! Then what's the point if it just takes more coins to buy stuff?"

"That's a complicated question and requires a lot of in-depth knowledge to really parse out the answer. First, you have to remember that even though we reduced the silver content in the coins, the kingdom decreed that their value was the same as the money that was already in circulation.

"That means that whether someone had a coin with 80% or 100% silver content, the merchant would be forced to accept them as if they were both of equal value. Of course, this only works for so long. Eventually, the market will adjust, and prices will rise.

"But since the kingdom minted and spent the coins first, we were able to pass off a mountain of them as if they were equal to their more valuable counterparts with a higher silver content. Since it takes time for the markets to catch up, we received a large first mover advantage when we debased the currency.

"And don't forget that the kingdom has price controls, long-term contracts, and debt payments. All of those can now be paid with coins that contain less silver or gold, meaning we can effectively reduce our debt obligations by debasing the currency and minting extra coinage."

Emilia still sat in the chair across from Lucian, but sometime during his long speech, she had begun to lean forward, as if lessening the distance between them would somehow increase her understanding.

The results of her method were akin to pressing a button harder on a video game controller in an attempt to make the character's attack stronger, but in the end, it didn't matter. Emilia had soaked up his words and understood them with ease. Though she still had unanswered questions.

"Isn't that a good thing?" she asked. "If the kingdom can afford more, then everyone benefits, right?"

"No. Such methods don't come without a price. Market manipulation by central forces can only end in disaster. Businesses have a more difficult time making a profit, and the people will find their wealth stolen from them as inflation eats away at their savings. It's a vicious cycle, and once it begins, it's very difficult to stop."

"Eh? So it's a bad thing?"

"Very bad. There will always be people who take advantage of others, but in general, the free market is much better at making good decisions than any centralized power. Putting control into the hands of a few will make it easy for them to steal the people's hard work."

Emilia looked thoughtful. "You keep mentioning stealing, but how exactly does inflation lead to theft?"

"To answer that, I think another demonstration is in order."

Lucian gave the book back to Emilia and retrieved the coin he handed her in exchange for it. Next, he took out several more coins, until there was a small stack on the table before him.

"As we said earlier, a loaf of bread is worth a full silver coin." Lucian slid one toward Emilia.

"Thank you for your purchase." She handed him the very same book as before.

"Now." Lucian held up a second coin. "Imagine the next coin only contains 50% silver. Would you trade it for a loaf of bread?"

"No. I'd like two coins, please."

"I'm sorry, but these are tough times. The kingdom has placed price controls on bread, meaning you can only sell them for a single silver coin each."

"Eh!? But that's cheating!"

"When you make the rules, it's not cheating. It's policy."

"Fine..." Emilia handed over another book, taking the half-silver coin in exchange.

"Ah, I'd like another. Except this coin is only 25% silver."

"It's getting lower!?"

"Like I said, it's a vicious cycle. But the generous officials who make the laws understand your plight. That's why they've raised the price ceiling on bread to two silver coins."

Lucian held his hand out, and Emilia reluctantly exchanged a loaf of bread for the two coins.

"Now..."

"Please, don't say it!"

"...12.5% silver."

"Argh! I'm going to be ruined if I keep selling them at these prices!"

"Don't worry, you can now sell bread for three silver coins. Aren't you grateful?"

Despite her reluctance, Emilia made the trade. Though she nearly had tears in her eyes as she handed the loaf over.

Emilia looked at the four coins which now rested in Lucian's hand. Next, her eyes fell on the single loaf of bread that still sat on her side of the desk. Knowing what was coming, Emilia decided to go on the offensive before he could even suggest another trade.

"I'm not selling it for four coins with only 6.25% silver in them! I'd rather eat the bread myself!"

"Ah, so you decided to shut down your business because the income you were generating didn't cover the cost and labor involved. Yeah, that's pretty common in a high inflationary environment. In any case, let's tally up what you earned. You sold four loaves of bread, but how many ounces of silver did you actually get?"

"Um, let's see. One, plus a half, plus two quarters..." Emilia did some quick, mental math. "A total of 2.375 ounces of silver. That's barely two ounces, yet I sold four loaves of bread!"

"In essence, you could say that by debasing the currency and manipulating the markets, I stole nearly two loaves of bread from you. That's two loaves that you worked hard to prepare that are now in my hands simply because I used financial trickery to my advantage."

Lucian held a silver coin up between two fingers. "You can think of money as a representation of the work you've done. The time and energy you spent is stored within this coin and given a value by society. And it's by trading this coin for goods and services that you can spend that stored up value.

"By stealing your bread, I've essentially stolen your hard work. Your time, effort, energy, knowledge—all of it was siphoned to me. That is the true essence of what it means to have your wealth stolen through the continued debasement and inflation of your currency."

Emilia's fox ears drooped. "That's terrible…"

"Agreed, which is why I want to make our coinage whole again. For the good of the people. They deserve a currency that is a true representation of their hard work, rather than a vehicle to transfer their labor to me.

"Of course, this demonstration was an extreme example. Real inflation usually happens over a sustained period, little by little so most people don't notice. It's easier that way. And without price controls, you could increase the cost of your bread to match the lower silver content within the coins.

"But as inflation continues, the people lose more and more of their purchasing power, making it difficult for them to afford the higher prices. In the end, the result is the same. Less for the people who actually build society, and more for those who rule it."

"But you're going to fix it, right?" Emilia looked at him with a hopeful expression.

"I'm certainly going to try. But I can't right now."

"Eh? Why not?"

"People are starving, our kingdom is in massive debt, and we're gearing up for a continuation of the war with the Esgares Empire after winter. There are simply too many problems at our doorstep."

"And things are only getting worse," Emilia said. "Will there ever be a good time to fix it?"

"Of course." Lucian let a smile form on his face. "Because I have what it takes to make that future into a reality."

Emilia found herself captivated by the confidence radiating from the young prince.

She had heard that Prince Lucian was a man of the people, but others warned her that it was likely a facade. She didn't know the truth, so she was quite nervous when she was first summoned to meet him.

But now, there was no doubt.

"Anyway," Lucian said. "I'm going on a little trip tomorrow morning, so make sure you're up bright and early."

"I'm going, too?" Emilia looked excited.

"Yep. I need the captain of my personal guard to protect me, after all."

"That's right! I'll have to be by your side at all times!" Her tail began wagging, making a soft noise as it repeatedly slid across the chair she was sitting in. "Where are we going?"

"To the province just east of the castle. When I was doing my research on the farming situation, I noticed something interesting. I'll give you the details on the way, since we'll have plenty of time to talk during the carriage ride."

Emilia had no clue what was so interesting about the province to the east. Regardless, a king does what a king wants, so she was bound to find the answers soon enough.

Chapter 15

"We should be arriving shortly, Prince Lucian." Emilia stared out the window, watching the passing scenery.

"How do you know that? No matter how much I look out the carriage window, it all looks the same to me."

"You see that wide patch of barren land with the brown grass?"

"Yeah."

"Well, that's not actually grass. It's a type of weed that commonly grows after a field has been harvested. Although, it's strange that the farmers allowed the weeds to grow to this extent. It's common practice to clear the fields of them during winter, otherwise next year's crops will suffer.

"Oh, and notice that the ground there is flatter than most of the surrounding land and has no trees? That's because it was cleared by people so they could grow crops. Though I'm curious why such great land is so poorly maintained."

"Ah, I get it now. It's farmland. Then that means that plot of land and that plot of land are fields, too." Lucian pointed out the window at several other weedy patches.

"Yes. Since there are so many, then this must be a large farm. And since we left the castle at the crack of dawn, the current position of the sun means about four hours have passed, which lines up with the estimated time of arrival."

"Wow. You sure know your stuff, Emilia."

"It's only natural since I grew up in a small village."

"Somehow, I doubt all the knowledge and insight you've shown me so far is normal."

"W-well, maybe I did a little bit of studying in my free time..."

A bit of studying was quite the understatement, considering Emilia spent the better part of the first half of her life with her nose in one book or another. She picked up many concepts the average person on this planet had scarcely been exposed to, due to the general lack of information available to them and the requirement that many children begin working from a young age.

As Emilia expected, the carriage was indeed nearing its destination. Since the horses were moving at a brisk pace, the carriage averaged around 20 mph.

Such a rate would be impossible for horses to maintain for an extended period back on Earth. But when buffed by magic, the horses didn't tire easily.

Normally, a high speed would leave all but the hardiest occupants feeling ill from the effects of motion sickness. But the carriage had been fitted with a special shock absorber that utilized a magically enchanted gem to soften the bumpy ride.

Together, the use of magic enhancements and enchanted technology gave this world many advantages over the medieval society Lucian studied on Earth. And these differences would only grow as he explored more of his new homeland.

This magitech really is useful in a lot of ways. I should spend some time soon and learn more about how it all works.

But for now...

The carriage came to a stop. From the window, Lucian saw a building that looked to have been recently constructed. It wasn't anything extravagant, but it certainly stood out among the other rough constructions in the rural lands that made up most of the empire.

In front of that building was a man whose clothes screamed anything but farmer. His tailored outfit wouldn't turn heads among the nobility at the castle, but it certainly stood out from the working class that Lucian had seen.

Of course, he wasn't wearing his best uniform by happenstance. A messenger was sent ahead of the carriage to inform the necessary people of their prince's impending arrival.

"Welcome, welcome!" The pale-faced man greeted him. "It's an honor to receive His Highness, Crown Prince Lucian!"

"Are you the official in charge of these farms?" Lucian got right to the point.

"Yes! I'm humbled that you would come all this way to meet with me!"

"I see. Then I will have you show me around." Lucian motioned for the man to begin the tour.

One thing he learned as a politician on Earth was that overly explaining himself would only get him stuck discussing the minor details of everything he planned to do. Rather than that, it was much better to move the conversation forward.

As the future king, there wasn't a person around who could force him to halt his steps when he showed his intent to move, so the guards and official had no choice but to match Lucian's pace.

"I'm afraid there's not much to see, Your Highness. It's just a bunch of dirt and weeds as far as the eye can see."

"Odd that the weeds have been allowed to overtake the farmlands. If left to grow, they will certainly diminish next year's yields."

"A-ah." The official was surprised to hear the prince knew of such details. "It's true that it would be good to pull them up, but the workers aren't slaves, so any work we put on them must be compensated with pay. And with our budget being what it is..."

"I understand. Since the farms belong to the crown now, it's our responsibility to upkeep them, rather than the farmers themselves."

"I'm glad you understand, Your Highness! I requested an increase to our budget, but so far, I've not received a positive reply."

You want more money to squander? Lucian thought. *You should feel lucky you even get to keep your position for a while longer.*

He kept his thoughts from his face as he looked over the fallow fields, wondering how many other farmlands across the empire were being run into the ground like the one before him.

I need to fix it. If I want to obtain the so-called levels from the Goddess, then I have to put an end to the famine.

Since my actions so far haven't leveled me up, I can only assume what I've done isn't enough, which means I need to take more drastic measures.

"I've arrived today," Lucian started, "to find a particular man. I'm sure you know him. He goes by the name of Ivan."

At the prince's words, the official's eyes lit up. "So you read my letters, Your Highness! I warned of Ivan's rebellious attitude for years. It's great to see he's finally getting what he deserves!"

"Yes, I read your letters. Ivan has a particular hatred for our new farming system. He was also the one who controlled this land before the change, so I'm eager to hear what it is about the new system he hates so much."

"Hah, he said something about it being his land. What the fool doesn't understand is that it was never his. The crown has always been the owner."

Lucian ignored the man's smile. "Bring Ivan to me. I'll be waiting for you in the administrative building."

"At once, Your Highness!"

The official practically skipped toward one of the homesteads that dotted the area, each house containing a farmer and his family. Once upon a time, they owned and ran these fields, but that all changed when the previous king set up the bureaucratic administration to oversee the farmlands in the empire.

Lucian and Emilia stepped into the recently constructed administrative building, where the decisions were made on how to run this farmland. As expected, it was quite a step up in quality and convenience compared to the average home, with many expensive magitech devices lying around.

Lucian ignored all of that and took a seat behind the desk, while Emilia stood behind him, like a guard or attendant. She was in fact his guard, so the arrangement only made sense.

"Thank you for your patience, Your Highness," the official said. "I brought the troublemaker."

A middle-aged man with tanned skin and dark brown hair stood behind the official. Unlike the man who brought him here, his clothes could only be called average. They weren't in bad shape, but he wouldn't exactly be setting any new trends, either.

Compared to Lucian's soft features and thin limbs, Ivan was like a beast with his toned muscles and leathery hands. But despite the physical differences between them, the farmer couldn't hide the terror from his face.

"Good job," Lucian said to the official. "You may go."

"U-uh, right."

The official reluctantly left the building, leaving Ivan alone with Lucian, Emilia, and a handful of guards. The man had wanted to stay and watch the prince tear the farmer down, but he couldn't find the courage to ask such a thing.

"Now," Lucian said. "Let's get down to business quickly. I don't like to waste time."

"Y-yes, Your Highness!" The farmer managed to find his voice, which Lucian appreciated.

"I heard from the one in charge here that you've been quite vocal on how the kingdom runs its farmland. I would love to hear what exactly you find so disagreeable."

"That's just … sometimes, men argue! Yeah, just arguments on long, hard days! Farming's not easy, so sometimes we just—" He closed his mouth after seeing Lucian raise his hand.

"Let me be clear. I'm not here to punish you, Ivan. I simply want a few answers. You once owned the farms around your homestead, correct?"

"Yes, until five years ago."

"Until the former king took the land."

"…" Ivan's fear shifted into frustration.

"During my research," Lucian continued, "I saw that these farms in particular performed very well compared to ones of similar size. Yet now, they've fallen to nearly half their previous output. Care to explain why?"

"It's…"

"It's what, Ivan?"

"It's impossible. How can we produce crops with all these restrictions? They won't let us properly prepare the fields because they don't understand how important it is! They want to grow crops that don't do well in this climate and soil just because they're more valuable once harvested!

"We aren't planting the crops at the right time, our watering schedule isn't right, and we're lucky if we're told to harvest at the right time! All because that man has to be in charge! No matter how many times I tell him, he just won't listen!"

"I see."

"Ah…!" Ivan finally seemed to realize that he just yelled all his frustrations at his future king.

"You said some interesting things, Ivan. I assumed it would turn out like this, but I simply had to make sure."

"Y-Your Highness! Please, forgive me!" Ivan got on all fours, his forehead pressed against the ground.

"Um." Emilia made a sound only Lucian could hear. "You're scaring him, you know."

"Ah," Lucian replied softly. "Sorry about that."

"Raise your head, Ivan." Lucian waited until the man did as commanded. "I need someone to help me revise the current laws and bring them back in line with how they were before the former king seized the farmlands.

"It seems to me that someone with both the experience of working the land and the guts to speak the truth would be the perfect person to fill such a position. It's fortunate that I managed to find him so quickly."

"W-what are you...?"

"I'm saying that you should pack your bags for travel, Ivan. Because you're coming back with me to the castle."

The farmer couldn't hide the dumbfounded look on his face as he peered up at his prince from his still-kneeling position on the hardwood floor.

And it wouldn't be the last time Lucian would see such an expression.

Chapter 16

"Well..." Lucian closed the door behind him. "I think that went as well as could be expected."

"Minister Walther wasn't happy," Emilia said. "About any of it."

"He'll have to get over it." Mia looked unconcerned. "There's nothing he can do when the crown prince gives him a direct order."

"That's true. I just hope he doesn't drag his feet out of spite." Lucian motioned for the girls to follow him down the castle halls. "If he does that, then it'll give me justification to appoint someone else to his position."

The morning after returning from his outing, Lucian met with Walther, the Minister of Production. As the one in charge of the administrative organization that runs the farmlands, Walther had to be brought into the prince's plan to rewrite the laws that defined the agricultural state of the empire.

Emilia and Mia joined him in the meeting, as did Ivan, the former owner of the vas farmlands they visited. In fact, Ivan was still in the meeting room with Walter as the two went over the first changes that needed to be made.

The Minister of Production was absolutely flabbergasted that Lucian had brought a common man in to provide advice on how to best rewrite the laws. But as Mia said, he had no choice but to obey.

"Why Ivan?" Mia asked. "What makes him qualified to help us?"

"I made a list of the most productive farms nearby, then did some preliminary research on them to find the ones where the previous owner was still living there. As for why I ended up choosing to meet with Ivan, it's because of the letters that official sent, claiming Ivan was vocal about his opposition to the new policies. I needed somebody with both guts and knowledge. Those two traits alone might be enough to see us through this mess."

"So you went to one of our empire's largest farms in search of someone that may or may not be able to help us?"

"I didn't have much choice. I simply don't have time to get bogged down in the minutiae of agricultural reform. And I'm no expert on the matter, so it wouldn't be an easy task for me. That's why I needed someone to take the task from my hands. But I can't trust the people here at the castle. Any one of them could have been involved in the assassination attempts against the royal family, so I had to look for outside help."

Lucian turned a corner. "And since planting season is only a couple months away, I needed to move quickly. I didn't have time for an extended search or long vetting process. He fits what I was looking for and can read. That'll have to be enough. Besides, I have backup plans in case things don't go as I want."

The two girls listened to Lucian's reasoning as they continued their walk through the castle hallways. Although they agreed with him, neither could have imagined a future king even considering the usefulness of a common farmer.

As Lucian mentioned before, he would be making decisions that many would see as odd. Depending on the perspective, it could be interpreted as welcome progress or a dangerous precedent. Of course, the common people would see it as the former, while the nobility would see it as the latter.

"I think I understand," Emilia said. "If you really want to make big changes, you have to be unpredictable. It's the same in combat. You won't win by targeting the opponent's body where he expects, otherwise he will be ready to guard the attack."

"Exactly, Emilia. Being a wild card has its benefits, especially since ... well, you know what I told you about who I really am. By making all these odd decisions, I can throw them off from whatever expectations they may have had for me."

"So it's not just for the reform, it's for their perception of you, too."

"Yep. And it won't be the last time I make decisions they find questionable."

Emilia made a thoughtful face. "But how do you even know if changing the laws back will bring production up to what it was before?"

"Not long before I was born on Earth, a country called Vietnam went through a similar agricultural change as the one here in the Almekian Kingdom. Land was taken from farmers and placed under the control of the government. The farmers were organized into collective groups to work the fields, and all the decisions were made by bureaucrats—specifically, accountants and administrators who were planning the economy through centralized control.

"The ones with generations of knowledge on how to actually produce food had no real voice. They could only do what they were told by people who had no idea what it takes to actually turn a field into a productive farm. Predictably, the output of food in the country fell. A lot. So much so that in just a few years, the previous relative abundance of food had turned into a shortage, then a full-blown famine.

"During that time, corruption was the norm, with the local administrators manipulating the numbers, imposing unfair fines on the farmers, skimming off part of their production, and many other underhanded things to enrich themselves. This was common practice all the way up the administrative chain, resulting in angry officials who blamed the exhausted and demoralized workers for the deficits.

"Eventually, after decades of mismanagement, the government reverted the laws, allowing farmers to once again own their land and grow whatever they pleased. After that, the economy of Vietnam exploded, becoming one of the fastest growing nations in the region. Not only did the people have enough to eat, but they produced an excess, allowing them to become net exporters and provide a source of income for the country, rather than be a burden as they had before."

"Wow..." Emilia expressed her thoughts with a single word.

Mia uncharacteristically joined the conversation. "And you think that's where we're headed if you don't revert the laws? Decades of famine and unnecessary corruption?"

Lucian nodded. "From what I've seen of it so far, we're already on the edge of that future. And there's no way I could sit by and let us fall into that dark pit."

During their long conversation, the three had been walking down the castle halls, but Emilia had noticed something strange. She looked around, as if curious about something.

"Um, where are we going, exactly? I've never been down this castle hall before."

"That's because it's not a place I'd like to go, given a choice." Lucian looked to Mia. "Maybe it'd be best if you went back to your room."

"No," Mia said without hesitation. "If we're going to the castle dungeons, then I want to come along."

What is it you have planned down there? Mia thought. *Or should I ask, which criminal do you plan to visit?*

No, the answer is obvious. But how do you intend to deal with him?

It was a conversation Mia wished to hear. She had put aside her doubts about her brother's new personality being a scheme. But she had been burned by him too many times before. She still carried an ounce of reservation, and she intended to keep hold of it until all her doubts had been extinguished.

"Your Highness." The guard saluted.

"I'm here to see the prisoner."

"Understood." He took a key and unlocked the heavy, wooden door.

Beyond was a set of dimly lit stairs, leading down into a subterranean dungeon where some of the kingdom's most important prisoners were held captive.

The ones below weren't necessarily the worst offenders. They didn't cause the most damage or take the most lives. In some cases, their crimes could even be considered relatively minor, compared to what was considered normal in their world.

But there was one thing about them that did stand out, one aspect that they each shared in one degree or another.

They had committed crimes against the kingdom itself.

This is terrible, Lucian thought as he walked down the dungeon's dark halls. *Their living conditions aren't just bad, they're inhumane.*

Trying not to peer at the unfortunate prisoners, Lucian followed the guard along the damp path. Even though he wasn't looking, he could still smell the death that saturated the air. It made him feel sick, but he had no choice but to endure. Such was his duty as the one who ruled.

This isn't just a dungeon, Lucian thought. *It's my dungeon. I own the walls that make up these cages, just as much as I do the ones in my room.*

Could I ... reform it? Make it better? Or would I only end up making things worse...?

This world doesn't have the same concept of forensic science as Earth. How could anyone be certain that someone committed a crime if they weren't caught in the act?

Without fingerprints, DNA samples, and surveillance video, it must be frighteningly easy to get away with crimes in this world. Which means...

Lucian looked upon the poor sap that he came to visit. The assassin that attempted to take his life a couple days ago sat rotting in a cell no different than the others.

On his body were fresh wounds. They weren't given to him during his assassination attempt. No, they were more recent than that, with some being as little as an hour old.

...Without harsh methods like torture to dissuade crime, would more innocent people become victims?

Or does knowing the terrible fate that awaits them turn even petty crooks into hardened criminals, thinking if they're going to be dealt with by a heavy hand, they might as well go all the way?

Is it worth having less crimes if the ones that are committed become more vicious?

Lucian was afraid. Afraid because he didn't have the answer. What if he messed up? What if he made things worse and more people suffered because he tried to instill his morals onto this world?

Those kinds of thoughts ran through his mind. As the ruler, he was responsible for this suffering. Yet if he made a mistake, he could be responsible for so much more.

It's heavy, Lucian thought. *This responsibility.*

Back on Earth, I could at least spread my burden out among the democratic voters and other elected representatives. No single man could make all the decisions.

But now ... now it's just me.

In a perfect world, the answer would come to him. But this world was far from perfect, and the same could be said of Lucian himself.

In the end, he could only grit his teeth and focus on the reason he entered this forsaken dungeon in the first place.

"Assassin," Lucian said. "I've come to hear the truth. Who sent you to kill me?"

The man looked up, meeting Lucian's eyes. Despite his terrible treatment, it was obvious the fire in him had not yet been extinguished.

The man wasn't the well-trained and equipped assassin who nearly succeeded in taking Lucian's life. That man had fallen from his wounds already.

No, the man was the decoy, the one who had engaged Lucian in discourse to distract him.

Yet even though he wasn't a proper assassin, the man's spirit refused to yield. Even now, his eyes threatened to burn a hole in Lucian.

"You ... damn prince!" He stood, with great effort. "You'll get what's coming to you, mark my words! The Goddess won't let such scum live in luxury forever!"

Lucian was a bit taken aback by his ferocity. "You've got some nerve calling me scum when you're the one who tried to kill me."

"Don't think I'll forget...! I'll never forget! It's because of you that my daughter never came home! Where is she!? What did you do to her!?"

"Your ... daughter?" A foreboding feeling crept up Lucian's spine.

"She was smiling when she left to meet the prince that had taken a liking to her. To meet you! But ... she never came home! I know it was you, wasn't it!?"

"I..." Lucian's mouth went dry.

This man. His daughter was one of the prince's victims...

He wasn't trying to assassinate me. He was taking justice into his own hands. Justice that would never be afforded him because of the difference in our status.

"Please don't accuse the prince of such things!" Emilia said.

"He doesn't know anything about your daughter." Mia backed her up.

"Lies!" the man yelled. "All lies!"

Emilia ... Mia...

...Thank you.

"I'm sorry for your daughter's disappearance," Lucian said. "But I had nothing to do with it. However, I understand now why you would seek my life, however misguided your actions may have been.

"So, in the spirit of justice..." Lucian looked to the guard who brought them there. "Release him and send him on his way."

"What!?" The guard couldn't hide his shock. "You want to let him go!?"

"This is an order from your future king. I want this prisoner released. All his belongings shall be returned to him, and his wounds healed."

"I ... I understand, Your Highness!"

Lucian turned back to the distraught father. "I hope you will find peace."

With those words, Lucian turned and began walking. Emilia and Mia joined him, both a step behind. That was good, because he didn't want them to see the conflict that still covered his face.

Dammit. It wasn't supposed to end up like this...

Chapter 17

The assassin who sought Lucian's life stepped through the gate that ringed the castle, setting foot back in the city that surrounded it.

They really let me go, he thought. *Even returned my things and healed my wounds. But...*

Don't think I'll fall for your lies, you damn prince!

The future king had built himself a nice reputation among the populace. This assassin assumed his release was to be used in some greater scheme to show his merciful side and hide the depths of his hidden cruelty.

As such, the failed assassin had no intention of disappearing quietly into the night.

I'll get my revenge, I swear it!

The man walked the city streets, but he wasn't headed anywhere comfortable like his modest home. Instead, the neighborhoods he passed through steadily deteriorated until no sane man would look around and feel comfortable.

Buildings? Decrepit.

Merchants? Swindlers.

Residents? Scum.

Perhaps that last one may have been a bit harsh. After all, there were many people who simply couldn't afford to move to a better neighborhood. It was unfortunate that they had to live in a hive of such villainy, but life wasn't always fair.

Regardless, no matter how you sliced it, the failed assassin had no business walking into such a district without good cause. But cause he had, as his friends nested in that place.

He stepped up to the door of a house and knocked. By the looks of it, there was nothing special about it. But it contained the one thing the failed assassin wanted more than anything else—a path to vengeance.

The door opened, revealing a man with a slender face. "W-what the hell!? You're alive!?"

"I'm alive. And I'm back to help again."

"Get in, now." Slenderface ushered the failed assassin inside, then quickly closed the door.

"Thanks. I'm sorry for failing, but next time I'll—guh!"

Slenderface grabbed the failed assassin from behind. "Shut the hell up, you idiot."

"What are you doing!?"

"We should be asking you that!" He tossed the man into the center of a room. "You were taken by the guards! What the hell are you doing back here!?"

The failed assassin looked around and saw the faces of his other conspirators. Along with them was a new face he didn't recognize, but no matter where he turned, he could only see hostility in their gazes.

A new recruit? He thought. *Probably to replace me.*

"Look, I know it's hard to believe, but they just let me go. But I still want my revenge, like before! So please, let me try one more time!"

"This is why I was against him joining," Slenderface said.

"You." The leader of the group looked to the unknown man. "Get out of here. It's too dangerous."

"Tch. What kind of timing is this? Our benefactor won't be pleased if this idiot brought them here."

"Brought them here?" The failed assassin asked. "Brought who?"

"The soldiers, you fool!" the leader roared. "Do you really think they'll just let you walk out of the dungeon out of the kindness of their—"

"Patrol!" A yell interrupted the leader's words. "They're coming this way!"

"I knew it!" He turned back to the unknown man. "Go! They can't find you here!"

The mysterious man turned and fled, heading into a room that contained a window.

The rest of the conspirators grabbed their weapons and made their way toward the far side of the house, intending to flee through the back door.

"What's going on!?" the failed assassin asked.

"Fool!" Slenderface shot him a glare. "You brought the soldiers right to us!"

"T-they followed me!? We have to get out of here!"

"We? No, you're staying. Someone needs to distract them."

"B-but they'll throw me back in that dungeon!"

"No they won't." Slenderface tossed the failed assassin a sword. "Because you're gonna die fighting."

"I...!"

Before he could collect his thoughts and respond, Slenderface had already left. The only one who remained in the room was the man who sought to avenge his daughter's death. Yet he had doomed the operation that worked to bring his desire into a reality.

I'm not going to die before I get my revenge! A way out! There's got to be a way—

A battlecry disrupted his thoughts. It came from the direction the other conspirators ran, which was where he now heard the sounds of battle.

I ... I'll go help them fight! Then they'll see that I'm worth keeping around...!

The failed assassin ran toward the battle, his sword held in a sweaty hand. The back of the house contained several men, each of which he knew, even by just seeing the hair on the back of their heads.

However, there was one head of hair that was turned his way. It sat just in front of the back door, blocking their path. Even as he watched, the hair zipped around like a blur, with each movement being accompanied by a splash of red and the scream of a man being cut down.

That hair...! It's her, the white hair from that day!

The young girl had surprised the failed assassin with her quick reaction when he tried to run the prince through. Even though she wasn't enhanced by magic at the time, there was nothing he could do to overpower her.

But this time, things were different. It was nothing like that day. Because right now...

"Vermin, you will be eliminated." Emilia's blood-splashed face warped into a satisfied smile. "But at least try to put up a fight first. It's no fun if the pests fall too easily."

"You damn monster!" the conspirator's leader yelled. "You and your kind—"

He was cut down before he could even finish.

What ... the hell! She's just one person! One little person! And we can't defeat her!?

All but two of his supposed companions now lay on the ground. But as the failed assassin watched on, even those two met their end.

Finally, the glowing, red eyes of the white hair turned to him, and his blood ran cold. The sword in his hand felt no more than a lead weight that would slow him down as he fled, and he wished nothing more but to drop it and run as far as he could from the approaching monster.

But he couldn't look away from those scarlet eyes, as if just by meeting her gaze, he had been struck with a paralysis spell.

Step by step, the bringer of his doom approached, her twisted smile encapsulating her desire to fight.

Even when she stopped in front of him, he couldn't bring himself to raise the sword. He understood. He knew just how worthless such an action would be. Perhaps by remaining frozen, his heart would beat a few more times before she decided to end it. That was all he could hope for now.

"You. You dared to seek the life of my prince."

The failed assassin's mouth moved, but no words came out.

"Any foolish enough to raise arms against him ... deserves only death!"

The failed assassin fell to his knees, his face turned up to the fearsome monster who held his life in her bloodstained hands.

Lucian stepped into the decrepit building the conspirators were using as their base of operations. Blood still covered the floor, but he was getting used to such sights by now.

Ignoring the signs of battle, he walked toward Emilia. He hated sending her to fight like this, but the girl had asked to be let loose. Besides, he needed her strength, and as his guard, she was responsible for his life and wished to end the criminals with her own hand.

Well, to be precise, only some of them died. The others were only wounded enough for capture. They had a lot of questions for them, after all.

"Emilia," Lucian said after reaching her. "Good work."

"Such vermin can't even be considered a warm-up. Why couldn't there be at least one capable warrior among them?"

"I'm sure you'll get a chance to fight such a warrior eventually."

"I had better. I can feel my skills wasting away with each passive day that goes by. If only I could get my other self to bring me out during training more often."

"Well, you know the laws with regards to casting enhancement magic on your kind. Not that the laws apply to me."

"Ah!" Emilia showed Lucian her fangs. "My prince, may I be so bold as to ask you to release me more often? There's nothing quite like spilling a little blood daily, don't you agree?"

"I'm going to have to disagree with you on the spilling blood part. But I'll talk to you once the magic wears off, and if both of you wish it, I'll bring you out more often."

"Truly!?" Emilia's eyes narrowed at the thought. "Please do your best to convince that girl to agree to my terms!"

You're that girl, though, Lucian thought.

Although Emilia spoke of her unenhanced self as if she were a different person, that wasn't actually true. They were one and the same, but their personalities were so far apart that they couldn't help but see themselves as separate entities.

According to tests done on white haired beastfolk, those whose enhanced personalities closely matched their original selves didn't experience such separation of identities. Only the ones who were normally calm and caring, like Emilia.

"In any case," Lucian said. "The immediate threat has been dealt with. And the man who tried to assassinate me is...?"

"Hmph. Of course I spared his life, as you asked. The soldiers have already taken him back into custody."

"Good. Thanks, Emilia."

She sighed. "It would be much easier to simply end his life."

"There's no way I can do that after what he said about his daughter. It'd haunt me for the rest of my life."

"Truly a man of honor. I suppose I don't hate that. So where will he be sent?"

"To the other end of our empire, with enough gold to start a new life somewhere."

"And if he returns?"

"I'll deal with that when the time comes."

"I see."

A soldier stepped into the room Lucian occupied. "Your Highness, we found something strange on one of the corpses."

"Take me to it."

The soldiers led Lucian out of the house and to a nearby alley. One of the men inside had attempted to flee through a window, but he had been cut down during his escape.

That corpse was dressed in much finer clothes than the rest of the men, so Lucian immediately assumed the man was the group's leader who had tried escaping at the expense of his men's lives.

But he was incorrect in his assumption.

"A handkerchief?" Lucian asked.

"Not just any handkerchief," the soldier said. "One embroidered with a house name."

Lucian eyed the embroidery. "House Almekia. The royal house..."

"My prince," Emilia said. "Could it be that the ones seeking your life are your own flesh and blood?"

"That ... may just be the case."

Chapter 18

"If it's a forgery," Mia said, "then it's a particularly well-made one."

Lucian looked between the two handkerchiefs on Mia's desk. "So you think it's the real deal?"

"If I had to choose, then yes. But that's only my opinion."

"Well, it's a valuable opinion to me."

After their outing to take out the rebels that were trying to assassinate Lucian, he and Emilia returned to the castle and immediately sought out Mia. As a princess, she was in a unique position to check out the handkerchief that was embroidered with the Almekian family crest.

She had her own handkerchief with the same design, which was a perfect match to the one taken from the rebel who tried to flee the scene. When placed side by side, the only way to tell the handkerchiefs apart was the color of the threads.

"Mia, you said that princesses can't take the throne, right?"

"Yes. We can only be married off to whichever man ascends, if it comes to that."

"But what about a king's relatives? Is there a line of succession in case the king dies before producing a male heir?"

"That largely depends on the reputation of the ones in question. If there's a close relative with support from the noble class, then he will likely take the throne. But if not, there may be a civil war to determine who will rule."

"A close relative with a good reputation..." Lucian thought upon a certain man he met at the party to celebrate his survival. "Mia, if the royal family had been completely wiped out, what do you think the chances are that our uncle Henrik would have taken the throne?"

"Uncle Henrik..." Mia made a thoughtful face. "He is well-known for his successful magitech business, giving him deep connections with powerful merchants. On top of that, being an Archduke and the brother to the king places him in a unique position of power..."

"So, it's likely."

"Yes, I believe he would be the first choice to rule, had you succumbed to the disease."

"Um." Emilia made a small sound. "Are you saying Archduke Henrik is the one behind the assassination?"

The foxgirl had just recently reverted from her Berserked state, and she was still embarrassed by her arrogant actions and comments, which were still fresh in her memory.

"He's the most likely candidate," Lucian said. "But we can't just assume without proof."

"Should you send someone to investigate him, then?"

"That's a little difficult. We have spies for missions like that, but I don't know if I can trust them with such a task." Lucian sighed. "It's really frustrating to not know who I can rely on."

"If investigation is difficult," Mia said, "then perhaps setting a trap is the better option."

"A trap, huh? Not a bad idea. What did you have in mind?"

"If he's truly after your life, then he will surely jump at an opportunity to do so. All we must do is pass information to him and only him. If an assassin appears, then we will know the truth."

"That's true, but it's also dangerous..."

"If you're unwilling to move before knowing the truth, then you have no choice but to risk something to find it."

"You're right. And I definitely won't arrest him without being sure. That'd make me no better than a tyrant jumping at every shadow that moves."

"Don't worry, Prince Lucian! I'll protect you!"

"Thanks, Emilia. I'll be counting on you." Lucian picked up a pen. "But I hope I don't have to be a liability forever."

Lucian placed the point of the pen onto Mia's desk, with the shaft standing vertically. The two girls watched the strange scene, both clearly confused about why he would put the pen in such a position.

"[Order]. Stand." Lucian said some strange words that only further confused the girls.

However, he ignored their stares as he removed his hand, and to their surprise, the pen continued to stand upright, as if frozen in place.

"Eh!?" Emilia was the first to respond. "Why is it standing!?"

"Magic..." Mia replied.

"Yep. Support spells weren't the only things I acquired recently. I also gained what's known as Command Magic, which lets me infuse inanimate objects with power to control them."

"I've never heard of such spells before."

"Really? I honestly thought it'd be pretty common since it seems useful for creating magitech devices."

"Yes, it would surely have many uses. Maybe..." Mia picked up her own pen nearby. "[Order]. Stand."

Mia removed her hand, and...

clack

The pen fell and rolled along the desk's surface for a short distance.

"It didn't work." Mia stated the obvious without a shred of emotion.

"Maybe there's a trick to it?" Emilia said.

"Don't know. But if it's a new type of magic, we'll need to study it to unlock the secrets to casting it."

"For now," Lucian said, "I'll be doing my own studies on it. Since it's impossible to enhance oneself and Emilia can't cast magic, I need to find any way I can to make myself stronger, even if it's just a little."

"Talismans."

"Yeah, I already had someone buy me a stockpile of powerful talismans." Lucian pulled one out from his pocket. "But compared to magic, they're lacking in power. I'd be at a huge disadvantage against a trained warrior enhanced with the real deal."

All eyes turned back to the pen, which still stood upright in defiance of gravity. Giving inanimate objects orders was a new type of magic, so it was uncharted territory with unknown potential. But the ones who stared at the pen couldn't help but let their faces grow stiff.

"W-what kind of use could magic like this have...?" Emilia asked softly.

"I ... don't know," Lucian admitted. "But I better find out quickly."

He grabbed the pen. It felt no different than normal in his hand, so he brought it to a piece of parchment and signed his name. The ink flowed as it should, with the pen gliding over the paper without an ounce of resistance.

When he finished, he released the pen, and it stood upright again.

"Emilia, give it a try."

"Okay." She grabbed the pen. "Eh...?"

Her hand moved, carrying the pen with it. However, it looked awkward, as if she were fighting against some unseen force.

"It's resisting," Lucian said. "So that means it will obey my will, but anyone else who tries to mess with the object will have to overpower it."

Emilia brought the pen to the parchment. "Yes, but it's not very strong. I can move it with just my hand, even if it's awkward."

She used the pen to write her name beside Lucian's. At least, that was her intent. But it only came out as indecipherable scribbles thanks to the difficulty of controlling it.

In the end, she gave up after just one attempt, frowning at the alien language she concocted.

To Lucian's surprise, Mia grabbed the pen next. She brought it to the parchment with surprising ease, then signed her name. Unlike Emilia's alien dialect, Mia's was actually legible, though it lacked the flourish Lucian had come to expect from her handwriting.

When she was done, Mia moved the pen back to its original location and released it. As always, it stayed upright, awaiting the next hand.

"Amazing!" Emilia said. "You managed to figure out how the spell works!?"

Mia shook her head. "No. I simply noticed that when you were holding it, the pen was only trying to remain upright like the order stated. It didn't resist any horizontal movements, only the tilting."

"Ah, so that's it! No wonder you wrote in such a strange way. You let the pen stay upright the entire time, so it had no reason to resist."

"Interesting," Lucian said. "So it won't fight me no matter what I do, but if others try to mess with it, it'll do its best to follow my order."

"But ... is it useful?"

"..."

The three of them looked at each other. Even if nobody wanted to come right out and say it, the fact was that such magic didn't seem suitable for things like self-defense.

"Well, I'm just going to keep practicing. Who knows, maybe I'll find a use for it after I learn more about how the magic works. But for now, let's discuss how exactly we're going to go about setting up a trap for Henrik."

There was still a lot of work to do, and many obstacles to overcome. But now that Lucian had two reliable allies, he felt that, just maybe, he could accomplish something great.

Chapter 19

"At least let me help you out of the carriage." Lucian stepped down the carriage steps and onto a nice road.

"Sorry, but I can't agree to that." Emilia scanned the street. "As your guard, it's my responsibility to check for dangers before you emerge."

"I get it, but we have a dozen other guards too, you know."

"One more pair of eyes never hurts."

Shaking his head, Lucian moved from the street and onto a walkway. However, he quickly ran into a roadblock in the form of a gate. It was the only entrance in or out of the place he came to visit, as a respectable wall rose from both sides of the gate, cutting it off from the rest of the city.

But such obstacles weren't a hindrance to Lucian. As crown prince, everything in the kingdom was under his control. It's just that abusing that power would ultimately create a rebellion as the nobility would begin to fear his actions more than a civil war.

Fortunately, Lucian didn't need to exert his influence today. He had an invitation from the property owner himself, Archduke Henrik Mathias Almekia. Lucian's uncle.

"Should we really be walking in there?" Emilia asked as they approached the gate. "What if he really is the one trying to assassinate you?"

"Don't worry. If he is the culprit, this is the last place he'd make a move against me. Too risky to take me out inside the walls of his own magitech factory."

"True, but what if he expects you to think that and wants to catch you off-guard?"

"Well..." Lucian turned to her. "That's why I brought you."

Emilia's white fox ears perked up. "Of course! I won't let you down!"

As expected, the gate was barely a speed bump for them. The grounds behind were large, but most of the space was taken up by the several buildings that sat within the walls.

Considering this was the middle of Almekia's capital city, land value was sky high. Only someone with immense wealth and influence would be able to construct a gated facility meant for the advanced research of magitech.

Someone like the late king's brother.

The man in question didn't make his appearance at the door to the main facility. Instead, a servant stood at the entrance, ready to receive them.

"Your Highness, we're pleased that you decided to pay us a visit today."

"I'm glad to hear that. Though it appears that my host is missing from this reception."

"My apologies. Archduke Henrik was engrossed in his work and sent me to direct you to his office." The servant bowed.

"I see. In that case, let's not waste any time." Lucian followed the servant through the door.

So Henrik wants to play games, does he?
I guess I should use some of the cards in my hand, them.

Etiquette was clear. When visited by someone of higher status, the host was expected to receive them. Henrik continuing his work and sending his servant sent a clear message.

The Archduke thought himself equal, or even superior to, Lucian.

Now inside, the servant motioned for them to follow him down a hall. However, Lucian had other plans.

"What are those men doing?" He pointed toward a wide-open area opposite to the hallway.

The servant followed his finger. "They are taking the material we prepared for use in our magitech products and moving them to their proper storage locations."

"So you process the raw material elsewhere, then send it here for use in your magitech items."

"Correct, Your Highness. The other two buildings you saw when you arrived are used as a warehouse and to process the raw material. But Archduke Henrik can give you the full tour with much more flourish than I."

Lucian looked left, where the servant was standing just within the hallway leading to Henrik. To his right, men moved various items that would be used to make the magitech devices.

And forward, a second hallway, where doors lined one of the walls.

Ignoring the servant's wishes, Lucian walked forward.

Reluctantly, the man followed. The guest he was asked to receive wasn't just a noble. It was his future king. There was no way he could do something like force him to meet with Henrik.

So all he could do was fall in line and hope that the crown prince would decide to heed his words.

"What's in here?" Lucian turned the knob before even waiting for an answer. "Locked."

"Ah, my apologies. We keep some of the rooms secure. We can't be too careful."

"Then bring me the key."

"C-certainly, I will try to obtain it. Should I request that Archduke Henrik join us here, as well?"

"Hm? Sure, bring him to me."

"As you wish." He left with more vigor than he'd shown until then.

Lucian didn't plan to just stand in front of the door, though. He turned around and walked into the open area, where a group of men were handling all the material.

He saw stacks of talismans, strange pieces of hammered metal, rocks of various colors, and a plethora of other random objects. Although he didn't know what most of them were used for, there was one that he recognized.

They're going to enchant those talismans, storing a variation of the [Enhance] spell for someone else to use.

Does that mean the rest of the items are going to be enchanted in a similar way?

Magitech was still mysterious to Lucian. He hadn't had time to study it in any depth, only just enough to not give away the fact that he only just learned about it.

As he was about to step toward one of the more interesting looking items, the sound of footsteps echoed from the hallway behind him.

Turning, he watched as the man he came to visit appeared from around a corner.

"Prince Lucian." Archduke Henrik gave a small nod. "I'm glad you made it here today. Though I wouldn't have guessed that you'd have gained such interest in magitech recently."

"This business is important to the future of our kingdom, so whether or not I have a personal interest is irrelevant."

And right now, I'm far more interested in you.

"I understand." Henrik nodded more deeply than before. "We're on the cutting edge of magitech research, and kingdoms aren't interested in street lights and shocks for carriages. Of course, we can make far more useful items than that."

"I'd like to see those items so I can determine their worth to the crown. Depending on what I see, I may be back to discuss a deal to supply the army with some of your more useful inventions."

Henrik nodded with a smile. "It's good that you're interested in my business, and of course I will give you a grand tour. But please do be careful. There are many hazards here, and I'd be very dismayed if something happened to you under my roof."

"It's good to hear that you care so much for my well-being," Lucian said. "But you don't have to worry. I know enough to stay safe."

The official reason for Lucian's visit was to inspect the magitech devices for potential use in the upcoming war against the Esgares Empire.

But the real reason was to meet with his uncle, Henrik. As the prime suspect for the assassination of the royal family, Lucian wanted to talk to him and see how he felt about the man.

So far, he wasn't liking what he was seeing.

"Then if you're going to give a grand tour," Lucian said. "Why don't we start with what's in that room."

Henrik followed Lucian's hand, where the locked door sat in the middle hallway.

"That's not a problem at all." Henrik pulled a keychain from his pocket. "Let me show you what we make here."

He stuck a key into the lock, then pushed the door open.

Within the room was a long table, stacked with some of the same items Lucian saw the men moving around a moment ago.

Standing along the table's two longer sides were people. Mages to be precise, their hands grasping the items placed in front of them.

"One of the less exciting rooms, I'm afraid." Henrik motioned to the items stacked up. "Common enchanted objects. Pumps, lights, shocks, and the like."

"To me, those are some of the most important ones. Advancing our technology will improve the lives of the ordinary citizens far more than weapons of war."

"Yes, yes." Henrik spoke in an almost tired tone. "A man of the people, as always."

"It's only natural to want to strengthen the kingdom. And the best way to do that is to nurture our greatest resource—the people."

"Are you suggesting we swap focus to devices such as these, rather than ones that will help us defeat the Esgares Empire?"

Lucian paused for a second. "No. Right now, we need weapons."

"As expected." Henrik turned back to the door. "It'd be great if such advancements would appear. But there's always a threat, a reason to make more weapons."

The archduke walked out.

After the war, definitely...

Lucian turned and followed his uncle out the door.

"I believe I have a far more interesting room for you to see."

Henrik led the way further down the hall. He passed another door, pointing to it and claiming that talismans were enchanted inside.

At the third door, he stopped, and the servant carrying the keys unlocked it.

"This is what you came to see, isn't it?"

Lucian looked around the room. "Explosive projectiles, right?"

Henrik walked over to a box of heavy stones. "Each one of these will be enchanted to explode, then catapulted into enemy formations. It's crude, but effective against both troops and fortifications."

"Yes. I'm familiar with how devastating such weapons can be."

"The only problem is that many defensive spells were created to deal with these weapons, limiting their usefulness."

"That just means we need to innovate again." Lucian eyed Henrik with a sidelong glance. "You must have people dedicated to finding new weapons. Have you had any success?"

Henrik stared at the table where mages were enchanting the stones. "Making magitech weapons has proven unreasonably difficult. It's not as simple as adding a spell to a stone and being rewarded with something powerful."

He turned to Lucian. "But that hasn't stopped us from trying."

Once again, he left the room.

Further down the hall, a final door sat. Just from looking at the thick lock, Lucian could tell this room was more important than the others.

"This is where we conduct our experiments." Henrik's hand wrapped around the handle, but he didn't turn it. "A word of caution. Don't touch anything. Even I can't say what will happen if you accidentally activate any of the devices inside."

After Lucian nodded, the door opened.

Like the others, a table dominated the center of the room. Atop it were stones about the size of golf balls, some red, others blue.

Only a few mages were inside, and their ages were noticeably higher than the ones in the previous rooms.

"The problem with making magitech weapons has always been the limited functions of magic cast on objects." Henrik picked up a red stone from a box. "If we enchant this stone to explode, it would need to be thrown at the enemy either by hand, with a sling, or some other method."

He picked up a blue stone. "We could enchant it to seek a target, but what good is that when it can't even put a dent in their armor?"

Henrik brought the red and blue stones together. "If there were a way to add both a seeking and explosive enchantment to a single stone, then we'd have a useful weapon that can replace the limited spellcasting ability of the average soldier."

He put the stones back into their boxes. "But unfortunately, such a method still evades us. Though that doesn't mean we haven't made progress. I suspect we will find a way one day, but it's hard to say when that will be."

Lucian had a limited understanding of how magic worked, so there was nothing he could say to contest Henrik's claims that advanced magitech weapons were still far off.

From his limited research into his new world's history, Lucian learned that magitechnology had only recently seen the advancements that allowed for things such as lights and pumps.

It was obvious that all the nations would be looking to unlock the secrets of magitech, making Henrik's business invaluable to the Almekian Kingdom.

Just wish someone else was in charge of it. Anyone else.

"It's unfortunate that we don't have an ace for the upcoming battles against the Esgares Empire," Lucian said. "But I suppose that's to be expected."

"Well, maybe in your next war."

"Let's hope this is the last one for a while. No, I'm going to make sure it is."

"Optimistic, are you? I guess that's a privilege reserved for youth." Henrik walked back to the door. "If you wish to see more, then I can have a servant show you around."

"No, I've seen what I came for. It would have been good if the result was better, but I can't change reality."

"I see. Then I hope we can live up to your expectations the next time you visit." Henrik walked out the door, continuing down the hallway.

What are you hiding, Henrik?

Were you really the one who infected the royal family and sent those assassins after me?

Those thoughts filled Lucian's mind as he watched Henrik's back shrink. Unfortunately, nobody would answer his questions.

Chapter 20

After the visit to Henrik's magitech facility, Lucian spent the rest of the day at the castle. He visited nobles, dealt with problems, and did some studying. At the end of the day, he found himself in Mia's room, alongside Emilia.

That was quickly becoming a common ending to his days, spending the final moments before bed with the two people he trusted most.

But it was getting late, and Lucian couldn't afford to stay up too long. He had an important ceremony in the morning.

So, after bidding Mia farewell, he and Emilia began the trip down the castle halls from his sister's room to his own.

Although Emilia was acting as the captain of his guard, she hadn't been officially named as such, so she was still sleeping in her barracks with the other white hairs. The castle's exit took her down a different hallway, so the two said their goodnights and separated.

Mia's position as Prime Minister was also an unofficial promotion, so her daily routine had yet to be impacted to any large degree. However, that was about to change.

They're finally getting their promotions tomorrow morning, Lucian thought. *Emilia's room is ready, and Mia's daily duties are all worked out.*

Now, we just need to make it official, and all the pieces will fall into place.

I wonder if they want to add a training regimen to our schedule. I'm sure Emilia would agree since she's already training every day, but it'd be nice if Mia learned some self-defense, too.

After all, there are people seeking my life, and that may spill over to–

When he turned a corner, Lucian's thoughts came to an abrupt end. The reason for that was...

"Hey, buddy. Been a while, hasn't it?"

"Rudeus...!" Lucian couldn't keep the anger from his voice.

"Are you ... angry? Or is that another game? Man, I'd really like it if you could be a little more forthcoming with me..."

"Angry!? I'm furious! Who wouldn't be, after being left to die at the hands of that minotaur!?"

"H-hey, I didn't expect you to jump in there like that! I was just setting things up like you always do! What's wrong with that?"

Lucian's arm came up, pinning Rudeus to the stone wall. "You don't know me. You have no idea what I want, so stop acting like you do!"

"What happened to you? Ever since you woke up, you're like an entirely different person!"

"Maybe I am. Maybe Prince Lucian died that day and I simply inhabit his hideous body. Perhaps it's best if you pretend that's the case. Because if I ever see you in the castle again, I'll have you thrown in a cell."

"No way…" Rudeus finally understood that this was no game.

Lucian released the young noble, who slowly slid along the wall until he was out of reach. After leaving behind a look between fear and bewilderment, Rudeus turned and fled.

After what he did, that guy actually had the nerve to show himself again!

He's lucky he was Lucian's close friend. Otherwise, I'd have already thrown him in a cell.

Despite his anger, Lucian understood that making a move against Rudeus would be dangerous. It was well known that the two were close, so suddenly arresting the young noble would make Lucian appear to have trust issues.

Such thoughtless actions would only cause others to doubt him, wondering if they would be the next to draw his ire. Since Lucian was about to make some questionable decisions with Emilia and Mia's new positions, he'd like to prevent going overboard.

Considering he may need to make a move against his own uncle soon, he was already worried that he was pushing the boundary of what he could get away with. After all, Lucian was never meant to be king.

Well, no use worrying about it tonight. I've got a big day tomorrow.

The prince stepped into his private chambers and decided to get a good night's rest in preparation for the ceremony in the morning.

"You're doing what!?" the Minister of War, Marcus, yelled out.

"I believe I spoke clearly, but just to make sure, I'll say it one more time. I'm making Emilia the captain of my personal guard. She'll outrank everyone else in matters related to my safety."

"I heard what you said! But giving a white hair such a position is desecrating the souls of those who perished to put an end to their world domination!"

"That was a long time ago, and Emilia had nothing to do with that war. She's proven herself to me, and I'm sure she'll perform her new role admirably."

"Who cares about any of that! They're dangerous, which is why we keep them on such a short leash!"

"My decision is final, so drop it."

Marcus looked like he had more to say on the matter, but even a hot-headed man like him had to think twice about openly disobeying the crown prince.

As Lucian expected, the news of Emilia's official promotion didn't go over well. The bias against white haired beastfolk was rooted in a deep fear, so having to take orders from one on matters of their future king's safety was a hard sell.

But this was something Lucian had to do. He despised the way Emilia's people were treated, and he had seen that they weren't some evil race of demons. To him, they were just people, albeit ones with concerning side effects to magic.

It'd be nice if I could help ease the hatred toward her people, Lucian thought. *Maybe after I defeat the God's Acolyte, I can work toward that goal.*

"Putting that aside," another voice said. "I would like to know why I need to report to the young princess. Don't you think you've taken this joke a little too far?"

Lucian looked to Walther, the Minister of Production. "It's no joke, Walther. When I'm out of the castle, Mia will oversee the work of the four ministers. You are to seek her approval before making any critical decisions."

"That's precisely the problem! Has she even been trained to perform such a critical role!?"

"Mia has had one of the best educations this world has to offer. You may be surprised at just how capable she is."

Lucian raised his hand just as Walther opened his mouth again. "Enough. If you have more to say on the matter, we'll discuss it in private."

With those words, the open defiance against Lucian's unpopular promotion of Emilia and Mia to the new positions came to an end. Yet, it was obvious that their feelings wouldn't fade just because he ordered them to stay silent.

Even now, he could see the ministers and officials in the meeting hall frowning as they discussed this turn of events amongst themselves. Perhaps they imagined their words couldn't reach Lucian because they're out of ear shot, but the prince had a hidden skill up his sleeve.

"They're not happy," Lucian said softly enough for only Emilia and Mia to hear.

"How did you figure that out?" Mia asked in a sarcastic tone.

"Haha, very funny. But what I meant was that we haven't heard the end of their complaints. Even now they're discussing what to do about it."

"But you're basically the king," Emilia said. "They have to do what you say, right?"

"Yes, but that doesn't mean I can just do whatever I want and not pay the price. Even if they can't disobey me, they can still get their revenge in other ways. In the worst-case scenario, they may even join ranks with whoever is trying to assassinate me. After all, if I were trying to kill me, I'd definitely use their frustration to my advantage and recruit them."

Lucian's eyes fell on his uncle, Archduke Henrik Mathison Almekia. Half the reason he was invited was due to his influence and popularity, but the other half was simply because Lucian wanted to see what the man would do once he heard of Emilia and Mia's promotions.

But despite keeping an eye on him during the meeting, Henrik hadn't made any suspicious moves or expressions. The man seemed to have a knack for maintaining his cool, which frustrated Lucian.

Hmm. Who's that man he's speaking to?

Archduke Henrik was standing separated from the other members gathered here, speaking privately to a single individual. He was so far out of earshot range that it'd be laughable to even try to eavesdrop.

However, despite that, Lucian still stared at the two men with intense concentration.

"...Doesn't matter," Lucian whispered. "He can make a fool of himself to his heart's desire. In the end, none of it will do him any good."

"Eh?" Emilia's voice entered his ears, but he ignored it.

"The next man is ready," Lucian continued whispering. "This one won't be so easily dispatched. There's no doubt this time. The young prince won't live long enough to see the crown placed on his head."

Lucian went silent, sitting back in his ornate chair. None here knew, not even Emilia or Mia. Nobody knew that Lucian could read lips.

So it's true. Uncle Henrik really is the one coming after my life.

But what do I do about it? Arrest him?

I don't have any evidence, just a handkerchief that could have come from anywhere and my own word that he's guilty.

Would anyone even believe me if I said I read his lips to find out that he's planning another assassination attempt? If I were a juror on a case with that kind of evidence, there's no way I'd convict him.

But wait ... does it even matter? I'm the king. Or, I will be soon. Should I even care about what others think is true or not?

No, I shouldn't do what I want without going through the proper procedures. That's a slippery slope that I don't want to slide down...

As expected of a man who wanted to do what was right, Lucian had a hard time deciding on how to act on the information he acquired.

It wasn't easy to make decisions that could have massive impacts on the lives of an untold number of people. Mistakes could mean not only repercussions for himself but also Emilia, Mia, and all the subjects he ruled over.

And since he was sent here to save the world, failure would likely mean every single person on the planet would suffer, were he to fail. With that kind of pressure, making a critical decision would be enough to cause most men to go bald from worry.

"What's wrong?" Emilia asked. "And what were you whispering a moment ago?"

"Ah, sorry. The truth is, I can read lips. And since Uncle Henrik was facing my way, I decided to listen in on his conversation, so to speak. And well ... he's planning another assassination attempt."

"Eh!? So he is the one!?"

"Yes. But I don't know what I should do about it. Maybe we can gather some evidence. Or we could keep going with our plan to lure him into some kind of trap. Maybe we'll find something we can use against him if we do that."

"But couldn't you just arrest him?"

"Yes, but would my accusation stand up in court? It's just my word against his right now."

"Doesn't matter," Mia said. "There's no need to go through something like a trial. All you have to do is sentence him."

"Judge, jury, and executioner. That's exactly what worries me..."

"Why? If you know you're right, then just do it."

"I just ... don't like that kind of power..."

"Then maybe you should renounce the throne."

"That's..."

In truth, Lucian would be overjoyed to give up the throne and create a republic, where representatives had their say in the kingdom's decisions. In his mind, it'd be a step toward creating a country that worked for the people, rather than the powerful.

I can't. I won't be able to rely on others to defeat the God's Acolyte and fix this world. I have to do it myself, which means...

...Acting like a king.

But it's more than that. It's one thing if Henrik comes after me, but I won't be his only target.

Emilia's life is at risk, too. Especially now that I've promoted her to the captain of my personal guard. There's no way they'd let her just return to her squad, were I to die.

And even Mia's in a difficult spot now thanks to me. Henrik didn't target her with the disease before, but there's no guarantee he hasn't added her to his list now that she has an important position.

I ... can't let Henrik have another shot at my life. At our lives.

"Emilia. Looks like I'm going to have to ask you to use your new authority immediately."

"Understood, Prince Lucian!"

"C'mon. Let's show my uncle what happens to those who plot against the crown."

I just hope I'm making the right decision...

Lucian stood from his chair. The sudden movement was subtle, but it was his first since the meeting began, making it noteworthy despite being mundane.

With what he hoped was a confident stride, he headed toward the corner of the room, where his uncle still stood speaking to his co-conspirator. Upon his arrival, the two men went silent, looking at Lucian with their usual expressions.

"Uncle Henrik. I'm glad you could make it to this meeting, despite your busy schedule."

"Of course. When I read the letter, I knew I had to appear and hear your words for myself. I wasn't quite sure what you had planned, but you certainly exceeded my expectations."

"I'm glad to hear that. It was certainly a surprise, wasn't it? Though the biggest shock is yet to come."

"There's more? And you say it will make your promotion of a white hair seem tame by comparison? Then by all means, you have my ear."

"Good, good. Then, Archduke Henrik Mathison Almekia." Lucian pointed directly at him. "You're hereby under arrest for high treason."

Silence.

Perhaps the ones at the meeting believed his words some sort of joke. But they were about to be relieved of such naive thoughts.

"Sir Henrik," Emilia said, stepping forward. "Please come quietly."

Her aggressive posture finally knocked the man out of his stupor. "What's the meaning of this!? High treason!? Have you gone mad, Lucian!?"

"I know of your plot to assassinate me, uncle. You already failed twice, yet you plan a third right under my nose. I won't allow it."

"W-what are you talking about? I'd never do such a thing!"

"Save your breath. I already know the truth." Lucian nodded to Emilia.

"Unhand me, you damned beastfolk!"

"No. Now come along."

Emilia dragged Henrik to a pair of guards that Lucian had motioned over. The two of them took the Archduke into their grasp, though they were careful not to be too rough. Prisoner or no, the man outranked them by orders of magnitude, and nobility were often treated with delicacy, even when under arrest.

"See to it that Archduke Henrik is locked in one of our more accommodating rooms."

"Understood, Your Highness!"

"You've gone mad, Lucian!" Henrik yelled. "We all knew it was coming, but to think your true self would come out so quickly! You'll destroy this kingdom with your insanity!"

Lucian watched on as his uncle was pulled from the room. He wanted to refute the man's words, but he knew now that some of the others understood what kind of man the former prince was.

They think I'm arresting him because of some vile scheme, like the prince loved before I took his body.

Or maybe they just think I'm getting rid of a rival. Perhaps it would be best if they thought that, rather than assuming I've given in to my madness.

"Now, then." Lucian looked at the second man. "I hope you're willing to be a little more forthcoming."

"I-I haven't done anything wrong!"

"We'll get to the truth eventually." Lucian motioned to Emilia, and the man ended up dragged off just like Henrik.

With the ones after his life safely imprisoned, Lucian could finally relax a little. However, the weight that was lifted from him was immediately replaced by another.

"I don't know what's gotten into you," the Minister of War, Marcus, said. "But arresting your own uncle before the crown is even placed on your head was an idiotic move."

The other people at the meeting looked at Marcus with white faces, as if they were eyeing a dead man who still stood on two feet.

"My words were true. Every single one of them. And in time, I will prove it."

I hope.

"Then you might want to work on that instead of playing around in the Royal Study all night."

"My business in the study is important. But I intend to conduct a thorough search of Archduke Henrik's estate starting right now. In fact, I was just about to call an end to this meeting so I can organize the search party."

"Good." Marcus walked to the door and let himself out.

"You're free to go," Lucian said to the others, who were still frozen in place.

Without exception, each of the ministers and nobles who were in attendance spared not a single glance toward the crown prince after he gave them leave. Soon, the only ones remaining in the room were Lucian, Emilia, Mia, and a couple of guards who appeared to be uncertain about whether or not they should stay or go.

"Looks like things are going to get a little messy," Lucian said.

"Don't worry!" Emilia smiled to cheer him up. "Once we find some evidence, they'll see you were telling the truth!"

"I hope that's how it goes..."

"Uncle Henrik is no fool," Mia said. "He likely wouldn't keep any incriminating evidence at his estate."

"In that case, we may have to dig around the affairs of the noble he was conspiring with. Or maybe get more information from the group of assassins we caught the other day."

"Yes. I'm sure we can find something of substance among our options."

And so, Archduke Henrik Mathison Almekia, the man Lucian caught plotting his assassination, now sat in a locked room in the castle's most defensible halls.

Chapter 21

"Your Highness." A soldier saluted Lucian. "Another stack of papers has been found in one of the rooms."

"Put them in the carriage with the others. Did you scan through them?"

"Yes. They appear to be more documents related to the province Archduke Henrik oversees."

"As expected. But we can't be sure that there's no evidence hidden in the stack. Sometimes, the best place to hide something is amongst a mountain of similar items."

"Right. We'll add them to the pile, then."

After the meeting, Lucian assembled a team and quickly departed for his uncle's estate. Once word spread that he'd been arrested, there was a chance accomplices would steal any evidence before it could be confiscated, so he had to move with haste.

They'd been searching the mansion for nearly three hours now, carrying off anything that seemed like it could contain evidence of the Archduke's involvement in the assassination of the royal family. So far, nothing concrete had turned up, but the pile of documents in the carriage continued to grow.

Just how many days will it take to sort through all those stacks of paper? Lucian shook his head at the thought.

I'll have to trust the task to others. I simply don't have time to scan each document with my own eyes.

Normally, the future king would leave a task like ransacking a manor to his men, but there Lucian was, overseeing it himself. Of course, it was because he didn't know who he could trust, making such an important operation one that he had to partake in.

Emilia raised her head from a map laid atop the table. "Most of the rooms have been thoroughly searched, Prince Lucian. The ones that remain are not likely to have hidden evidence. I don't see Archduke Henrik hiding it in the kitchen where a maid prepares all his food, for example."

"Yeah, you're right about that. Then I suppose we can leave the rest to the men. We've already got enough to sort through, anyway."

"Your Highness," a guard says. "At your command, we will find any evidence you wish for."

"By find, you mean plant it?"

"Yes. I guarantee it will prove the archduke's crimes."

"I see. Yeah, I suspect that's a common solution. However, I won't be going that route."

"Then how about getting one of the assassins we captured to sing? With a little persuasion, they'll say anything we want."

"No, there's no need to go that far. I'll be doing this the right way."

"Understood, Your Highness."

How troublesome. Seems the ones in charge in this world have no qualms doing whatever they want as long as it benefits them.

That'll make any real evidence we find suspect, as people no doubt expect me to plant it.

A sudden thought occurred to Lucian. "Soldier, was the manor unoccupied when you arrived?"

"No, the archduke's family was inside."

"And where are they now?"

"We imprisoned them, of course." The man sounded proud of his actions.

Ah, crap!

Because Lucian knew with certainty that his uncle was working with the assassins, he sent a squad of soldiers to inspect the place before he arrived to make sure there wasn't a trap waiting for him there.

There wasn't. Instead, only the archduke's wife and children were present, along with their servants. Now, all of them are being held captive in Lucian's name.

"Listen up," Lucian said to the guard. "I want you to send word that Archduke Henrik's family and servants are to be released without exception."

"Released, Your Highness?"

"Yes. I won't arrest those who had no hand in the plot to assassinate me."

"But ... releasing them would be dangerous, wouldn't it? What if his son revolts? The man may be young, but his family has many allies."

"I'll deal with that if it happens."

"Understood. I'll send a message right now." The guard saluted, then left the room.

Emilia watched him as he walked out. "It's good that they're going to be free, but isn't it normal to confine a noble's family alongside them?"

"Is it? I guess things like that did happen long ago, but they haven't done anything wrong, so what justification do I have to arrest them?"

"Um. To protect yourself, I think? And since you'll be king soon, that means protecting the kingdom too, doesn't it?"

"I ... guess so. But in that case, where do I draw the line? If I just do whatever I want and justify it by saying I'm too important, then how many innocent people will end up suffering?"

"I don't know..."

"Well, you're in good company. Because I don't, either."

Despite his reservations, Lucian decided to follow through with his command to release the archduke's family. His conscience wouldn't allow him to place children under arrest for the crimes of their father.

He only hoped he wouldn't come to regret that decision.

Since their work at the estate was all but complete, Lucian and Emilia took the carriage filled with documents and went back to the castle.

As stated, he simply didn't have time to go through all the information himself, so he left it with a team of officials tasked with finding incriminating evidence about the archduke's involvement in any assassination attempts.

As for Lucian and Emilia, they went to their usual place. In other words, the Royal Study.

"Finally!" Emilia happily trotted toward a bookshelf. "I can continue my sorting!"

Lucian took a seat behind the desk. "You love it that much? At this point, I was considering hiring someone else to take care of it since you have actual responsibilities now."

"Absolutely not! I can't leave this task to anyone else!"

"Well, since I come in here so often, I guess there's no harm in letting you have at it."

As he spoke, Lucian was organizing a stack of papers. However, they had nothing to do with the ones they took from Archduke Henrik's estate. No, just like Emilia had her duties, so too did Lucian.

Even though he was only the crown prince, a kingdom needed a ruler at all times. Hence, he was king in all but name already, which meant he had to perform certain royal duties.

Among those responsibilities, one was to sign decrees and other legal documents into law. Some were changes requested by the ministers, while others were born from his own desires.

He already knew most of what was written on the papers, as he had discussed them in several meetings. Yet now they were ready for his signature, so he had to comb through them once more to ensure nothing was added to them at the last minute.

"Hmm." Lucian held his pen over the signature line of the first document. "[Order]. Sign my name."

He released the pen, and as expected, it signed Lucian's name on the line, perfectly replicating his signature.

"Amazing!" Emilia watched on, even as she continued sorting.

"I don't know about that, but it is interesting. I've done a few tests now, and I realized that the objects are more intelligent than I thought."

"Intelligent? Is it alive?"

"No, I don't think it can be considered alive, but—well, it's best to show you."

Lucian quickly read over the next document. When he didn't find anything worrisome, he placed it beneath the pen. Although he put it off-center, the pen compensated by moving to the line and signing in the correct spot.

"Oh, it moved! It really is smart!"

"Yeah. It seems to know what I want, even if I don't say it directly."

Next, Lucian took a blank page from a drawer and put it beneath the pen. However, there was no reaction.

"It didn't sign," Emilia noted. "Because there's no line?"

"Looks like it. I'm still learning about this skill, so I wasn't sure what it'd do, but it seems to understand that I only want it to sign on lines like these." Lucian put the next document under the pen and watched as it signed his name.

"Wow. Command Magic is really interesting! I wonder if you can order all the objects around you to do everything for you!"

"Unfortunately, there's a limit to the number of things I can cast it on. Three, to be exact. And there's a size limit, too. Mass, actually, but that's not the point. Anyway, I intend to run some more comprehensive tests when I have time. I'll need you for that, Emilia."

"Me? Sure! I'll help however I can!"

"Then it's a date."

"A-a date!?"

"Ah, haha. It's a figure of speech. Don't think too deeply on it."

"O-oh..."

Lucian was already reading the next document, so he didn't pick up on Emilia's disappointment.

Chapter 22

A few days later, Lucian sat in the Royal Study, preparing for an upcoming meeting. But this meeting would be different than any he'd had before. In his new world, at least.

Until now, all the people he'd met with had been his subjects. Even when asking a favor, Lucian had been in a dominant position of power simply because he was their next king. But today, that was going to change.

"Um." Emilia stood stiffly next to Lucian's desk. "It's past time for the meeting, isn't it?"

"Yeah."

"Shouldn't we be going, then?"

"No. Not yet."

"I see." Emilia didn't see at all.

"I'm a king," Lucian said, sensing her confusion. "It's only normal for me to be busy. I don't have time to sit and wait for a guest who may or may not arrive on time. At least, that's what I'll say if he asks."

"Ah." Emilia perked up. "Is this the art of negotiation?"

"Pretty much. If I were sitting there waiting for him when he arrives, it'd only make me look desperate. Since we're buying so much food in the middle of winter, he probably already suspects we're in a bad spot. The last thing I want to do is solidify that suspicion in his mind from the very beginning."

"Wow. I read about meetings like this in a book once! The protagonist, he—well, he died. But he was great at negotiating!"

"Let's try to do a little better than him, then. I'd rather not die again any time soon."

Lucian continued staring at the open book in front of him, but he had already stopped reading the contents. He couldn't hear anything, but from the corner of his eye, he saw Emilia's ears twitch. That could only mean one thing.

"Let's go." Lucian stood from his chair.

He walked to the Royal Study's only door and gave it a pull. What appeared before him was the surprised face of a guard, his arm raised to knock on the door.

"It's time to meet this merchant." Lucian walked past the guard, Emilia on his heels.

Lucian had released the emergency stock of food to halt the starvation in the kingdom's towns and villages, but that was only a temporary solution. More food was needed. Not only to replenish the emergency supply but also to keep prices stable through the rest of winter and spring.

Fortunately, there was one kingdom that the countries in the region could rely on when it came to trade.

The Villnore Kingdom bordered Lucian's on its northwest side. It was the country that sat between Lucian's Almekian Kingdom and the Esgares Empire that he was at war with, limiting the border that the two warring countries shared.

In terms of size and military strength, the Villnore Kingdom was far inferior to both of its neighbors. But what it lacked in power, it made up for with influence.

The Villnore Kingdom sat on a valuable piece of land. Or rather, it was the water it controlled that gave it value.

In Earth terms, it was equivalent to having control of the Mediterranean Sea. The connections, influence, and trading power of such countries would far exceed that of its more landlocked neighbors.

And that was precisely the case with the Villnore Kingdom. In fact, it was that very country that the Minister of Production had been selling most of the luxury crops that Lucian's kingdom had been growing.

From there, the goods would make their way to any number of other kingdoms scattered through the region. Or perhaps the nobles and wealthy merchants who lived in the Villnore Kingdom would keep it all for themselves.

People like the merchant they were about to meet.

They had to take several turns and go down a flight of stairs, but the total distance was rather short. And since Lucian had long since memorized every hall and room within the castle, he no longer needed anyone to lead him around.

Before long, the meeting room's door came into view. The guard on standby pushed it open just as Lucian reached it, letting him step through without slowing his stride.

A table dominated the room, large enough for a dozen people to comfortably sit. In fact, one person was already doing so. However, it wasn't the merchant Lucian expected to see.

What's going on? Why is there a young woman here? The merchant was supposed to be a middle-aged man.

Could it be that he sent his assistant to initiate the meeting, while he's going to show up whenever he wants?

Lucian took great care to start the negotiations with as much of an advantage as he could get. If he were made to sit and wait for the merchant to show up, it'd be like admitting he was desperate to make the deal.

Should I send her on her way until the merchant is ready?

Or is there a more elegant solution here...

As he thought through his options, Lucian never stopped moving. The table had many chairs, but since it was oval, it had two main seats.

Currently, the young woman occupied one of those seats, though she had stood when Lucian entered the room. That left the other open for Lucian. He took it, settling into the padded chair with confidence, even though he felt no such poise in his mind.

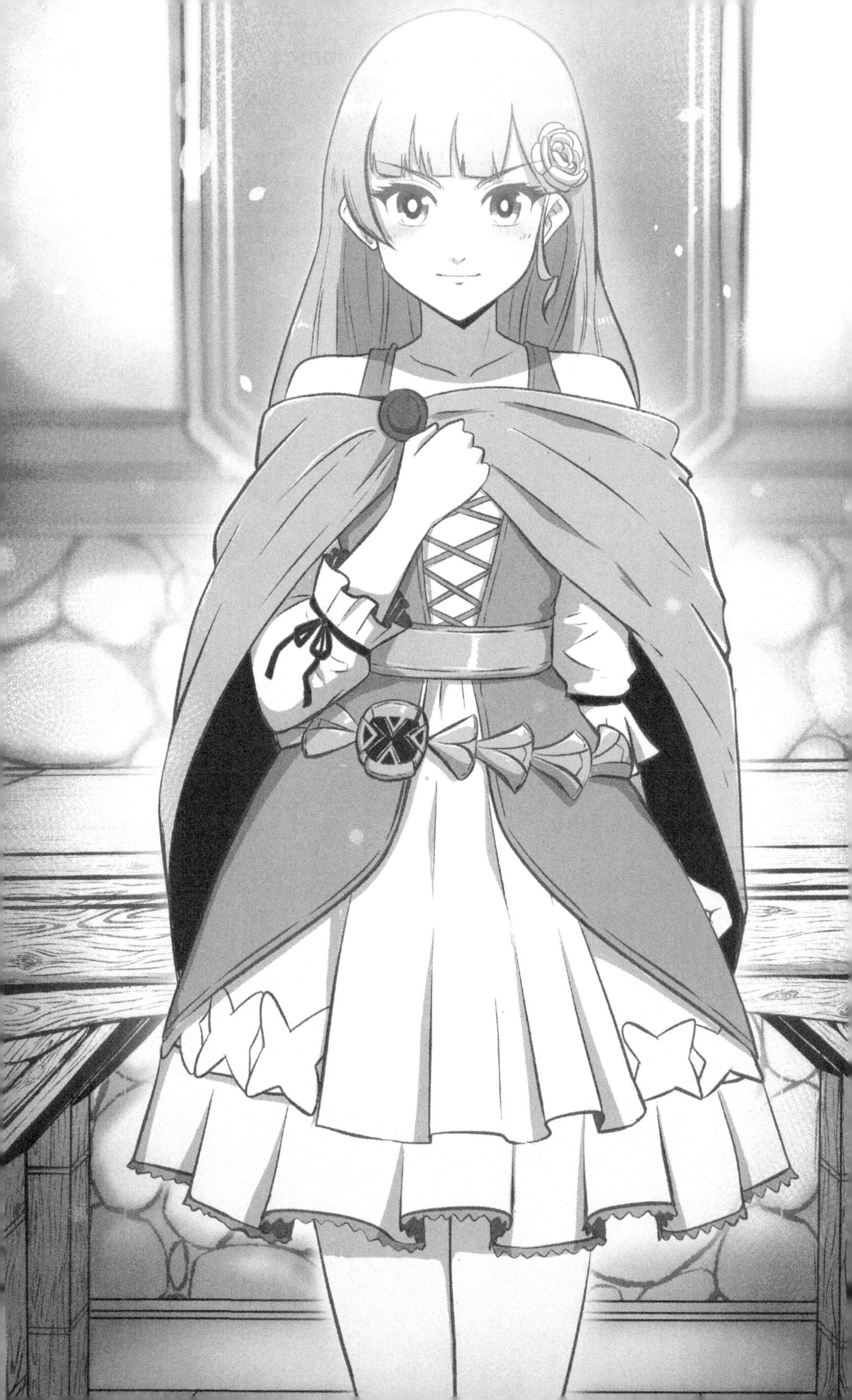

Only after he sat down did the young woman do the same.

No, wait. This girl, is she really...

The young woman had long, brown hair that could be found anywhere. But the same couldn't be said of her dress.

Lucian spent many years on Earth mingling with what was basically nobility. He had met with and negotiated with powerful politicians, business tycoons, influential geniuses, and more.

When wading through the high society on Earth, presentation was half the battle. Dressing well, following proper etiquette, and looking confident amongst some of the world's most powerful people was the only way to earn any form of acceptance.

That, and following their orders. It was that part which got Lucian into trouble in his last life.

But he had spent enough time in their ranks to pick up on who did or didn't belong. And right now...

She's no assistant. An exorbitantly expensive dress, an eye for etiquette, and confidence in the face of a foreign ruler.

She's definitely here to negotiate.

But then, where is the merchant who was supposed to arrive?

The owner of a large trading guild, The Golden Coast, was scheduled to meet with Lucian to discuss the deal. But he instead sat face to face with an unknown woman.

Although a lot of thoughts ran through Lucian's mind, only a second had actually passed since he sat down. Having come to the conclusion that he would be conducting the deal through this young woman, he decided to start the negotiation by clearing the air.

"Before we begin," Lucian said. "Would you like to start by introducing yourself and explaining why The Golden Coast's owner isn't here today?"

"My apologies for the surprise, Your Highness. My name is Alma Vastelle, and it's my pleasure to meet you." Alma gave Lucian a seated bow. "My father fell ill during our trip here and is currently resting in our lodgings."

"The owner's daughter, Alma Vastelle." Lucian finally understood the situation. "I hope your father's illness isn't too serious."

"We brought a great healer, so he should be fine soon. But there was no way he could present himself in such a condition, hence why he sent me."

Lucian eyed her hand, where a ring sat. "Before we begin, let's have a look at your seal."

"Certainly."

One of Lucian's men set down a small, inked pad and a piece of parchment.

Alma removed the cap on her ring, then pressed it into the inked pad. After that, she moved her hand to the parchment and placed her ring on its surface. When she raised it back up, the inked seal remained on the paper.

The man who set the items down collected them back up. Taking the seal Alma left on the parchment, he checked it against the official record of their seal, looking for defects.

"It's correct," the man said.
Lucian nodded. "Then Alma, why don't we start the negotiations."
This is perfect, Lucian thought. *She's young and inexperienced, which will make negotiating a favorable deal that much easier.*

And once she seals the contract with that ring, her father won't be able to back out.

I just need to take control of the discussion and set her expectations where I need them. That way, even after she talks me down, I'll walk out the winner.

"Alma." Lucian gave her a pleasant smile. "I'm quite sure we can find a price that will make both of us happy. Here, take a look at how much we intend to spend on this deal."

He handed a document to one of his servants, who delivered it to Alma's side of the table.

"These numbers are..." Alma put the document down, meeting Lucian's eyes. "...Within our expectations."

"Oh?" Lucian was genuinely surprised. "It's so much gold that I wouldn't have been surprised if you thought we accidentally added an extra digit."

"You wouldn't have called my father here if it were anything but an excessively large deal. Otherwise, it'd have been better to simply make an agreement through your foreign dignitaries."

"I guess you wouldn't be some of the wealthiest merchants in the famous trade kingdom of Villnore if you couldn't infer at least that much." Lucian picked up a quill and dipped it into some ink. "As for how much food I wish to purchase with the gold..."

He started writing on a piece of parchment that contained a list of foodstuffs he wished to purchase. Potatoes, corn, grain, dried fish, salted pork, and more were written on the page.

Now that he'd met Alma and decided how he wanted to do the negotiations, he was able to confidently fill the numbers in to get him to the position he wanted to be in.

When he was done, he handed the parchment to the same servant. It made its way to Alma's hands, with the young woman checking his numbers in silence.

"I see. We can certainly gather this much from our many guild partners. But there's only one problem." Alma set down the parchment and looked to Lucian. "There's not enough gold to cover the cost of buying and transporting this amount of food."

"My kingdom will handle transportation once it crosses into our border, cutting out over half the distance you need to escort the shipments."

"I'll take that into consideration, Your Highness. But even with the reduced transportation cost, the numbers you're giving me simply don't add up."

"Then let's hear some numbers that make more sense to you."

"Let's start by cutting the food in half." Alma didn't wait for his response, her quill already marking out Lucian's numbers and replacing them with her own.

Half? I was expecting around 30%, but she's cutting them in half from the beginning?

He did start his negotiation at a place he knew wouldn't hold, but he was still surprised at how aggressively and confidently Alma sliced his numbers in half.

Lucian thought she would be intimidated to be negotiating with a foreign ruler without her father here to back her up. She was only a few years older than his body in this world, putting her around 20 years old.

With the sudden weight of her task, Lucian thought to lead her by the nose until he ended up where he wanted. But it seemed this negotiation wouldn't be that easy.

"Cutting them in half is a bit extreme." Lucian held his arm out. "Production Report, please."

"Certainly." Emilia reached toward a stack of documents on a small table.

After quickly pulling out a parchment, she placed it in Lucians outstretched hand and returned to her position, standing just behind his right shoulder.

"From recent records," Lucian said, looking at the report, "your kingdom was blessed with a surplus harvest this year, as were several others in our geographical region. Meaning, there was little demand for you to sell your harvests."

Lucian met Alma's eyes. "I'm sure you're aware, but your kingdom produces each of the listed food items in large quantities. If selling it wasn't profitable during harvest season, then there's only one other option. You must have preserved it and put it into storage. I wonder how many people in the Villnore Kingdom are begging for a way to get rid of their excess supply of food. Maybe it wouldn't be so hard to find buyers at my asking price, if that's the case."

Alma's expression didn't change, but she did sit in silence for a heartbeat longer.

"It's true we've got an oversupply of food in our granaries, but our members aren't fools. They know what their stock is worth in the dead of winter. Asking for prices equivalent to harvest season would only get us laughed at. And besides..." Alma raised her arm. "Countryside report, please."

"Understood." A slightly older woman standing behind Alma pulled out a document from her pouch and placed it on the oval table.

"While we were traveling here," Alma said, "we of course sent scouts to check the status of the towns and villages we were passing near. There were many lacking adequate food supplies for the winter, especially at your kingdom's edge."

Alma ran her finger along the report. "As we got deeper into your land, the situation improved, with most towns suddenly having an abundance of food. Too sudden, in fact. After some questions, we learned that the Almekian Kingdom had released its stock of emergency food to quell the famine.

"Our guild, The Golden Coast, is made up of many members, each powerful merchants in their own right. Were they to hear of your kingdom's dire need for food, you'd be lucky to get half what you asked for to begin with. They didn't rise to the top by cutting deals to those in need, after all. Thinking of it that way, isn't my counteroffer quite reasonable?"

It was Lucian's turn to sit in silence for an extra heartbeat.

She really did her research. I was hoping to hide our situation as much as possible, but they were already searching for our weaknesses from the moment they stepped foot in this kingdom.

"As I'm sure you know," Lucian said, "our battle against the Esgares Empire didn't end well last summer. In fact, they've made themselves comfortable in one of our northern provinces."

"Seafaring Report, please." A document was placed in Lucian's outstretched hand. "I was surprised to learn that we weren't the only kingdom the Esgares Empire set their eyes on during the recent warring season."

Lucian put the report down on the table. "The Madina Sea is the reason your kingdom is so wealthy. Everyone knows that. But it's also your biggest weakness, which is why your naval strength is second to none."

He tapped on the report. "And yet the Esgares Empire claimed a section of the sea that your kingdom uses to trade, cutting you off from some of your trading partners. It can only be seen as an attack against a kingdom so reliant on their seafaring activities."

Lucian looked back up to Alma. "But the Villnore Kingdom never retaliated. If you wanted, you could reclaim that section of the sea by force, given your powerful navy. The fact that you haven't can only mean one thing. You're scared to go to war with the Esgares Empire."

He sat back in his chair. "My kingdom is the only one that can match them in strength. It's only because of our many battles against them that others in the region have been able to remain free from their influence."

Lucian held up his hand, showing Alma the seal ring he wore. "What use is a trade agreement when the Esgares Empire invades with its legions? If we let their domain spread, they won't be negotiating deals with you as equals. They will be making demands and expecting you to obey.

"I wonder how many trade deals you've already lost due to them claiming part of the Madina Sea. Just imagine how much worse it would get if they were allowed to spread their influence unchecked. Likely, you'll be absorbed into their empire, like many other kingdoms before."

Geopolitics was a complicated subject. Another nation could be an enemy and ally at the same time. Such was the case with Almekia and Villnore.

But when it came to the Esgares Empire, both kingdoms were in agreement that they were not to be trusted.

The Esgares Empire expanded into the geographical region about a hundred years ago. Their capital sat far to the north, but their influence reached all the way to the Madina Sea where the Villnore and Almekian kingdoms lay.

The Empire was always looking to expand, with many of the smaller kingdoms it conquered being absorbed. When they first arrived, it was the Almekian soldiers who put an end to their advance, killing their king in a decisive battle.

Turned out, the Esgares Empire had a long memory, as the relations between it and Lucian's never recovered.

Now, a hundred years after their arrival into the region, the Esgares Empire was once again using its massive resources to conquer the land around the Madina Sea.

In other words, the Almekian and Villnore Kingdoms.

A trade kingdom like Villnore was essentially run by its powerful guilds. At least, they had more influence over the king's decisions than the nobles did in Lucian's kingdom.

That meant Alma's guild wasn't just in the business of making money. They also wanted to make sure the kingdom that provided that money making opportunity stayed independent from the approaching Esgares Empire.

Over the last few days, Lucian had done his research on Alma's kingdom, and he intended to bring any and all arguments to the negotiation table to ensure he got the best deal possible.

"The whispers of war can be heard everywhere these days," Alma said. "But my king isn't a fool. He understands that we can't defeat the Esgares Empire alone. It would be much easier if you routed them, as your kingdom did before.

"Stability report, please." Alma's outstretched hand received a document. "It's no secret that the Almekian Kingdom has been unstable for a while now. This very famine is proof of that. There was plenty of opportunity to buy food during the harvest season, yet you wait until your people are starving in the middle of winter."

She looked down at the report. "From records of our imports, it's clear that productivity in the Almekian Kingdom has declined. You often run a trade deficit against us, but that deficit has grown substantially over the last few years, meaning you haven't been able to produce valuable goods at the same rate as before.

"Furthermore, there's been an increase in refugees crossing our border from your kingdom. And can you blame them, considering the Crown Prince just arrested his own uncle for assassinating the royal family? It seems the political instability runs deep."

Alma met Lucian's eyes again. "Given all this, many wonder if the Almekian Kingdom is even capable of putting an end to the Esgares Empire's expansion. And your recent loss to them on the battlefield hasn't helped dispel those thoughts."

Lucian saw where Alma was going, so he already had his argument ready.

"Guild report." It appeared in Lucian's hand. "Speaking of instability, didn't one of your five major guilds recently collapse? What was the cause again? Enormous amounts of greed and corruption, if our reports are correct. Perhaps your kingdom isn't so different from my own."

"Financial report." Alma's assistant placed it in her hand. "If our estimations are correct, the Almekian Kingdom is in massive debt. Perhaps that's the real reason you're desperate for a good deal today?"

"Citizenry re–" The report Lucian was asking for appeared on his desk before he could even raise his hand. "Thank you, Emilia."

"It's my pleasure, Prince Lucian."

Alma's assistant frowned. While Lucian had been fighting his battle, Emilia was engaged in one of her own.

She's quick to pull out the requested report, Emilia thought. *But if I can anticipate what Lucian will ask for, then I can have it ready even faster!*

Alma's assistant refocused on the two's negotiations. When Lucian finished his remarks on the Villnore Kingdom's citizenry, the assistant immediately reached into her satchel.

"Magitech re–" It appeared in front of Alma before she could finish. "Thank you, Teta."

"It's my pleasure, Mistress Alma."

Having met Emilia's challenge head on, Teta stood ready to deliver the next report.

What a fearsome opponent.

But I won't lose.

Emilia put all her focus on Alma's words, trying to decipher which arguments Lucian would use to counter.

One by one, the prepared documents vanished from Emilia's table, with Lucian's becoming more crowded as the negotiations continued.

"From the number of attacks on your merchant ships," Lucian said, looking at a report, "you seem to be losing against a simple band of pirates. And with the most powerful navy on the Madina Sea, at that."

"I'll have you know." Alma looked at a similar report on her side of the table. "Piracy has been cut in half in just the past year, all thanks to His Majesty's efforts."

"Yes, even my report notes the decline in piracy, but is it really true? Such a sudden drop in a year means something big must have happened, but we haven't heard of any raids on large pirate towns. Aren't you just making claims to save face?"

"Absolutely not. Once more time passes, you'll see that the reports are true. We really did destroy a large piracy operation."

Lucian nodded, as if convinced. "Then how? I'd like to update the report now, if you don't mind."

Alma set her report aside. "That's not something I can discuss here."

"Interesting."

She's willing to talk about a lot of things, but that one topic is off the table?

"Well, the fifth merchant's guild of yours was disbanded at the same time, so I suppose that could have led to a drop in piracy, somehow."

"..." Alma stared back in silence.

"The merchant guild..." Lucian dug through the pile of reports and pulled out the one related to the disbanded guild. "Like you said, Villnore's king himself moved against the guild. Only someone like him has the power to completely dismantle such a powerful organization."

Lucian looked up from the report. "But there's no mention of why he decided to break up the guild. Quite strange, isn't it?"

Alma still sat without a report in front of her. "What do you mean no reason was given? The guild was corrupt, so the king removed them."

Lucian shook his head. "No, I think it was something else. Something more personal. There's a reason why he decided to destroy the guild, rather than simply trying to clean up the corruption."

He tapped a single fingertip on the wooden table. "The guild must have been moving against the king. Or at least, against the kingdom. But what could a merchant's guild do that puts a trade nation like Villnore in jeopardy?"

Lucian took one report in his right hand, and one in his left. Placing them down side by side, he looked at their respective titles.

"Piracy and guild reports. Hey Alma..." He met her eyes. "Could it be that the dissolved guild was running the piracy ring?"

Alma sat in silence. As the daughter of another guild leader, she had all the detailed information on exactly what happened to the guild that was destroyed.

Her king ordered everyone to keep their silence on the matter, as there were several embarrassing failures for the crown and guilds. Plus, the Villnore Kingdom had plans. Plans that required keeping the truth hidden.

Knowing all that, Alma opened her mouth to respond to Lucian's deduction. "Yes, you're correct."

"Alma...!" Her assistant, Teta says in surprise.

"It's fine. He already knows it's true." Alma didn't take her eyes off Lucian. "The fallen guild was pirating our own kingdom's ships for nearly a decade before we realized what they were doing. And so, the king eliminated them."

"If I were Villnore's king," Lucian said, "I'd want to keep that secret, too. But Alma, that's not the real truth you're trying to keep hidden, is it?"

"What do you mean?"

Lucian pulled out the Villnore Kingdom's trade report from the stack. "From the records here, it seems the destruction of one of your five major guilds only had a minimal impact on your trading activity. That makes sense, considering the guild members were likely absorbed by the remaining guilds."

He picked up the piracy report again. "But what happened to the pirates that guild was using to ransack ships?"

Lucian slid a final report toward Alma. It was still far out of her reach, but he made sure she caught a glimpse of the title written across the top. It was a war report.

"I thought it was strange," Lucian said. "Your kingdom made no move against the Esgares Empire, even after they took part of your waters. But that's not really the case, is it? After all, if the enemy's expanding into the Madina Sea, then you might as well put those pirates to work ransacking their vessels."

This time, Alma didn't give any indication that he was on the mark. But Lucian was confident in his assumption.

He felt that if the pirates had been absorbed by the king, then it made sense why the rate of piracy fell alongside the guild. If they had just tried arresting the pirates, they'd have scattered and been forced to continue their piracy to survive.

Yet from all the reports Lucian read, there was no indication of that.

They're definitely trying to strangle the Esgares Empire's efforts to claim the sea.

But...

"Give up," Lucian said. "Your little piracy tactics won't work against the Esgares Empire. They've got far more land and resources than you. Even my kingdom can't match them."

Alma sat unmoving. "We do what we can, when we can. Even if it's only a little, it's better than nothing."

"I guess that's true. It just goes to show what kind of situation our two kingdoms are in." Lucian sat back, leaving the reports stacked in front of him. "And why we should be cooperating. My kingdom is set to continue our war against the Esgares Empire in the spring. But my troops won't fight on an empty stomach, and I can't leave my citizens to starve."

"I can't speak for the king, but right now, I do speak for the members of my guild." Alma placed her elbows onto the table. "There's no love for the Esgares Empire. They are a threat to our independence, and each of us would like to see them expelled from the region."

She took Lucian's original food request, the very same one which she cut down by half at the beginning of the meeting.

Her quill moved, marking out the numbers she wrote on each line and replacing them with new ones.

Finally, she held the parchment up, and the servant took it, placing it before Lucian. He picked it up, checking over the numbers.

"This is..." He looked back to Alma. "...more than acceptable."

"I just hope our investment gives us the return we desire."

Teta began gathering all the reports laid out on Alma's side of the table. Seeing that, Emilia got to work doing the same on her side.

"Strange," Alma said, looking at Emilia. "I thought your white hair a bodyguard, but she's your assistant."

"Actually, she's both. Captain of my personal guard, to be exact. But she's also my research partner. A very organized one, at that."

"I see. If she managed to keep up with Teta, then she certainly has promise."

Soon, the reports were all retrieved, leaving the table clear.

Although they had decided on the numbers, there were still documents that needed to be read, signed, and sealed by both parties.

Lucian and Alma would be working together for a little while longer.

The rest of the meeting went by quicker than either of the two expected. Details were hammered out quickly, and at the end, two seals were inked onto the trade agreement.

"I believe everything is in order." Lucian handed his copies of the agreement to Emilia. "We can consider the meeting officially over."

Alma remained seated. "It was a productive discussion, in many ways."

"I agree. I got far more than I expected, along with a favorable trade. I can't ask for any more than that."

"Then..." She stood. "Perhaps we will meet again at another negotiation table."

Lucian also got to his feet. "Yes, I look forward to that day. And I'll make sure to be even more prepared next time. I hope you enjoy the rest of your stay here at the capital."

"It's my first time here, so I plan to visit a few attractions."

"First time, huh?" Lucian looked to Emilia. "It's been a while since we went out to the city for fun, hasn't it?"

Emilia's eyes lit up. "Yes, almost all our trips out are work related."

"Yeah, but I think we should have some free time now." He turned back to Alma. "How would you like a royal escort for the day?"

Alma didn't look surprised. "I suppose it'd be rude of me to refuse a tour by the crown prince himself."

"Good. I've got a few great ideas on places you'll love to visit. Let's go to a clothing store first, and I'll buy you something you'll be proud to show off back home."

"Something fashionable within your kingdom, is it? Perhaps it'd be a good chance to judge the item's reception in my kingdom to know whether or not I should try introducing and advertising that style."

"Exactly." Lucian went along with it, despite her reasonings being far beyond his intent.

Just accept it as a gift, would you?

Then again, it's obvious she was molded from a young age to take over the guild from her father. Letting a potential trading opportunity pass her by is probably unacceptable.

"Anyway," Lucian continued. "We need to get a few things ready before we go out to the city. I'll meet you at the southern gate in half an hour."

"That's reasonable." With that, Alma and Teta left the meeting room.

With no reason to stay, Lucian and Emilia did the same. Unlike Alma who was going toward the castle's exit, Lucian started walking back to his room.

He wanted to change into something more casual. But more importantly, he needed to make sure he was fully prepared for the trip out.

"What do you plan to buy for Alma?" Emilia asked as the two walked down the castle halls.

"About that." Lucian looked to her. "I'll be relying on you."
"Eh? Me?"
"I don't have a clue about the fashions in this world. I barely kept up with the basics in my old one."
"Ah, well if it's fashion, then I have absolutely no confidence." Emilia certainly made the claim with confidence.
"Huh?"
"I didn't get out much, so I never really had to worry about dressing up. And when it came to fitting in, I had bigger problems than what I was wearing."
"That ... makes sense."

Now that he thought about it, Emilia almost always wore her military uniform. When she changed into something else, it was usually something from the castle wardrobe.

He couldn't think of a single time he'd seen her dressed up in her own outfit.

Hmm. We're going to a clothing store with Alma. Should I use this as a chance to buy her something nice to wear?

Lucian didn't have any eye for fashion, but he wasn't worried. A king couldn't rely on just one solution, not when the fate of an entire kingdom was counting on a favorable outcome.

"I need to visit her anyway," Lucian said. "So it won't hurt to ask her opinion on what to get Alma."

"Visit who?"

"Mia. I was going to get her to cast [Enhance] on me before we go out. And now, I'm hoping she's got an eye for fashion."

"Ah, Princess Mia certainly does. She's always dressed so well."

"True. She really likes to look and act mature. It's easy to forget she's only 11 years old."

They reached Lucian's room, but Emilia didn't enter with him. He was going to get changed, after all.

Walking up to his massive wardrobe, Lucian picked out one of the sets of clothing that was pre-selected by the maids to match. It made choosing his outfits much easier, considering his lack of fashion.

After quickly getting changed, Lucian finished by fastening his sword to his belt. When it was secured, he drew it, looking at the purple-tinted metal that made up the blade.

He ran his fingers across the smooth metal, passing over strange runes etched on the blade's side. Like a talisman, the runes enhanced the weapon, giving it more mass without increasing its weight and letting it cut deeper than should be possible.

His clothing had similar runes hidden on the inner lining. When worn by someone also enhanced with magic, the result was a warrior that couldn't be matched by anyone on Earth.

Let's just hope I don't have to use my sword this time.

He sheathed the blade and stepped out of the room. Emilia was waiting for him, and together, they headed toward Mia.

After a soft knock, the pattering of feet was followed by the door's opening.

Mia was finely dressed, as usual. She had a particular blue-white dress that she liked, which she was currently wearing. But she also wore a variety of outfits, each meticulously put together.

The only question Lucian had was whether she was choosing her outfits or if the maids paired them up for her, as they did with him.

"Hey, Mia. Can we come in?"

"If you wish." She stepped aside, giving them room to pass by.

"Thanks."

"Pardon the intrusion." Emilia politely accepted her invitation to enter.

"Okay, Mia," Lucian said after his sister closed the door. "I've got a very important question to ask you."

Mia was caught a bit off-guard. She had just closed the door and turned back to her brother, only to be told that the discussion was a serious one.

"What is it?" she asked in her usual dry tone.

Lucian pointed to her closet doors. "I have to know. Do you pick out the clothes you wear yourself, or do the maids put together outfits for you?"

"Huh?" Mia had a hard time following her brother's line of thought.

"You're always wearing outfits that can catch even a noble's eye, so I was wondering if that was because of your fashion sense or the maids."

"I ... see." She still didn't understand why he was asking, though. "If you must know, I choose my own clothing each morning, piece by piece."

"Alright!" Lucian gave Emilia a thumbs up. " We're in business."

"Congratulations, Prince Lucian!"

"Um." Mia looked between the two mysteriously excited people. "Care to explain what's going on?"

"Oh, right. Sorry about that. Mia..." Lucian smiled at his little sister. "You want to come to the city with us?"

Mia stared at her brother, wondering what kind of situation she just got roped into.

Chapter 23

"Thanks for waiting." Lucian stopped just in front of Alma.

"We only just arrived."

"Excellent timing, then." Lucian motioned to the side. "And allow me to introduce my sister, Mia. She'll be accompanying us on our trip out to the city."

"Pleased to make your acquaintance, Princess Mia." Alma gave her a bow. "It seems the tales of your silvery-blue hair weren't exaggerated. It suits you well, I might add."

"It's good to meet you, Alma." Mia returned the bow. "And thank you for the compliment."

As usual, Mia spoke the bare minimum required of her. She was never one to ramble, and that was especially true whenever she was meeting a new acquaintance.

Lucian had already taken note of that but wasn't quite sure why she was so reserved. It couldn't be helped that he had trouble figuring her out since he'd only known her for a short while, but he was sure Mia wasn't shy.

She'd met many powerful people through her life, and from what Lucian had seen so far, she'd never shown signs of being nervous around them.

Maybe she just likes to stay behind her walls.

But Alma said something interesting. Mia's silvery-blue hair is quite a sight, but she made it seem like it was rare.

Now that I think about it, I haven't seen anyone else with hair quite like hers.

His new world hosted a variety of hair colors that didn't exist on Earth. It was quite a culture shock at first, but he got used to it quickly. So fast that he stopped seeing things like blue hair as strange at all.

But he hadn't realized until now that Mia's hair was so unique.

"You met her already, but..." Lucian motioned to his other side. "This is Emilia. As stated, she's both my personal guard and a trusted companion. Please treat her well."

"I'm happy to meet both of you." Emilia bowed to Alma and Teta.

"Consider the sentiment returned."

"And me as well," Teta said.

"Then since introductions are done..." Lucian stepped up to a nearby carriage. "Why don't we get this trip started."

As the primary guest and a visitor to his kingdom, Lucian held his hand out to Alma first. She took it without hesitation, letting him guide her into the carriage.

Mia was next, followed by Teta. Lucian intended to let Emilia enter after Mia, but when he met her gaze, she returned it by shaking her head.

"As your guard, I should be the last to enter."

"Maybe. But right now, you're not just my guard. You're my companion on a trip out to the city. And besides..." Lucian put his other hand on the hilt of his sword. "Things are different this time."

Emilia still clearly remembered her near failure the last time they tried to enjoy a day out in the city. She told herself she wouldn't make that mistake again, that she would be extra vigilant.

But Lucian wanted her to enjoy the time spent with them, rather than worrying about an assassin that may or may not appear.

Of course, Lucian intended to keep an eye out in her stead. As someone who lived nearly a full life on Earth, he'd already had many experiences like going shopping with friends.

But Emilia hadn't, her heritage as a white hair closing those doors to her.

At the very least, he wanted her to enjoy days like this. Especially considering the dangerous times that lay ahead.

"Thank you." Emilia took his hand and entered the carriage.

After stepping inside, Lucian rang a bell, signifying that they were ready to start moving. The coachman already knew the destination, so all the passengers needed to do was wait until they arrived.

Lucian knew he couldn't rely on Mia to start a lively discussion, and Emilia was reserved due to her white hair. Fortunately, he was used to these kinds of social situations, so he decided he'd initiate a conversation himself.

And he knew exactly what he wanted to talk about.

"What's it like living in such a major trade city?" Lucian asked. "Almost anything you can think of moves through your kingdom's capital at some point. I can only imagine all the exotic items you've seen."

"I've certainly seen treasures many of your nobles can't even fathom. Items from far-flung regions, their kingdom's names barely known to us, much less their culture. In fact, hunting those elusive artifacts isn't only exciting, it's good business."

Alma adjusted her sitting position. "Crowns of magicite, the king whose head it once sat on long forgotten to history. A ceremonial amulet, the meaning of the art adorning it limited only by your imagination.

"There are a lot of interesting items in the world. And you never know when you'll find something unexpectedly powerful. You should know what kind of items pass through the Villnore Kingdom. Your family has purchased many of them from us." Alma looked to Lucian's sword.

"That's true." Lucian placed his hand on its hilt. "They may be powerful, but I still end up shaking my head when I think of all the gold we've spent buying them."

"We've got plenty more when you're ready for the next purchase."

"Please spare me. You know how my kingdom's finances are right now."

Lucian figured a bit of jovial back and forth would help lighten the mood. And since he gave Alma a chance to boast about her kingdom, she ended up getting engaged in the conversation.

Plus, talking about the good parts of the Villnore Kingdom was nice, considering the fact that both of them had spent so much time disparaging each other's kingdoms during their negotiations.

And since Lucian was about to show her some of the better parts of his own kingdom, he intended to use the carriage ride to let Alma talk about hers.

The trip went well, giving their outing into the city some momentum as they arrived at their first stop.

"Grand Heritage Designs?" Alma read off the shop name. "Quite a title for a clothing store."

"It's one of the best in the city," Lucian said.

At least, this is where Mia suggested we go. I've never heard of this store before today.

"Let's go see what it has to offer this time." Lucian led the way through the door.

Once inside, he looked around and nodded.

Yep. I have no idea what I'm looking at.

He once again confirmed that he had no eye for fashion in this world. He could put together a coherent outfit with ease, but as with any culture, certain pieces must fit together in specific ways, like how a tie complemented a suit.

This is why I brought my secret weapon.

"Mia," Lucian said. "What do you think of the selection today?"

"It's winter, so many of the items were made to provide warmth. The variety in style and color is acceptable, and I'm already seeing several outfits that I believe will match Alma well."

"Good, good." Lucian breathed a sigh of relief. "Then how about I let you take the reins here. Let's see what you can come up with."

"Alright." Mia stepped forward. "Please follow me."

Lucian had a plan. Though that plan essentially boiled down to following Mia around while she and Alma went through the clothes.

But there were other steps too, some of which were known only to him. A surprise would make the trip more memorable, after all.

While Mia and Alma picked dresses off a rack, Lucian looked around at the clothes that surrounded him. He didn't know the world's fashion, but if it was just a dress, then all he had to do was find one that looked nice.

"Emilia," Lucian said. "Follow me."

She looked around warily, wondering what had caught his eye. Nothing stood out to her, so she just traced his steps until he came to a stop.

"Did you find a nice dress for Alma?" Emilia asked.

"No, I'm leaving that completely up to Mia, like we discussed. But I did find the one I'm looking for." Lucian pulled a dress off the shelf.

"Ah, it's very pretty. That light shade of purple is really nice, and the frills are cute."

"I agree. And it's a more casual dress than the uniform you're wearing."

Emilia looked down at her outfit. "Uniforms are practical. And I didn't really have time to change, so..."

"I know. If we weren't coming here, we'd have made time for you to put on something more fitting. But since we are here, I can just do this." He held his hand out to Emilia, the dress in his grasp.

"Eh?" She took it out of reflex. "Why am I holding it?"

"Because you're going to try it on. If you like it, then it's yours."

"Ah!" It dawned on her. "I don't really need something like this. The outfits I borrow from the castle are more than enough!"

"Nonsense. You've got a high rank now, so you need to fill up your own wardrobe. And something nice like this is the perfect place to start."

Emilia looked at the frilly, lavender dress in her hands. Until she started visiting the castle, she could only dream of wearing such luxurious outfits. And now, she was being gifted one that even a high noble would wear with pride.

This still feels so unreal, Emilia thought. *My life is nothing like it was before.*

Just by being near Lucian, her future had been altered so completely that she still hadn't adjusted. The fact that she needed her own wardrobe never even occurred to her.

He's right. If I'm going to be by his side, then I need to look like I belong.

"I understand, Prince Lucian." Emilia held the dress close. "I won't disappoint you."

"There's not really any reason for me to be disappointed, though?"

"You're right. There's not even a tiny chance that I will fail."

"Are we talking about the same thing?" Lucian shook his head. "Nevermind. It looks like Mia's ready, so let's go see what they picked out."

The two of them made their way back to the others, where Mia, Alma, and Teta each held dresses and accessories in their hands. They weren't going to buy all of them, it was just part of the plan Lucian and Mia concocted before meeting up with Alma.

More specifically, Mia and the girls would narrow it down to a few choices, then leave the final decision up to Lucian. That way, he could be sure he was getting an outfit that Alma could proudly wear back in her kingdom since the choices had been filtered by those who know the fashion.

At the same time, since he was making the final decision, he was living up to his words of choosing a gift for her here. It was the best possible outcome for everyone involved.

He'd just have to come up with a way to thank Mia later.

"All three of them are great choices." Lucian looked between the outfits. "But there's one clear winner."

He walked up to Teta, who held a pink dress in her hands. Compared to Emilia's, it had more flaps and folds in the cloth, rather than ripples and frills. But the design of the dress would be better suited for a humid place like a seaside city.

Lucian didn't know that, though. He only picked it because he thought it'd look nice next to Emilia's lavender dress.

The reason he said it with so much confidence was because people's opinions would often follow when speaking with enough conviction. Even if it was her least favorite out of the choices, her opinion could be overturned just by hearing him praise the dress.

Two of the outfits were put back onto the racks, leaving only the one Teta was holding.

"If we're going to buy it," Lucian said, "then you might as well wear it."

"You want me to wear it now?" Alma was a bit surprised. "But it hasn't been tailored to me yet."

"I'm sure they can make some quick adjustments." Lucian waved over the owner. "These two would like to try on their new outfits."

"Yes, Your Highness." The woman motioned for Emilia and Alma to follow her.

Alma did so, her steps containing a bit of hesitation. Lucian completely missed that fact, though.

Unlike the cramped closets that passed for changing rooms in most places, the shop they were in had an actual room meant for trying on and adjusting clothes.

There were partitions on one of the walls, but Emilia didn't intend to use them. As a soldier, she was used to changing her clothes around her female companions. And since the shop only sold clothes for women, there wasn't a single guy in the changing room.

With a practiced hand, Emilia's uniform ended up folded nicely on a nearby table. It happened so quickly, while Alma hadn't even begun unlacing her dress.

"Please, allow me." The tailor began to help her undress.

Guess there's no choice...

Alma gave up, letting the tailor get to work. She had been raised to be self-reliant, so she didn't use maids to help her get dressed. Her outfits were always made to be put on by just the wearer, unlike some noble wardrobes.

Being helped in and out of her dress was only slightly embarrassing. More important was the man standing just on the other side of the door she was looking at.

Just knowing that he was aware that she was getting changed was enough to nearly make her blush.

No. Alma shook her head. *Just don't think about it.*

She turned her head, looking for something else to focus on. What filled her vision was Emilia holding her lavender colored dress, looking oddly determined about something.

White. Alma calmly noted the color of Emilia's underwear. *How practical. As expected of a soldier.*

While Emilia was putting on her dress, Alma looked down at her own exposed body. Unlike Emilia, hers was pink, with laced edges in an intricate design. The color was a near perfect match with the dress Lucian picked out for her, but she would never dream of telling him that.

After putting on her dress, Emilia looked at herself in a mirror. It was a bit loose on her, but the tailor would fix that before she left.

More importantly...

Cute. Emilia pulled at the skirt. *And it belongs to me?*

It was even finer than her mother's best dress. Much more so, in fact.

This just means I'll have to work even harder!

With a boost of determination, Emilia turned from the mirror and looked at Alma, who was just about to put on her new dress. Or rather, the tailor was going to put it on for her.

Maybe she's not familiar with how to put on that style of dress?

Emilia certainly didn't know all the nuances, but she had managed to figure out hers pretty quickly.

Wait a second! She saw something that made her completely change focus. *I lose again!?*

Emilia looked down at her own chest, then back to Alma's.

Why can't I win!?

No, I'm still growing. I'm definitely still growing, right?

Emilia paused to think about how she looked a year ago, when she was 16.

I'm not growing...

No, this is how I want it! Emilia raised her fist into the air.

A slender form makes it easier to evade enemy attacks! This is exactly how I want it, okay!?

"Emilia?" Alma tilted her head.

"Ah, haha..." she lowered her hand. "You look really cute, Miss Alma. I think pink is the right choice! Ah, but I already saw that you agree."

"F-forget what you saw." Alma cleared her throat. "But you don't look any less fantastic, Emilia. You picked out a nice dress."

"Ah, Prince Lucian picked it out for me. To be honest, I was surprised."

"I see. He certainly knows fashion well. I'll remember that."

"Ah. Haha..."

Back outside the dressing room, Lucian and Mia waited patiently for the girls to finish. Since the dresses had to be altered a bit, it took even longer than normal.

But the wait was worth it.

"How does it look, Prince Lucian?" Emilia lifted the hem just a bit.

"You look amazing, Emilia. I hope to see you in beautiful dresses more often."

"Understood! I definitely won't fail!"

"I'm still not sure what there is to fail, though..."

He turned to Alma next. Since he first set eyes on her, she had always exuded confidence. But right now, she seemed a little vulnerable.

Maybe she doesn't like the dress and doesn't want to say it?

Hmm. Girls can be hard to read...

"You look stunning, Alma." He decided to ignore his doubts and compliment her anyway. "That dress was definitely the right choice. It really accentuates your natural charm."

"I guess charm helps during negotiations..."

"Hah, that's true. Though I don't think you need any more help at the negotiation table."

"I'll take every edge I can get."

"I noticed. I had to work really hard because of that." Lucian shook his head. "But what do you say we move on to the next destination. We've still got a lovely day ahead of us."

The five of them stepped out of the store and back into the carriage.

The royal tour continued for several more hours. But the one acting as the tour guide wasn't Lucian, or even Emilia. It was Mia.

She was the only one who was actually familiar with the city. Emilia had arrived from the countryside and spent most of her time in the barracks.

And Lucian was Lucian. Or rather, he wasn't Lucian, which was the problem.

He did spend a bit of time studying the city and its landmarks, but that was a far cry from being familiar with them.

That didn't stop him from acting like he knew what he was talking about, though. Just like he was doing as he and the girls entered a local park.

"Actually, this isn't well known to outsiders, but..." Lucian lowered his voice. "Some say this park is haunted by the spirits of the tribe that once owned these lands."

"Haunted?" Alma looked between Lucian and the park.

Lucian swept his hands across the air, motioning toward the park's entrance. "It was here that they had their religious temple, before we came and conquered them. When Almekia's capital was founded, nobody wanted to build on the land that had such a powerful history, so it was made into a park."

"That's good then, right?"

He shook his head. "It wasn't enough for the spirits to find peace. Those who come here at night..."

Alma gulped. "W-what happens to them?"

"They..." Lucian met Alma's eyes. "...usually mistake other people's voices as spirits. Or maybe an animal was scurrying around in the bushes. Either way, it's probably not true."

"Huh!? But what about the tribe and the temple!?"

"Ah, that's real. Maybe. It's hard to know with so few records of that time."

"Hah..." Alma let out a breath. "Well as long as there aren't any spirits..."

"Don't worry, even if we run across a ghost, we'll be fine." Lucian turned his head. "We have Mia here."

"Why me?"

"Hmm. Something tells me you'd get along well with a spirit. Maybe it's your even temperament? I think a spirit's rage would be quelled just by being near you."

"Do you even hear the words coming out of your mouth?"

Lucian nodded, though not at Mia's words. "Yeah, we'll be just fine."

"I-I hope so..." Emilia's small voice came from his other side. "Ghosts are..."

A hand clutched his sleeve. Tracing the arm, Lucian saw that it belonged to Emilia. Although she was holding his clothes, her eyes were set on the park's entrance which still sat in front of them.

"Just stick close to me, Emilia," Lucian said in a confident voice. "And I'll stick close to Mia."

"Don't put your hopes on me."

With a shrug, Lucian finally took a step toward the park. In his hand was a blackberry pastry, a snack he got from a nearby sweets shop.

Each of the girls had their own delicious pastry, though none of them had taken a single bite yet to confirm whether or not they were actually as tasty as they looked.

As they stepped through the entrance, Emilia's hand clutched his sleeve tighter. And if Lucian was right, Alma was walking just a bit closer to him than before.

But fortunately—or perhaps unfortunately—the story Lucian told was just that. A story. The truth was lost to time.

"What a great spot to relax." Lucian overlooked a small flower garden.

Nearby was a gazebo, perfect for enjoying some snacks and refreshments.

Lucian led them to that gazebo, taking a seat at the octagonal bench within. The girls piled in around him, while the ever-silent guards stood around the perimeter.

"What did you think of the capital?" Lucian asked Alma.

"You have a long history contained within this city, with a dedication to tradition. It's quite different from my kingdom, where the influence of other cultures can be easily felt."

Alma unwrapped her pastry. "It lacks the excitement of my kingdom's capital, but it feels as if everyone here is focused on the same goals. Back home, there are so many forces swirling that problems often arise, as you discerned with the dissolved guild."

She finally took a bite, taking her time to chew before swallowing. "And the sweets are good."

"Wow." Lucian nodded. "I'll consider that high praise coming from you."

"Just stating my initial impressions. Don't think about it too deeply."

Lucian finished a bite of his pastry. "Who knows, maybe I'll be giving you my first impressions on your city soon enough."

"Yes. Depending on what my king decides, we may have the chance to meet again soon."

"When you see him, please deliver a personal message. Tell him that no matter what he chooses to do, it won't stop what's coming. The only question is, how well prepared will he be to meet it."

Alma digested Lucian's words as she finished the last bite of her pastry. "I'll pass on your message."

The crunching of twigs could be heard as several pairs of feet walked toward the same gazebo where Lucian and the others sat.

Seeing them, Alma stood from her spot on the bench and turned to Lucian. "It was a pleasure, Prince Lucian. I don't expect we'll meet again before I leave the city tomorrow, so I'll take this opportunity to wish you a pleasant crowning ceremony."

Lucian stood, as well. "Thank you. I'm confident it will go well. Take care, Alma. And you too, Teta."

"Thank you, Your Highness." Teta bowed.

With that, the two young women met their escorts at the gazebo's entrance and began the walk back out of the park.

"I'm a little confused." Emilia watched their backs. "Are we going to the Villnore Kingdom soon?"

"Maybe. I won't know until I hear what their king has to say."

"This was just a trade deal, right? Why is Villnore's king getting involved?"

Mia wrapped up her half-eaten pastry. "The trade negotiation wasn't the only battle taking place. Our kingdom just lost its ruler and crown prince, leaving Lucian to ascend to the throne. Foreign powers are curious what kind of king he will become."

"Ah! So they were testing us?"

"Yes. Villnore's king will hear every detail of the meeting in order to learn of his neighboring kingdom's new ruler."

"So that's how Prince Lucian knew we might be meeting them again. If the king approves of Alma's report, we could end up going there."

"Yeah," Lucian said. "But I don't know if I managed to impress Alma. To be honest, I'm shocked at how well the people in this world negotiate. I thought I was prepared, but I only just managed to get the results I wanted."

He stood from his bench, looking at the path Alma took when she left. "If that's the kind of people I'll be going up against at the negotiation table, then I need to work even harder. I wonder if—woah!"

"What's wrong!?" Emilia leapt to her feet, scanning the park for danger.

"It's nothing to worry about." Lucian ran his eyes left to right, as if reading a message only he could see. "I was just surprised at this pop-up—or rather, the Divine System Interface, as it's called."

"Eh? You mean that thing where you learned your magic?"

"Yeah. I can look at it anytime, but I didn't bring it up. It just popped up on its own. But there's a reason for that." He looked at the two girls. "Looks like I leveled up again."

Level up! Congratulations on solving Almekia's food crisis!

Please select a skill from the list below.

[Physical Resistance I] [Extended Chant I] [Pain Resistance I]

Lucian quickly read the names of the skills available to him, but unlike the last time he leveled up, none of them stuck out as the obvious choice. Though there was one that he immediately ruled out.

"[Extended Chant I], again? I still don't see how it's useful in any way."

"Eh?" Emilia sat back down. "Is that one of the skills you learned?"

"No, I haven't learned it. It's just one of my choices. The others are [Physical Resistance I] and [Pain Resistance I]. I'd read the descriptions to the both of you, but it's pretty obvious by their names alone."

"Hmm." Mia let out a thoughtful sound. "I believe either of the two resistance skills would be the wiser choice."

"Me too!" Emilia agreed. "If I had to choose one, I'd pick [Physical Resistance I]. Anything to help you survive."

Lucian nodded. "Yeah, dulling the pain would be nice, but [Physical Resistance I] essentially does the same thing, just with physical attacks only. But it has the added benefit of lowering the damage I take at the same time."

He concentrated on the skill, and it disappeared from the list. He didn't feel any different, but [Physical Resistance I] appeared on his skill list, so he was sure he'd obtained it properly.

"Since I get to choose two skills per level up, another one has appeared. But it doesn't seem that great. It's called [Alchemy I], and it lets me craft stronger potions. Seeing as how I don't even know how to craft them, I don't really see how it'd be useful to me."

"In that case," Mia said. "[Pain Resistance I]."

"Done." Lucian eyed his two new skills. "It's good that I got some upgrades, but this level seems a bit ... lacking."

"Compared to the two schools of magic you managed to unlock last time, I agree."

"Yeah. My first level up was a game changer, whereas this one just gives me a few passive bonuses. Still, it's better than nothing. Plus, let's not forget why I leveled up in the first place."

"The food crisis is over."

Lucian nodded at his sister's words. "Yeah. I guess getting Alma to agree to our terms was enough to solve it. Add in that farmer, Ivan's, work to revert our agricultural laws alongside the release of our emergency food supplies and it seems it all added up to the completion of the quest."

"Congratulations, Prince Lucian!" Emilia showed him a wide smile. "The people's lives are already getting better under your rule!"

"Yeah. Yeah, you're right, Emilia. Now I just need to solve the other hundred tasks, and maybe I can turn the Almekian Kingdom into one I'll be proud to lead."

Down the path Alma used to leave the park, she and her entourage were just stepping back onto the road outside the entrance. A carriage awaited them, one that any noble would be proud to ride in.

She and Teta were the only ones to get in, with the rest escorting her from the outside.

The ride was short, compared to the cross-kingdom journey it took to get to the city. When she stepped out of the carriage, an inn stood before her.

She already had a room, so she walked in and went straight to the hall where it was located. However, she didn't step into her room. Rather, she knocked on the next door over.

It opened a sliver, but when the man saw that it was Alma, he let the door swing open.

"Alma, welcome back." He stood aside, letting her enter. "I hope he managed to at least provide some entertainment for you."

"Indeed he did, Father. He even brought me around the city after the negotiations."

Alma's father scoffed. "He was that desperate to impress you? What a fool, thinking that would work on the greatest negotiator our kingdom has seen in generations."

Alma's father was supposed to be sick, but the man didn't show any sign of illness. Of course, that was because he was perfectly healthy.

The reason he didn't go to the negotiations wasn't due to physical reasons. He simply wasn't needed. Alma was by far the superior negotiator, and that held true no matter who she was compared to in the Villnore Kingdom.

She came prepared, certain that the second prince would prove himself incompetent and untrustworthy.

However...

"Father, I lost."

"Of course you did, nobody could beat you in–" His words stopped, even as his mouth hung open. "Wait, you lost!?"

"I agreed to deliver food at nearly harvest season prices."

"What!? Why would you agree to something like that!?"

Alma stared out the window, recalling the meeting. "Despite attacking him from so many angles, he never once flinched. Time and again, he'd find a counter to my argument, digging deep into our kingdom's state of affairs.

"He's a couple years my junior, but when I stared into his eyes, I saw a depth that shouldn't be possible for someone his age. Competence, far beyond what I thought to find."

Alma turned back to her father. "If—no, when Prince Lucian becomes king, Almekia will find itself with its first great ruler in many generations."

Chapter 24

"What's next?" Mia asked.

"Let's see." Lucian ran his finger across a page in a notebook. "The emergency stockpile of grain has been delivered to most of the needed towns, we've got a shipment of foreign food on the way, I finally have a few people I can trust in you and Emilia, and my uncle's assassination attempts have been thwarted. I'd say that's some good progress in just a couple weeks."

"Yes, but that still leaves many tasks incomplete. What about the national debt, debasement of the currency, or the war with the Esgares Empire? Do you already have plans for dealing with them?"

"Well ... it's not exactly a plan. But I've got ideas."

Mia sighed. "As king, the responsibility falls on your shoulders. We can't afford to fail, not if what you told us about the upcoming collapse in civilization is to be believed."

"I-it's fine!" Emilia said. "I'm sure your ideas are amazing, right?"

Lucian looked away from Emilia's hopeful eyes. "If it's war, then my confidence is ... lacking might not be the right word. Zero, maybe?"

"Eh!? But you're a powerful mage and warrior, aren't you!? Doesn't that mean you can lead us to victory!?"

"Being strong doesn't mean I have the strategic knowledge to win a war. To be honest, I planned to find a general I can trust to help guide me. That should be the Minister of War, Marcus, but I don't know how much I can rely on him..."

As with all the ministers, his allegiance was questionable at best. Putting the fate of his kingdom in the hands of such a man didn't sit right with Lucian.

"If only we had as many strategic geniuses as the dark elves," Mia said. "We'd have no shortage of commanders at our disposal."

"The Dark Elves? They live in the rocky land to the east, right? I didn't know they were known for their intelligence."

"It's not something spoken about very often, since our relationship with their people is rather strained. It'd be a bad look for us humans if we praised their exploits on the battlefield."

"I guess that makes sense. But–"

Lucian cut off his words at the sound of a horn. It wasn't one he'd heard since coming to this world, but it still put him on edge.

It brought to mind memories of fire drills and tornado alarms, filling him with the sense that something was wrong. After tearing his eyes from Mia's bedroom door and looking back to the girls, he knew his intuition was correct.

"An attack!?" Mia said in shock.

"Prince Lucian, please stay behind me!" Emilia put herself between him and the door.

Since they were in Mia's personal room, there were no guards sitting outside the door. Lucian loathed the idea of dragging soldiers with him while in the safety of his own castle halls, so there was no telling where the nearest men were stationed.

However, unlike before, the prince was prepared for battle. He carried his sword with him, even here. Though he only did so with the intention of growing accustomed to having it at all times, he said a silent prayer for his decision to do so.

Emilia crept closer to the door, with Lucian a few steps behind and Mia as far from the combat area as her rather large room would allow.

Step by step, Emilia closed in on the door. When she finally got within arm's length, her hand came up, wrapping around the handle. However, she didn't twist it. Rather, her two fox ears began to twitch, as if picking up sounds only she could hear.

"Fighting," Emilia said. "But it's distant. Several halls away."

Lucian turned to his sister. "Stay here and lock the door. Emilia and I will go find out what's happening, but cast enhancement magic on me first."

"A-alright." Mia looked fearful, but she knew she'd only put herself in more danger if she went outside.

After a short chant, Lucian felt Mia's magic fill his body. The strength was leagues above a simple talisman, giving him the confidence to step out into the hallway where soldiers were fighting and dying.

"Let's go, Emilia."

"Yes, Prince Lucian!" She gave the knob a twist, and the outside hall came into view.

There wasn't anyone waiting for them, so they stepped in the direction where Emilia heard the fighting. Now that they'd left the room, even Lucian could hear the yelling and clashing of metal. He wanted to hurry to the battle, but Emilia warned him that other enemies could be behind each corner, so they had to be careful.

After only a single turn, a group of armored men appeared in the hall before them, rushing in their direction. They had the common equipment worn by castle guards, but that didn't necessarily mark them as allies. Not in this situation.

"Halt!" Emilia yelled. "Stop and explain the situation!"

The men obeyed, stopping several paces in front of the now captain of Prince Lucian's personal guard. She was effectively their commander now, since all soldiers stationed within the castle were considered personal guardsmen for the king, even if they weren't technically part of the Royal Guard.

"Commander! Your Highness!" The soldier saluted. "Enemies have infiltrated the castle! Their numbers are low, but they're putting up a fierce resistance!"

"Who are they?" Lucian asked. "And do you know why they're here?"

"I don't know why they attacked, but as for who they are–they're soldiers. Our soldiers."

"What!?" A bad premonition surfaced in Lucian's mind. "Our own men..."

The prince turned his head, looking at a wall. Or rather, he was looking at where the wall met the ceiling. Though in truth, he was peering in the direction of a certain room which lay beyond.

"Prince Lucian," Emilia said. "Do you think..."

"Yes. Lead the way. We can't let him escape."

"You men." Emilia motioned to the three soldiers. "Follow me."

"Yes, commander!"

The two of them had turned into five, all of which now made haste through the castle hallways. The room they sought was on the top floor of the castle, so they were required to go through many turns and up two flights of stairs.

The halls on the upper floor of the castle were eerily silent. There weren't as many people up there as the lower floors, but there was still a noticeable difference between how empty it was now compared to a normal day.

The doors strewn about the castle halls were all shut. That was often the case for most doors, but there would always be at least a few open here and there. But not a single open door could be seen right now.

The group neared a bend in the hall, but as they grew closer, they slowly came to a stop.

"That's..." Lucian eyed a splash of red on the floor and wall.

"Blood," Emilia finished.

The soldiers held their weapons in battle-ready grips as they neared the bloodstain. It was only a small splash of red, but the shape of the stain made it obvious that more awaited them around the corner.

The nameless guards were the first to reach it. They charged around the bend, shields ready to intercept any attacks. However...

"It's clear, Your Highness," one of the guards said. "But..."

Lucian stepped around the corner and saw exactly what he had feared. Five bodies were strewn about the corridor, each wearing the armor of a castle guard. And not a single one of them stirred.

"Dammit," Lucian said. "How could this happen..."

These were my men...

They were under the employ of the kingdom to protect this castle, to protect me.

And now they're dead...

During his time on Earth, Lucian had only seen corpses on television programs. Although he got his first look at lifeless bodies during the raid on the assassins, they were the remains of criminals who were after his life. He felt surprisingly little remorse at their demise.

But seeing his own men murdered inside the castle was an entirely different story.

I'll make them pay. Whoever was behind this will definitely regret it!

The group continued on past the bodies. Unlike Lucian, none of the others seemed to take more than a cursory glance at them while they passed by. The brutality of this world was a far cry from the one that Lucian came from, and the people who grew up in it had long since become accustomed to their harsh reality.

When they arrived at their destination, they found that unlike the rest of the doors, the one for the room they came to visit was wide open, with two guards lying slain at the entrance. Not a single sound could be heard coming from within, but they still had to step inside to make certain of what they feared.

"I knew it." Lucian peered around the empty room. "They were after Henrik."

"This is dangerous," Emilia said. "If they're willing to go so far as to break Archduke Henrik out of his imprisonment, then they won't stop with just this one attack."

"I know. Henrik has the support of a lot of powerful people. If they're making their move, then that means this isn't just a jailbreak. It's a declaration of war."

"A coup..." Emilia looked worried. "But if we look on the bright side, at least he's proven his treason with his actions now."

"That's true, but I don't know how much help that'll me now that he's escalated it this far." Lucian stepped out of the empty room. "C'mon. Let's get back to where the battle was taking place. There's still a chance Henrik hasn't made it out of the castle."

"Right! Let's go, men!"

They quickly retraced their steps, until they arrived back on the second floor, where the sounds of fighting had echoed through the halls. However, no yelling or clashing of metal could be heard anymore.

In its place were the thumping of countless pairs of boots as soldiers ran down the pathways. When a squad saw Lucian, they stopped what they were doing and saluted.

"Your Highness! We've secured the second floor!"

"Good work." Lucian kept his distance, still unsure who these guards truly owed their allegiance to. "And what of the first floor?"

"Another squad went down to check the situation, so I'm not sure if they're still fighting down there."

"Then lead the way, we're going to find out."

They met several more groups of wandering soldiers as they moved through the halls, but rather than getting them to join, Lucian told them to continue their patrol. He couldn't be sure that there were no more traitors hidden around, and Mia's room was on the second floor, so he definitely wanted to make sure she was safe.

As for the group he was with, the soldiers he commanded to lead the way brought them to the first floor using the most direct path. When they arrived, no sounds of battle could be heard, but many soldiers ran about, just like they did on the floor above.

It was an easy enough task to find the one in charge of the men. Marcus, the Minister of War, stood in a circle of soldiers. He had taken command shortly after the fighting broke out, and it was through him that order had been maintained during the chaotic attack.

"Marcus."

"Your Highness. I see the men were able to find you and secure your safety."

"Something like that. But we've got a problem. Archduke Henrik has escaped."

"Tch. So that was their goal. I sent some men up to check on him, but they haven't returned."

"Slain. We found them in the hallways."

"I see." Marcus rubbed his beard. "Whoever ordered the attack had soldiers wearing our own armor. Without a doubt, they belonged to a noble. And since someone recently released Archduke Henrik's family from their prison, I'd say the culprit is obvious."

Lucian nodded. "I know. His family likely organized the invasion to free him. And if they're willing to go this far, then they won't stop with just one attack."

"Yes, but there's a bigger problem here."

"What kind of problem?"

"Nobles are allowed to have personal guards within the city, but those men weren't guards. They were soldiers."

"Ah, so that's what you meant. You're suggesting that they brought some of their army into the city. If that's true, then we'll need to be very careful, since we don't know how many men they snuck in."

In the Almekian Kingdom, only the king was allowed to have soldiers stationed within the capital city and its surrounding countryside. The reason for that was simple. If nobles were allowed to freely move their troops within reach of the king, then it'd be a simple matter to take the throne by force.

Like most medieval countries on Earth, the Almekian Kingdom relied on the nobility in charge of each province to maintain their own individual armies. When the country needed to wage war, the nobles would send their soldiers to the king, who would lead them under a unified banner.

This system spread the burden of maintaining the army to each province, decreasing the financial burden to the crown. And since each province essentially had its own army, it allowed the nobility to better secure their land against criminals and foreign invaders.

But the system did have its drawbacks. Although the soldiers answered to the king, they spent most of their time under the command of the noble in charge of their territory, meaning their allegiance was ultimately to their liege, not the crown.

Due to a turbulent period in the Almekian Kingdom where the nobility fought for the right to rule the country, a law was passed to ban the movement of troops in the king's personal province, where the capital city sat.

However, according to the Minister of War, Archduke Henrik had managed to sneak in soldiers from his province, which his family used to assault the castle and free him from his captivity.

"How many men do we have in the city?" Lucian asked.

"Around 200 in and around the castle. Most of our men are still in the north, preparing to battle the Esgares Empire in the spring. If we include the city guard, we can add another 500. But city guards don't have the same level of training and equipment as real soldiers."

"We need the guards to keep the peace in the city, but we should gather a hundred of them and bring them into the castle grounds, just in case. For the rest, have them scour the city for Archduke Henrik. I want him found."

"As you wish." Marcus barked some orders, and men started moving.

This is turning into a real mess...

Chapter 25

"Report!" a soldier yelled after walking into the room.

Lucian motioned for the others to go silent. "Speak."

"A group of city guards has been ambushed. The ones who escaped say they were attacked by our own soldiers."

"So they've shown themselves. Where did this battle take place?" Lucian waved the messenger over to the city map sprawled atop the table.

"Around here, Your Highness."

"So they're in the warehouse district. Henrik has several storage buildings there where he keeps supplies for his magitech business, so he likely hid his soldier's equipment there until he was ready."

If they're gathering their equipment," Marcus said, "then that can only mean one thing."

"Yeah. They're preparing for battle."

This was an outcome that they were expecting, but that didn't mean it was a favorable one. The best result would have been the recapture of Archduke Henrik, followed by the subsequent surrender of his accomplices and soldiers.

However, it seemed that future was not to be. Upon this realization, Lucian began to ponder his alternatives.

Should we march to the warehouse district and subdue them? Or is that what they want?

Could they have let some of the city guard escape so we would know where they are? If that's the case, we could walk right into their trap.

But what else can we do? Sit behind the castle walls and wait? What if they have more troops hiding outside the city? We'll be giving them time to gather up for an assault on the castle.

All eyes were on Lucian. As the ruler, it was up to him to decide how to deal with the army at their doorstep.

When he accepted the responsibility of carrying the weight of the world's future on his shoulders, he knew it wouldn't be an easy task. But only now was he truly feeling the weight of that burden.

The time had finally arrived, the time when he would truly be put to the test. With a single word, he could send countless men to their deaths, even if he won the day. And if he were to lose...
This world would be finished...
The God's Acolyte would take over and bring about a disaster.
Emilia, Mia, and everyone else would suffer a horrible fate.
Lucian met the eyes of all the important people in the room. Emilia. Mia. Marcus. Generals and advisors. One by one, he took in the faces of those who were putting their faith in him.

Then, he stood.

"Henrik seeks to tear this kingdom in half. He pits friend against friend, brother against brother—and in my case, uncle against nephew. All in search of the crown that rightfully belongs to me.

"This kingdom—our kingdom—is already facing its most turbulent years. Famine, unrest, and wars plague our lands. I know each of you understand because I've seen many of you dealing with such problems.

"That's why I won't allow it. I won't allow Henrik to throw us into a bloody civil war! Today, we march. We will meet them on the battlefield and show that traitor what happens to those who put their own selfish desires ahead of our very kingdom!"

Nods of approval follow Lucian's speech, with Emilia and Marcus showing the most outward support for his decision. The Minister of War even had a sinister smile on his lips. He loved the battlefield, so he had no problem stepping onto it here in Almekia's capital city.

"I'll gather the men," Marcus said. "We'll leave as soon as we're ready."

"Good. In the meantime, we'll be going over a few plans. Join us here before we march so we can fill you in on—"

"Report!" A new soldier yelled as he entered the room.

"Speak."

"Troops sighted in the city streets! They're marching straight toward the castle!"

"What!? They're attacking us!?"

"How many men?" Marcus asked.

"We're not sure," the soldier replied. "Several hundred at least. Maybe more."

"Tch. So they have at least as many as us. No, they must outnumber us. Otherwise, they wouldn't be so bold as to march to the castle walls like this."

Is this a good thing? Lucian wondered. *If they come to us, we'll have the defender's advantage, right?*

He was no tactical genius, so all he could do was wonder about the implications this turn of events would have.

However, he couldn't afford to look incompetent in front of the kingdom's most influential people. He didn't even want the soldiers in the room to hear him ask Marcus what they should do now that things had changed so much.

As he was concocting a way to lead the conversation in a direction that would both give him the answers he needed and prevent him from looking incompetent, a savior appeared.

"What do we do, then?" Mia asked.

"It'll take at least a half-hour to gather all the men from their stations," Marcus said. "We can set the rally point near the gate, and when we're ready to move out, we'll have more information."

Lucian nodded. "That sounds like a good plan. Gather our forces behind the wall and prepare to meet them in the streets or to defend the walls, depending on what our scouts say when we're ready."

"Then I'll disperse the orders." Marcus took his leave from the room, along with several other commanders.

Lucian spared a glance toward Mia. The young princess knew that Lucian didn't have the strategic training to make critical decisions on the fly, and she also understood how important it was to keep that fact hidden for now.

With a simple nod, Lucian expressed his gratitude toward her for speaking up when he couldn't. Seeing that, his sister merely looked away.

Embarrassed? Lucian barely kept the wry smile from his lips. *You should be a little more honest.*

"Well," Lucian said. "I suppose we should head to the meetup spot ourselves. It'd be good for morale if I'm on the front line with the men."

"I agree, Prince Lucian," Emilia said. "And you can make decisions more quickly if you can see the situation with your own eyes, rather than relying on messengers."

"Precisely. Mia, you stay in the castle. I'll keep you informed in case things change."

"Understood."

Lucian, Emilia, and Mia all exited the meeting room at the same time, but that's as far as they could go together, as Mia's room was in the opposite direction of the castle's main exit.

When Lucian stepped outside, he realized that it was already well into the afternoon. Since it was the middle of winter, the days were short, with the sun already starting its final stretch toward the horizon.

He shrugged off the chilly air and stepped toward a large space of empty ground between the castle and wall. It was often used for gathering troops for various dispatch missions, so it could hold a few hundred people in formation without getting crowded.

There were already men standing around, with more arriving each minute. When they saw their prince walking up to them, they immediately straightened their formations and stood tall. The new arrivals quickly fell into place among their companions, and the semblance of a fighting force began to form.

Lucian was only vaguely familiar with the tactics used by his army. He had read a bit about them when he had spare time, but it wasn't a priority. Until now, he assumed any major battles would be months away, when the war against the Esgares Empire started back up in the spring.

That lack of foresight had come back to haunt him. But at least he had someone he could rely on.

"Emilia, I'll be counting on you to help guide my decisions."

"You can rely on me, Prince Lucian! I studied all kinds of tactics during my training!"

"Good. Then don't hesitate to speak up if you think we need to make adjustments, since I likely won't be able to tell a good decision from a bad one."

"Understood. I'll keep a close eye out and inform you if needed."

The gathering of soldiers continued for a good fifteen minutes. From Lucian's estimates, most of the men were already standing in the open space, and that assumption was backed up by the large decrease in new soldiers arriving each minute.

Marcus seemed to be finished with whatever task he was working on, so Lucian stepped up to him and the several commanders who stood with him.

"We're nearly finished gathering the men," Lucian said. "And it took less time than we imagined."

"Yes, Your Highness. Though we're still waiting for the report on the enemy's movements."

"None of the scouts have returned?"

"Not yet. But I told them to report back within a half-hour, so they should be arriving shortly."

Lucian looked out over the men. "Two hundred soldiers and a hundred city guard. Depending on the size of my uncle's army, our available strategies may become very limited."

"As long as we have our storehouse, we have enough food to survive for weeks. If we can get a messenger out of the city, we can call for reinforcements."

"True. As long as they don't have an overwhelming number of troops, there's bound to be at least one gap to sneak through. We just–"

"Your Highness!" a man yelled.

Turning, Lucian caught sight of a soldier rushing toward him. He didn't know who the man was, but none of the others made any moves to stop him, so he merely watched on as the soldier came to a stop.

"Reporting enemy movement!" the man said. "Archduke Henrik is preparing to surround the castle walls! Estimated size of his army is 700 men, with 400 being soldiers and the other 300 being city guards he conscripted into his ranks!"

"So he has over double our numbers," Lucian said with a frown.

"It's not as bad as I feared," Marcus said. "With the walls, we can hold against a force that size for quite a while. And if they try to take the castle, the defender's advantage may be enough to obtain an outright victory."

"That's true." Lucian secretly felt relieved. "Then we man the walls and send a messenger to gather some reinforcements. Like you said, with the food from the storehouse, we can survive at least a couple weeks if we ration–"

An explosion silenced Lucian mid-sentence. All heads turned to the source of the loud sound, where they saw smoke rising from a building.

"T-that's..." Lucian started. "...The storehouse!"

It seemed Archduke Henrik didn't intend to let them drag the battle out.

Lucian, Emilia, and Marcus rushed toward the sound of the explosion, bringing along a healthy number of soldiers.

When they arrived, they saw the castle's storehouse billowing plumes of dark smoke through the open door. A red light was glowing behind the thick smoke, making clear that the crackling sound that filled the air was indeed the roar of flames.

"Water," Lucian yelled. "Quickly!"

He wasn't sure what to expect. Men gathering buckets of water from the castle's well, perhaps. But what he definitely didn't anticipate was a group of soldiers rushing to the smoke billowing from the open door, their hands completely empty.

"Goddess of war, bring out a tsunami!" Marcus yells.

The other soldiers' words were drowned out by all their chants blending together. But when they finished...

Water magic! Lucian thought. *Of course!*

But wait a minute! Aren't they destroying the food with those powerful spells!?

Lucian watched on as several different water spells burst from the mages' hands, disappearing into the flaming storehouse. Even someone as inexperienced in magic as Lucian could tell that the water conjured by the mages didn't have the force of a mere firehose. Rather, it contained the power of a destructive spell that would be used in battle.

The reason was obvious. The men were soldiers, not firefighters. They only knew how to conjure water for the purpose of destruction. Something like a gentle stream to fight a raging fire was simply not in their repertoire.

It's ... working? No, it's definitely working.

The hiss of water hitting flames was overpowering even the roar of the fire, while the dark smoke was now interlaced with white steam.

Unfortunately, the guards posted at the storehouse didn't stand a chance against whoever set the fire. Their bodies were lying on the ground, looking as if they didn't even know they were under attack.

How many infiltrated the wall? And are they still here?

Lucian looked around the castle grounds, but he wasn't even sure what he was really looking for.

Then again, there's always a chance that it was one of our men who set the fire...

His eyes fell back on the storehouse that was still billowing smoke.

There's nothing I can do here. I can't even cast offensive magic like these mages.

But what I can do is boost the morale of the soldiers still standing in formation near the wall. They've got to be worried about everything that's going on.

"Marcus," Lucian said. "See to it that the fire is put out. I'm going back to the wall."

"Fine."

"Let's go, Emilia."

"Understood, Prince Lucian."

The two left the still flaming building, heading back to the lines of soldiers who stood in formation near the wall.

As expected, many of them were looking at the pillar of smoke that rose from the storehouse, with their hardened expressions hiding whatever it was they thought about the situation they were in.

Lucian couldn't afford to have them lose their nerve, so he stood at the head of the formation and ran his eyes over his soldiers. The rigid training the men went through taught them to always focus on their commander at times like this, so most of them were already eyeing Lucian, waiting for his words.

"The cowardly Archduke tried to sabotage our supplies. But the fire is already retreating thanks to the efforts of Marcus and his men. Fear not, for such an underhanded tactic can only mean one thing. Henrik fears us. He knows he cannot win and is desperately looking for a way to defeat us by any means necessary.

"But he will fail. I, Lucian Valesti Almekia, am the true heir to the Almekian Kingdom, and I won't allow a usurper to take the throne with a bloody revolution!" Lucian unsheathed his sword and raised it high. "I'm going to put an end to Archduke Henrik's schemes with this very blade, even if I have to battle my way through his entire army to reach him!"

He lowered his sword and swept his gaze over the men. "Any who stand victoriously beside me when the fighting stops will receive a reward worthy of their bravery! So raise your swords high, and let me hear your courage!"

Lucian once again raised his weapon into the air, but this time, it was alongside hundreds more, topped by the shouts of soldiers preparing for battle.

"Down with Archduke Henrik!" Lucian yelled.

"""Down with Archduke Henrik!""" a chorus of voices followed.

For the next several minutes, Lucian continued to throw fuel onto the fire of his men's enthusiasm. Having hundreds of men shouting alongside the clanking of their metal equipment made him feel as if the battle had already begun.

Perhaps in a way, it had. Victory wasn't just obtained on the field but also in the hearts and minds of the ones who were destined to fight. Many battles in history had been lost before the first weapon was even swung.

"Prince Lucian," Emilia said. "Do you really plan to do battle with Archduke Henrik?"

"Sorry, Emilia. It just kind of came out, and it's too late to take my words back. Besides, I spent countless hours studying history before coming to this world, and the kings who led their troops into battle gained the undying dedication of their men, while those who cowered in the rear lost their respect. As things are, I can't afford even a small drop in morale."

Emilia nodded. "It's true that soldiers will follow their king into nearly any battle, but it also gives the enemy an easy target. They know that if you fall, so does the army."

"You're right, which is why I apologized to you. After all, I'll be relying on you to protect me."

"Of course! I won't lose, no matter what!"

Lucian looked back over his little army of three hundred. Their cheers were dying down, but his words had their intended effect.

I just hope this will be enough to get them to fight after Henrik's army shows up at our doorstep.

When they realize we're outnumbered 2 to 1, will they still cheer for me?

It seemed his question would be put to the test quicker than he thought because a scout came rushing up to him at that precise moment.

"Your Highness! Archduke Henrik approaches!"

"Okay men, it's time to show these rebels what it means to challenge the soldiers who protect the royal castle!"

Marcus arrived at some point, having left the extinguishing of the fire in the hands of one of his men so he could help get the soldiers set up in their proper stations.

As for Lucian, he got out of their way. He didn't really have any experience on matters like this, so it was best to let the professionals handle it. Besides, he felt that overseeing the work while others handled the details made him seem more like a king.

"Let's go to the wall," Lucian said after most of the men had left the staging area. "I want to see the army for myself."

Emilia stepped forward. "Then please follow me, and be careful of arrows."

"Alright."

Not sure what I can do against a sniper, though... Lucian kept his thoughts to himself.

Once on the wall, he had a clear view of the approaching army. They marched down the main roads that led to the castle walls, like a parade. But rather than bringing joy and entertainment, this parade was only after one thing. Blood.

Are they going to attack as soon as they reach us?

Or are they going to surround us and starve us into surrendering?

Did they attack our food supply for that reason, or were they just trying to demoralize us?

...War isn't easy.

Henrik's army finally reached the walls. Or rather, they got as close as they could without putting themselves into attack range of the archers and mages. Still, it was close enough that Lucian could see the faces of the soldiers, even if he couldn't make out much detail in their features.

"Marcus," Lucian said as the Minister of War walked by. "What's the status of the storehouse?"

"With it, we had weeks of food in case we had to last through a siege. But now ... a couple days at best."

"Not enough time to call for reinforcements, then."

"No. We've got no choice but to fight now."

A small force broke from Henrik's army and marched forward. As they drew near, it became obvious that they wanted to speak. Though the Archduke himself wasn't among the men.

He's afraid of making himself a target while attempting to negotiate, huh? Well, I don't have that luxury.

Lucian made his way to the section of the wall where the men were approaching. By the time he got there, Henrik's soldiers were already within speaking distance. Or shouting distance, to be exact.

"His Majesty Henrik Mathison Almekia is an understanding ruler!" a soldier yelled from below. "Any who throw down their arms will be forgiven! And the one who brings us Lucian's head will be rewarded with riches!"

"You want my head? Then tell Henrik to come and take it!"

"Prince Lucian! You are outnumbered over 2 to 1, and your food supply has been set ablaze! You have no chance of victory nor time to call for reinforcements! Surrender now, and maybe His Majesty will show mercy!"

"Like he showed mercy to my father and brothers? Or how he mercifully sent an assassin to finish the job? No, I've had enough of Henrik's mercy for one lifetime!"

"Even so! His Majesty still wishes to avoid bloodshed! He's giving you until tomorrow morning to think upon his kind offer! We hope that by the sun's next visit, you'll be wise enough to accept!"

Lucian turned from the group, indicating that he'd heard all he needed.

Giving me until the morning? It's almost dark, so don't pretend like you're doing me some kind of favor when you just don't want to fight at night.

No, could it be he plans to send an assassin?

Or is he hoping my men mutiny after seeing their numbers?

No matter what his reason, I can't waste this chance.

"Emilia. Let's get ready."

"Understood. But what are we going to do?"

"We're going to drastically increase our chances of victory while we still can. Well, either that or we're going to mess up and get killed."

"Eh!? What do you have in mind?"

"There's still a group of soldiers who haven't been dragged into this battle, and I'm going to go get them."

Lucian led the way back down the wall, heading toward the castle.

Chapter 26

The pattering of soft footsteps echoed down a stone corridor. Unlike most of the people in the building, the one walking down the dark hall was wearing a pair of shoes, rather than boots.

Although Liliana—or Lily, as she was known—was walking slowly, it wasn't because she was relaxed. Rather, it was the exact opposite. She could barely contain her anxiety, which was why she was pacing in the hallway in the first place.

What are we going to do? What are we going to do?

Lily reached the end of the hall, so she turned and began pacing in the other direction.

The Council should be the ones to make this decision, not me!

How am I supposed to choose which side to take in a civil war!?

No, are they really giving us a choice? From the way Archduke Henrik was talking, it was clear he expected us to help him take the castle...

Lily stopped in front of a door. Sleeping within were nearly two dozen white haired beastfolk. At least, they should be sleeping. But Lily doubted they could force themselves to sleep after the events that transpired today. She sure couldn't.

If only the archduke would allow us to speak with the council...

Lily reached to her head and rubbed one of her squirrel-like ears. It was a habit of hers when she was lost in thought. She could never get rid of it, and it was those types of gestures that made her especially poor at games like poker.

However, unlike the other beastfolk, Lily's hair was a dark brown. She wasn't here in the white-haired garrison as a trainee like Emilia. Rather, she was a representative of sorts, answering to the Council of Elders who watched over most of the beastfolk in the Almekian Kingdom.

Even though they were labeled as dangerous and had their rights restricted, white-haired beastfolk were still part of her race, which meant it was the council's responsibility to make sure they were treated humanely.

As humanely as soldiers training for war could be, at least.

Is the archduke really going to make them fight against the crown prince?

They're just trainees. The contract says they can't be conscripted until they finish their training. But...

Lily thought back on her discussion with Archduke Henrik. In the end, she managed to maintain the white hair trainees' neutrality, but she expected him to return. He even left guards to protect the white hairs, or so he claimed.

But Lily knew the real reason he left his men was to prevent them from escaping until Henrik could return with whatever he intends to use as an excuse to conscript the trainees.

Emilia. I hope you're safe.

Emilia had been with Prince Lucian when news of the civil war broke. That meant if the white hairs were to be conscripted by Henrik, there was a good chance they'd end up fighting against her.

Lily turned from the door where the male trainees were sleeping. Although she had been doing a lot of thinking, she wasn't any closer to the answers.

She began her pacing again, walking down the stretch of hall that led toward the girl's sleeping quarters. But before she could make it two steps, a scream stopped her in place.

It echoed down the hall, making it hard to know where it came from. However, there were only so many possibilities in the small garrison.

What's going on!? Are we under attack!?

The door next to Lily opened. As expected, the white hair trainees were wide awake. When they heard the scream, they naturally wanted to know what was going on, with their unofficial leader, Sigurd, opening the door.

"Stay in your room," Lily said to Sigurd.

"But what about—"

Another yell reached their ears. Afterwards, the sounds of clashing metal could be heard in the distance.

"Without enhancement magic, you can't fight soldiers," Lily said. "And we don't have authorization to enhance you."

"But still...!" Sigurd visibly disagreed.

"Get geared up, but don't leave the room. I'm going to go find out what's going on."

"That's too dangerous, Lily! You don't even know how to fight!"

"That means I'm not a threat, so I shouldn't be a target. Hopefully..."

Sigurd obviously didn't agree with Lily's order, but she outranked him. As a soldier trainee, he had no choice but to obey her orders.

The door closed, and Lily heard the white hairs within putting on their equipment.

Ohhhh! Why is everything going crazy all at once!?

Even though she called it crazy, Lily already had a good idea of what was going on. The archduke had stationed his own men around the garrison. Lily thought the real reason was to prevent the white hairs from leaving, but there was another reason for Henrik to station his men there.

Has the battle between Archduke Henrik and Prince Lucian already begun?

But the sun only went down a few hours ago. Weren't they going to wait until the morning?

No matter how much she thought about it, Lily wouldn't find the answers in the stone hallway. So, she started walking toward the sounds of battle.

What am I doing!? I'm not a soldier!

But I can't send the others out until I know what's going on!

Ohhh! I hope I don't end up regretting this!

Lily tiptoed around a corner and peered down another hall. Her first priority was to make it to the girls' room, where the female white hairs slept. They were stationed on the other end of the building, but the fighting hadn't yet reached them.

That meant Lily had an opening to make it to them and tell them the same thing she told the males. Gear up and stay inside.

Seeing that the hall was clear, Lily dashed down it, her eyes focused on the far wall, where the corridor turned and led to the girls' room.

Precisely halfway down the hall, another path intersected it. It led toward the garrison's only exit, and it was there that she had heard the sounds of battle.

Lily wasn't a soldier. Even though she had a military rank, she was an administrative officer, meant only to help manage the white hair trainees at the facility. If she were a soldier, perhaps she would have noticed that the fighting had already ended.

Lily reached that intersection with the path that led to the exit. She had intended to run right by it, but when she passed it, she took a glance and saw a figure standing within.

In that frozen moment of time while Lily was running past the intersection, she saw the glint of a sword held in the person's hand. From its tip dripped a thick, red liquid, coloring the stone floor one drop at a time.

The sight was so shocking that Lily stopped dead in her tracks, staring down the hall toward that figure. That's when she noticed.

Red eyes, glowing in the darkness, and...

...White hair!?

The figure had long since noticed Lily. They had already taken several steps toward her in the time it took for Lily to realize what it was that she was seeing.

Lily gulped. But she didn't run.

"Lily," the figure said after coming to a stop. "You're coming with us."

"Emilia..." Lily looked into her fierce eyes. "Why are you here...?"

"Isn't it obvious? I'm here to collect you and my companions. There's no way we're going to let Archduke Henrik conscript you into his army."

"That ... is what I expected. But that look, you've been enhanced by magic. Does that mean..."

"Correct," a voice called out from behind Emilia. "I enhanced her myself."

"Prince Lucian!" Lily fell to one knee.

"Stand. We don't have time for formalities. We need to get the others and leave before reinforcements arrive."

"Ah, right!"

Lily had become obedient because of the sudden appearance of Emilia and the prince, but when she thought about it, having the trainees conscripted by Lucian wasn't any better than having them conscripted by Henrik.

No, isn't it worse? I heard the archduke outnumbers the prince by a lot. Doesn't that mean they're in more danger by fighting for him?

Despite her thoughts, Lily had no choice but to lead the two toward the trainees' rooms. Since the men already understood what was happening, she decided to start by turning around and taking the prince to their room first.

She knocked on the door, and Sigurd opened it.

"Lily and ... Emilia!? You're enhanced!"

"Aren't you forgetting to greet someone, Sigurd?" Emilia said with an arrogant tone.

"Ah, Prince Lucian!"

"Don't even think of formalities," Lucian said. "Just come with us."

Sigurd looked to Lily, who nodded. With that, the nearly two dozen male white hairs filled the hall, falling in line behind Emilia.

They visited the girls' room next, and after a quick explanation, the girls fell in with the others. Since there were less than a dozen females, Lucian ended up leading a group of around 30 white haired beastfolk back to the garrison's front entrance.

When Lily stepped foot outside, she finally saw the extent of the fighting that had taken place. Nearly twenty soldiers were lying on the bloodied ground outside the barracks, some near the entrance, others strewn throughout the facility's yard.

Not everyone on the outside was on the ground, though. The camp's commander was standing next to a group of soldiers, their armor an almost perfect match to the ones worn by the dead men. In fact, some of them were a perfect match, as Lucian and his soldiers didn't take this facility without casualties of their own.

"Commander," Lucian said after they met up with the soldiers. "We're vacating the training facility."

"Yes, Your Highness." He didn't sound disturbed about the whole incident.

"Everyone, follow me. We've got a way to get over the wall, but we need to hurry before the enemy–"

Lucian cut his words short when the sound of marching boots began to fill the air.

"Tch. They're here already. Let's go!"

There were nearly 40 of them now, but only a handful were actual soldiers. The rest would have to be protected during battle, especially since a white hair couldn't cast magic on their own. They'd be at a huge disadvantage against properly trained and enhanced soldiers, if it came to a fight.

Fortunately, the wall that surrounded the castle wasn't far. The training facility for white hairs was deemed too dangerous to keep within the castle walls, but having it too far from their center of power was risky, as well.

So, it was built just a stone's throw away. Far enough that the king could sleep without fear of a group of white hairs suddenly going berserk in his home but close enough that they could keep a tight leash on their prized weapons.

In just a couple minutes, the wall appeared. With a quick whistle from one of the men, three ladders dropped down.

Lucian motioned toward the female beastfolk. "Go."

Three at a time, the trainees began to climb. After several batches, the girls were all either on the ladder or atop the wall. So, the boys lined up next.

But before a single one could get their feet onto the first rung, the sound of marching boots began to fill the air.

"There they are!" a soldier yelled from down a road. "They're escaping over the wall!"

"Emilia!" Lucian yelled.

"Easy prey."

Lily watched in horror as an entire squad of soldiers appeared from around a corner. They had at least twice as many battle-ready fighters as her group, and they didn't hesitate to charge right at her and the beastfolk she was with.

However, a white blur zipped across her vision, heading straight toward the approaching men.

Emilia, no!

Lily looked toward Prince Lucian, who had ordered the girl to charge right toward over a dozen armed and trained soldiers.

Why!? Is she just a tool to buy time!?

No matter how powerful a white haired beastfolk was when enhanced, defeating so many battle-hardened soldiers was impossible for a mere trainee. Even one as strong as Emilia.

But what she didn't realize was that Emilia wasn't enhanced by just any mage.

W-what the...

This is ... Emilia!?

The girl hit their ranks like a whirlwind, tearing through them with reckless abandon. But despite being alone, it was the soldiers who began hitting the ground.

By the time Lucian's men finally got to the battle to support Emilia, nearly half the enemies had been wiped out.

Together, they cleaned up the rest without a single lost life. On Lucian's side, anyway. Plenty of the enemy's lives were lost during the encounter.

With the battle complete, Emilia walked back to the wall and looked at the ladders. The last of the beastfolk had finally begun climbing, but that wasn't what interested Lily at the moment.

She's ... bleeding.

Several cuts on Emilia's body dripped red blood. But the young girl didn't seem to pay it any mind, as if the wounds weren't even worth considering.

Lucian, however, thought differently.

"You're too reckless," he said. "You should have waited for the soldiers and engaged as a team."

"And let them steal my prey?"

Lucian sighed. "Well, let's get over the wall before anyone else shows up."

The prince motioned for Lily to take one of the ladders, while he and Emilia took the others. Finally, the soldiers came up last, and the ladders were pulled up.

Over 40 people stood on the walkway atop the wall, most of which were white hair trainees. The operation had been a success, but that didn't mean everything would suddenly fall into place from then on.

Is he going to make them join the battle? Lily thought. *To fight and die, even though they're not even done training?*

That's...

She looked at Prince Lucian. The man was already directing everyone toward a guard tower where they could use the stairs to get down from the wall.

...No better than what Archduke Henrik had planned for them.

Chapter 27

"Has there been any retaliation from our mission?" Lucian asked.

"No, Your Highness," a soldier replied. "There hasn't been any activity reported anywhere on the wall."

"Good. But the night is still young, so we can't count out the possibility that Henrik's waiting until the right time."

"Understood. We'll keep a careful watch and perform a change of shifts in sections, rather than all at once."

At Lucian's nod, the man exited the meeting room to return to his post. He was the captain in charge of organizing the guards, including where the individual squads were posted and when they would change shifts.

Lucian was glad to have someone else to fill that role, since he was sure he'd only mess it up if he took charge. Marcus could do it, but as the Minister of War, he had his own responsibilities to deal with, so he oversaw the captain's work, rather than performing it himself.

Although it was Lucian's idea, Marcus was the one who drew up the plans on how to successfully rescue the white hairs. Now that they'd completed the mission, it was time for a little debriefing to get everyone up to speed.

That's why they all sat in the castle's large meeting room, the trainees included. Over 40 people occupied the chairs within, filling the room to capacity. Looking around, most had white hair, matched with a worried expression.

"Now," Lucian said. "Let's deal with the most pressing issue."

Lily stood from her chair. "Your Highness, my name is Liliana, and I'm the current Council of Elders representative stationed within the training facility."

"Yes, I've heard. You're in charge of making sure that the trainees are treated fairly, aren't you?"

"That is correct. They may have white hair, but they're still beastfolk, like me. The crown and council struck a deal, ensuring that they wouldn't be trained as sacrifices for the army. Hence why they always appoint a representative to oversee their training."

Lucian nodded. "Understandable. Considering the stigma against them, I suppose it's a fair deal. Unfortunately, we're unable to contact the Council of Elders in our current situation, so you'll have to speak on their behalf."

Lily flinched. "A-about that. According to the contract, the trainees can't be forced into war until their six months of training are complete. I know this is a difficult predicament, but these young beastkin are still unprepared for battle!

"In fact, some of them arrived a few weeks ago, and they've only just begun combat training! There's no way they can fight against an army of hardened veterans, even when enhanced! I know many people think that a white haired beastfolk are fearsome warriors, but without training, even they're not capable of defeating a real army!"

After her long speech, Lily slowly sat back down into her chair, looking more horrified by the second.

What was I thinking!? I'll be thrown in a cell for sure! Or worse!

There's no way he'll just let thirty powerful soldiers sit idle while he fights for his very survival, even if it means breaking the contract the royal family made with the council!

Lily hoped that the sweat drop she felt sliding down the side of her face was only a figment of her imagination. Or at least that nobody had seen it.

Lucian sat back in his chair at the head of the table. "Emilia told me of the contract long ago. However, she still decided to fight for me, regardless. Do you know why?"

Because you forced her to? Lily didn't voice her real thoughts, of course.

"Umm ... I'm not sure..."

"Care to explain, Emilia?"

"Of course, Prince Lucian."

The young girl swept her gaze over Lily and the white hairs, her trainee companions.

She no longer lived with them, ate with them, or trained with them. Her new position as the captain of Lucian's guards tore her away from that life. But she hadn't forgotten.

"I know how many of you feel," Emilia said. "Uncertain about what fate awaits you once you're shipped off to war. Worried that the lip service they give us about white hairs being treated fairly is nothing but a lie to get us to the battlefield.

"I had those same fears. Some of you even shared yours with me. We're a feared and hated race, after all. If we're treated so badly in society, then why would it be any different in the army?

"Many of you only joined because you had no other choice. Nobody will give work to us, and nobody will buy anything we make. The world is full of doors, but they're all closed to us. Except for the one you chose.

"But Prince Lucian opened a door for me that I never dreamed of stepping through. He cast away the darkness of uncertainty and set me on a path filled with light. And it's one I chose to walk of my own free will.

"Now all of you have a choice to make. The contract prevents Prince Lucian from forcing you onto the battlefield, but there's nothing stopping you from going if you choose to do so. I know it's a lot to ask when you're not even fully trained, but if you want to give our people a chance to become truly accepted by this world, then we need Prince Lucian.

"Unlike everyone else, he doesn't discriminate against us, not even a single bit. If he ascends to the throne, then perhaps the doors that have been closed to us all our lives will truly begin to open. For me, that's a future worth fighting for."

Emilia bowed her head to the trainees. She wasn't ordering them as the captain of the Royal Guard. She was asking them. Asking them to risk their lives for the prince she had come to adore. In her mind, such a speech could only be topped off with an honest bow.

There was a moment of silence in the meeting room. Many of the trainees were simply too stunned to respond, having had the choice placed in their individual laps. But there was one among them who was able to keep up with the sudden turn of events.

"You're asking them to choose?" Lily asked. "What if they say no?"

"Then they can stay in the castle until the fighting is over," Lucian said.

"Just like that? You're going to let a powerful fighting force sit the battle out?"

"The contract is clear. I don't have the authority to make them fight, and I'm not going to break the terms of our deal just because things are grim. If we have to, we'll fight without a single one of them."

Lily was shocked. "Then why bring us here? Because you were afraid we'd become your enemies if Archduke Henrik got his hands on us?"

"Yes, I won't deny that removing you from the battle is beneficial to me, since Henrik would likely field you against us. And at the same time, there's a chance I can voluntarily acquire your aid in the upcoming battle, so there's no downside risk. But the most important factor was putting you in a position where you are free to choose, rather than coerced with threats. And I believe here is the only place where you can truly decide your own fates."

Lily looked to the thirty trainees that she was responsible for. She always knew they'd be shipped off to war. That was precisely what they trained for.

But only after they were ready.

Right now, most of them only had a couple months of training, not nearly enough to step onto a battlefield. Especially the newest arrivals, who had only been with them for a few weeks.

Is the prince really just going to let them hide in the castle?

Nobody would allow a group of white hair warriors to sit idle in this situation, even if they're trainees.

Lily turns back to Prince Lucian. "Can we have some time to discuss this amongst ourselves?"

"That's fine. You have until tomorrow morning to decide. We'll need to adjust our plans based on everyone's decisions, after all."

"Thank you."

"Then, you can use a few of our empty rooms." He turned to Emilia. "Would you like to join them for the night?"

"Yes, I would love to."

Lily and the trainees followed Emilia out of the meeting room and down the hall. It was in these rooms that they would stay the night. And it was also here that they would decide their own fate.

"These two are empty." Emilia pointed to a pair of doors. "If we get some bedrolls, the guys should be able to fit in them for a night. There's another room around the corner for the girls, and you can have your own room if you wish, Lily."

"No, I don't mind staying with the girls tonight."

"Understood. Then…" Emilia waved over a castle maid. "Please gather enough bedrolls for everyone here and place them in these rooms."

Emilia took the young woman around, showing her the three rooms Lily and the white hairs would be staying in. Afterwards, the maid acknowledged her order and set off to start the task.

A particularly expressive girl couldn't hide her excitement any longer. When Emilia returned, the girl spoke before anyone else had a chance to get a word out.

"Wow!" Sara said. "I can't believe the people in the castle actually listen to you. That's amazing!"

"Even I'm still getting used to it. It's fine when Prince Lucian is with me, but it feels strange to give out orders when he's not around."

"But you looked really cool doing it! I'm so jealous, Emilia!"

"I-I don't know about looking cool, or anything…"

Sara might as well have had sparkles in her eyes as she looked at Emilia. The two had become close, despite Emilia putting in little effort to be her friend.

"Rooms are nice and all," Sigurd said. "But where can we talk about what we want to do tomorrow? We can't exactly fit in a single room."

"There's a smaller meeting room nearby that we can use. I'll lead you there, then go request some refreshments."

"Man, life in the castle sure if different, isn't it?"

"Yes. It's convenient. But also restricting."

Sigurd nodded. "Yeah, I don't think I could sit behind these walls all day. Just not for me."

With Emilia seeing to their needs, Lily and the white hairs piled into the meeting room, preparing to decide whether or not they were going to step onto the battlefield by Lucian's side.

Chapter 28

It was a late night, but Lucian eventually went to sleep. He had no choice, if he wanted to be ready for what was coming in the morning.

But it didn't take long for that morning to arrive, the reality of his precipitous situation hitting him with the force of an exam that he had failed to study for.

At least there wasn't an attack last night. That could have ruined everything.

No, maybe it would be better if he did attack. I wonder how much of an advantage the walls really give us...

After throwing off his covers, Lucian immediately made himself presentable. The last thing he wanted on a day like this was for the soldiers' crown prince to come out looking as insecure as he felt.

As was often the case, Lucian was up before the sun. That meant he lacked a full night's sleep, but there were just too many things to do both before bed and after waking. Time waited for nobody, even a tired prince.

Stepping out of his room, Lucian made haste to the meeting room they used quite often. He was the first to arrive, so he took his seat and waited, trying not to look too tired.

It's times like this that I'd like a nice, hot cup of coffee.

Unfortunately, he hadn't passed by any maids on the way there, and he wasn't about to send a soldier out to fetch one. If the men had to go without, then so should their ruler.

"Morning, brother." Mia gave him a small bow for appearance's sake. "You awoke even earlier than normal."

"Guess I was a bit excited about today."

Excited, he said. More like nervous, but that wouldn't be very kingly.

"So you're going through with it," Mia said.

"Yeah. If we're going to do battle eventually, then I might as well take the initiative, right?"

"I suppose..."

The door opened again, and Emilia stepped through. She looked saddened to see that she was the last of the three to arrive, even though it was only by a few seconds.

She had an even later night than the other two, though. Lucian gave her a mission, and of course the hard-working fox-eared girl wouldn't let something like a lack of sleep prevent her from finishing it.

"Good morning, Prince Lucian." She took her place diagonally behind him.

"Hello, Emilia. How did it go last night?"

"I have high hopes for several of them."

"I'm glad to hear that. And what about you? Did you sleep well? It's been a while since you spent the night with your fellow white hairs, hasn't it?"

"Ah, yes! They bombarded me with so many questions! About what I do now, how I'm treated, where I get to go, and a lot more! We were always close because of our situation, but I was worried that might have changed. It didn't! They were as talkative as ever!

"Ah, of course I left out the stuff I can't say. In fact, every time I told them I couldn't talk about something, they seemed to get even more excited! I guess everyone likes a good mystery, huh? They were always some of my favorite types of novels, so I can see why!"

Lucian cracked a smile. "Sounds like you had some fun. That's good. I hope we have many more nights like that ahead of us."

The door opened again. This time, it was the final major player in their castle defense, Marcus. The man was a warrior, through and through. Large body, commanding voice, and a tone that demanded obedience.

He strode into the room seemingly without care about whatever was going on inside. Instead, he headed directly to the table and began to move pieces around on the map.

When Lucian first met Marcus, he didn't have much faith in the man. He was one of the four ministers, making him a candidate as the assassin looking to take out the royal family. He was also loud and vocal, ignoring the typical etiquette that other nobles followed.

But when things turned sour, Marcus was the only one of the ministers to rise to the challenge, going so far as to lead Lucian's defense against a numerically superior foe.

It's no wonder he became the Minister of War.

With his help, winning this battle might not be so hard, after all.

"Made a few changes to the wall defense last night," Marcus said to nobody in particular.

"Was there a problem?"

"No, but it's good to keep the enemy guessing. They probably spent a good amount of time yesterday going over our men's positions. Now that time and effort was wasted."

"Ah, makes sense. Good work, Marcus."

The man didn't reply. He was fully focused on his task of updating the pieces to their new positions.

"By the way, Marcus. Why is it that you decided to fight with me?"

"What do you mean?" His hand never stopped.

"The other ministers just so happened to leave the castle the day of the invasion, yet you stayed behind. Wouldn't it have been easier to join Archduke Henrik instead of fighting an uphill battle with me?"

"I wouldn't be so sure that the other ministers defected. I received a message the morning of the attack. Someone asked to meet me in town to discuss something of 'vital importance'. If I had gone, I'd likely have been captured by the archduke's men."

Lucian's eyes widened at the revelation. "So the other ministers could have gotten a similar letter and are being held captive? That certainly makes sense, though you were likely their primary target for obvious reasons. By the way, what did you do with the letter?"

"Tossed it in the fireplace, of course. I don't have time to meet with some coward who won't even sign their name on the letter."

"Hah." A genuine laugh escaped Lucian's mouth. "Well, that stubbornness worked out in our favor, that's for sure."

Marcus turned toward one of the guards. "Bring the beastfolk. If they're sleeping, wake them up."

"They're awake," Emilia said. "And they're ready."

"Good. Then I expect them here on the double."

The guard saluted, then left. When he returned a short while later, he was trailed by thirty beastfolk with white hair, and one with brown.

Lily was at the head of her group of trainees, as if acting as their captain. She didn't have any fighting experience, but there were more types of battlefields than just one where armies clashed.

As an administrator, Lily had been to many meetings. Although her position was only supposed to be an intermediary between the trainees and the Council of Elders, she had no choice but to take charge now that she was cut off from the council.

She's dedicated, I'll give her that, Lucian thought.

It'd be nice to have someone like her on our side after we squash the rebellion.

"Care to take a seat?" Lucian motioned toward a chair meant for Lily.

"If it's all the same, I'd prefer to stand."

"That so? Well, the decision is yours." Lucian turned his gaze to Lily's white hair companions. "Speaking of decisions, I assume you've come to one about our request?"

"Yes..." Lily looked hesitant. "The trainees will be–"

"Please," a young white hair man said, "allow me."

"Sigurd. Sure, you can be the one to say it."

"Thank you." Sigurd met Lucian's gaze. "Your Highness, as Emilia said, all of us chose to join the army because there are almost no other paths for us. We can't even live in a city without constant harassment. People think we should be fighting for them, giving our lives so that they can be safe.

"But none of them ever stop to think about what we want. Although nobody forced us to join the army, it's essentially the only way for us to live in this kingdom. So, when you said you were leaving the decision in our hands, of course none of us wanted to fight. We never did, from the very beginning.

"But you gave us a choice, Your Highness. When almost nobody else would, you left it up to us to decide our own fate. And I think that makes you worth fighting for. In fact, all of us agree. We will be joining you in the battle."

"Sigurd..." Emilia said softly. "Thank you. We won't disappoint you!"

"Then it's settled." Lucian sat back in his chair. "But I can't take all of you."

"Huh!?" Sigurd looked flabbergasted.

"Liliana said some of you had only just arrived at the training facility before all this mess started. I can't send anyone without at least a couple months' worth of training."

"It's true that some of us are fresh, but they'll still fight."

"No, I can't agree to that." Lucian looked to Lily. "Select only those who have at least two months of training. The rest will wait in the castle."

"Alright." She called the names of one trainee after the next. "All of you will remain here, as His Highness commanded."

The trainees separated into two groups, one that will be fighting and one that won't. Lucian counted the group that would be joining him on the battlefield, noting that 21 of the 30 trainees met the two months requirement.

"Um, Your Highness." Lily spoke with a bit of reservation. "Do you already know where the trainees will be fighting?"

"I do have a plan for them already, though we're still working out the details of the battle plan overall."

"Ah, I see. Well, um, you don't intend to send them in alone, right?"

"Alone? Why would I do something like that?"

Lily relaxed a little. "It's just that many soldiers don't trust them after they've been enhanced, since..."

"Ah, since they go berserk. Well, there's no way I'm sending under trained soldiers on a suicide mission, if that's what you're worried about. In fact, I planned on keeping them with me."

Lily gave him a look of surprise. "With you, Your Highness?"

"Having them with me means there's no need to worry about how the other soldiers would feel to be fighting alongside them. And since I don't care about the prejudice against them, it doesn't bother me at all."

"I see. I guess that's for the best, then."

"It is. But forget about that for now." Lucian motioned to a guard. "Go to the kitchen and tell the cooks we're ready to eat."

While the man was gone, Lucian and Marcus began to go over some of the finer details of the upcoming battle. There were still a lot of unknowns, so they could only hope that they were prepared enough to deal with whatever Archduke Henrik had planned.

But not everything was going badly.

Henrik forced our hand by destroying our food supply, Lucian thought. *Now, we have no choice but to abandon our walls and attack him. If we don't, we'll starve and my own men will likely hand me over.*

But that also means he's giving us the initiative. Even if he has twice as many men, we'll be the ones who choose when and where to attack.

Maybe that advantage will be enough...

The cooks arrived. Many of them. So many that the trainees began to openly gawk at all the freshly cooked food that began to fill the table.

Along with it came the smell of various cuts of meat, flavored with the best spices in the entire kingdom. It was a meal literally fit for a king.

"Well," Lucian said. "Eat up. We'll need the energy soon enough."

"Us too?" Sigurd asked.

"Of course. Why do you think I asked them to bring in so much? I can't eat it all by myself!" He turned to the nine beastfolk who were sitting the battle out. "That includes you. You better not go back to your rooms hungry."

"But ... weren't we low on food?" Lily asked.

"I had all the food in the storehouse brought to the castle. The cooks have been working hard through the night to make a feast. Not just for us but for all of the soldiers. If they're going to risk their lives to protect me, then I can at least give them a meal worth eating."

"Does that mean ... we won't need a stockpile of food?"

"That's right. Because in a couple hours, the battle will begin. Whether we win or lose, the food won't do us any good sitting here uneaten."

And so, Lucian and those who fought for him were in the final moments of their precarious peace. After their meal, preparations for combat would truly begin.

Chapter 29

"There," Marcus said, pointing toward the enemy army. "A weakness in their defense."

Lucian looked out over the wall's edge, directly where Marcus was pointing. However, the prince couldn't see this supposed opening. There were fewer enemy troops gathered in front of him, but the same could be said of many sections of the wall.

I'll just have to rely on Marcus for things like this. There's a reason he leads our army in the wars.

"Then we exploit that weakness," Lucian said.

"We'll attack from there." Marcus pointed to the nearest gate. "You and the white hairs charge the opening. Once you're behind their line ... the rest is obvious."

"Attack Archduke Henrik and end the battle."

"Right now, we have the advantage of surprise. They don't know when or where we'll attack, but as soon as we start moving troops, they'll prepare for battle."

Lucian nodded. "I'm ready."

Lucian looked out over the streets below. Although it was early, the sun had already begun its ascent in the sky, giving him plenty of light to see. Soldiers were scattered about, watching his men for signs of movement.

Because both sides had the same armor, Henrik had outfitted his men with red tabards to prevent friendly fire during an intense melee. The sight of hundreds of men standing in blood-red outfits was certainly an unnerving sight.

Most of the soldiers were near the gates, the only exits Lucian had. But because the enemy troops didn't know what Lucian had planned, they could only spread out to cover the perimeter of the castle wall.

Once they realized Lucian was making his move, they'd quickly adapt. That meant the first few minutes were crucial to the success of the plan.

Break out of the castle wall, establish a foothold, and attack the weak point.

Marcus was tasked with creating that foothold, giving space for Lucian and the white hairs to break through the soldiers and attack Henrik.

The Archduke's flag flew well behind the main body of soldiers. Knowing he had the advantage, the man opted to sit in safety, rather than step onto the battlefield himself.

Lucian didn't have that luxury.

"The general will be guarded by his most powerful warriors," Marcus said. "Even if you reach him, winning won't be easy."

Lucian nodded. "I know. But it's the only chance we've got to put an end to this uprising here and now. If he escapes, he may come back with another army."

"Just don't forget that the enemy has the same victory conditions. If they capture you, we'll be defeated then and there."

"I know. But I can't afford to play it safe."

Lucian still wasn't aware, but the subtle changes to his temperament were due to his new body. Although small, a fragment of the former prince still lived inside him in the form of his hormones, chemical makeup, and latent memories.

Those little bits influenced the man formerly known as Thomas George Hamilton. The politician from Earth would have had a much more difficult time accepting the recent events he had experienced, were it not for those changes.

However, there was a common saying that society was nine meals away from anarchy. Although modern people on Earth often virtue signaled their superiority to people of the past, their grandstanding would cease if they were forced to go even three days without food.

The plan's already in motion. From here on, the battle has effectively begun.

The small army at Lucian's disposal couldn't attack from the wall, so word was spread to the commanders to bring their squads to the southern gate, where the assault would begin.

It would only be a matter of time before the enemy noticed his troop's movements, so speed was a necessity. As the one in charge, Lucian made sure to be one of the first to arrive, Emilia at his side.

"Prince Lucian, how many of us are you going to enhance with your powerful magic?"

"If I cast it on too many at once, the effectiveness will drop, right?"

"Yes. It's best to only enhance a single person at a time, but if you have to use it on multiple, it's said that three is a good number, and never more than five."

"Hmm. Then let's go with three. The rest will be enhanced by the other soldiers."

If only I could use my magic on everyone. We'd easily be able to win this battle...

Unfortunately, rules existed that limited what a mage could do. With the long cooldown on casting support spells, it wasn't easy to enhance more than a handful of soldiers.

The men were still gathering, so all Lucian could do was wait for everything to fall into place.

The white hairs were already lined up behind Lucian, looking nervous. He felt those same nerves, but he couldn't afford to show them to anyone.

"Sigurd, was it?" Lucian looked at the white hair who gave the speech this morning.

"Yes, Your Highness."

"You're the most experienced of the trainees, and I heard you've got some skill with the sword. I'll be enhancing you, Emilia, and..."

"Her, Prince Lucian." Emilia pointed to a female trainee.

"Yes, her. You three will receive my magic, while the rest are enhanced by soldiers."

"I understand," Sigurd said. "But is it fine to spread your magic out between the three of us?"

"No problem." Emilia responded in Lucian's stead. "The prince's spell is really strong. You'll see soon."

"Right. Then I have no complaints."

Even without any expertise on the battlefield, Lucian could tell that Marcus and the soldiers were nearly ready. The influx of men from the walls had slowed to a trickle, while the ones near the gate stood in a battle-ready formation.

"They know what we're up to," Marcus said. "We should expect a tough battle on the other side of that gate."

Lucian looked to the gate in question. "That's what I anticipated from the beginning."

There wasn't any more time to spare. Nearly all the men were ready, Lucian included. As ready as he could be, anyway.

So when Marcus turned to him with a look like he was expecting orders, Lucian raised his hand, drawing the men's attention.

"Open the gate!"

The gate standing between Lucian and Henrik's army creaked. Then, it began to rise.

"Attack!" Marcus shouted as soon as the gate was high enough for the men to run through.

Suddenly, a wave of bodies moved forward, matched by the deafening clanking of their metal armor as they ran.

There were three hundred men but only one gate. Like a poorly thought-out highway, the gate acted like a choke point, preventing the men from rushing out all at once.

Lucian could only watch on from the back lines as several hundred men squeezed through the opening a handful at a time.

Soon, other sounds began to cut through the noise. Battlecries, yells, and the clashing of metal on metal.

Just behind that gate, men were fighting. Screaming. Dying.

All under Lucian's command.

Soon, it was Lucian's turn to rush forward. The bulk of his men had already made it out onto the streets beyond the gate, opening the path for him and the white hairs.

Lucian and his entourage filled the space outside the gate, stepping onto the battlefield. For now, they were still in the safety of the foothold provided by Marcus' surprise charge. But they wouldn't be in the backlines for long.

"That way!" Lucian pointed to the right, where a street ran parallel to the wall.

"Everyone, follow me!" Emilia took the lead, rushing down the path that would bring them to the weak spot Marcus saw from the wall.

Lucian ran in the very center of the group, along with several other human soldiers. Surrounding them were the white hairs, Emilia at their head.

Fortunately for the group, Marcus managed to engage most of the enemies stationed nearby. However, when stepping onto a battlefield, it was inevitable that they'd be confronted with soldiers.

"Enemies ahead!" Emilia yelled.

"It's time, then!" Lucian turned to the humans he brought with him. "Cast!"

Several chants filled the air, the soldiers using their unique variations despite all casting the same spell. Lucian's voice was among the ones chanting, the prince secretly relieved that his words would be lost in the sounds of battle.

"Divine Goddess, grant them power! [Enhance]!"

Lucian could feel the energy ripped from his body. With it went some of his strength, leaving him feeling winded.

But the reverse was true for Emilia. His spell hit her like a scorching fireball, enveloping her with a power that couldn't be matched by any other mage she'd ever met.

That same strength filled Sigurd and the third white hair he targeted. And with it emerged the fearsome personas that sat dormant within each of their special kind.

"Finally," Emilia said with a smile. "I get to have some fun."

Sigurd stepped forward. "If there are any left for you when I'm done."

"Don't think you can hog all the excitement for yourselves." A third white hair spoke from the group.

Without exception, each of the 21 leaked a deadly bloodlust so thick that even an untrained warrior like Lucian could feel it.

No wonder Emilia advised against casting our magic until the last moment.

It was standard knowledge in the army that enhancing white hairs should only be done at the last minute.

Having enhanced Emilia several times now, Lucian understood why. But being surrounded by nearly two dozen white hairs, each in their Berserked state, really emphasized why the army adopted the practice.

"Emilia!" Lucian yelled. "Don't forget the objective!"

"Hmph. I don't need a reminder."

That was all the response Emilia had time for. The enemy soldiers were close enough that from a warrior's perspective, the battle had already begun.

He'd seen it from the wall, but up close, the red tabards that Henrik's men were wearing to distinguish themselves made the squad of soldiers look like they were already soaked in the blood of their enemies.

Ahead of Lucian, the unmistakable sound of clashing metal rang out as the two sides finally met. Even though he wasn't in the skirmish, Lucian still flinched when they charged into each other.

I hate this. Just standing here while they risk their lives in battle...

As he was, Lucian would only be a liability if he fought. He was enhanced by a normal soldier, so he wasn't lacking in strength. But he couldn't afford to be recognized.

Like the white hairs, Lucian was wearing a normal soldier's outfit, making them appear like any other group fighting in the streets. If the enemy were to find out that his group contained the crown prince that they're fighting to depose, then the entire might of the army would be turned against them.

It truly was a risky and desperate plan. But one that would reward them with a decisive victory if they could pull it off.

As expected of a group of Berserked white hairs, Emilia and the others quickly overwhelmed the soldiers they faced. Though a large part of that was due to the enormous strength of the three white hairs Lucian enhanced.

So that's the difference between a normal white hair and one I enhance.

I only used a quarter of my mana, yet the three I cast the spell on are so much stronger than the others.

The more mana he put into his spells, the greater the effect. But unlike the first time he used the magic, he couldn't afford to drain himself until he could barely stand. Not on the battlefield.

Yet even though he held back, the three he enhanced were quicker, tougher, and stronger than the rest. So much so that even Lucian could easily see the difference.

"W-white hairs!?" A soldier's voice cut through the noise.

Standing just in front of the man was a girl whose helmet had been knocked off, revealing her white hair and furry ears. Such a sight on the battlefield was feared by the average soldier, especially when it was unexpected.

"Now that you know," Emilia said. "You die."

The enemies who fought until now began to waver at the revelation that they'd been fighting berserked white hairs all along. In seconds, they crumbled under a ferocious assault, panicked soldiers turning their backs and running with all their might.

A bloody scene played out before Lucian. Men cut down as they fled, chased by the rampaging berserkers that even veteran soldiers feared.

Not good! If we get all spread out, we'll never break through to Henrik!

"Emilia!" Lucian yelled.

A girl turned, and Lucian could see her red eyes staring back at him. That one glance was all she gave him before looking away.

"Get back here, trainees!" Emilia shouted. "Or we'll leave without you!"

Fortunately, most of the enemies were defeated in the chaos, meaning there wasn't much prey left for the berserked beastfolk to chase. A few did manage to flee, though there was a bigger problem than that.

"We're missing two," Emilia said after they regrouped.

Lucian looked around. "I don't see any of ours on the ground."

"They gave in to the thirst and chased the men who retreated."

"That's bad. By themselves, they'll probably run into a group of soldiers and get killed."

"..."

Sara. Emilia looked in the direction her friend had run off.

Sara was particularly bad at controlling her berserked state. Emilia had told herself that she'd keep an eye on her, but she too had given in to the bloodlust until Lucian called her name.

Emilia wasn't the only one who was nervous.

What do I do? Lucian thought.

Do I leave the two missing white hairs and keep going? But they're just trainees. Ones I brought to the battlefield...

There's no time. We can't look for them and make it to Henrik before the enemy figures out our plan. Especially now that soldiers have seen us.

Lucian looked to the white hairs who did return. Many of them were already looking toward another nearby battle, as if itching to join the fight.

I need to decide fast. They won't sit idle for long.

"Sigurd," Lucian said. "Take two others and find the missing trainees. When you get them, meet back up with us."

"Tch." He made a sour face. "Looks like I'll need to teach those two a lesson when I find them."

"Save it for after the battle. For now, just secure their safety."

Sigurd pointed to two white hairs, then the three of them ran off in the direction their missing companions had gone.

Did I make the right choice?

Nobody answered Lucian's internal question.

There was no time to reflect on his decision. Lucian could only hope that Sigurd could find the two white hairs that went missing and bring them back.

With the soldiers defeated, the path ahead was clear once again. The group rushed forward, still heading toward the weakness in Henrik's defensive positioning.

If we can just reach that spot, we'll have a direct path to Henrik. Then this battle will be over.

In Lucian's mind, the quicker he could end it, the better. His men were essentially fighting each other. That's what it meant to wage a civil war.

We can't afford these cracks in our kingdom, not if we want to defeat our real enemy.

It was Lucian's responsibility to find a way to heal the kingdom's wounds. Yet he was stuck battling for the right to even sit on the throne.

Maybe I can—

"Incoming magic!" Emilia's shout interrupted Lucian's thoughts. "Shield's up!"

Although the group was away from the front line of the battle, spells had been landing nearby the entire time. But unlike the previous volleys, the current one was aimed close to their location.

Whether it was chance or a conscious decision to hit them, Lucian wasn't sure. All he knew was that bright spheres of fire and rocks the size of his head were flying right toward them.

Protected by several rows of shield bearers, Lucian could barely even see the sky in the direction of the magic. All he could do was hide behind the white hairs who were protecting him.

A deafening boom made his ears ring as the wall of flesh and steel shook from the power of the spells. Even without being hit directly, Lucian could feel the force of the spells with his own body, making him worry for the ones who shielded him from the magic's power.

Is Emilia alright!?

Perhaps he should be equally worried about all his companions, but he couldn't help single out Emilia in his mind.

"Shields down." Emilia's voice calmed his mind. "Anyone injured?"

Nobody spoke up.

That kind of power hit us, and they didn't even get hurt?

Some were bruised or bloodied from the magic, but nobody sustained any serious injuries. Lucian was beginning to realize just how powerful people could become when enhanced with support spells.

That fact was doubly true for white hairs, who received even more power than an average soldier.

"Good job," Lucian said. "Now let's—"

"I see the mages!" A white hair shouted, interrupting him. "Let's get them!"

Several white hairs vocalized their support, looking to Emilia for the order to charge.

Hey, I'm supposed to be the one in command.

"A bloodbath." Emilia smiles. "That sounds fun."

"Wait." Lucian made his voice as commanding as possible. "Save it for when we meet Henrik. We can't get bogged down here."

"Tch. At least send a few of us to deal with them."

"No. I promised to keep them with me for their safety as much as my own. I won't send them off into a dangerous battle alone."

In their berserked state, the white hairs had almost no regard for their own safety. That meant it was up to Lucian to look after them, even if he had to go against their desires.

No wonder the army has a special division just for the white hairs. Controlling them in battle is no easy task.

Fortunately, Lucian managed to rein in their focus and get them back under his command. Before they could catch sight of more prey, the prince ordered them to move again.

The spot Marcus pinpointed finally appeared ahead of them. It was an alley for a section of the city that was recently rebuilt after a raging fire that engulfed several streets, destroying many of the buildings.

Because of changes to the layout, the alley in front of Lucian ended up connected to several others, forming a small network of paths behind the buildings.

One of those paths ended behind enemy lines, and from their limited information, it wasn't defended.

If we can get behind them, we can force Henrik to fight us without the protection of his army.

And with Emilia and the other white hairs, our chance of victory against him and his personal guards is high.

That was the crux of the plan. Take a powerful fighting force and ambush the enemy general, defeating them before he could use the full might of his army, which easily doubled the size of Lucian's.

The sounds of battle still raged nearby, but Lucian ignored them, ordering everyone into the alley. It was a tight squeeze, with only a few able to stand shoulder to shoulder in the cramped space between the buildings.

They passed an intersecting alley, but the group continued forward.

One.

Another intersection, but still they pressed on.

Two.

Ahead, the alley curved to the right, but Lucian needed to go left, which is why...

Three. This is it.

"That way." Lucian pointed to the left path of the intersecting alley.

"You heard him." Emilia was the first to turn, and the others followed. "And this takes us to the battle?"

"It ends on the same street where Henrik set up his command post. We'll be behind him, so we should be able to force a fight."

"That's all I need to know."

The mouth of the alley came quicker than Lucian expected, with the group finding themselves on a wide, open street.

Pointing left again, Lucian directed Emilia in the direction of Henrik's command post. The road bent, but Lucian was certain he didn't make any mistakes through the city streets and back alleys.

He was at the right spot, and just beyond the curve was the man who started the civil war in a bid to take the crown. Which meant...

The final battle is just ahead.

And it's win or die.

Chapter 30

"There they are!" Lucian yelled as his group rounded the bend.

"There's even enough prey for all of us."

As Emilia said, plenty of soldiers were packed around the command post. There was no way Henrik would send every man to fight, leaving himself vulnerable.

It seemed the Archduke made the right decision, as Lucian managed to sneak around his defensive line and was currently rushing toward the command post's rear guard.

"Just remember," Lucian said. "We have one goal. Capture Archduke Henrik."

"Or slay him here and now."

"If needed, then yes."

The enemy soldiers spotted Lucian's group nearly as soon as they came into view. Over a dozen men scrambled into formation, making a line to break the charge.

More enemies were behind them, some still unaware that they were about to be thrown into a sudden battle.

We need to find Henrik quickly! If we get bogged down in a big battle, he could use that time to escape!

Lucian looked from one helmeted man to the next, trying to find his uncle, Archduke Henrik. But no matter where he turned, all he saw was another typical soldier.

Where is he? Did he run already?

Having Henrik get away meant Lucian and his group would have to fight their way through an ever-increasing number of soldiers to corner him.

But there wasn't any more time to worry about that at the moment.

Shouts filled the air. Battlecries, released by both sides as the lines of warriors clashed in the center of the road.

A mass of bodies pushed against each other, weapons slamming into metal breastplates and helmets. The noise was so deafening that Lucian could barely make out the voice in his own head.

I don't see him! Lucian continued looking, protected in a pocket like a quarterback.
Then who's leading the forces from the command post!?
He swapped objectives, instead looking for anyone who might be the general.
There!
A man could be seen barking orders, also protected like Lucian.
If we capture him, can we end the battle!?
Or at least find out where Henrik is!?
The situation was bad, with the main target of the surprise attack nowhere to be seen. But if Lucian could at least capture the one in charge, perhaps there was still a chance to salvage the operation.
"Emilia!" Lucian once again called for his trusted companion.
However, she didn't answer.
Dammit! She's pushing too far forward!
Emilia had been front and center during the initial charge, and she'd already carved a hole in the enemy's defenses.
Henrik's soldiers were starting to realize that they were facing white hairs, sending a wave of fear through the enemy ranks.
Because of that, Emilia was able to push deep into their line. Too deep to hear Lucian's voice when engulfed in the sounds of battle.
No choice, then!
Lucian was fully armed. His powerful sword had been unsheathed since the beginning of battle, but he had yet to put it to use.
That was about to change.
Since it was obvious that the white hairs would go berserk once the fighting began, the human soldiers Lucian had with him were tasked with personally protecting the prince. Those five men had yet to engage in the melee, giving Lucian at least a few pieces to move as he pleased.
"Follow me!" He yelled to those five men. "We're going for Emilia!"
The battle had just started, but the line between the two forces was already devolving into an unorganized mess. That's just how it was when white hairs were berserking through enemy ranks.
They may be several times stronger than an enhanced soldier, but they were just as hard to control as they were powerful. Lucian could barely keep them from rushing off whenever they pleased, much less actually getting them to fight shoulder to shoulder.
The prince squeezed between two white hairs, the two warriors nearly swinging on him in their frenzied state. Fortunately, there was just enough reason in their eyes to realize who he was.
His five men opened the path wider, giving him a clear view of Emilia up ahead. She was facing off against a fresh wave of soldiers who'd just arrived at the battle, without a single white hair ally by her side.
So reckless!

A weapon whizzed nearby, Lucian picking up a blur in his peripheral. He swung his own sword, nearly on reaction, catching the blade before it could hit his body.

Lucian's men lunged at the enemy, taking him down and leaving the prince standing with his sword stiffly raised in the air.

Dangerous. That could have been the end of me.

He didn't have time to even feel the fear. The path to Emilia had been opened, and he couldn't afford to miss the chance.

"Emilia!" Lucian yelled again, now much closer to her.

Thankfully, she stopped her advance into the enemy ranks and took a few steps back. When allied white hairs began stepping in and covering her flanks, she turned and met Lucian's eyes.

"What?"

"I found the commander, but it's not Henrik. We need to capture him and find out where the Archduke is."

She followed Lucian's finger. "Fine."

Emilia literally grabbed the shoulders of two other white hairs, yanking them from their battles. The berserked warriors didn't look happy at having their fun interrupted, but when she shoved them in the direction of the commander, they found more opponents to fight.

With a few more forced adjustments to the battle line, Emilia had the white hair force more or less fighting to break straight through to the commander. It was a simple and effective way to get the berserked warriors to put pressure on a particular point in the battle line, but Lucian knew it wouldn't last long.

Already, the white hairs were losing focus, chasing enemies and engaging whoever happened to be just in front of them.

But it put a dent in the line, and that was all Emilia needed.

The commander could only look on with a shocked face as Emilia broke through the weakened formation. She appeared before him so quickly that the man barely had time to raise his sword.

That weapon was knocked aside before he could finish a single swing, and without hesitation, Emilia grabbed the man by his breastplate and hurled him into the sky.

Lucian watched with shock as the commander came flying over the heads of soldiers, both allies and enemies. With a crash, the man hit the stone road near Lucian's feet, screeching to a halt a few steps away.

Before the commander could even get back to his feet, Lucian's human soldiers surrounded him.

"Where is he!?" Lucian yelled at the downed man. "Where is Henrik!"

"Tch." He looked up. "If it ain't the damn prince himself."

Lucian motioned for his men to lift him. "Tell me where Henrik is hiding."

"Hiding? Hah! Idiot, you think he's cowering in fear of your little army? If it weren't for your damn white hairs, you'd be a corpse already."

"Then where is he? On the front lines?"

"You won't get anything out of me." The man smiled. "Even if he's a great strategist, Marcus can't win this battle. It won't be long now. You and your little army are done for."

Damn!

Lucian looked toward the wall, where Marcus still held against an army twice his size. He couldn't see much, just a mass of bodies pressed against each other, locked in fierce combat.

But he knew where Marcus was, and he was sure that he would be overwhelmed before long.

Is that their goal? To take down Marcus?

Lucian was just a prince, not even the original crown prince. Compared to Marcus, who was a seasoned general and the Minister of War, Lucian could be considered an afterthought.

Was this command post just a decoy all along?
What should I do...

Looking around, Lucian saw that the battle had devolved into a mess. Most of the enemy soldiers had been killed or routed, which meant the white hairs were splitting in all directions, chasing them down or hunting more prey.

He had already lost sight of many, with others still growing smaller as they rushed off toward more enemies.

There's no way I can gather them all up in time.
But I can't just leave them here to get spread out and picked off one by one...

Just then, Emilia fell from the sky, landing beside Lucian.

"There he is."

Lucian looked in the direction of Emilia's gaze. Off in the distance was a familiar face, one that he was hoping to see.

"Sigurd! We need to regroup with him!" Lucian motioned for the human soldiers to bind the commander. "Let's go, Emilia!"

The two ran toward the white hair Sigurd, who was engaged in battle with several soldiers. Around him were a few other white hairs, including one of the two who disappeared after the first battle.

Emilia looked off into the distance. Sara was one of the two who vanished after their first encounter, but she hadn't returned with Sigurd.

"New orders, Sigurd," Emilia said after joining his side.

"Again? And I was just starting to let loose."

"Then you'll be glad to hear what I want," Lucian said. "Defeat the rest of the soldiers at the command post, then take the white hairs and come back to the wall where our soldiers are fighting."

"Clean up? There are hardly enough here to entertain me."

"You'll get a chance to fight again after you meet us at the wall."

"Fine. And you?"

"Emilia and I are going to find Henrik. He wasn't here at the command post, but I have a good idea on where to find him."

"Don't end the battle too quickly. I'm finally warmed up."

"Then hurry and clean up here so you can get back to the real fighting."

"And Sigurd," Emilia said. "Keep an eye out for Sara."

With that, Lucian and Emilia rushed back through the same alley they used to flank the enemy. From there, they could get back to the wall unchallenged, and hopefully make it to Marcus before Henrik could spring whatever trap he had planned for Lucian's Minister of War.

"Enemies." Emilia smiled as she spoke.

"Let's find a way around." Lucian grabbed her hand. "This way."

He took off across the open street, only stopping when he reached the curb on the other side. He would have kept going in order to find a better path around the enemy soldiers, but a huge wall blocked him.

They had reached the wall that surrounded the castle, but Henrik's men controlled the street that led back to the gate where Marcus was fighting. Getting back to him would be a challenge.

How do we get by?

From his hiding spot, Lucian peered down the street. The backs of enemy soldiers filled his vision, though he didn't know how many rows deep the enemy formation was.

There can't be that many. He had less than a thousand men to start, and there are men fighting all over.

Should we break through? With Emilia's strength and the element of surprise, maybe we can do it.

Lucian turned to Emilia. The young beastfolk girl had been in several battles already, and it showed. Blood coated her outfit, and not all of it belonged to the enemies she slew.

It was said that a berserked white hair knew no pain. Many would fight until all the strength in their body ran out, something Lucian saw first-hand when Emilia battled that minotaur.

She has to be tired and injured, even if she doesn't know it. Just how much more can she take before it gets dangerous?

Lucian wasn't sure, but he didn't want to push her to that limit again.

It'd take too long to sneak by. Who knows how much time it'd take to look for another way through.

Lucian looked around for anything that might help him get through to Marcus. He didn't see any openings, nor any friendly soldiers that might be able to help him.

Only an empty street blocked by enemies and littered with the bodies of fallen warriors. He did take note that most of the slain were enemy soldiers.

The surprise charge out of the gate gave his men the upper hand in the early minutes of the battle, but the tide had turned, with Henrik's men using their numerical advantage to surround Lucian's soldiers.

At this rate, won't we lose?

As Lucian stood looking at the corpse-laden street, an idea occurred to him.

Henrik outfitted his men with red tabards to distinguish his men from mine.

It was a necessity so his soldiers would know who their enemies were, since the men's armor was otherwise identical.

The only difference is the red tabard...

"Emilia, I have an idea."

"About time. I was getting bored. And how long do you intend to hold my hand? Do you think I'm a child?"

"Just a little longer." He pulled on her arm. "Come on."

He brought her out to the street, where several soldiers were sprawled on the ground.

They're really dead...

Since arriving in that world, Lucian had seen things he never imagined. But until now, he had taken a hands-off approach, letting his guards and servants handle most of the messes while he watched on from a distance.

Others may have seen it as just the crown prince dictating to his subjects, but the truth was that Lucian didn't want to dirty his hands.

He once lived in a world of peace. One where the brutality of human nature had been mostly tamed.

But he wasn't on Earth anymore. People fought in his name, dying at his command. And yet Lucian stood by, still reluctant to even touch the corpses of the men whose deaths were the result of his actions.

But he couldn't keep his hands clean forever.

He reached down, pulling the red tabard off the fallen enemy soldier. He did the same for a second man, then tossed it to Emilia.

She frowned as she caught the tabard. "You want to blend in with the enemies?"

"It's the easiest way to get past them. We'll pretend to be on their side, then push through the ranks until we reach our men."

"We'll be attacked by our own forces."

"I have a plan for that."

Since both Lucian and Emilia were outfitted in normal armor, they looked no different than the average soldier. It was a necessity to keep their identities hidden while they snuck around to the command post, and with the simple addition of the red tabard, they could swap sides in an instant.

In short order, the two were equipped with the enemy's colors. Now undercover, they dashed toward the backs of Henrik's soldiers. But rather than attacking, Lucian and Emilia began looking for a weakness in the battle line, somewhere they could push through to get to their real allies on the other side.

"There!" Lucian pointed to a part of the battle lines thin enough to see through.

As if charging to fill the gap, Lucian and Emilia rushed through the opening. Lucian's own soldiers moved to stop them, but they were no match for a white hair.

Emilia broke through their defense in a quick charge, without shedding a single drop of their blood.

Lucian's helmet rested in his hands, revealing his face and long, blonde hair. When the men realized who he was, they immediately stopped their attacks.

"Where's Marcus?" Lucian asked a nearby soldier.

"There, Your Highness." He pointed to the battle line.

Lucian saw a man with thick, black hair, wielding a greataxe against the enemy soldiers.

No, not just any soldiers! He's fighting a white hair!

As Lucian watched, a second white hair leapt into the sky. With a massive sweep of his greataxe, Marcus knocked the white hair's attack aside.

Even against two, Marcus stood his ground. The problem was the third.

"Gah!" Marcus spat blood.

"Marcus...!" Lucian yelled.

The third white hair's sword went straight through Marcus' body, its tip stained red with his blood. When the white hair pulled his weapon free, Marcus fell to the ground.

Lucian ran toward the Minister of War who led his troops in this battle, but one of the white hairs caught sight of him. The berserked man's arm blurred, and a whizzing sound filled the air.

"Wha–!?" His vision swam as someone yanked on his arm.

"Careful, Prince," Emilia said. "Those three white hairs are battle-trained."

Lucian looked behind him. Just as Emilia pulled him, a knife had passed by his ear. That blade now sat hilt deep in an unfortunate soldier, the same one who had pointed him toward Marcus.

"Well, well," a familiar voice said. "The prince finally shows himself."

"Henrik!" Lucian yelled his uncle's name. "Let Marcus go!"

The archduke looked down at the injured man. "And why should I? I gave him a chance to join me, and he refused. Now that he's lost, his life is mine to take."

"I'll never..." Marcus said with difficulty, "...join the coward who murdered the king."

"My brother was a fool who only obtained the crown because he was born first. He nearly ruined this kingdom, and his incompetent heirs would be the end of us. You should be thankful that I plan to rid us of them all."

Henrik looked to Lucian. "Once I finish the job, there will be nothing standing between me and the crown."

The archduke motioned with his hand, and a sword fell.

"No...!"

Nobody paid heed to Lucian's yell, and with the flash of a blade, Marcus was slain.

"Now." Henrik looked to Lucian. "There's only one more obstacle."

This can't be happening...

Are we ... going to lose?

Lucian always intended to confront Henrik, but he was supposed to have a small army of white hairs beside him.

Now, only Emilia remained. She never even completed her training, while Henrik had three white hairs who'd all stepped on many battlefields.

The strategy had fallen apart. Marcus was dead. And Lucian was trapped in the center of a battle that his men were losing. Once they realized that their true leader, Marcus, had been slain by the enemy general, morale would plummet.

I was never important. These men only fought because Marcus was here.

Nobody cares about the second prince who lucked out and had the crown fall into his lap.

They won't rally, no matter what I say.

Already, he could see some of his nearby men faltering after seeing Marcus' fallen body. Soon, they would route, and the battle would be lost.

There's only one chance. I have to kill Henrik!

Only by returning the favor and felling the enemy commander could Lucian salvage the battle. But he had to do it quickly, before his men began to flee.

"Emilia." Lucian spoke with no apparent emotion. "Get out of here. I'll handle the rest."

"Have you finally lost your mind? There's no way I'm leaving such an exciting battlefield."

"I figured you'd say something like that. The moment I promoted you, I tied your fate to mine. There's no running, for either of us. Which is why..."

Lucian spoke his chant again, and the magical energies flowed from him, seeping into Emilia.

"Oh?" Emilia held up her hand. "Now this is more like it."

Lucian wiped the sweat from his forehead. "Put a lot of mana into that one."

"Put too much, and you'll faint."

"I can still fight, and you're going to need the strength against them."

The three white hairs stood just behind Henrik, ready to protect him against any threats.

There's no way I can face those berserked warriors, which means I have to rely on Emilia to hold them off.

While she does that...

Lucian's grip on his sword's hilt tightened as he looked at Henrik.

"I suppose we should end this," Henrik said. "There's no need to waste the lives of more soldiers on this pointless battle."

"I was thinking the same," Lucian said.

Henrik looked to Emilia. "A single white hair against my three? And she's only a trainee, no matter how high a rank you gave her."

"You're going to find out exactly why she's the captain of my personal guard."

"I hate to waste the life of a white hair, but she simply chose the wrong side." Henrik waved to his three guards. "Kill her."

The sound of screeching metal rang out as Emilia and the other three white hairs clashed.

But Lucian didn't have the luxury of watching her battle. He had to fight his own.

"I know how practiced you are with that blade." Henrik eyed Lucian's sword. "But it won't do you any good this time."

"Say that after it's covered in your blood."

"You brought this on yourself, you know. If you weren't such a psychopath, maybe I wouldn't have had to slay you and your family."

"You're right. Prince Lucian was a terrible person. Even I hate him after hearing about everything he's done. Acting like a saint, then betraying people and forcing them to battle a minotaur. Maybe I shouldn't blame you for trying to get rid of us. I'd probably do the same if I were you." Lucian looked to Marcus' body. "But right now, I don't care about any of that!"

"Speaking of yourself in third person? You really have lost it." Henrik pulled something from his coat pocket. "All the more reason to rid this kingdom of you."

"You want the crown?" Lucian raised his sword. "Come and take it."

"It's not me who's fighting for the crown in this battle," Henrik said. "It's you."

Lucian spared a glance at the battle that raged around him. The prince's men were getting pressured on three sides by Henrik's larger force, and the only reason they hadn't been defeated already was because of the castle wall that prevented a full surround.

But that would only last so long. Left to play out, Lucian was sure his men would lose the fight.

Then I'll end it myself!

Lucian kicked the ground, dashing straight to Henrik. But the Archduke had other plans.

"Get him." He stepped behind two soldiers.

Tch! More bodyguards!

The pocket Lucian stood in was more in Henrik's control than his. Henrik had more men nearby, and Lucian had to attack into him.

That gave the Archduke more pieces to play with, and he wasn't shy about using them.

Fortunately for Lucian, the two men protecting Henrik were normal soldiers, not white hairs. But even with that...

A sword whizzed by Lucian's ear, just barely missing him.

The second man was a hair slower, but his attack was far more difficult to dodge, forcing Lucian to take it with his sword.

Can I even defeat two soldiers!?

As usual, the prince was relying on his body's muscle memory to carry him along. But Henrik's personal guards weren't pushovers.

The men were battle-hardened, while Lucian was just a regular guy in a trained prince's body. Even if he could somehow hold his ground, he wasn't sure how long even that would last. And since he just spent a good portion of his mana enhancing Emilia, he was already feeling sluggish.

Lucian sidestepped a sword, then met the second with his own. By the time he was ready to attack, the first man was already swinging at him again.

With no time to go on the offensive, Lucian could only backpedal against the combined assault of his two opponents.

"Is that all you have?" Henrik asked, watching from a safe distance. "Princes are trained by the best warriors, yet you only obtained that level of skill? Perhaps I was overestimating you, after all."

Lucian didn't have the luxury of a response. All he could do was try to survive and hope for a miracle.

"Stay still, brat!" one of the soldiers yelled.

Of course he wouldn't do what the man asked when the outcome would be certain death. In fact, Lucian started moving faster.

Another attack whiffed, and this time, Lucian had an opening. His sword arced, hitting the man squarely in the side.

Without time to even judge the attack's effectiveness, Lucian was forced to parry the second soldier's strike. After backing up and getting some breathing room, he saw the man he hit holding his side, blood flowing through his fingers at steady pace.

"Damn!" The wounded soldier yelled. "Keep him busy for a minute!"

The man took out a bottle from somewhere. The red liquid inside was familiar to Lucian, though he'd never tried drinking any.

A healing potion!

The soldier downed the bottle while Lucian was still dealing with the second man. By the time he found an opening to attack again, the wounded soldier was already rejoining the battle, though he did so with a wince.

It felt as if all his progress had been undone. The soldier was still wounded, but he fought with nearly as much ferocity as he had before Lucian's attack.

Enhanced soldiers really are on another level.

He could feel that same strength running through him. A power that would make even the best trained athletes on Earth jealous. And all it took was a little magic.

Lucian spared a glance to Emilia. She was facing three berserked white hairs all alone, and it wasn't easy, despite the powerful enhancement spell Lucian used on her.

Unfortunately, with each drop of mana used, a person's physical strength would fade. Since Lucian had to fight his own battle, he couldn't afford to fully enhance Emilia. It would leave him too weak to defend himself.

I just hope it was enough for her to win.

As the two soldiers re-engaged, Lucian realized that about a third of his strength was gone because of his [Enhance] spell.

If I had my full strength, wouldn't these two men be easy to defeat?

It was useless to think about what might have been, if he had played his hand differently. But the thought that he did somehow outclass these seasoned warriors gave Lucian a bit of confidence.

He clashed with them again, finding it just a little easier to fend off their attacks. Maybe it was the injury he gave one of them, or perhaps it was his own strength that was slowly returning alongside his mana.

Either way, it wasn't long before Lucian found himself poised to take advantage of another opening. And this time, he knew he could put everything into his attack.

Lucian gripped the hilt of his sword, his eye on the very same soldier he wounded already.

This time, I'll–

Movement caught his eye. With a glance, Lucian looked toward Henrik and saw the man with his arm outstretched. But that wasn't the movement he saw.

Hurtling toward Lucian was a red stone, seemingly glowing with a crimson hue.

In an instant, the stone reached Lucian, moving at a speed that even the enhanced prince had a hard time reacting to.

What is–!

With a flash, Lucian's vision was engulfed in what felt like a small sun. A thunderous roar assaulted his hearing, deafening him to all the other sounds on the battlefield that had seemed so loud before.

The smell of something burning was the only sensation that stuck out to him, along with a numb pain where the rock had exploded.

His thoughts were a mess, and he could barely tell up from down. All he knew was that he absolutely had to keep hold of his sword.

Stumbling, Lucian backpedaled as best he could. Somehow, he managed to keep from collapsing, despite his vertigo.

After what felt like an eternity, his senses finally began to return. Just in time to see the sword before it entered his gut.

"Guh...!" Lucian grunted.

He desperately swung his sword at the soldier that stabbed him, but the man dodged, pulling his sword free from Lucian's body at the same time.

"Ugh." Lucian held his stomach, where a deep wound gushed blood.

If it weren't for the [Physical Resistance I] skill he recently obtained, Lucian was sure the injury would have crippled him. Even as it was, he knew his situation had suddenly become dire.

"I told you." Henrik pulled out another red stone. "Your skill with the sword wouldn't help you."

"What ... are those things?"

"The latest prototype magitech weapon. You do remember that I showed them to you during your recent tour, don't you?"

"You said ... they weren't ready."

"A lie, I'm afraid. What you saw was research on how to further improve them. The stones themselves are ready for use." Henrik held the stone toward Lucian. "And what better time to test it, if not against you?"

The crimson rock flew toward Lucian without Henrik even needing to throw it. On top of that, it moved in an impossible arc, tracking Lucian as he moved to dodge it.

The stone exploded, engulfing Lucian in another burst of light, sound, and fire. Fortunately, he had managed to avoid a direct hit, but he still smelled something burning, and his senses were overloaded.

Despite that, he managed to parry a soldier's follow-up strike. Just barely.

Panting, Lucian finally got a second to breathe. But Henrik was already holding another one of his magitech weapons, and his two bodyguards were preparing for a full assault.

The very next clash between them could very well decide the fate of the entire battle.

Chapter 31

Ow...

Lucian winced as the wound in his gut throbbed. He wanted to take out the healing potion he kept in a padded pouch, but he'd have to use both hands to hold and uncork it, giving Henrik and his two bodyguards a huge opening.

Unlike the enemy soldier, Lucian didn't have anyone to cover for him. Looking to the side, he saw Emilia still embroiled in a fierce melee with the other three white hairs.

Even though it felt like a long time since the battle began, the truth was that barely a minute had passed. When fighting enhanced soldiers, it would take time to wear them down, meaning he couldn't count on Emilia winning her fight in the immediate future.

Lucian was thankful for the extra endurance granted by [Enhance], though. It was only because he'd been magically powered up that he could even stand after taking something like a sword to the gut. Not to mention the grenade-like explosions that landed two hits against him.

It's a miracle I have the strength to keep fighting. Magic really does change the rules in this world.

His sword held before him, Lucian stood against the two enemy soldiers. Henrik still clutched the magitech stone in his hand, but the one in his palm was blue instead of red.

Lucian didn't have a chance to wonder what that meant, as the two bodyguards decided it was time to continue the battle.

Ignoring his wound the best he could, Lucian parried one of the swords coming at him. Knowing he couldn't block the other, he was already moving away from the blade before he even parried the first.

I can see it.

Lucian deflected another attack.

I can see exactly what they're going to do.

Lucian wasn't just reacting to them anymore. Without even realizing it, he had begun anticipating his opponents' moves.

"Damn brat!" One of the soldiers stepped back, a fresh wound on his thigh.

"I can win." Lucian was surprised at his own confidence.

"You ain't gonna do nothing but die!"

The man lunged at Lucian, but his blade never reached the prince. Another parry, another retaliation, and another fresh splattering of blood.

"Incompetent." Henrik said with a frown. "Move. I'll take him down myself."

The blue stone leapt from Henrik's hand, flying straight toward Lucian.

However, the prince was ready for it. The red stone's blast was blinding and deafening, but the damage was minor, and the effective range was short. Otherwise, he'd risk hitting his own men with the magitech weapon.

As long as I hit it with my sword, I should be able to avoid the damage. Even if it explodes, I'll be far enough from the blast that it won't blind me like the last couple.

Back on Earth, he wouldn't have the confidence to hit a baseball from an accomplished pitcher.

But he wasn't on Earth anymore.

Lucian stood ready as the blue stone zipped through the air toward him, the sword held aside almost like a batter just before his swing.

Now!

His arms blurred, his blade seeking the blue stone that tracked him like a guided missile.

kachink!

The sound of metal hitting stone filled Lucian's ears, just as the vibrations of the impact reached his hands.

Got it!

The blue stone...

kaboom!

The sun itself exploded into existence just in front of Lucian. At least, that's what it felt like to him.

Sight, hearing, and even his consciousness were in complete disarray, just as they were when the red stone blew up directly on him.

But the blue stone Henrik used was far enough from him that he was confident its effects would be minor. Turned out, he had underestimated what he was dealing with.

"Ugh..." Lucian sat up. "What was that..."

"Hah." Henrik sounded happy. "Just another weapon we've been developing. It's for power, but you have to be careful, or..."

Lucian looked around, still a bit dazed. The two soldiers were standing, but they were both a bit unsteady on their feet, as if still recovering from a sudden attack.

The blast affected them, too.

Now Lucian understood why Henrik didn't use the blue stone from the beginning. It was too powerful, catching allies in its area of effect.

But after losing patience with his men, he stopped caring about keeping his allies safe and decided to speed up the fight with a deadly magitech item.

Even though the two bodyguards were in the weapon's effective range, they didn't sustain nearly as much damage as Lucian.

Perhaps in a miraculous twist, the men would be angered at being collateral damage. But the world wasn't such a simple and convenient place.

Lucian got a leg beneath him just as the first man swung his sword. With a clank, he knocked the weapon aside, sending it to the stone road on which Lucian knelt.

Putting strength into his still numb legs, the prince pushed himself to his feet.

Another sword sought his flesh. Lucian saw it slicing through the air, held in the second soldier's sweaty and dirty hands.

Ugh...!

Lucian stumbled. He didn't know if it was a concussion or if he was just getting exhausted, but the sudden exertion of getting back to his feet made him lightheaded.

Before he knew it, the soldier's sword was too close to parry or dodge.

Crap...!

Lucian put up a desperate defense and hoped just to survive the attack, watching as the weapon arced straight toward his body.

A white blur flashed across his vision. When it vanished, the soldier had disappeared.

Looking to his left, Lucian saw the man who was just about to land a clean strike on him. He lay in a heap on the ground, a blade sunk deep into his body.

Emilia pulled her weapon free and stood up straight. She was covered in blood, both those of her enemies and her own. The same berserked light glinted in her eyes, but she barely had a second to spare before she had to tear her gaze from Lucian.

"Die already!" a male voice yelled.

As soon as he spoke, the white haired beastfolk Emilia had been fighting attacked her again. The two's battle put Lucian's to shame. The speed of their weapons outclassed his by a wide margin, and each strike seemed to carry enough power to break through the defense of an average enhanced soldier.

Just as quickly as she arrived, Emilia was gone. Looking around, Lucian saw that one of the white hairs was already on the ground, leaving Emilia with only two opponents.

But she's probably nearing her limit, just like me.

The wound in his gut was deep, and it has had time to bleed for a while now. The explosions had taken their toll as well, with Lucian still feeling the effects of the last one messing with his senses, even now.

But fortunately, Emilia didn't just save his life. She also bought him a few, precious seconds.

With a pop, a cork was pulled free. In a single gulp, Lucian downed the healing potion he kept in his padded pouch, giving him some much-needed recovery for the fight ahead.

Just one bodyguard left. Then I'm coming for you, Henrik.

Chapter 32

The air whistled as Lucian's sword cut through it. It was only a small sound compared to the clashing metal that rang throughout the battlefield, but it stood out to the prince as his weapon arced toward Henrik's final guardsman.

Unlike before, Lucian wasn't defending or countering. He was attacking.

Henrik's magitech weapons made it difficult for the prince to fight a defensive battle. He had to break through and capture Henrik before those deadly explosions could wear him down.

The sword made contact, sending a shock through Lucian's arm as the guard blocked with his own weapon.

Having known that it would be parried, Lucian was already in position to strike again. He was done retreating and playing it safe. No, Lucian had stepped forward, into his attack.

It was a risky tactic. A seasoned warrior could take advantage of the aggressive maneuver. But Lucian didn't have the luxury of a proper duel. He had to win, right then.

Moreover...

I can see your mistakes!

Somehow, Lucian knew where to move. His forward foot pointed right at the guard's exposed side, the man's sword still held high after using it to parry.

Lucian's sword blurred, moving in a way that would be impossible for a swordsman on Earth. But when wielded by a body enhanced by magic, the laws of physics could only bend to the warrior's will.

A flash as the silvery sword passed through a beam of light, followed by a spray of red. Finally, the thump of something hitting the ground.

Lucian thought he heard a scream mixed in somewhere, but he did his best to block it out.

Looking at the downed guard, he saw that the man was still alive, but it was obvious he was finished. Not even an enhanced soldier could fight after receiving a wound as deep as the one Lucian gave him.

Meeting Henrik's eyes, Lucian saw frustration in them. He brought along three white hairs and two personal bodyguards, yet one by one, they were falling.

With his two remaining white hairs still battling Emilia, there wasn't anyone standing between the two royals who sought to rule the Almekian Kingdom.

Although Henrik looked annoyed, he didn't show any fear. A blue stone was already sitting in his hand, while his other carried a sword.

"Not bad," Henrik said. "But don't forget, I was also a prince. I received the same royal combat training as you. If it's just a single, wounded youngster like yourself, then victory is already mine."

Lucian touched the wound in his gut. "Even with this, I can defeat someone who's spent the last decade in a magitech facility instead of on the battlefield."

Henrik tossed the blue stone up, catching it with the same hand. "Time well spent. Even if my skills have dulled, I can make up for it with the powerful spells I have at my fingertips. No mana cost, no delays between casting. Just magic, whenever I wish it."

"Until you run out of those stones. You can't have more than two dozen that size before they start to weigh you down."

"That's more than enough to finish you."

The short conversation was just what Lucian needed to give the healing potion time to close his wounds. He had even gotten a little lightheaded from that short battle with the final guard, but it had already faded.

There was a major problem, though.

As I thought, the enhancement magic is starting to run out.

The healing potion had already closed the wound on his stomach, but the pain seemed to be getting worse. The sword in his hand felt heavier, and his exhaustion was getting deeper.

All signs that [Enhance] was wearing off. In five or ten minutes, he'd be nothing but a normal man, surrounded by an army of enhanced soldiers.

He was sure that if he reached for a talisman, it would only give Henrik a chance to strike. That meant he either had to end it with the strength he had remaining, or he needed to find an opening large enough for him to enhance himself with a talisman.

Lucian moved the same moment as Henrik. He started from several paces away, but that distance would disappear in an instant, if Lucian were to dash straight toward the Archduke.

Unfortunately, there was something preventing the prince from bringing the fight to melee.

A blue stone flew from Henrik's hand, straight toward Lucian. The prince knew it was coming, so he moved to dodge the explosion. However, rather than running from the stone, he stepped diagonally toward it.

The magitech weapon arced toward Lucian, tracking him like every time before, but as he suspected, the magitech weapon had a hard time making quick turns. That meant running from it would only give the stone more room to make the wide turn it needed.

An instant after Lucian passed the stone, a violent boom shook the ground as it exploded.

The force of the explosion hit Lucian, making him grit his teeth. But his feet remained securely planted on the ground.

"You realized–" Henrik tried to say something, but Lucian attacked without stopping to listen.

Two swords clashed, both held by warriors trained in the royal court.

"You sure are eager to die, aren't you!" Henrik lashed out with his sword.

"People are dying around us!" Lucian swept an attack aside. "I can't let the battle go on any longer!"

"Oh, drop the act! I know what you truly are, nephew! A monster, willing to do anything to get what you want!"

"You don't know half of what you think you do!"

As Lucian expected, Henrik's skills had dulled over the years. With another quick exchange, he managed to knock Henrik's sword aside, opening a path to his body.

The archduke's battle coat was colored red as Lucian gave Henrik his first wound of the battle. With a grunt, Henrik leapt back, pulling something from a pocket.

Lucian gave chase, trying to keep Henrik from getting enough distance to use his magitech weapons.

Even though Henrik only managed to put a single step between himself and Lucian, he didn't hesitate to activate the stone in his hand. It flew from his palm, straight toward the approaching Lucian.

A red stone...!

Lucian realized his mistake just as the red stone burst into a brilliant, white light.

Unlike the blue stones that exploded like a fireball, the red ones barely did any physical damage. But like a flash grenade, they could disrupt the senses of anyone nearby.

Can't see...!

Even though his vision was gone, Lucian still swung his sword. It clanked against something metallic, releasing a sharp sound.

Still impaired, Lucian leapt back to get out of the reach of Henrik's sword. He expected to be followed or blasted with another magitech weapon, but no such attack came.

Finally, his vision began to return, and Lucian understood why Henrik didn't follow up on his initial strike.

He was affected, too.

Henrik rubbed at his eyes, as if trying to dispel the effects of the red stone. He was only a single step further from the stone when it exploded, so he couldn't escape the blinding effect, even by closing his eyes.

"Didn't even have time to turn away," Henrik said. "But it matters not. This battle is mine."

He pulled out another stone, but Lucian's vision was still blindingly white. So much so that he couldn't even tell what color the magitech weapon was.

Blue. It's definitely a blue stone.

He wants to finish this fight right now.
I can't get hit by the explosion. My strength is already draining. If I take any more damage, I won't stand a chance, even in melee.
Henrik raised his hand, and the stone flew from his palm.
Lucian dove aside as the magitech weapon zipped toward him. Before he even hit the ground, a massive explosion rocked the area. The intense shockwave made his ears ring, even as he hit the road and rolled.
Lucian raised his head, pushing himself to his feet. As soon as his eyes regained their focus, he saw another stone in Henrik's hand.
This time, he could at least see well enough to make out blue color.
Before he could even steady his legs, Lucian was forced to leap again. A heartbeat slower this time, the powerful boom of the magitech weapon hit him, adding cumulative damage on top of his already injured body.
Trailing smoke, Lucian emerged from the explosion, rolling over the cobblestone road.
Ugh...
With effort, Lucian got a hand beneath him and raised his head, looking toward Henrik. Yet another blue stone sat in his hand, but he seemed in no hurry to use it.
"It really is a pity," Henrik said. "Not you, of course. It's a pity that I'll have to execute so many valuable white hairs for siding with you. And during a time of war, no less. Perhaps I can spare some, use it as an example of how forgiving I can be. What do you think?"
Lucian pushed himself back to his feet. "Hah...hah..."
"Hmm. Guess it's useless to ask for advice from someone who wasn't even able to secure the crown, despite being so close. Then how about I give you some advice, instead." Henrik held out his hand, the blue stone sitting on his palm. "Try to be more aware of who your real enemies are."
With those words, Henrik activated the magitech weapon, sending the blue stone hurtling toward Lucian.
I have to dodge it...!
Although the thought passed through his mind, Lucian's body didn't move.
Time crawled. But it didn't stop. The blue stone that marked his death approached.
So much was his focus on the magitech weapon that he knew exactly how many heartbeats until it would explode.
Three.
I can't be killed here! Emilia, Mia, the white hairs who put their trust in me! If I don't win, all of them will be...!
He'd only been in this world a short time, but there were already many people whose fates were intertwined with his own. Were he to fall, so too would they.
Move!

He yelled at his body, but his feet remained planted. Something was wrong. Something he didn't quite understand. Whatever it was, it kept him from leaping to safety, as he had done before.

Two.

Ah, that's why.

It's too late. Even if I dodge now, I can't escape the blast.

It's over...

Lucian watched on as the blue stone slowly grew larger.

If only I hadn't stopped to think. If only I had just jumped when he activated the stone.

No. It wouldn't have mattered. Not as I am now...

The [Enhance] spell had mostly run out, leaving Lucian aching and exhausted. His physical strength was fading, and with each passing second, he would just get weaker.

The wound in his stomach throbbed with each beat of his heart. His senses were numb from the numerous explosions he'd endured. And his body was heavy. So heavy.

One.

Who cares!? I'll survive this explosion, no matter what I have to sacrifice in the process!

Lucian raised his heavy arm.

As long as I have one good arm for my sword, I don't care about anything else!

The magitech weapon hit his open palm, and Lucian could feel the magical energies held within the stone begin to erupt.

"[Order]...!"

Zero.

Metal clashed. Men screamed.

But no explosions could be heard.

Slowly, Lucian brought in his outstretched hand, still holding the blue stone in his grasp. The weapon was silent, as if it had never been activated in the first place.

"A dud," Henrik said. "Talk about atrocious timing. But that's to be expected from a prototype."

He pulled out another blue stone. "Let's end it for good this time."

The magitech weapon flew from Henrik's hand, threatening to take Lucian's life that had just been miraculously saved.

It was Lucian's perfect chance to fix his mistake. To move now, before the stone got too close to dodge.

And yet he simply stood in place, watching as the explosive weapon drew near.

A sword clattered to the ground, and an empty hand reached out.

Drawn to Lucian by magical means, the stone hit his open palm.

"[Order]."

Silence fell over the two royals. As silent as a battlefield could be. It may have still been loud, but the deafening explosion Henrik expected never erupted.

"What...?" Henrik stared at the two blue stones sitting in Lucian's hands. "Two duds? That can't be right..."

"Uncle Henrik." Lucian spoke with such confidence that he even surprised himself. "I don't blame you for poisoning the royal family. From what I heard, they were destroying this kingdom. Who knows, maybe you would have made a better king. But..."

Lucian stretched out one of his arms, a blue stone resting on his palm. "I have things I need to do, too. Missions to accomplish, people to protect. And if needed, I'll crush anyone who gets in my way, even you!"

"[Order]! Kill Henrik!"

The blue stone came alight with power, leaking a mana that far exceeded what came before.

Then, it leaped from Lucian's hand, heading straight toward Henrik.

"Wha–!"

A thunderous boom drowned out Henrik's voice as the blue stone exploded. The archduke was so shocked to see his own supposed dud flying toward him that he didn't even have the chance to put up a defense.

With one of his hands now free, Lucian picked up his sword and charged. He was injured, slow, and weak. But he could run, and that was all he cared about.

"Henrik!" Lucian yelled as he sliced at the shadow that moved within the cloud of smoke.

"Gah!" A pained grunt came from beyond the smoke, along with a splattering of blood.

Lucian's next attack found only air, the shadow shrinking as Henrik retreated. But the prince didn't have time to play it safe, leaping into the cloud of smoke and dust.

"Brat!" Henrik met Lucian's sword with his own. "How did you do that!?"

"Why would I tell you!" Lucian swung again.

Henrik was off-balance, with scorched skin and a fresh wound on his chest. By all accounts, Lucian had the upper hand, and he sought to leverage that advantage before his uncle could recover.

But despite the situation being perfect for a turnaround, the prince's sword couldn't find Henrik's flesh.

"Slow!" Henrik knocked Lucian's sword aside. "It's over, nephew! Look at you! You can barely even stand!"

"You..." Lucian's sword arced again. "...haven't won yet!"

Like before, he only found air. Even if he was the better swordsman, Lucian was fighting against odds that would make any gambler recoil.

His [Enhance] was gone. His wound was bleeding again. His stamina was drained. And his body ached all over.

Under those circumstances, the injuries he finally managed to give to Henrik seemed minor.

Yet he kept up the assault, putting everything he had left into his sword arm. Henrik was so focused on keeping the sharp edge from finding his flesh again that he seemingly forgot Lucian had two hands.

And in the other one was...

"[Order]! Kill Henrik!"

"Oh shi—"

Lucian's hearing vanished, save for the massive boom that drowned out all other sounds. The explosion was so bright that he had to squint, holding his free hand in front of his face to shield it from the blast.

Just like last time, the blue stone left a massive smoke cloud behind, covering Henrik's figure. But Lucian knew what he needed to do. It was the only thing he could do.

Attack.

"Right there!" Lucian felt his sword sink deep.

"Guh..."

"It's over, uncle." Lucian looked at Henrik as the smoke cleared. "Surrender."

"Me ... surrender...?" Henrik grabbed the sword still stuck in his gut. "Like hell!"

A blue glint caught Lucian's eye. His gaze drawn to that brief flash of light, he realized exactly what Henrik had planned.

"Let's see which one of us survives!" Henrik raised his hand, and a blue stone leaped from his palm.

Crap! I gotta stop it!

Lucian reached for the magitech weapon. Only by touching it could he activate his Command Magic and take control of the stone.

He was sure. Sure that if he took another explosion, he'd be finished.

His fingers sliced through the air, desperately closing in on the blue stone. Just one touch. A single finger was all he needed. Then victory would be his.

Everything disappeared. Light, sound, feeling. All taken by the explosive power of the magitech weapon hitting his defenseless body.

Was he floating? Or was he dead? Lucian couldn't tell, not without his senses. He could barely even think.

All he knew was that the pain and exhaustion was finally gone. He could relax, finally able to sleep after such a brutal battle.

...ucian.

Tired. So tired.

Prince Lucian.

He just wanted to let go, to slip into the darkness.

Prince Lucian. We're going out to the city again soon, right? Next time, I want to try a milkshake!

He couldn't see, yet somehow, Emilia's face appeared before him. She was smiling, with just a bit of strawberry shortcake on her cheek.

When you're king, maybe I can do something for my parents. They sacrificed so much for me...

Emilia never said it, but Lucian knew she felt guilty for being a burden because of her white hair.

We're going to win this battle. And after that, we can finally start fixing this kingdom!

Win. The word stirred something in him. He couldn't feel anything, not even pain. But the thought of losing everything and everyone hurt more than any sword or magitech weapon.

Win...

I ... have to win!

Lucian's eyes snapped open. With his blurry vision, he could just barely make out the glimmer of steel.

He couldn't feel his body, but he threw every last ounce of strength into it. Even with everything he had left, the best he could muster was to twist his torso.

A tiny achievement, one that would normally be worthless. But in this case, it was the only thing that prevented Henrik's sword from sinking into his chest.

"Awake ... are you?" Henrik spoke with difficulty. "Would have ... been much easier for you if you just kept your damn eyes closed."

"This new life has been ... nothing but difficult." Lucian watched as his uncle raised his sword with unsteady hands. "But just because it's tough ... doesn't mean I'm going to give up."

"Save it for the Goddess." Blood dripped from Henrik's raised sword. "Goodbye, nephe–gah!"

The sword that was poised to take his life clattered to the ground. The hand that held it reached up, wiping the fresh stream of blood that spurted from a gaping wound.

Henrik turned. White and red covered his vision, Emilia's distinctive and cursed hair covered in a thick layer of blood.

"Goodbye, Archduke." Emilia swung her sword.

Lucian wanted to turn away, but he didn't even have the strength to do that. He could only watch on as Henrik was decapitated right in front of him.

With a single strike, the enemy commander became just another corpse on the bloody battlefield.

Lucian stared up at the bloodied Emilia. It wasn't just from her enemies, either. Wounds of various sizes covered her, some nearly as bad as the one on Lucian's stomach.

She's injured that badly, but she can still stand so confidently.

Enhanced white hairs really are on a different level than regular soldiers.

During his battle with Henrik, Lucian barely had time to see how Emilia was faring against the three white hairs. But what he saw when he took glances made him feel like his own fight were nothing but a schoolyard scuffle by comparison.

The way the white hairs fought truly lived up to their title as Berserkers. An aggressive and fearless combat style, with seemingly no care for self-preservation.

He knew his magic could power Emilia up beyond that of a normal mage, but seeing her fight three battle-hardened white hairs and win really cemented that fact in his mind.

"Are you just going to lie there?" Emilia asked, looking down on Lucian.

"Moving hurts..."

"The battle will go on until the soldiers realize one of the generals is dead." Emilia lifted her sword. "Which is just fine with me."

Lucian twisted his body, turning over onto his stomach. "It's not fine with me."

With a push, he got to his knees. After fighting off a bout of dizziness, he finally managed to get his feet beneath him and stand.

Emilia tossed his sword, and Lucian snatched it from the air. Raising it above his head, he let out the loudest shout he could muster.

"Victory is ours!"

In the chaos of battle, his voice was just one among many. But the nearby soldiers had been aware that the two generals were battling it out.

Before Lucian even declared victory, enemy soldiers who knew the outcome were already fleeing. They served under Henrik's personal banner, so when he fell, so too did their reason to fight.

Soon, word spread through the entirety of the enemy's ranks. Within minutes, the battle lines had dissolved into a stampede of soldiers, some running, others chasing.

They're trying to cut them down as they run.

Lucian realized that his men weren't content with just letting the enemy flee. Many were giving chase, the bloodlust of battle having taken them over.

Such scenes were common. Unlike white hairs, regular soldiers didn't go berserk when buffed with magic. But the [Enhance] spell did push a warrior to fight, to defeat the enemy.

For many, that translated into intense bloodlust. Useful for keeping morale up, but having an army scatter and give chase can be dangerous if exploited by a competent commander.

But Lucian didn't care about the tactical aspects of their bloodlust. He only wanted to limit the number of lives lost. The battle was already over, and he wanted the fighting to stop.

"Where's Marcus, he–" Lucian went silent for a second. "He's dead."

"Why Marcus?" Emilia asked. "You're the crown prince. These are your soldiers."

"You're right..."

Lucian started walking. He felt like he'd fall if he moved too fast, so he kept his steps slow. He needed to look confident, like a king. Even if he didn't feel it.

Although many of his men were pursuing the enemy, there were still those who decided that chasing them wasn't worth it. Magic affected everyone differently, though some were simply too wounded to keep fighting.

"Soldier." Lucian called out to one of his men. "Are you able to cast [Enhance]?"

"Y-yes, Your Highness."

"Then use it on me."

After a short chant, much needed strength flowed in Lucian.

"Spread the word," Lucian said. "The battle is over, and all remaining enemy soldiers are to be captured alive."

"Understood!"

Lucian turned, heading to another soldier. One by one, he sent the men to spread his command. It was still a bloody end to a fierce battle, but he wanted to think he managed to save at least some lives by sending the men out to stop the needless deaths.

"This would normally be the time you give a grand victory speech," Emilia said. "But there's a distinct lack of men here to listen."

"That's fine by me. I'm not in the mood to give one."

The battle had been tough in many ways, and Lucian wanted nothing more than for all of it to be over.

But as the future king, he had to play the part of a powerful and confident ruler, even if that was the last way he felt.

Chapter 33

"Thank you, Your Highness." The soldier stood, crossed one arm over his chest, then bowed.

After his show of etiquette, the man returned to the line of warriors standing before the throne.

Each of them had performed exceptionally well during the battle yesterday, prompting Lucian to reward them. It wasn't just praise from the future king that he offered. There was a sizable pouch of gold, as well.

Sizable compared to a castle guard's annual pay, anyway. It was akin to a rounding error for the Almekian Kingdom.

Sitting on the throne was, of course, Lucian. He was thankful for this world's magic, as only a single day had passed since the battle, yet he didn't feel the least bit exhausted.

Even his injuries were healed, including the deep wound in his stomach. And since healing magic was applied in time, his injuries didn't leave a single scar.

But even though he felt fine, Lucian was still ready to be done with the ceremony. There were still so many things he needed to do, and that list only grew thanks to Henrik's coup.

When the final part of this ceremony finally arrived, Lucian was grateful it was almost over. But at the same time, he was dreading this moment.

The white hair trainees stepped forward, taking the place of the soldiers. Lucian's advisors warned him against rewarding the white hairs, but he couldn't agree to leave them out after how they fought for him.

Or more precisely, how they died for them.

Three trainees, dead because of me.

If I'd have been more prepared—more capable—then they wouldn't have had to die.

He brought 21 to battle, but only 18 returned alive. Considering that he lost control of them and abandoned them in the enemy's backline, Lucian felt like he had failed to live up to his promise.

After all, he did say that he'd keep them by his side. It was his way of assuring them that he didn't plan to enhance them and send them rushing off to their deaths.

Yet in the end, that's precisely what happened.

He looked over the faces of the 27 remaining white hair trainees, along with their representative, Lily. Even the ones who didn't fight were called, since Lucian wanted to give them the same offer as the others.

"Liliana." Lucian spoke in his diplomatic voice. "Your trainees performed exceptionally well on the battlefield yesterday. Allow me to congratulate you on training such fine soldiers."

"Thank you, Your Highness. They work hard every day to live up to your expectations."

"Yes, I see that. Which is why I wanted to give them an offer."

"An offer?" Lily looked surprised.

"Yes. I'm in need of a specialized unit under the direct command of my personal bodyguard, Emilia. And I want each of them to be a white hair, just like her."

"That's a very tempting offer, Your Highness. I'm sure many of them will think deeply upon it."

"Yes, I hope so. We'll discuss the details soon, so be prepared."

With that, the trainees stepped away from the throne, heading to the back of the room before being escorted out.

Emilia spent the entirety of the ceremony standing by Lucian's side. She'd managed to keep her usual expression since the beginning, but that façade cracked as she watched the retreating backs of her white hair companions.

Sara, Emilia thought. *I'm sorry that I couldn't protect you.*

She was saddened by all three of the white hairs' deaths, but one in particular hit her hard. Sara was too nice for her own good, but when enhanced, she became exceptionally reckless.

Emilia knew that, yet she had still failed to protect her.

I lost control so many times. How am I supposed to protect anyone when I can't even remember when it really matters?

War was always in their future. And war meant death. But that didn't make the pain of losing a friend any easier.

Despite her feelings, Emilia kept her expression neutral as the ceremony continued.

"Finally." Lucian sat down behind a familiar desk. "Those formal occasions really like to drag on."

"True," Emilia said. "But it was exciting."

"I don't hate them. I just have too much to do, and entertaining nobles isn't really high on my list. I really just wanted to hand out the rewards and leave."

"If you're so busy," Mia said. "Then why are we in the Royal Study?"

"Because this is the only place I can get some peace and quiet. Which means, I have time to look over these..."

Lucian put his hand on a stack of parchment on the desk. It wasn't a huge pile, but depending on what it contained, it could take several dedicated hours to look through them.

"What's in the stack?" Emilia asked. "Can I help?"

"Yeah, I'd definitely appreciate it if you two would help me. As for what's in here..." Lucian picked up the first piece of parchment and placed it in front of the two girls.

"A financial document?" Mia scanned the paper. "And it's related to Henrik's magitech business."

"Yep. Since he committed high treason, I banished his family and seized all his assets for myself. Which means Henrik's magitech factory is now mine. And the first task when taking over a business is to assess its finances."

"I see. I don't know how useful I will be, but I suppose I'll help out."

"Ah, me too!" Emilia showed enough excitement to make up for Mia's lack of energy. "It's just reading, but with numbers."

Lucian nodded. "Well, basically. I just want a quick overview to make sure the business is healthy. It wouldn't be funny to take control of it, only to find out it loses tons of gold each year."

The distinctive sound of parchment filled the Royal Study as Lucian sorted the documents into three equal piles, one before each person at the desk.

"As for what to look for, each document will have–"

A knock on the study door cut Lucian off. It was rare to be disturbed while he was in this room, but it did happen from time to time. Normally, it was only after he spent too much time inside, so it was strange that he would be needed right after arriving.

Emilia answered the door. "Yes?"

"Pardon the interruption," the servant said. "But Mr. Sampson was insistent that he needed to speak with you."

"Sampson." Lucian had a sour look on his face. "I suppose I don't have a choice. Send him here."

"As you wish."

The door clicked closed, and the faint sound of the servant's footsteps could be heard outside.

Hearing Sampson's name really put Lucian in a bad mood. So much so that he decided not to even start on the financial documents until after the meeting.

As the owner of the kingdom's largest bank, Sampson held a lot of power. The man even gave massive loans to the royal family, putting Lucian in a difficult spot when dealing with him.

Bankers are dangerous, no matter what world I'm in.

Sampson arrived and saw Lucian sitting behind the desk, flanked by Emilia and Mia. A chair was left empty for him, but the man didn't intend to take it.

The aging banker gave Lucian his usual bow, his hat placed over his heart. "Thank you for meeting me on such short notice, Your Highness."

"I'm always available for my closest business partners, Sampson."

"I'm happy to hear that because we may be working together even more from here out. Though it'll likely all be done through my assistants after today."

Lucian raised an eyebrow. "What do you mean when you say we'll be working together?"

"I'm referring to this." Sampson placed a piece of parchment onto the desk.

Lucian scanned the document. He was surprised when he saw that it had to do with Henrik's magitech factory, but his surprise was about to transform into utter shock.

"You're taking possession of the factory!?" Lucian couldn't help but shout in surprise.

"As per the agreed terms with our loans, possession of the business transfers to me upon Henrik's inability to pay his debts. And since he's no longer even in this world, I believe those conditions have been met."

Lucian continued reading from Sampson's parchment. "If these numbers are right, then Henrik was drowning in debt. And you loaned it all to him?"

"I believe you will find the numbers accurate, Your Highness. And it was only through our investments that Henrik was able to build such an amazing business. Though perhaps we did loan a bit too much. That's why I need the business, to ensure I at least get most of my coin back. Of course, if you wish to take control of the business, I'm more than willing to negotiate a contract to transfer the loans to the crown."

"More debt." Lucian shook his head. "I'll need to go over these numbers first. You'll be hearing from me soon, Sampson. And I expect you to answer, not your assistant."

"I'll see what I can do to make myself available, Your Highness."

After giving another bow, Sampson left the Royal Study.

Lucian sighed, still looking at the parchment listing the massive amount of debt Henrik's magitech business had accumulated over the years.

It couldn't be easy, could it?

Epilogue

The heavy clacking of wood echoed around the stone room.

Lucian pulled on his sword, sending the blade toward his opponent. A swift block put an end to the offensive strike, but it was just one of several, meant to pressure them into making a mistake.

Attack after attack was met with the opponent's blade. But each strike drew just a bit closer than the last.

Finally, an opening.

Lucian pivoted his foot, his eyes set on the gap in his opponent's defense. It was the perfect chance to land a clean hit.

Too perfect, Lucian thought.

With a flash, he scanned his opponent's stance and realized why he felt uneasy about attacking.

His opponent looked off-balance, but according to Lucian's estimation, their center of balance, stance, and foot positioning were still fine. There should be no reason why a trained fighter like his opponent would be vulnerable.

And that's when Lucian noticed that they were leaning ever so slightly in the direction they would need to move to avoid Lucian's attack.

In other words...

A trap.

Lucian stilled his hand, deciding not to strike.

As expected, his opponent effortlessly stepped in the direction he anticipated. Such a move would have allowed them to avoid his attack and get the upper hand in the next engagement.

Fortunately, he had listened to his instincts.

"Good job," Emilia said, lowering her training sword. "I thought for sure you were going to attack."

Lucian relaxed, exiting his combat stance. "I almost did. But something about the way you were standing caught my eye."

"Yes. Learning to read your opponent's next move is vital for a warrior. You really catch on quick."

"It's not really me." Lucian looked at his hands. "My body just seems to remember."

"As long as you become strong, that's all that matters."

"That's true. I'll use whatever I can get my hands on. Or rather, I don't have much of a choice."

Emilia had already placed her training sword back on the rack, but Lucian still held onto his.

"Do you want to keep sparring?" Emilia asked.

"No, it was a good place to stop, but I think I'm gonna do another round of practice swings before bed."

"If you wish. Then I'll get comfortable."

"There's no need to stay and watch. It's already late, so you should take some time for yourself."

"Eh? I don't mind, though."

"I know, but it's still good to relax sometimes." Lucian motioned around him. "We're in the castle's training room. What are the chances that an assassin would just happen to show up?"

"Um, really low."

"And that's why you should take some time off."

"I guess you're right." Emilia visibly relented. "Then I will see you again tomorrow, Prince Lucian. It's an exciting day, so I hope I can sleep well."

"Yeah. I'm finally being crowned tomorrow. It seemed so far away ... until it wasn't."

"Ah, that means I'll need to start calling you King Lucian."

"I'm going to miss hearing you say 'Prince Lucian, Prince Lucian' all the time."

"I don't say it that much!"

"You don't? Maybe it's just my imagination, then."

"That must be it." Emilia nodded sagely. "You're hearing voices. Maybe we should visit another soothsayer to make sure you're not being haunted."

"Oh, another date, is it? I think that's a great idea. After I'm crowned, let's find an excuse to go to town."

"D-date..." Emilia's eyes wandered the room. "M-milkshake."

"That's right, you wanted a milkshake. Guess I'll get one, too."

"Then we should definitely go! To get milkshakes!" Emilia turned toward the exit. "Goodnight, Prince Lucian."

"See you tomorrow, Emilia."

The white haired beastfolk girl practically skipped her way down the hallway.

"Now..." Lucian looked at the training sword in his hand. "Actually, let's use the real thing."

He placed his wooden weapon on the rack, right by the one Emilia used.

Reaching down to his waist, Lucian pulled on his weapon's hilt. The gleaming, purple-hued sword sang as it left its sheath, the vibrations continuing even after he completely freed it.

Stepping up to a training dummy made of straw, Lucian stood with his weapon held between him and his unmoving opponent.

"King, huh?" His blade sliced the air, sinking into the straw. "It feels like I've already fought the final battle. But it was just a small skirmish compared to what's coming soon."

It'd been nearly a month since Henrik's death. That meant the end of winter was fast approaching. And when spring arrived...

"War." Lucian took another swing. "We're going back to war."

A single battle was tough for Lucian. But now he was going to fight many more in an attempt to stop the God's Acolyte that was causing problems in the world.

"I hope we can—"

The creaking of a door caused Lucian to go silent. There was only one door in this room, so his eyes immediately went to it.

A sliver of darkness sat between the door and its frame. As Lucian watched, that sliver grew wider, slowly revealing the staircase that sat behind the door.

But there was something else. Something far more important than the steps that led down to the gladiator arena.

"Hey, buddy." A young man stepped through the open doorway and into the training ground. "Been a while, hasn't it?"

"Rudeus." Lucian raised his sword. "Why are you coming from the gladiator arena?"

"Isn't it obvious? I was waiting for you. Thought that annoying white hair would never leave."

"You were waiting for me in there, even after I told you to never show your face to me again?"

"Hey buddy, before our falling out, I couldn't help but notice something weird." Rudeus came to a stop a few paces from Lucian. "You were really weak."

"You came to kill me because you're stronger? And what do you think will happen to you after?"

"Don't worry about me, I'll be alright. You should be more concerned with yourself. Not that it'll do you any good."

"Does that mean you have accomplices?"

"Who knows?" Rudeus shrugged. "I don't think it'd help you, even if you knew."

"That so?" Lucian picked up the shield leaning against a training dummy. "Then forget I asked."

"A shield?" Rudeus shook his head. "You really are a completely different person from before. You never used to use shields."

"They're useful." Lucian raised it into position. "I'd rather not get stabbed in the gut again."

"Not like it matters either way. Shield or no, you don't stand a chance against me."

With his hand hidden behind his shield, Lucian secretly released the power of the talisman he held between his fingers.

Compared to a real enhancement spell, a talisman could be considered weak. But it was the best Lucian could do at the moment. He and Emilia had been training without magic, for obvious reasons.

That meant Lucian just had the strength of a normal person before using the talisman. But the same couldn't be said of Rudeus.

From the way he walked and stood, Lucian could tell he was enhanced with magic. Fighting him directly should have been a terrible decision. Yet Lucian didn't back down.

The two warriors stood opposite each other, just as they did a month ago when Rudeus first brought him there.

But unlike that time, this wasn't mere training.

Rudeus blurred, his sword cutting the air at the same time.

Lucian's shield met it in the middle, the force of the impact sending a shockwave through his arm. Another attack followed, again sending a jolt through his body.

With the magic fueling him, Rudeus stood several steps above Lucian in strength. Even just from the initial engagement, it was obvious that the soon-to-be king would need a miracle to win.

"Weak!" Rudeus yelled. "What happened to you!?"

Lucian sidestepped an attack. "It's not worth telling you."

"Bastard!" Rudeus swung with all his strength. "Do you know how much effort I put in to becoming your 'best friend'!? And now it's wasted!"

A heavy blow impacted Lucian's shield. "So that's what you were after from the beginning? Getting close to the crown?"

"Of course! What better way to lift my family up than by having a prince for a friend?"

"How pitiful."

"I don't need your pity!" Rudeus lowered his stance. "I just need you to die!"

A flurry assaulted Lucian. He hadn't even had a chance to strike back, only barely able to keep up with Rudeus' speed thanks to the power of the talisman.

But it seemed the young noble finally decided to end the battle, unleashing a combination attack that Lucian couldn't fully defend against.

One of the blows knocked Lucian's shield aside, exposing his body. Seeing the perfect chance, Rudeus didn't hesitate. His blade closed in on the soft flesh no longer protected by the shield.

Clang!

Rudeus' sword was met with unexpected resistance.

"Gah!" The young noble looked down at his stomach, where Lucian's sword pierced him. "Your shield...! "Impossible!"

Lucian stood behind his shield, both hands on his sword's hilt. "You're right that I'm weak. Too weak. But I have my own way of fighting, and I'm confident that it's enough to beat you."

Lucian pulled his sword from Rudeus' body, causing the young noble to grunt.

The shield still protected the prince, despite the fact that he wasn't even holding it. Nothing was attached to it. It simply floated in front of Lucian, as if it had a mind of its own and a desire to protect him.

"What kind of magic is that?" Rudeus faltered for the first time. "Your shield is moving on its own!"

"Yeah, that's what happens when I use my Command Magic. After a lot of experiments, I realized that ordering a shield to protect me would be a good way to not get stabbed."

"No way. You're just trying to trick me." Rudeus readied his sword again. "That shield won't matter if I just kill you!"

One strike after the next sought his flesh. Yet Lucian merely watched as the shield thwarted them all.

Now!

Between two attacks, Lucian lashed out with one of his own. It slid through Rudeus' defenses, landing another clean hit.

"Dammit!" Rudeus backed away, now bleeding from two deep wounds. "What's going on!?"

"You should have listened when I told you to stay away. I was willing to let you go, but now that you've gone this far, it's too late."

Lucian held out his hand, the sword in his grasp. "[Order]. Kill Rudeus."

As soon as he loosened his grip on the hilt, the sword came to life. It zipped toward Rudeus with clear purpose, catching even the enhanced noble off-guard.

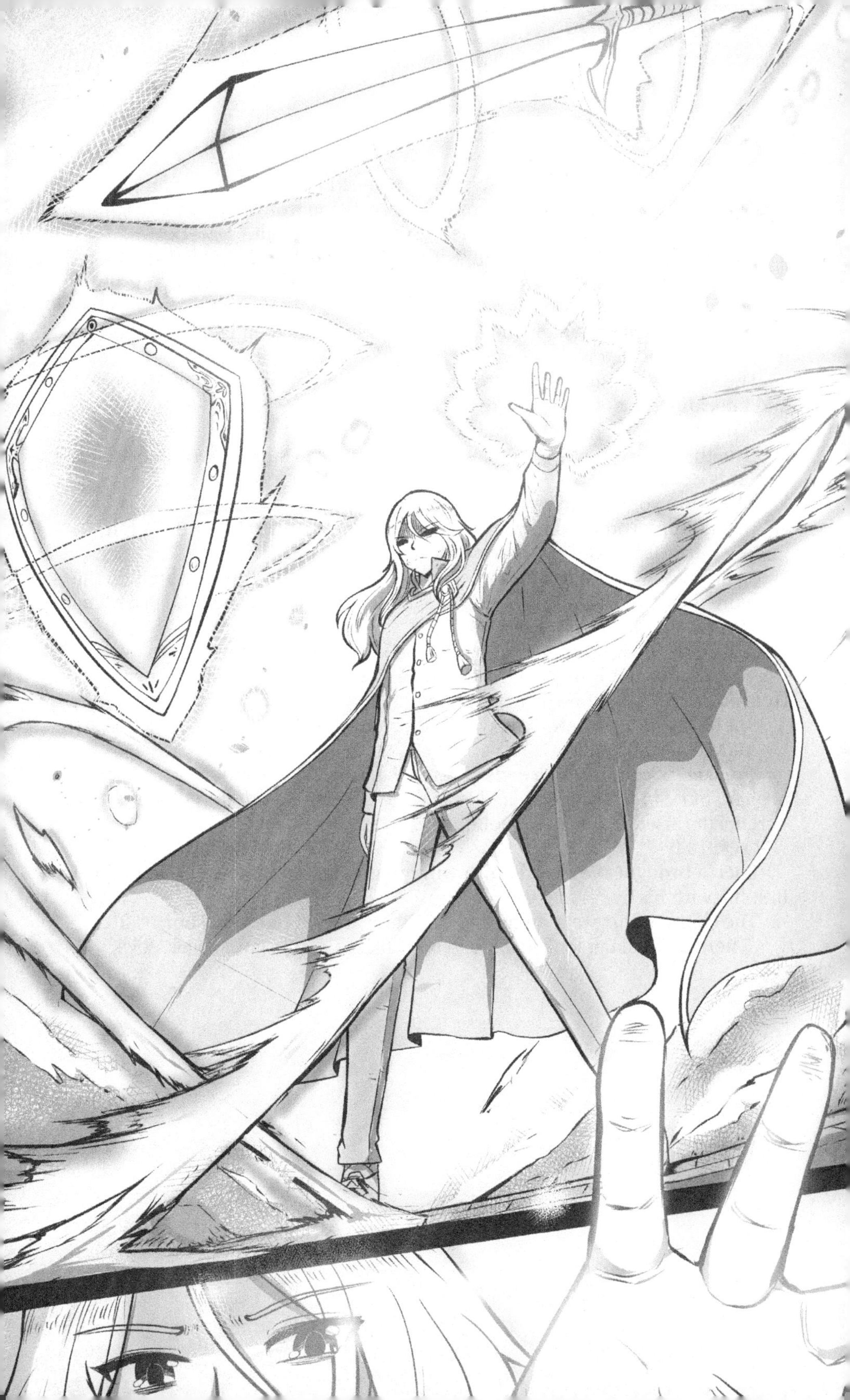

"W-woah!" He batted the weapon away with his own.

"It's useless."

Lucian's sword struck again. Without the need for a wielder, the angles of attack were far different. A stab from above, a swipe from below, and a spinning cleave that'd be impossible if anyone were holding the hilt.

The string of attacks continued, with even more of Rudeus' blood spilling.

Lucian just watched on as his former friend fought against his magically enchanted sword.

Soon, the inevitable happened. Rudeus was unable to judge the next attack, having never faced a weapon without a wielder.

The sword's tip hit Rudeus' stomach at full speed, burying itself up to the hilt and knocking the noble to the ground.

"This can't be..." Rudeus coughed up blood.

"No, this is how it has to be. It's the only way I can survive long enough to save this world."

"What are you ... talking about?"

"It's nothing you need to worry about." Lucian grabbed his sword's hilt, pulling it free from Rudeus' body.

As always, he could temporarily cancel the magic effect just by holding the enchanted object. Looking down on the noble, Lucian squashed the last of his resistance.

Until now, he had managed to not kill a single person. Even Henrik was slain by Emilia, not him. And the guard he injured before his showdown with Henrik survived the injury Lucian gave him.

But he knew. He knew the day would come when he'd have to take this step. And now, it was here.

No, I've killed with each order I gave that led to someone's death. I can't pretend like I'm not responsible just because I wasn't holding the sword.

Lucian raised his weapon, holding it in a sweaty grip.

"Wait! I'll—"

Lucian brought the sword down without giving him time to speak, taking his first life with his own hands.

The clatter of his weapon hitting the stone ground followed shortly after.

"There's..." Lucian looked at his bloody hands. "...No going back now."

Extra chapter 1

"All hail King Lucian!" A chorus of voices shouted.

From the castle's highest balcony, Lucian looked down on the cheering crowd. Thousands of soldiers and citizens showed up to witness his coronation.

Although he was sweeping his gaze over the people below, he wasn't looking at them. That was because something popped up in his vision as soon as the crown was placed on his head.

You leveled up! Congratulations on becoming king!

Please select a skill from the list below.

[Extended Chant I] [Talisman Making I] [Magical Resistance I]

Hey, does the system want me to pick [Extended Chant I] that badly? Well, too bad.

He selected [Talisman Making I] instead. He had already begun to learn the art, so having a skill to enhance it would do him a world of good.

The skill that replaced it was [Physical Resistance II]. It was the first time he'd seen a tier 2 skill, but he didn't choose it. Rather, he went with [Magical Resistance I] to round out his defenses.

Level 4. Is that good, or bad? I guess there's no way to know since I have nobody else to compare myself to.

He wanted to go try out his new talisman skill, but he was in the middle of one of the most important ceremonies of his life. He couldn't afford to just walk out.

Lucian was no stranger to ceremony. Back on Earth, he had spoken at countless rallies and events, each containing their own small flourishes.

But even he had his limits. The morning had been full of celebrations, even before the crowning ceremony. At noon, the crown was placed on his head, after which, the celebrations only increased.

More hours passed, until it was midafternoon. The massive celebration had died down, and Lucian left center stage. The party continued inside the castle, but by then, the nobles were just using it as an excuse to enjoy themselves with the castle's food and wine.

As for Lucian, he managed to sneak off with Emilia under the guise of taking a break after all the ceremonies. He was tired, of course. But being enhanced with magic made such minor issues pointless.

"Hey, Mia." Lucian sat down in one of her chairs. "I couldn't help but notice you snuck off after my coronation."

The young princess continued swinging her legs as they hung off the side of her bed. "Too many people."

He took off his crown and placed it on the table. "Well, I can understand that. But next time, take me with you."

"Impossible. It's your job to deal with it."

Lucian let his head fall loosely into the soft cushion behind him. "That's true. I just hope next time I have such a large crowd gathered, I can actually interact with them."

Emilia stepped in front of him. "You're king now, Prince Lucian. I'm sure you'll have many chances to speak to them."

"You're probably right. Though I still have tradition to think about, which means I'll need the two of you to help me out."

"Of course! We'll do whatever we can. Right, Mia?"

"Sure."

"See?" Emilia smiled at Lucian.

"What a massive difference in enthusiasm." He stood from the chair. "But thanks. If we work together, I'm sure we'll be just fine."

"Yeah!"

Without a word, Lucian walked to Mia's door and opened it. A maid was standing outside, holding a strange box that looked almost like a serving platter covered with a square lid.

Emilia had sensed the arrival of the maid outside, but she didn't feel like it was a threat. Turned out, Lucian had summoned her in secret, carrying a mysterious box.

"Thanks." Lucian took the box, then turned back to the girls. "I had a hard time deciding. I was always bad at things like this. So…"

He walked up to Mia and held the box out. "…I hope you like it."

"Me?" She took it from Lucian's hands.

"I told you, didn't I? That I'd get you a gift for all your help."

Mia seemed to hold the box a bit more carefully, but she didn't move or say anything in response.

"Well," Lucian said. "Don't keep Emilia waiting."

"Yeah! I want to see what it is!"

"I suppose…"

Mia put the box down on her desk. As usual, it was completely free of clutter, giving her plenty of room to open the gift.

The only thing that covered it was a square lid, the handle rising from the top. Mia grabbed that handle and lifted, revealing…

"A kitty!" Emilia watched the little kitten with a smile.

"Since you spend so much time in your room, I thought you might like a companion." Lucian thought back to the teddy bear he saw under Mia's covers. "Especially at night."

Mia didn't respond.

Lucian hadn't forgotten the story of her brother's wicked deeds. He had given the five-year-old Mia a kitten, only to force her to watch as he fed it to that minotaur a few months later.

"I told you that you could watch me and decide for yourself if I'm worth trusting," Lucian said. "I don't care if that takes five months, five years, or longer. I'm confident that you won't find a trace of your brother in me."

Finally, Mia raised her hand. She unlatched the cage door and reached inside. With a gentle hand, she picked up the kitten within, who protested at being handled.

"Th—" Mia pulled the kitten close. "Thank you."

And I've already decided, Mia thought.

To trust one more time.

Lucian showed a relieved smile. "I'm glad you like her. You should give some thought to her name. I was never good at naming, so—"

"Luna."

"—so, don't expect much help from me, is what I was going to say. But wow, you already have one picked out?"

"Yes. Luna."

"Well Luna, looks like we'll be seeing each other a lot from now on."

The kitten's only response was to meow louder.

After getting Mia's room set up for their new, furry companion, Lucian decided to bring up the next topic.

"Hey, how about we take a page from Mia's book and sneak out?"

"Eh? Where are we going?"

"I'm suddenly in the mood for something sweet." He grabbed the crown, placing it back on his head. "How about we see what your favorite pastry shop has for sale today."

"If it's sweets, you can leave the taste testing to me!"

"That's the spirit." He looked to Mia. "You ready?"

"Me?" Mia looked up at him from the edge of the bed, Luna nuzzled in her lap.

"Why do you look so surprised? Of course you're coming."

"I suppose it's good to get out sometimes." She placed Luna down onto the bed beside her.

"Let's make it more than sometimes, alright?"

Mia slid off the bed, landing on her feet. "Not likely."

She walked over to her wardrobe and picked out a blue dress. Turning, she looked at Lucian wordlessly.

"Alright, I get it." He turned toward the door. "I need to change too, so I'll meet you at the intersection between our rooms."

Emilia left the room alongside Lucian, excitement covering her face.

"You really like going out, don't you?"

"Yes, but that's not why I'm excited."

"That so? Then why?"

Emilia turned toward the direction of her room. "Just wait and see, Prince Lucian."

She trotted off and disappeared around a corner.

"How playful." He turned in the opposite direction. "But 'Prince Lucian', huh? Didn't you just say I was king now?"

With a shrug, he walked off toward his own room.

He changed clothes quickly. More quickly than the girls, meaning he was the first to arrive at the intersection they agreed to meet at.

After a bit of waiting, someone appeared in the hallway.

"Ready," Mia said.

"You look impeccable, as always."

"It's part of my responsibilities."

"Then I'm glad you're so dedicated."

The two waited patiently for Emilia. Her room was a bit further away, so it couldn't be helped that she would arrive last.

Soon enough, another figure appeared down the same hallway. A young woman, with furry, white ears and a lavender dress.

Emilia came to a stop in front of Lucian, looking up at him with a hidden smile. "I'm ready, Prince Lucian."

He spent a long second looking at her. "You look fantastic, Emilia. I'm really glad you chose that dress."

"It's my favorite. You bought it for me, after all."

"Then let's show it off to the people of the city."

"Yes!"

Lucian looked at Mia, then back to Emilia. "Shall we?"

The three of them started down the hallway, heading toward a fun and memorable day out in the city.

Extra chapter 2

And then, Lucian mounted his mighty steed and went to beat up the God's Acolyte before riding off into the sunset with Emilia.

A truly wonderful ending, where every single person lived happily ever after.

"Now do you understand why I chose Lucian?" the Goddess asked the young immortal. "Everything worked out, just like I predicted."

"Wow." He looked at her with reverence. "I can't believe I ever doubted someone as intelligent and beautiful as you."

"Hm! Hm! Hmmm!" She soaked up the praise. "Such results are only natural for me."

"Yes, I see that now." He knelt before her. "Please, will you bestow upon me just a fraction of your magnificence, my Goddess—no, my majestic and heavenly mistres~~—"

The Goddess' journal was violently ripped from beneath her pen.

The young immortal looked down at her, the book she was writing in dangling from his grasp.

"What the hell are you writing!? As if I would ever say something so ridiculous! I wouldn't even think it—no, the very concept doesn't even exist to me!"

"How rude," the Goddess said. "I was just trying to write a happy ending for everyone."

"At least wait until he actually beats the bad guy before writing that part of the story! And what about me? Don't I get a good ending?"

"Eh?" She started acting bashful. "Wouldn't anyone be happy to worship me~?"

"I see." The young immortal nodded in understanding. "So you're truly that far gone. A pity that a Goddess would lose her sanity. But as a cheeky brat once told me, not everyone can handle immortality."

"Oh, what a wise friend. I'm sure we'd get along very nicely."

The young immortal imagined what would happen if the two were to team up on him. "Never. I'll never introduce you!"

He took a look at the ridiculous story the Goddess had been writing before he snatched the journal away.

Why did she write this? There's no way it was just to annoy me.
...
No, maybe it was just to annoy me.

He re-read the few paragraphs she managed to scribble, trying to find what she was telling him.

The Goddess was annoying, but she was also ridiculously ancient, even compared to some of the others he'd met with infinite lifespans. The young immortal knew that anything she said or did could be a hint to some piece of knowledge or understanding.

"You sure do like writing," he said. "Can't you just will the finished book into existence?"

"Yes, though it's not quite an act of will. You know that's not how our power works."

"I know, but just roll with it. Why sit and write with a quill? Don't you have other worlds to oversee besides just this one?"

"Many other worlds. But if a god does their job right, they don't have to do anything at all!"

"You sound just like my old manager..."

"Another wise friend." The Goddess placed her finger beneath her chin. "With so many intelligent people around you, I wonder just where you went wrong..."

The young immortal gave her a smug smile. "It all started when I met this particularly annoying Goddess..."

"Oh my, how rude." She took on a wise expression. "You shouldn't speak of others in such a way when they're not here to defend themselves."

"I'll keep that in mind for when I leave here." He held up the journal. "But you never answered my question. Why write it with your hands?"

A book appeared on the table in front of the Goddess, right where the journal sat before. The cover reminded the young immortal of a cheap fantasy book, though that was likely just to mess with him.

"This book contains the adventures of this world's previous summoned hero. A grand tale, filled with adventure, but also tragedy. A hero I chose to save this world centuries ago, and one that set it on the course to prosperity."

She picked up the book. "I didn't just will this recording of his journey into existence. I lived it, experiencing the many powerful emotions he and his companions felt. Hope, fear, anger, sadness, regret, and finally, salvation. Though perhaps it wasn't the salvation he was hoping for."

She put the book back on the table, looking up at the young immortal. "I'm not just writing Lucian's tale. I'm feeling every single emotion as him, without exception. The fear of losing Emilia to the minotaur. The anger at Rudeus and Henrik. The frustration of not having the power to protect everything he cares about. I felt it all."

The young immortal stood in silence, considering her words. He had personal experience with the same powerful emotions Lucian must have been feeling since his reincarnation.

Living through such things again didn't sound like a very pleasant experience. But he knew the Goddess wouldn't be doing it just for fun.

"So that's it," he said. "You're learning. You experience their adventure to see how the one you picked saves the world so that next time, you can use that knowledge to pick an even better candidate as hero."

"That's right. Even for us gods, using heroes is rare. It's been centuries since I've had to use one like this." She motioned to the book that was still sitting in front of her.

"Twice in a row on the same world. What bad luck."

"Perhaps. Or perhaps it's not a coincidence."

The young immortal pondered on her words. He still held the journal where she'd been recording Lucian's story, and those few ridiculous paragraphs were still etched onto the current page.

Looking at it again, a certain passage stuck out to him.

"In these idiotic paragraphs, you asked if I understood why you chose Lucian. Well, the answer is no. You didn't even choose him from this world, going so far as to negotiate with the god of Earth to get his soul. There's got to be a reason for that."

"Oh, finally catching on?"

"You didn't need him." He placed the journal back on the table. "You wanted him. Him specifically."

"Indeed, I did. If it's him, then..." She shook her head. "No, it'll be much more enjoyable to see your reaction when you realize the truth."

The young immortal looked at the center of the table, where a projection showed Lucian enjoying a late afternoon out in the city with Emilia and Mia.

"Lucian Valesti Almekia..." He leaned closer to the projection. "...Who are you?"

Afterword

Hello, and thank you for reading Volume 1 of my newest series, Assassinated King! Let's start off with the question that's likely on many minds: 'What's up with the leveling system!?'

Well, you see, Lucian is a king, and a king needs to lead, right? How could he do that if he had to go grinding for all his levels? As you read, the Goddess created the system for him, and of course she didn't want him running off to the far-flung edges of the known world to fight powerful monsters just so his numbers would go up.

So instead, wouldn't it be great if he could get more powerful by doing kingly things, like solving national crises? At least that's what I—I mean, that's what the Goddess was thinking.

'But where are my stats and stuff!? I want numbers! Lots of numbers!' Ah, about that ... this series will be quite light on the numbers, as you could no doubt tell. I have another series called The False Hero that's a lot crunchier with the numbers.

Simply put, I didn't want to write the same series twice. So where Lucian was reincarnated, Lutz was summoned. Where Lucian has a progression-based leveling system, Lutz has a traditional experience-based one. Where Lucian is a respected prince, Lutz is condemned hero. Where Assassinated King is third person, past tense, The False Hero is first person, present tense.

They are both familiar isekai that most light novel readers will recognize, and they both contain their fair share of anime-like tropes. But I wanted them to be as different as possible in many other ways, especially since I'm writing the two series at the same time. I want to be able to bounce between the two and not feel like the only real difference is the character names.

Anyway! Yeah, that's how it is. But if you enjoyed Volume 1 of Assassinated King, then I assure you that the series will only get better from here. Volume 1 did a lot of setting up. Heck, Lucian didn't even really get his unique powers until the Epilogue!

That may seem like a long time just to showcase his strengths, but I plan on this series being rather long. Don't be surprised if the volume numbers run into the double-digits. The False Hero is on Volume 8, and I plan to release 4 or 5 more before that series concludes.

Hmm. This afterword is getting rather long, so I'll end it here. But I'd like to once again thank you for reading Volume 1, and I hope to see you soon, when Lucian's journey through his new world will truly begin!

Social Media

For early access, extra content, and updates, follow me at:

Website: http://www.thefalsehero.com/

Patreon: https://www.patreon.com/MichaelPlymel

Facebook: https://www.facebook.com/michael.plymel.79

Discord: https://discord.gg/Wc2cYpPMt3

Reddit: https://www.reddit.com/r/TheFalseHero/

Copyright

Assassinated King, Volume 1
By Michael Plymel

This book is a work of fiction. Any similarities to persons or places are strictly coincidental.

Copyright © 2023 Michael Plymel
Illustration by: Aditya Novianto

Made in the USA
Las Vegas, NV
03 February 2025